CARNIVORES OF LIGHT AND DARKNESS

ALAN DEAN FOSTER

ASPECT®

WARNER BOOKS

A Time Warner Company

For Absalom . . .
Who burned to know how to read.

Cape Cross Station, Skeleton Coast, Namibia
November 1993

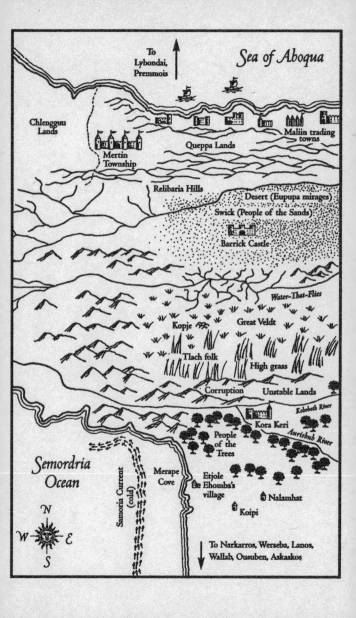

I

T WAS THE MORNING AFTER THE SENSUOUS SECOND FULL MOON
f Telengarra, which heralds the coming of the spring rains,
hen little Colai came running into the village to cry that
ere were dead people washing up on the beach. And not just
ad people, but people of unnatural aspect attired in strange
othes, whose pale faces were unmarked by ritual scars yet
metimes overgrown with hair.

Most of the village was not yet awake when the frantic boy
me running and shrieking past the houses. At first his
other thought it was a trick. She caught him and shook him,
gry that he should disturb everyone's morning for the sake
a joke. Then she saw something that, like a piece of grit,
d become caught at the bottom of his eyes, and stopped
aking him. Together they hurried to the house of the chief.

Asab was just emerging as they arrived. He fumbled to ad-
st his fine musa-skin cloak with the impressive dark blue
ripes and the phophilant headdress with its sweeping crest
intense red and yellow feathers. He was clearly upset at
ving been rousted from his sleep before normal cockcrow.

Hastily donned, his headdress kept threatening to slip from his head.

"I saw them, I saw them!" In addition to Asab, a crowd had begun to gather around Colai and his mother as the boy declaimed breathlessly.

"Now, child," the chief intoned solemnly, "what is it you think you have seen?" Other men and a few of the women clustered close, rubbing sleep from their eyes while fighting back the sour morning taste of recent dreams.

"Dead people, Chief Asab! Many of them, very different from us." The boy barely paused for air as he turned and pointed. "On the beach. Above where the mussels and the tyrex shells grow!"

Sleepy faces glistening with a reluctance to believe turned to the tall, lanky head of the village. Asab briefly considered the child's harangue before finally frowning down at the anxious, panting youth.

"We will go and see. And for your sake, boy, there had better be something on the sand besides shells and dried sea noodles!"

While barren of all vegetation save a little grass and a few hardy weeds, the beach was not devoid of wood. Gigantic logs cast ashore by the cold Samoria Current littered the sand and protruded from rocky outcroppings where they had been hurled by violent storms. Interspersed among the unbranched, well-traveled forest giants were the whitening bones of demised sea creatures large and small: whales and serpents, birds and batwings, fish and stoneaters. From such bountiful detritus did the villagers recycle useful materials for their homes and barns.

"There!" Colai pointed, but the gesture was unnecessary. Everyone saw the hungry dragonets circling over the spot.

There were a dozen or more of the little black scavengers. Wings folded, another four or five sat on the sand picking at irregular lumps that on closer inspection resolved themselves

nto perhaps a dozen human figures. Ululating and waving
heir spears as they approached, the villagers frightened the
arrion-eaters away. Hissing their displeasure, the raven drag-
nets rose into the transparent air on noisome, membranous
vings, content for now to circle slowly overhead. They would
vait.

Truth to tell, if anything Colai had understated the matter.
The bodies were more than passing strange. Just as he had
laimed, several showed faces matted with hair, mostly black
or brown but some as yellow as the gold that Morixis the
Trader brought from the far southern mountains. The figures
vere clad in an excessive amount of clothing, all of it dyed
overbright and some fashioned of cloth so fine it was soft as
a little girl's tears.

On top of this barbaric display of color most also wore
armor of heavy cured leather of a type unknown to Asab or
any of the other village warriors. Scenes that showed men
ighting with one another and strange animals and buildings
vere deeply embossed on breastplates and leggings. With so
much weight to carry it was a wonder that any of them had
been washed ashore.

Asab and two of his best warriors knelt beside one man.
With one exception, all the bodies on the beach were shorter
nd stockier than the average villager. They were also exclu-
ively male.

"See." Tucarak ran a finger along the dead man's exposed
heek. It was cold with the damp of the sea and infused with
eath. "How smooth the skin is. How untouched." With his
ther hand he traced the curving scar, a sign of manhood, that
ecorated his own cheek.

"And how pale," added a disapproving Houlamu as he
ose. "Who are these men, and where do they come from?"
aising his gaze, he squinted out to sea. Nothing was to be
een save the dark, chill water, not even a lingering cloud.

There were only the endlessly rolling waves and the amazingly homogeneous deep blue of the morning sky.

"Well, they are dead, and I am sure they would not want their dying to be wasted." With that Asab ceremoniously began the salvaging of the deceaseds' belongings, beginning with their curious apparel and assiduously examining every bulge and pocket for anything, however foreign and exotic, that might prove useful to the village.

"Can we safely eat them, do you suppose?" Tucarak held a blood-and-salt-water-soaked shirt up to the sun. "They look like men. So they should taste like men."

"Ho-yah," agreed Asab. "We will let old Fhastal try a bit of leg. She will eat anything." The chief chuckled softly. "If it does not kill her, we will know it is safe for the rest of us."

Houlamu contemplated the proposed dismemberment with distaste. "You can eat them if you wish. I only eat what I know. Or who I know." He nudged another of the limp bodies roughly with the butt of his spear.

"These are plumper folk than the Koipi or the Nalamhat." As he spoke, Tucarak was tugging hard on the corpse's unusual footgear. It was much too awkward and heavy to be worn on Naumkib feet, of course, but cut into pieces it might provide the makings for a couple of pairs of serviceable sandals. "If anything, I would think they would taste better than our neighbors."

While the chief and his warriors debated the deceased visitants' suitability for the cooking pot, other members of the tribe wandered up and down the waterline in search of other bodies. Among the searchers was a particularly tall warrior, tall even for a Naumkib, whose somber aspect was the subject of much good-natured gibing among his peers. In response to the frequent jokes made at his expense, Etjole would always smile tolerantly and nod. He was not one to spoil the fun of his hunting companions even when he was the butt of their entertainment.

"Help . . . me. . . ."

The words were barely audible, and for a moment Etjole Ehomba thought they were only subtle distortions of the surf-music, sprinkled upon his innocent ears like wind-blown foam. Having paused momentarily, he started to resume his walk, convinced he had heard nothing.

"Please . . . by whatever god you pray to . . . help me. . . ."

Not foam, not wind, but the dying utterances of a man very like himself. Halting, Ehomba looked northward along the shore with a tracker's experienced eyes, sweeping the rocks and sand for signs of life. Eventually, he found it—or what was left of it.

The man was younger than himself, sturdily built, and clad in the most elaborate garments anyone had yet seen on the bodies on the beach. His fine leather armor extended down to over his upper arms and legs, but it had not been enough to preserve him. There was a great hole in his right side, through which glistening red flesh and pale white bone were clearly visible. Ehomba wondered how he had survived even this long with so deep a wound. It was ragged around the edges, clear evidence of a bite. Whatever had done it had bitten clean through the thick, tough armor. A big shark might have made such a wound, he knew. There were many sharks in the waters offshore from the village. Yes, it might have been a shark—or something else.

The man's hair was straight, shoulder length, and golden. Very different from the thick braids that were bound up in a tight bunch at the back of Ehomba's neck. He marveled at the wispy strands. Leaning forward, he wiped sea slime and sand from the pallid face. At his kindly touch, the other's eyes opened. They were a delicate, diluted blue, but not yet entirely dimmed, and they focused immediately on him.

"You . . . who are . . . ?"

"I am Etjole Ehomba, of the tribe of Naumkib. You and many others have been cast ashore on the beach below our

village. Your companions are all dead." His gaze flicked
briefly over the cavity in the younger man's torso. "You are
dying too. I know a little medicine, but not enough to help
you. Not even the old wise women of the village could help
what I see. It is too late."

The stranger's reaction was not what Ehomba expected.
The man's eyes grew suddenly, shockingly wide. Reaching
up, he clutched the taller man's wool overshirt and used it to
pull his ruined, bleeding upper body off the sand until his face
was only a foot away from that of his finder. In light of the
terrible injury he had suffered, the effort of will required to
accomplish this feat was nothing short of astonishing.

Staring straight into Ehomba's eyes, he hissed in his odd,
uneven accent, "You must save her!"

"Save her? Save who?" Ehomba's bewilderment was absolute.

"Her! The Visioness Themaryl of Laconda!" Remarkably,
and with what invisible reserves of strength one could only
imagine, the man was shaking Ehomba by the front of his
overshirt.

"I do not know of what, or of whom, you speak," the herder
responded gently.

Exhausted by this ultimate physical exertion, the wounded
stranger collapsed back on the sand. He was breathing more
slowly now, and Ehomba could sense Death advancing flu-
idly across the surf, choosing as its avenue of approach, as it
so often did, its friend the sea.

"Know that I am Tarin Beckwith, son of Bewaryn Beckwith, Count of Laconda North. The Visioness Themaryl was
my countess, or my countess-to-be, until she was carried off
by that pustulance that walks like a man and calls itself Hymneth the Possessed. Many"—he coughed raggedly, and blood
spilled from his lips as from an overfull cup—"many of the
sons and masters of the noble houses of Greater Laconda took
a solemn oath never to rest until she was returned to us and

her abductor punished. To my knowledge, I and my men were the only ones to track the monster's ship this far." He paused, wheezing softly, praying for breath enough to continue.

"There was a battle this morning, on the sea. My men fought valiantly. But Hymneth is in league with the evils of otherness. He cavorts with them, delights in their company, and calls upon them to help defend his miserable self. Against such foulness and depravity even brave men cannot always stand." Once more the watery blue eyes, the life fading from them, fastened on Ehomba's own. "I pass on the covenant to you, whoever you are. I charge you, on the departure of my soul, to save the innocent Themaryl and to restore her to the people of Laconda. With her abduction, the heart has gone out of that land, and all who dwell within it. I, Tarin Beckwith, place this on you."

Ehomba shook his head slowly as he gazed down at the stranger. "I am but a simple herder of cattle and harvester of fish, Tarin Beckwith." He gestured with the tip of his spear. "And this is a poor man's land, spare of people and resources. Not a place in which to raise armies. I would not even know which way to begin searching."

Raising himself off the sand with a second tremendous effort, Beckwith turned slightly at the waist and pointed. Sunlight glistened off his visible intestines. "To the northwest, across the sea. There! Having defeated the only ones capable of following him, Hymneth the depraved will feel safe in returning now to his home. I am told it lies in the fabled land of Ehl-Larimar, which is far to the west of Laconda. Seek him there, or find another who will." Once more, clenching hands clawed at Ehomba's simple attire. "You must do this, or the innocent Themaryl will be forever lost!"

"You expect too much of me, stranger Beckwith. I have a family, and cattle to watch over and protect, and—"

Ehomba halted in midsentence. His encumbrance delivered, the life force spent, the spirit of Tarin Beckwith of Laconda had at last fled his body. Gently but firmly, Ehomba disengaged the insensible fingers from his shirt and laid the upper part of the destroyed body down upon the cool sand. It lay there, teal blue eyes staring blankly at the sky, as the herdsman rose.

It would be a privilege, he knew, to consume a chop cut from the flank of so brave and dedicated a man. When the time came for the sharing out of the food, he would make a point of making this claim to Asab.

As to the dead man's trust, there was nothing he could do about it, of course. He had spoken him the truth. There were family and herd and village responsibilities to look after. What matter to him the troubles and tribulations of a people from far away, or the carrying off of one woman?

Suarb and Deloog came running over. They were young men, not yet acknowledged elders, and they nodded to him respectfully as they knelt by the now motionless form at his feet. There was excitement in their voices, and their eyes were alight with the pleasure to be found in something new.

"Etjole, you found this one, but you do not take his belongings." Suarb eyed him uncertainly while Deloog gazed at the heavily embossed leather armor, openly covetous.

"No. I have no interest in such things. They are yours if you want them."

Elated at their good fortune, the two youths began to strip the body of useful material. As he yanked on a pants leg, Deloog watched the taller, older man curiously.

"These are fine things, Etjole. Why do you not take them?"

"I have been given something else, Deloog. Something I did not ask for and do not want, and I am not sure what to do with it."

The youths exchanged a glance. Ehomba was known for sitting and saying nothing for long periods of time, even when he was not guarding the herds. A peculiar man, for certain, but kindly and always helpful. The boys and girls of the village, and not a few of their parents, thought him peculiar, but nice enough in his own quiet fashion.

So the two young men did not make fun of him behind his back as he walked away from them, up the beach toward a point of rocks. Besides, they were too excited by their booty.

Working his way up into the rocks, Ehomba found a flat, dry place and sat down, positioning his spear in the crook of his right arm and resting his chin on his crossed forearms. Small waves broke themselves against the cool, gray stone. Farther up the coast, seals and merapes played in the surf, occasionally hauling out to dry themselves on the sun-warmed beach. The merapes would crack clams and abalone to share with the seals, who did not have the benefit of hands with which to manipulate rocks.

Out there, somewhere, lay lands so distant he had never heard of them, exotic and alien. A place by the name of Laconda, and another called Ehl-Larimar. A woman being taken from one to the other against her will. A woman many men were willing to die for.

Well, he already had a woman worth dying for, and two children growing up strong and healthy. Also cattle, and a few sheep, and the respect of his contemporaries. Who was he to go searching across half a world or more on behalf of people he did not know and who would probably laugh at his untutored ways and plain clothes if they saw him?

But a brave and noble man had charged him with the duty as he lay dying. As it always did, the sight of the sea and the waves soothed Etjole. Yet he remained much troubled in mind.

Half the day was done when finally he rose and started back to the village. All the bodies had been removed from the beach, leaving only the dark stains of blood to show where they had lain. Come high tide, the sea would cleanse the sand, as it cleansed everything else it touched.

That night there was a solemn feast in honor of the

strangers who had died on the shore below the village. Everyone partook of the cooking, and it was agreed without dispute that wherever they had come from, it was a land of plenty, for their flesh was sweet and uncorrupted. As he ate of Tarin Beckwith, Ehomba pondered the unfortunate man's final words until those around him could no longer ignore his deep concern. Not wishing to lay his melancholy on them, he excused himself from the company of his wife and their friends, and sought out old Fhastal.

He found her by herself off to one side of the central firepit, sitting cross-legged against a tired tree while chewing with some difficulty on the remnants of a calf. Though white as salt, her hair was fastened in neat braids that spilled down her back, and she had decked herself out for the evening in her finest beads and long strips of colored leather. She looked up at him out of her one good eye and smiled crookedly. The other eye, blinded in youth, gleamed chalky as milk. Given her few remaining teeth, it was no wonder she was finding the meat tough going.

"Etjole! Come and sit with an old woman and we'll give the young girls something to gossip about tomorrow!" Her grin fell away as she saw that his expression was even more serious than usual. "You are troubled, boy. It clouds your face like smoke."

Crossing his own legs beneath him, he sat down beside her, waving off her offer of meat, broiled squash, or bread. "I need your wisdom and your advice, Fhastal, not your food."

Nodding understandingly, she picked at a strip of gristle caught between her remaining back teeth as she listened to him tell of his encounter with the dying stranger on the beach. When he had finished, she sat silent in contemplation for a long moment.

"The stranger placed this burden on you as he lay dying?" When Ehomba nodded, she responded with a terse grunt. "Then you have no choice." Idly she fingered the lightly browned slices of squash in her bowl. "Are you or are you not a man of conviction?"

"You know that I am, old woman."

"Yes, I do. So we both know what this means. You must finish this man's work. One who dies in another's arms is no longer a stranger. Like it or not, he bound himself to you, and in so doing, his mission was bound to you as well."

The man seated across from her sighed heavily. "That is also how I interpreted what happened, and it is what I feared. But what can I do? I am only one. This Tarin Beckwith had many warriors with him, and they were not enough to save him or allow him to succeed."

Fhastal sat a little straighter. "They were not Naumkib. They were from outside the stable world."

He was not persuaded. "They were still men. That is all that I am."

"No it is not." A gnarled fist the color of spoiled leather punched him several times in the upper arm. "You are Etjole Ehomba, herder, fisherman, father, warrior, and tracker. The best tracker in the village. Can you not track that which is not seen as well as that which is?"

"That is not so great a skill. Tucarak can do it, and so can Jeloba."

"But not as good as you, boy. You know that you must do this thing?"

"Yes, yes. Because this Tarin Beckwith, whom I do not know, put it on me as he died. This is not fair, Fhastal."

She snorted, her nose twitching. "Fate rarely is. If you want me to, I will explain it to Mirhanja."

"No." He uncrossed his legs preparatory to rising. "I am her husband, and it is my responsibility. I will tell her. She will not take it well."

"Mirhanja is a good woman. Give her more credit. She understands honor and obligation." She fumbled a slice of fried pumpkin into her mouth. "How old is your boy?"

"Daki will be fourteen years next month."

Fhastal nodded approvingly. "Old enough to do a turn or two looking after the herd in your stead. Time he started doing something useful. The little girl will have a harder time accepting this, but her tears will pass." Reaching down, she removed one of the many colorful fetishes that hung in bunches around her neck. It was a fine carving of a woman, done in the shiny gray horn of a stelegath. As he leaned forward, she slipped the cord from which it hung over his head.

"There! Now I can go with you. I have seen the Unstable Lands in my dreams, and now I can travel with you to see them in person."

He smiled fondly as he studied the figurine hanging from its cord of sisal fiber. "You mean that this image can go with me."

"Oh no, big handsome!" She cackled gleefully. "It is the image you are speaking to right now, the image that the village children make fun of and call names behind my back." She pointed to the necklace. "That is the real me."

For just an instant, he thought he saw something in her blind eye. Something flickering, and alive. But it was only a trick of the weak light, distorted by the cook fire.

"I will carry it as an amulet," he assured her, not wanting to hurt her feelings. Fhastal meant well, but she was a little crazy. "So that it will bring me luck."

"If you'd carry it somewhere else on your body, it might bring *me* luck." She laughed madly again. "I hope that it will, Etjole." She made shooing motions at him, like a mother hen guiding one of her brood of chicks. "Now then—go and see to your wife, so that you may lie with her before you leave. Make your farewells to your children. And be sure to stop by Likulu's house. She and the other women will gather some small things to give you to take on your journey. Meet me tomorrow by the stone lightning and I will set you on your way. I can do no more than that."

He straightened. "Thank you, Fhastal. With luck, I may be able to return this woman to her people and return home in a month or two."

He did not believe it as he spoke it, but that did not matter. Fhastal did not believe it either. Without discussion, they chose to connive in the illusion.

II

MIRHANJA TOOK IT HARD, AS ETJOLE HAD KNOWN SHE WOULD. He tried to explain slowly and carefully, not forgetting to include the confirming conversation he'd had with Fhastal, reminding his wife again and again why he had to go.

"If I did not do this thing, then I would not be the man you married."

Lying next to him, she reached over and hit him hard on the chest, a blow arising out of frustration as much as anger. "Better half a live man unconvicted than a whole one dead! I don't want you to go!" She pressed tighter against him, her thigh curling over his flat stomach. She was nearly as tall as he, but in this she was not exceptional. The women of the Naumkib were famed for their statuesqueness.

"I have to. He who betrays a dying man's obligation is himself dimmed forever in the sight of the heavens."

"But you don't want to go." She kissed him ferociously on the neck.

"No," he confessed as he turned to her in the bed, "I do not."

"Tucarak would not go. Not even Asab."

"I do not know that, and neither do you. But you do know me."

"Yes, damn you! Why must you be such a good man? You are going to try and save a woman you have never met, of a tribe you do not know, from a land no one has ever seen, for a man you knew only for a moment as he lay dying. I know the depth of a warrior's obligations, but can you not be even a little bit of a knave just for me?"

"You are so beautiful." He was running his fingertips light as a summer breeze over her forehead and back down across her hair, smoothing out the curls, trying to smooth away her fears as well. But despite his best efforts, they kept springing back up again, just like the curls.

"And you are a fool!" She placed gentle fingers on his lower lip. "And I am cursed because that makes me a fool's wife."

"Well then, Mrs. Fool, at least we are well matched."

"Promise me one thing, then." She looked over at him, her eyes moist. "Promise me you will not stay away long."

"No longer than is necessary—wife."

"And that while you are gone, when the nights are cold and lonely, you will not lie with the beautiful women of far-off lands, but will remember that I am here, waiting for you."

He smiled, and the love he felt for her poured out of him like water from a cistern. "No live woman could compare with even the memory of you, Mirhanja." He covered her then, feeling the warmth of her surge up and around him, and she sighed beneath him even as he wondered when next he might feel a part of her again.

Early the following morning Daki stood solemnly watching, maturing in the moment, but Nelecha would not let go of the leather strips that hung down and over his woolen kilt. For so slim a child she had a lot of energy, all of which she put into crying "No, no!" over and over, until her eyes were red from the seeping and her throat was sore. Eventually, reluctantly, hopelessly, she let herself be gathered up in her mother's arms.

He and Mirhanja had made their own farewell the previous night. Several of Ehomba's closest friends among the men of the village had come to see him off. He did not tell them he was going to meet Fhastal or they would have laughed at him. As it was, there was no laughter. Only firm handclasps and sympathetic waving of hands as he turned and started off along the coast path. They understood why he was going, but he could tell that, tradition notwithstanding, several among them disagreed with it.

"Asab could make you an exception. As chief he can do that," Houlamu had told him before he started on his way.

"Yes, but *I* cannot make myself an exception, and it is myself I have to live with the rest of my days," he had replied.

"A short life it's liable to be, too, in the Unstable Lands," his friend had muttered.

"I will track my way clear," he assured them.

"In the Unstable Lands? Where people are swallowed up by unreality, by things that should not exist?" Tucarak was dubious, his tone bordering on the spiteful. "Who comes back from those places? No one goes there."

"Then how can you say that no one can come back?" Ehomba challenged them, but try as they might they could not think of anyone foolish enough to have attempted such a journey. Not in recent memory.

As he crossed the point of rocks that led to the seal and merape beach, he paused to pick up a handful of the wave-washed thumb-sized gravel. The merapes preferred the purchase the sandless beach gave their hands, and the seals, their friends, went along with this choice. Carefully he dumped the handful in a small wool sack and put it into a pocket, then buttoned the pocket shut. Homesick in some far land, he could pull out the pebbles and they would remind him of the village, his friends, his family. Few of his fellow warriors would have understood. Already burdened with sleeping roll and leather backpack, no one else would have chosen to add ordinary beach pebbles to the load.

He looked back. The village was already out of sight, but he could see the fires from individual houses rising into the pellucid sky. Sight of his home, reduced to smoke. What would congeal out of the smoke that lay ahead? He pushed on.

No one knew when the bolt of lightning had turned to stone and embedded itself in the bank of the creek, but there was no mistaking its shape, or the way it made everyone's skin tingle and hair stand on end when walking over it. This phenomenon made it a favorite haunt of the village children, but none were running back and forth along its tormented petrified length today. It was too early for that kind of exploratory play.

As promised, Fhastal was waiting for him in front of the unnatural natural bridge. "Good morning, big handsome." She took notice of his pack, his best overshirt and kilt, the necklace of colorful, hand-painted and -drilled beads strung on a leather thong around his throat, the elongated spear he was using for a walking stick. In leather sheaths slung across his back were two additional weapons: the short sword fashioned from the scavenged jawbone of a whale that had been carefully lined on both sides with the inch-long, razor-sharp teeth of a great white shark, and the slightly shorter sword the village smithy, Otjihanja, had forged from one of the hundreds of lumps of nickel-iron that had fallen from the sky in archaic times and now littered the plain to the southeast of the village lands. "Ready to begin the thing, I see."

"As I must. As the covenant binds me to do." Despite his determination, he was already having second thoughts. The dying Beckwith's words were fading.

But try as the herdsman might to shut it out, the stranger's face would not.

She grinned knowingly, showing an alarming paucity of front teeth. "You don't *have* to do this thing, Etjole. No one in the village will think the worse of you if you change your mind now."

"I will," he replied laconically as he looked past her. Beyond lay the barren north coast, and farther still the river Kohoboth, that marked the southern edge of the Unstable Lands. "The warrior Tarin Beckwith said that the woman Themaryl would be taken to a country far to the northwest, across the great ocean. How shall I cross it?"

"You must keep traveling north," the old woman told him. "Make your way through the Unstable Lands until you come to a place where the making of large boats is a craft, and take passage on one of them across the Semordria."

He looked down at her. "Is there such a land?"

"In my youth I heard tales of such kingdoms. Places where people live by knowledge that is different from ours. Not greater, necessarily, but different. It is likely you may find passage there. If not"—she shrugged—"you may freely return home knowing that you tried your best."

"Yes, that is fair enough," he admitted, content with her conclusion. "Obligations do not wait. Best I be on my way."

A gnarled hand grabbed his wrist. There was surprising strength in that withered arm. The one good eye stared up at him while the other seemed to turn in upon itself.

"You must come back to us, Etjole Ehomba. Among the Naumkib, it is you who stands the tallest. And I am not making a joke about your height."

"I will come back, Fhastal. I have a family, and herds to look after." Bending down to plant a kiss on the aged, parchmentlike cheek, he was startled when she shifted her face so that her lips met his. Her tongue dived into his mouth like a wet snake and he felt half the breath sucked out of him. As quickly as it had happened, she pulled away.

"Don't look so surprised, big handsome." The smile she gave him took forty years off her life. "I am old, not dead. Now then, be off with you! Discharge your obligation as best you can, and may the spirit of this Tarin Beckwith count itself supremely fortunate to have departed this world in your arms and not those of another."

He left her there, waving atop the little ridge of rocks among the ghost trees as merapes squabbled for seafruit on the pebble beach below. He watched until she turned and disappeared, beginning the long hobble back toward the village. It would have been interesting, he found himself thinking, to have known Fhastal in her youth.

Better to devote his thoughts to the journey ahead, he told himself. Resolutely, he turned away from the ridge, the village, and the only life he had ever known, and set his gaze and his feet firmly on the path ahead.

He passed the rest of the sheltered cove with its barking seals and chittering merapes lying on the glittering gravel just above the steep shore break. One of the merapes threw an empty oyster shell at him, but it landed well short of his legs. Funny creatures, the merapes. They could be playful or vicious, depending on their mood of the moment. Not unlike people.

Beyond the village lay untold stretches of empty coast, for his clan inhabited the last mapped settlement this far to the north. Traveling to the south he would have been in familiar territory. Though Wallab and Askaskos lay a goodly distance down the coast, their people and those of the village knew of one another, and engaged in regular commerce and trade. Beyond those villages was the larger trading town of Narkarros, and still farther the villages of Werseba, Lanos, and Ousuben. The farther south one journeyed, the more fertile the lands became, the better the pastures. But someone always had to live

on the fringes of the known world, his father had told him
more than once, and that choice had fallen long ago to the
Naumkib.

North of the village the grass gave way to sand and rock in
whose bleak confines only the hardiest plants could eke out
an existence. Few animals lived there, and those that did had
been rendered permanently mean and ill-tempered by their inhospitable surroundings. Expecting to encounter nothing specific, Ehomba was therefore prepared for anything. Where
potential strife was concerned, he retained an entirely open
mind.

That evening a gale rose up off the sea, indifferent and unfriendly. It blew all that night and the next day, forcing him to
walk with a scarf over his face and his eyes locked nearly shut
in a permanent protective squint. The harsh wind-blown
grains blasted his face and scored his arms. But he was not to
be so quickly defeated, and certainly not by mere weather.

"Go back to the open sea!" he yelled into the gusts more
than once, raising his arms and shaking his spear at the ocean.
Off to his left, the great flat green-black sweep of the Semordria roared its challenge, vast and cold. "Leave me be! I am
only a man just begun on his journey, and this is not fair!"

The waves exclaimed on the shore and not even seabirds or
the Soft Ones answered, but when he emerged the next morning from his makeshift shelter of blanket and driftwood, the
wind had stopped. Given up, he decided with satisfaction,
only to be replaced by a cousin of gentler mien.

Had he been traveling inland, the dense fog in which he
now found himself enveloped would have created many problems. As long as he followed the coast, however, he could not
lose his way, not even in the thickest mist. Not with the echo
of the surf to guide him. If he kept it always on his left, for
some distance yet it would guide him due north.

Using scraps and splinters of driftwood still dry from having been buried in the sand, he struck sparks off a convenient

ock with his sky-metal sword and made a fire. Blanketed by
he fog, the morning was chill. Tea and jerky were his break-
ast, the tea warming him, the jerky providing his mouth with
xercise in the absence of conversation. He sat huddled be-
eath his blanket, an island of life and warmth in the gray
nist, sipping his drink and slowly chewing on the stubborn
trip of dried meat. The smoke from his fire and the steam
rom his cup fought for space with the fog. In the mist-en-
ulfed silence, all that could be heard beyond the dying
rackle of the fire was the sound of unseen waves coming
shore on the shrouded beach.

Done with the frugal but adequate meal, he rolled his blan-
et tight and resecured it to the top of his pack. There was no
eed to scatter the ashes from the fire or douse them with
vater—there was little here to burn. No danger of a grass fire
n the absence of grass, or of a forest fire in the absence of a
orest. Orienting himself by the sound of the surf, he resumed
is trek northward.

He did not know how far the impenetrable sea fog ex-
ended. No one did. For as long as the Naumkib could re-
nember, theirs had been the northernmost settlement of the
outhern peoples. The perpetual fogs kept them from expand-
ng northward, and probably kept people living to the north
rom moving south. He knew that he had to keep the sound of
he ocean always close. Lose it, and he might wander around
n the fog forever—or at least until his food ran out.

His expression set, he lengthened his stride. The fog clung
amply to him as if trying to hold him back, but he pushed re-
ntlessly forward, scattering it with sheer determination.
Torth was where he had to go, and nothing was going to keep
im from getting there.

III

T̲HE LAND DID NOT GROW STEADILY GREENER AS HE WALKED
but it became clear that the Earth was trying harder. Pockets
of brush began to appear, and then clumps of smaller, more
diverse vegetation that huddled close together beneath the
protection of overhanging trees. Some he recognized, like the
ivory-nut palms and salt-tolerant casuarina pines, while others were new to him. There was one tree in particular, with
long spreading arms, that was ripe with both nuts curved like
a courtesan's eyebrows and large purple fruit. Winged caterpillars gnawed on the round leaves, while flightless butterflies
crawled along the branches in search of flowers or rotting
fruit to suck.

In one grove where he stopped to drink from a small, com-
paratively clean pool, a troop of monkeys appeared overhead.
They marched along the branch in single file, perfectly in
step, following their leader. He wore a headdress made from
the empty husk of a gourd. Necklaces of nuts and shells
flopped against his hirsute brown chest. As was the nature of
monkeys, all were armed. Several carried small bows and ar-

rows, while the rest were equipped with tiny spears that had been whittled from hardwood sticks. There were no females or infants in the troop. Those, Ehomba knew, would be waiting back at a carefully chosen treetop bivouac for the males to return.

"Halt!" he heard the leader suddenly exclaim. Instantly, the rest of the troop assumed a fighting stance. As Ehomba stepped back from the edge of the pool, shaking water from his hands, he was careful not to reach for any of his own weapons. A dozen miniature bows were already trained on him.

Using his long arms and prehensile tail, the troop leader descended from the tree in a rush of anarchic branches, until he stood confronting the herdsman. Ehomba politely took a seat, a move that reduced his great height and left him eye-to-eye with the three-foot-tall monkey. Necklaces jangling, sharpened stick in hand, the troop leader approached warily to extend a limp hand, in the manner of edified monkeys.

"I am Gomo."

The herdsman gently enveloped the strong, limber fingers in his own. "Etjole Ehomba, of the Naumkib."

"I do not know that tribe of men." Overhead, the other members of the troop began to relax. Keeping their weapons close at hand, they spread out among the branches. Several began snacking on the moist, tasty leaves of the tree while others set about gathering the purple fruit, placing the dark orbs in crude sacks they carried slung over their narrow shoulders. The rest relaxed by grooming themselves or their neighbor.

Ehomba gestured loosely to the south. "I have come from down the coast, to fulfill an obligation to a man who died in my arms."

Gomo scratched vigorously at his tailbone. "Ah! Your path is chosen for you, then."

The herdsman nodded. "And what brings my small cousins to this place? The bounty of this tree?"

The monkey leader shook his head. "Bounty of a different kind, I hope. We are looking for help." Straining to see behind the human, he noted the strangely tipped spear and other unusual weapons lying on the ground. "You are a warrior?"

"A herdsman. But all the men of my village are also warriors. One never knows when raiders may come out of the interior, hoping for easy plunder." He smiled thinly. "They do not find it among the Naumkib."

"I understand what you say about human raiders," Gomo replied sagely. "That is a problem the People of the Trees do not have. We hold among us little that humans find of value."

"Difficult to maintain a herd in the treetops," Ehomba agreed. "Even a small steer or sheep would have a tough time grazing in the branches."

"Oh-ho!" Gomo doubled over and slapped his belly. Reflecting the laughter below them, the other members of the troop joined in, their raucous chattering momentarily drowning out every other sound in the grove.

When his chest and stomach finally stilled, Gomo turned serious once more. "Half a warrior would be more help to us than none." He scrutinized the human from head to toe with great deliberation. "And you are almost tall enough to make not a half, but two. You could help us."

Ehomba looked past him, gazing significantly northward. "I have told you where I am bound and why. My family waits for me to return. I have no time for side trips or excursions."

The monkey edged closer, bringing his pungent smell with him like a loose coat. "You are following the coast? North of here the trees thin once more and the country turns desolate. But inland it rapidly becomes greener, especially along the banks of the Aurisbub. That in turn flows into the great river Kohoboth. Upstream from their confluence lies the human town of Kora Keri, where one such as yourself would find rest, food, shelter, and information on the lands farther north that are a closed mystery to me and my people." He sat back, one hand on his spear-stick, his long tail flicking back and forth behind him. "Of course, if you already know all this, then I am wasting my time telling you about it."

"I did not." It was always wise, Ehomba knew, to be honest with a monkey. Unlike their human cousins, they could be sly, but only rarely were they intentionally deceptive.

"Our forest home lines this side of the Aurisbub. If you would help us," Gomo went on, "I myself would guide you to Kora Keri. Of course, you could continue on your way up the coast, but you would make much better time via the inland route, in the company of unlimited fresh water you would not have to carry on your back, all manner of available food, and a town for your immediate destination."

"You are right—I would."

"We would not ask you to stay among us more than a night or so."

"You mean a day or so."

"No." Gomo brooded on troubles unseen. "Our travails strike us at night, when we are at our weakest."

The herdsman sighed. "What is your trouble, Gomo, that you need the services of a warrior?"

Learned, limpid eyes looked up at him. "We are plagued, man, by a flock of slelves."

Ehomba nodded knowingly. "I have seen them, but they do not bother our flocks."

"No. They would not. Man and his weapons and warlike ways they shun, but of the People of the Trees they have no fear." Bitterness sharpened his words. "They come among us at night and steal our food. Several times now they have tried to take some of our children. The females are frantic, and we are all weary from lack of sleep. Sooner or later the slelves will wear us down, and then there will be tragedy instead of inconvenience." Too proud to beg, he lowered his voice.

"We cannot offer you gold or silver, Ehomba. Those are man-things and we do not keep them. I can promise only guidance, and gratefulness. I will understand if your obligation weighs too heavily on you to let you detour even a little from your predetermined path."

Ehomba considered the request, and the monkey seated solemnly before him. After a moment he rose abruptly, using his spear to lever himself upward. Startled, the members of the troop leaped about in a sudden, mad fit to regain their weapons. Their leader hastened to calm them.

"Peace! The man has something to say!"

Tilting back his head, the lanky herdsman peered up at the slim bodies within the branches. "Nothing is predetermined. I will help you—if I can."

His response inaugurated an even greater racket than before among the members of the troop. They leaped joyously from branch to branch, flung handfuls of leaves into the air, and did somersaults on narrow tree limbs without a single spill. When they began to quiet down, Gomo rejoined them, scampering up a trunk and swinging himself effortlessly back into the branches.

"This way, friend Ehomba." From his perch he used his spear-stick to point northeastward. "It is not far to the Auris-bub, and we need to hurry. In order to look for help, we had to leave the females and young in the care of juveniles and sil-verhairs. They will be wishing anxiously for us to return."

Ehomba nodded as he followed along below, occasionally glancing up into the branches to check the troop's direction. "Just don't expect me to travel through the trees. I am no monkey."

"No," Gomo agreed sadly. "Your kind has lost that ability and that freedom. We feel badly for the tribe of men."

Although the vegetation grew steadily denser as they moved inland away from the coast, there were still places where the troop was forced to drop to the ground and walk upright. Out of the trees, they were at their most vulnerable, and their alertness was correspondingly heightened. At such times they tended to shed their monkey bravado and cluster closer to the tall, well-armed human.

Once, they saw a patrolling leopard. A reversed female, her yellow spots were prominent against her black body. She only glanced in their direction. Of more concern was the herd of hairy elephants that lumbered past close on their southern flank. But despite the presence of young among them, the elephants, hot within their woolly coats, were interested only in reaching the river and assuaging their thirst. A couple of matriarchs bellowed in the troop's direction, raising both trunk and curving tusks, but did not swerve from their course. The troop paused briefly to let the herd get well ahead. It would not do to stumble into the migrating behemoths in the middle of the night.

The members of the troop shared their meager rations with the man in their midst, and he accepted the nuts and berries and fruit more out of politeness than necessity. Still, it was good to be able to conserve his own stores. One never knew when the future might prove less accommodating.

Eventually a line of taller trees appeared ahead, stretching unbroken from south to north. Birds and small dragons and squeaking pipperils flocked above it while rodents mowed the shorter grasses in long, disciplined ranks. Unlike the barren coast, this was clearly a region of abundance.

"Yonder lies the Aurisbub," Gomo told him as his troop broke into a gamboling trot. "We are a little south of where we should be. When we strike the river we will turn north, and soon I will be back in the bosom of my family."

"I wish I could say the same." Mirhanja's warmth was already a too-distant memory.

"I am no seer, Ehomba, and so cannot prophesy the end of your journey. But by traveling along the Aurisbub to the Kohoboth and then to Kora Keri, I *can* predict that you will achieve it sooner." He slipped a long, lanky arm around the human's thighs. "Come now. We are close to friendly faces and places."

The explosion of joy that greeted the appearance of the troop was something to see. Females and young came pouring, tumbling out of a clutch of trees that grew close to the river, setting up a din that had to be heard to be believed. The acrobatics the herdsman had witnessed earlier were as nothing compared to the circus that now ensued. The scene of reunion was one of utter and unrestrained monkey mania.

When families had been reunited and juveniles and oldsters relieved of their duties as guardians, Gomo introduced him to the members of his own family circle. For the rest of the day and on into evening, he was forced to tolerate the attentions of two incredibly energetic, playful youngsters. They clambered all over him despite periodic admonitions from their parents to cease and desist. For the young monkeys, it was as if a wondrous perambulating, talking jungle gym had wandered into their midst, exclusively for their enjoyment. At Gomo's urging, Ehomba would smack them off his head or shoulders when their antics grew too distracting. But he could not bring himself to do it often. They were small, innocent, brown bundles of pure unadulterated fun. The thought that if something was not done they might become food for marauding slelves was a sobering one.

There was very little moon that night as Ehomba sat in the crook of the orange-pod tree looking out at the silvered river and listening to Gomo chatter on beside him. Nearby, he could see monkey families settling down for the night, females clutching their infants close to their breasts, juveniles piled one atop the other, males sleepily doing their best to stay alert and on guard. In keeping with the beauty and tranquillity of the surroundings, it should have been a setting of pastoral contentment. Instead, unspoken threat saturated the air with tension.

"They always come from there." Gomo pointed. "From across the river. They must live in the taller trees on that side."

"At least you can see them coming." Years of standing watch over flocks day in and day out had sharpened Ehomba's night vision to the point where it was far more sensitive than that of the average person. Something flapped slowly as it made its way downstream, and he tensed momentarily before unbending: It was only a perffus, dragging the surface of the river for fish with its hooked wingtips as it glided along silently above the water. As he followed its progress, the flier's right wingtip suddenly dipped and jerked as it lanced a bug-hunting fish just below the gills. Quickly transferring the catch to its beak, it flapped mightily to straighten out and regain altitude. The last Ehomba saw of it was a flash of silver from the unlucky fish as predator and prey disappeared into the trees on the far bank.

But the movement there did not cease. Instead, it multiplied as a dark mass emerged from the wall of forest. It grew larger as it drew nearer, and in doing so resolved itself into individual shapes.

Gomo sounded the alarm. Half asleep, terrified females and infants were herded into the largest trees, where the bigger branches would offer some protection. Armed males gathered to protect them, while a strike force of the best fighters clustered around their leader. They would attempt to ward off the attackers before they could harry the more vulnerable members of the troop. The tribe's cries of panic and agitated chattering roused every animal along the river.

Ehomba clutched his spear firmly as he hunched down next to Gomo. The air around him was thick with the musky odor of the troop, but he hardly noticed it. As a herdsman, he had lived around and among animals all his life, and their smells did not bother him.

"It's them," Gomo murmured unnecessarily as he gestured with his spear-stick. "Why won't they just leave us alone?"

"You are easy prey." Ehomba seemed to become one with the tree, hardly moving. "I can see several problems with your defense already."

The troop leader's eyebrows lifted. A lesser individual might have construed the human's observation as an insult, but the desperate Gomo could not afford the luxury of indignity. "Is that so? What, for example?"

"No time. Tell you later."

In the absence of moonlight it was impossible to count the number of attacking slelves. They were more than a handful and less than a horde. Within moments they were in among the trees, diving at the troop, trying to reach the unarmed females with their infants. The monkeys screamed defiance, jabbing at the night fliers with their spear-sticks, firing feathered arrows at the dark shapes that darted between the branches. In the feeble light it was almost impossible to take proper aim at a target.

Ehomba fought alongside them, roaring the battle cry of his village and thrusting with his much longer spear even as he wondered what he was doing there. Then a shrill, piercing scream rose above the general cacophony and confusion, and he knew. An infant small enough to fit in the palm of his hand had been wrenched from its mother's arms by one of the attacking slelves. Piteous to hear, the wretched, hopeless cries of the little one were soon swallowed up by the noise of battle.

The herdsman was not as agile as his companions, but his great size gave a number of the invaders pause. It took several moments for them to realize he was no monkey, and in that time he wounded one aggressor and ran his spear through another. It fell to earth, tumbling over and over as it clutched at itself, mortally injured.

Then, just like that, it was over. The slelves withdrew back across the river, hissing and chattering among themselves, leaving the troop to count its losses. These consisted of the infant Ehomba had seen abducted and one old female who had been unable to free herself from the clutches of a pair of assailants.

An exhausted Gomo rejoined his human friend. "Two lost. Without you, my friend, it might have been much worse." He slumped heavily on the branch. "It will be worse. They will come again tomorrow."

"Why don't you just leave this place?" Ehomba asked him. "Move to another part of the river?"

The troop leader favored him with a jaundiced eye. "Don't you think we've tried that? The slelves track us, following our progress. To free ourselves from them completely would mean abandoning the entire length of the Aurisbub. It is a difficult choice. This is a good place, full of food. And there are no other troops here to compete with."

Ehomba nodded slowly. "I can understand your position."

"Yes. The living here is good. The water is clean and we have plenty to eat. It would be a paradise for us if not for the slelves."

Folding his arms over his chest, the herdsman leaned back against the trunk of the tree. "I admire anyone willing to stand up and fight for their chosen home. Tell me, Gomo, were the slelves here before you?"

The troop leader looked up sharply. "Whose side are you on here, man?"

"The side of those who do not steal children from their mothers." At this, Gomo relaxed. "But I have lived long enough to know that in such conflicts the truth is rarely as obvious and straightforward as either of the combatants would like others to believe."

"We offered you our assistance in return for your help in fighting the slelves. Slurs I can get for free."

"Don't be so sensitive, Gomo." Ehomba jabbed playfully at him with the butt end of his spear. "I have taken your side. But since I was very young I was taught always to examine both sides of a rock before picking it up. One never knows when there might be a scorpion on the other side." He straightened. "Now, let us see what these slelves of yours look like close up."

Instantly Gomo put aside his irritation with the tall human. "You have some ideas?"

"Perhaps," Ehomba replied noncommittally. "First I need to make sure of what I am dealing with."

The slelve he had speared lay where it had landed, sprawled on the grassy ground, one wing crumpled beneath it. With a total wingspan of more than six feet, it was an impressive creature. Covered in fine gray and beige fur, the humanoid body was slim and no bigger than a juvenile monkey. Two six-inch-long antennae protruded from the fuzzy forehead. The nostrils were wide and large, the ears pointed and batlike, and the great oversized eyes closed. A spear fashioned from sharpened wood lay nearby where the slelve had dropped it. Ehomba picked it up. Suitable for carrying by a flying creature with limited lift capability, it was made of a much lighter wood than the monkeys favored. But the tip was as sharp as a sewing needle.

Reaching down, he picked up the dead body in one hand. It weighed surprisingly little, much less than a monkey of comparable size. Much slimmer build, he saw, and bones that might be partially hollow. But the mouth was filled with needlelike teeth that were as sharp as the tip of the wooden spear, and the pointed nails on hands and feet hooked downward for grabbing and holding on.

"What do you think?" Behind Gomo, a clutch of males crowded close to listen. Several were bleeding from nasty bites and scratches. One had a heavy bark bandage on his upper arm where a spear had penetrated the lean flesh.

Ehomba found himself staring across the river in the direction of the trees where the invaders had disappeared. Tilting back his head slightly, he studied the sky. Even though they had no idea what he was doing, the assembled males copied his every move. Perhaps they thought imitation would bring understanding. Monkey see, monkey comprehend, he mused.

"You must have some relief from these depredations or you would have been forced to leave this country by now. Do the slelves only attack when the moon is sleeping?"

Gomo nodded slowly. "Mostly, though, they will sometimes come when there is as little as a sliver showing. It depends"—he choked back emotion—"on how greedy they are feeling."

"Needy and greedy," added another member of the troop. Around him, his companions gave voice to their fury and frustration.

"I see." The man in their midst turned from the river to gaze down at them. "Then they will come again tomorrow night."

"In all probability." Gomo unloaded a vicious kick on the limp body of the dead slelve. "It is the time of the month that suits them."

"Then we must make ready. We will need some things."

"You *do* have an idea." The troop leader's eyes shone with eagerness.

Ehomba nodded. "I think so. It cannot hurt to try it. If nothing else, it will surprise them."

Gomo put a long-fingered hand on the herdsman's arm. "Tell us what to do."

IV

AFTER SEEING TO THE SETTING OF A NIGHT WATCH, GOMO AND
the other members of the troop retired to an uneasy sleep, leaving Ehomba to contemplate his plan in silence. If it worked, it
might well free the troop from the depredations of the slelves
forever. If not, he would try something else. Though he was
dismayed at the delay in his journey, he had given his word
that he would try to help. And he had told Gomo the truth in
one other matter.

He didn't much care for a people who stole the children of
others.

The following morning the monkeys responded to his directions with an alacrity that bordered on the hyperkinetic,
rushing to and fro in response to instructions almost before he
could finish explaining what he wanted them to do. As the intent behind his directives became clear, Gomo began to smile
more and more frequently.

"I think I understand what you have in mind, man. You intend to make the slelves easier to see. So that we can make
better use of our bows and arrows?"

"No." As he spoke, Ehomba watched the monkeys rushing to carry out his instructions. "That is not my idea at all."

The troop leader, who thought he had figured it all out, looked momentarily crestfallen. "Then I have to confess that I don't understand."

"You will." Ehomba raised his voice to a pair of peripatetic young males. "No, not there! Higher up! Yes, that's better." He returned his attention to Gomo. "That is, you will if it works."

His refusal to explain further left the troop leader pensive, but willing to wait.

Although it hardly seemed possible, the new night brought a darkness even deeper than that of the one that had preceded it. In the dead tree they had chosen for their frontline outpost, Gomo crouched next to Ehomba. Together they surveyed the line of trees that rose like a leafy stockade on the far side of the Aurisbub.

"A perfect night for the slelves," the troop leader whispered. "I would be surprised if they chose not to make another foray." His voice fell. "Especially after their success last night."

"If this works, that will be their last success." Ehomba was quietly confident.

"I pray that it is so. I am deathly tired of having to console mothers made vacant by the slelves."

"We will know soon if you will have to do so again." Ehomba raised an arm and pointed.

The dark mass came boiling out of the far treetops, forming an ominous smudge against the night sky that blotted out the stars. To the intently focused Ehomba it seemed bigger than the one the night before. His suspicion was confirmed by Gomo.

"There are more of them tonight. In addition to the one you killed, we slew several yesterday. They are not used to multiple losses. I think we made them angry." He concluded with a quietly triumphant gesture that was a recognizable obscenity to any primate.

"Probably you did," Ehomba agreed. "In addition, they know that I am here."

Gomo looked up at the human squatting stolidly on the branch alongside him. "You are not worried, or afraid?"

"Of course I am worried. I am always worried when I know that something is coming to try and kill me. But I am not afraid. The first time a little boy is guarding cattle at night and hears a distant dragon roar, he either loses his fear or is never sent to guard the herd again." In the darkness, he smiled at the monkey. "I am a good herdsman."

The troop leader nodded sagely. "I hope you will prove as good an undertaker." A hand came up to rest gently on Ehomba's knee. "For a human, you possess almost enough natural nobility to be counted a monkey."

"They're coming." Ehomba tensed. "Make ready."

"Everyone knows what to do. You briefed them thoroughly. My people will not let you down." With that final quiet assurance, Gomo went silent.

There were indeed more of the slelves than before. Their swooping, darting movements as they crossed the river suggested agitation as well as anger. To find a human in the monkeys' midst must have surprised them. To find one fighting on behalf of his fellow primates had surely left them enraged.

Onward they flew, brandishing their spear-sticks and small knives, intent this night not merely on abduction but on murder. Their collective demeanor suggested an intention to deliver a lesson to the monkeys: that resistance was futile, and that death would always be met with more death.

Rising from the branch on which he had been kneeling, Ehomba raised his spear above his head and waved with his free hand. "Here! We're over here!"

Like a dark river, the flush of slelves shifted in midflight to home in on the dead tree. Spears were drawn back in readiness for throwing. The high-pitched squealing of the attackers rose until it drowned out the sound of the river, of the forest.

Gomo held his ground, or rather his branch, silently, but several of the other armed members of the troop found themselves stealing nervous glances in the human's direction. What if his plan didn't work? they found themselves wondering. After all, it was a human and not a monkey plan, and everyone knew that the People of the Trees were vastly more clever and devious than any ground dweller. Still, none of them ran, as much out of fear of what Gomo would do to them if they did than from any terror of the approaching slelves.

Certainly Ehomba waited a long time, until the slelves were virtually upon them. Then, swinging his spear in a wide arc to clear a path through the first of the attackers, he shouted at the top of his lungs, "Now!" and scrambled down the tree trunk as fast as his clumsy human arms and legs would carry him.

His descent was not nearly as agile as that of his companions, but he still made it before the monkeys at the bottom removed the covers from their fire gourds and tossed the blazing containers against the base of the dead, lightning-hollowed tree. The troop had spent the previous day filling as much of the empty trunk as they could with a loose packing of dry leaves, twigs, flammable tree sap, and anything else that would burn fast and hot. They had done their job well. Converted almost instantly into a giant torch, the dead bole exploded in flame. Yellow-red tongues of fire erupted skyward, temporarily splashing the night with light that was brighter than that of morning.

Arrayed in the surrounding branches and on the ground, grim-faced members of the troop prepared to do battle. Their watering eyes struggled to adjust to the sudden, intense illumination. But if the human was right, the nocturnal slelves would have a much more difficult time handling the abrupt, unexpected flare of brightness. If his assumptions were cor-

rect, those attackers flying closest to the unexpected blaze
ought to be momentarily but thoroughly blinded. The actual
result, however, was different in a fashion quite unforeseen by
the meticulous herdsman.

Gomo was gesturing madly with his spear-stick. "See!
They are not blinded."

"No." Ehomba stood next to the troop leader and watched
the tree-torch light up the night sky. "It is worse for them than
that."

The monkeys waited for the fighting to begin. And waited,
and stared in amazement.

Reacting like moths, the night-dwelling slelves found
themselves irresistibly drawn to the towering blaze. Mesmer-
ized, they darted up and down, in and about the length of the
blazing tree. And like moths, an individual would swoop in
too close to the conflagration, only to be consumed. One after
another the slelves incinerated themselves, erupting one after
another in a burst of flaming wings and charred bodies whenever they crossed into the critical zone.

Instead of finding themselves in a desperate fight for survival, the monkeys found themselves with time to cheer,
jumping up and down and turning somersaults as they gleefully watched their enemies annihilate themselves in individual bursts of incandescent flame. A few of the slelves
managed to resist the lure of the giant torch, but they were as
blinded as Ehomba intended they should be. Fluttering
dazedly toward the river, they flew into trees and branches,
stunning themselves and becoming easy prey for the ran-
corous, vengeful monkeys.

It was all over within an hour. Near the end, the females
and children emerged from the place of hiding where they had
been sent for safety to cheer the final vestiges of the jubilant
massacre. Ehomba took no part in this sorry business, prefer-
ring to stay on the sidelines and let the monkeys take out their
frustrations on those who had for too many seasons stolen

their children. When the troop was finished, not one slelve who had crossed the river was left alive.

Lingering behind, something barely glimpsed from the corner of his eye caught his attention. No member of the troop saw it, being fully engaged as they were in the slaughter of the surviving slelves. But Ehomba did. He froze, one hand stealing toward the sky-metal blade that hung ready for use against his back.

The bulging teardrop shape was a black smudge against the firelit sky. Two burning red eyes of pure vileness glared back at him above a mouth-slit that reminded him of a sword cut on ebony skin. When it parted slightly, the mouth shape bled malignance. As he watched, it darted through the air and took a bite out of the firelight. Not the fire itself, only the light. Slowly he slid the iron blade halfway from its scabbard, doing his best not to draw the nebulous entity's attention.

Then, on its own, it whirled and departed. Perhaps the light of the fire was too intense for it, he thought, or the taste not to its liking. In any event, it was not the illumination from the fire it was after but the light of triumph being expressed by the victorious monkeys. That was what its kind would truly delight in consuming. As soon as he was sure it was gone, he let the blade drop back into its sheath.

Something touched him. Turning sharply, he saw Gomo at his side. The troop leader had recoiled in response to the tall human's reaction. "What's wrong, friend Ehomba? You had the strangest look on your face just then. I have never seen you so tense, or so rigid."

Solemnly, the herdsman pointed in the general direction of the blaze. "I saw something by the tree."

Leaning slightly to his right, the troop leader peered past him. "I was looking in the same direction. I saw nothing."

"They are very difficult to see, for men as well as monkeys. It takes the eye of an experienced tracker. It was an eromakadi."

Gomo made a face. "I do not know that animal."

"It is not an animal. It is one of those creatures that lives in the spaces that fill the gaps in the real world. An eater of light. Not the kind of light that comes from the sun, or even from a fire like that." He pointed again at the flaming tree. "The eromakadi thrive on the light that comes from a new mother's joy in her babe, or an artist's delight in a new way of seeing the world around him. When they fixate on quarry, they are relentless. They are responsible for much of the misery in the world. We do not see them a lot in the south, where life is hard and there is little of glowing happiness for them to prey upon. The elders of my village know them, and from infancy all Naumkib children are taught how to recognize and deal with such creatures."

"I see." Gomo considered. "From what you tell me, I think I am glad I cannot see them."

"They are all around, but very sly and unpredictable. Some days they are themselves preyed upon by the eromakasi, the eaters of darkness, but this is uncommon. Unlike the eromakadi, the eromakasi seek to avoid confrontation." He turned toward the river. "It does not matter. I thought we might have to deal with this one, but it was quite a small specimen of its kind, and it did not stay long. Perhaps it smelled a greater happiness or inspiration elsewhere and went to seek it."

"I hope so," Gomo replied with feeling. "I dislike the idea of having to fight something I cannot see."

"It is very difficult, both for men and for monkeys. The next time you are severely depressed, or extremely unhappy, you can almost be certain that an eromakadi is close by, gnawing at your disposition."

Even though the night was warm and the heat from the burning tree prickly against his fur, Gomo shivered slightly. For all his disarming simplicity, it seemed that the tall human was in possession of knowledge that was denied to the People of the Trees.

The dead tree torch burned for another hour, and the embers that were its legacy glowed all through the remainder of the night, but as Ehomba had surmised, the surrounding jungle was too green and too damp to do more than smolder at the edges of the fire. The few nearby boles that did catch alight soon burned themselves out, the incipient blazes smothered by humidity, sap, and lingering dew.

Later, Gomo sought him out again, this time to offer congratulations. "Except for the eromakadi creature, which only you saw, it went much as you said it would, Ehomba."

"No," he replied reflectively, "not as I said it would. I thought they would be blinded. I did not expect them to be enraptured."

"Well, you expected them to be dead, and that is what they are." A spidery hand reached up to clap him on the side. "The People of the Trees are in your debt 'til the end of time!"

The herdsman smiled politely down at the troop leader. "Until I reach Kora Keri will be sufficient."

"It was something we would not have thought of. When we chose to remain in the trees while humans and apes went down to the ground, we forswore the use of fire." Gomo shook his head and stuck out his lower lip. "Fire and trees make a poor mix. Fire in trees is much worse." Using the tip of his spear, he tapped his friend on the shoulder. "That is the trade you humans made when you came down out of the trees. Freedom for fire."

"I suppose. I was not there at the time the decision was made so I was not given the choice."

"Oh-ho! A mastery of drollery as well as strategy. I will miss you, friend Ehomba."

"Perhaps, but your troop will not." He indicated the trees where males who had been prepared to die had joyfully reunited with their mates and offspring. The shapes and sizes and gruntings and chatterings of the reunion differed from what he would have encountered back in the village, but the tender domestic scene still left him feeling homesick. "They will be glad to see me gone."

Gomo turned to follow the herdsman's gaze and sniffed. "Yes, it's true. Humans make them uncomfortable. Especially tall, fighting humans like yourself." He looked back up at his newfound friend. "Where are you bound?"

"Finally? Truth to tell, I'm not sure of the exact location. For now, to the north. Hopefully to find someone to carry me across the Semordria to a land I have never heard of before—a place called Ehl-Larimar."

The troop leader frowned. "I've never heard of the place, either."

"A dying foreigner charged me with trying to save a beautiful woman from the embrace of a man she does not love or want."

Gomo considered the man's words, rubbing his chin with an index finger longer than that which could be found on any human. "Let me see if I understand: You have left behind your country and your family to go to a place you do not know, for a man you never knew, to fight an enemy you have never seen, on behalf of a woman you have never met."

"That is a very good summation, Gomo."

The monkey leader grunted. "And humans say we monkeys are stupid." He shook his head slowly. "Why are you doing this? If the fellow is dead, he no longer can trouble you."

"I am doing it because I have to. Because it is the kind of person I am," Ehomba explained frankly.

"You could turn around right now." Like hovering dragonflies, Gomo's fingers fluttered toward the south. "Say to anyone who asks why you are returning that you tried but could not get through. The dry lands stopped you, a river stopped you, an angry crocodile stopped you. No one need know otherwise."

"I would."

"Twaddle. An answer worthy of a hero. Or a fool." Hairy brows tried to mate as the troop leader leaned close and peered up into his friend's face. "I wonder. Which are you, Etjole Ehomba?"

"I don't know. Maybe both. Of one thing I am certain, though. It is in my nature to ask many questions. Before I am finished with this, that is one whose answer I will have."

Gomo nodded. "I hope you are not a fool. Fools die quickly and easily, with none to mourn them, and after what you have done for us this night it would grieve me to see you dead." Drawing back slightly, he straightened and smiled. "But in the end we are all dead. Tonight we live." He pointed to where other members of the troop were piling fruits, nuts, edible shoots and bugs in a delectable heap. "There will be a celebration. See? Preparations have already begun. If you think you humans know how to have a good time, then you have never partied with the People of the Trees! Come, Etjole Ehomba. Come and relax and forget your burden for one night! Tomorrow we will start upriver toward Kora Keri. Tonight, maybe we can help you forget who you are."

Ehomba rose from where he had been sitting and staring out at the river and the piles of incinerated slelves. What had the delicate flying creatures left on the other side of the river when they had flocked to attack the People of the Trees? Females and infants, now huddled in futile wait for their fighters to return? He strained, but could hear no sounds of wailing, no distant echoes of lamentation. It was as well. Too much death could cling to a man, like a bad odor no amount of soap could wash away. Turning to follow Gomo, he glanced down at a blackened corpse from which the wings had been singed and found himself wondering idly if it would be good to eat.

Gomo had not been bragging. The celebration began much as expected. What he had failed to mention was the monkeys' talent for seeking out fermented honey and fruit juices and combining them in ways no human had ever considered.

Ehomba awoke the following morning with a head that throbbed as if he had spent the night in the midst of a cattle stampede with the occasional steer using his skull for a football. His sorry condition engendered much good-natured jesting among the members of the troop. These chittering jibes and sallies he bore with his usual good humor.

The entire troop escorted him north. When Gomo had mentioned the location of Kora Keri, Ehomba had imagined he could find it himself simply by following the river north. But as he soon saw, it was not so easy as that. Numerous islands thick with jungle split the river into dozens of channels, not all of which flowed north. A wrong choice would send a traveler meandering in the wrong direction or, even worse, back the way he had come.

But the troop knew exactly where they were going. Following a road through the treetops that was invisible to him but wide and obvious to his companions, they pushed on past deceptive forks and mendacious tributaries, forging as straight a line as possible given the preponderance of dense vegetation and the occasional swamp. Without his active, agile guides Ehomba knew he might well have become hopelessly lost.

Of course, he could have continued as he had originally planned, turning west until he struck the coast again and then following it north. That would have kept him going in the right direction. But he would have missed Kora Keri and its amenities entirely.

River serpents broke the surface in the deeper channels. They posed no danger to the arboreal troop. Of more concern were the dragondines that skimmed low over the river. Whenever one of these swooped too near, the monkeys retreated into the trees where the leathery-winged fliers could not go and waited there until it had glided past. Yellow eyes glared balefully at the unreachable prey that taunted from the cover of entwined branches.

Before very many days had passed they reached a place where the river became a broad, slow, single channel. Descending from the branches, Gomo strode proudly to the grassy riverbank and dipped a finger in the murky liquid. Straightening, he turned proudly to Ehomba and pointed westward.

"We have reached the confluence of the Aurisbub and the Kohoboth. From here, the water flows west into the Semordria." Pivoting, he gestured in the opposite direction. "On the far bank a day's journey from here lies Kora Keri. You will have to find a way to cross the river. This is where we must leave you now to begin our journey back home. To a home that is safe now, where even children may feel free to play in the treetops and scamper along the water's edge."

Hands held high over his head, he waddled up to the herdsman and wrapped long arms around the human's waist. The powerful, slim arms gave a sharp, quick hug. "Good-bye, Etjole Ehomba. I will always think of you as a hero, because to believe you a fool would cause me too much pain."

Reaching down, Ehomba gave the troop leader's shoulder a friendly squeeze. "Believe me, it does my digestion no good to think of it either."

Raising his spear over his head with the shaft held parallel to the ground, he made sure his pack and weapons were secure against his back. Then, to the surprise and delight of the troop, especially the young ones, he plunged into the Aurisbub, showing Gomo that it was not necessary for him to find a way across.

Behind him, the female monkeys set up a lilting ululation that followed him as far as the middle of the river, where the coppery tonal palette of their combined voices became lost amid the swirling babble of running water. Here where the river was broad, the current was very weak. He was a strong swimmer, and the far shore was already looming near.

He grew gradually aware that he had company.

The frog was the biggest he had ever seen. Between its extended legs and its body it was at least as long as his arm. Dark green with black spots, it swam parallel to him on the surface, kicking once for every three strokes of his while tracking his progress with great bulging eyes. These were covered by some kind of transparent mask or goggles to which was attached an upward curving tube manufactured from some exotic, bright blue material. In addition, strange webbed footwear of the same matching blue substance covered the frog's feet, and it was clad in a false skin of some shiny turquoise-hued fabric.

"You swim well," the frog commented as it kicked along.

"What are you wearing?" Ehomba's arms pulled him through the water even as his legs pushed him forward.

"Mask, snorkel, fins, wet suit. I'm a great believer in redundancy, man. When others of my kind must turn away and flee, these let me get by in those places where the water turns to liquid methane." Behind the mask, one bulging eye winked knowingly. "There's good hunting in liquid methane, if you know where to look and don't let the cold get to you."

Ehomba rolled onto his back and continued kicking. "I've never heard of such a thing."

"There are many extraordinary places in the world where most folks fear to go, man. But not me." It grinned at him, but then it was always grinning. Like most frogs, this one couldn't help it. "A friend of mine is an eagle with no taste for amphibians. You ought to see his jet backpack."

"What manner of magic might that be?" Ehomba inquired. But there was no reply, for the outlandishly equipped batrachian had already arched its limber spine and dived, to be

seen no more. The herdsman did not dwell on the strangeness
of what he had seen or what the frog had said. There was indeed much that was odd in life, and a man who allowed it to
trouble his mind would find his time on Earth forever dominated by nagging second thoughts about the stability of his
cosmos.

His right foot struck something hard and unyielding, and
for a moment he tensed. But it was only the bottom of the
river, coming up to greet him. Emerging from the shallows, he
looked back the way he had come. Though he could see
clearly to the far bank, there was no sign of the troop. Having
made their farewells, they had, as Gomo indicated they
would, started on the way back to their southern forest.

Water dripped from him, drying as it fell, while he checked
his gear to make sure nothing had been lost in the crossing.
Assured that all was intact, he turned to the east and resumed
walking. In the warm, humid atmosphere that clung to the
river, the breeze created by his fast pace swept across his sodden clothes and helped to cool him.

He made a solitary camp that night by the river's edge. In
the absence of the chattering, hyperactive monkeys, the silence that engulfed him was stupendous. The stars seemed to
edge closer, as if interested in inspecting the lone man
crouched next to the small fire, eating by himself in the darkness.

He thought he felt something brush against him. A chill like
a thin stream of ice water ran down his back and he whirled,
but if there was anything prowling the night, it was no more
palpable than darkness itself. He saw nothing. Taking a deep
breath, he lay down and wrapped himself in his blanket. If
something wanted to take him while he slept, there was nothing he could do about it. A man must sleep. He would rely, as
always, on his tracker's intuition and alertness to awaken him
if anything approached too near. Even an eromakadi, though
he was not too worried about that.

After all, there was clinging to him no exceptional brightness, no radiant happiness, and therefore nothing to make him particularly attractive to those malevolent ephemera that haunted the margins of what most men falsely believed to be an immutable reality.

V

MORNING BROUGHT RENEWED DETERMINATION TO PRESS ON. Just as Gomo had promised, the cultivated fields that marked the outskirts of the city by encircling Kora Keri like a verdant necklace soon came into view.

To say that the town was a colossal disappointment might have been too strong a conclusion, but at first glance it certainly was not what Ehomba had either expected or hoped for. In fairness to Gomo, the troop leader had never ventured an actual description of the municipality. He had only said that Ehomba might find useful directions or assistance there. It was good, the herdsman reflected as he walked toward the gate in the defensive mud wall that encircled the community proper, that he had hoped for nothing more.

From what he could see, Kora Keri had little to boast of but size. There were no towering temples, no marble palaces, no architectural marvels rendered in stone and brick. Though clearly a much poorer place than he had expected, the town was also far more populous. Plenty of activity was visible beyond the gate, through which a line of horse- and camel-drawn wagons, buffalo carts, giant cargo-carrying sloths, and pedestrians was slowly filing. A brace of husky guards checked bundles and packages, though for what manner of contraband Ehomba did not know. Fetching up against the back of the line, he patiently awaited his turn to enter.

"Well, a stranger stranger than usual." The guard rubbed at an itch beneath the brim of his tightly wound, bright blue turban and gawked at the tall herdsman standing before him.

"From the south, I would think." Approaching Ehomba, one of the other guards sniffed ostentatiously at the visitor. "This one stinks of sheep and cattle—and something else." He inhaled again and made a show of analyzing the aroma, like some degenerate oenophile pondering a particularly pungent vintage. "I've got it. Monkey! He stinks of monkey."

All five of the sentries on duty laughed while offering their own crude comments. One stepped up to poke the herdsman ungently in the ribs. "Tell me, herdsman: What are the hidden meanings of this distinctive perfume? Does it mean that when you are not consorting with sheep, you like to screw in the treetops?"

"You'd better watch your step in Kora Keri," another advised gleefully. "The whores here prefer hard coin, not bananas." Once more the mirth was general.

In response to this widespread jollity Ehomba offered no comment; he simply stood and waited patiently for a remark worth responding to. Wiping at his eyes as the laughter finally began to fade, the officer in charge confronted the traveler with something resembling formality. Behind him, the line waiting to enter the inner city was growing longer, and murmurs of impatience could be heard rising from drivers and tradesfolk.

"So then, monkey lover, what is your business here?"

"I am only passing through." Ehomba maintained a straight-ahead gaze and did not look at the guard.

"Passing through, eh?" The officer winked at his men, who

were thoroughly enjoying themselves at the stranger's expense. "Passing through to where?"

"To the north," Ehomba explained candidly.

"Really? You'd best not go too far north. It is said there is big trouble brewing there." He took a step back and fingered the hilt of the sword scabbarded at his waist. "One gold piece entrance fee."

Ehomba frowned slightly. "I did not see anyone else paying an entrance fee."

The officer's expression darkened. "You need to look closer, then. Maybe there's something wrong with your eyes." His voice darkened. "If not, a little partial blindness can be arranged." Reaching down, he drew the sword partway from its scabbard.

The herdsman turned to meet the threatening gaze. "I do not want any trouble."

"Then don't go looking for it." With his other hand the officer extended an open palm. Nearby, his men tensed.

"I am a simple herdsman. I have mostly cattle and some sheep, but no coin. My village is a poor one."

The officer shrugged. "Not a problem. Turn around and go back to it."

Ehomba eyed the other side of the gate longingly. He could hear the sounds of a bustling bazaar, smell meat and vegetables being cooked in oil with exotic spices, understand many of the come-ons of unseen hawkers and barkers. "I have come a long way and am very tired. I need food and rest."

"Go ask your friends the monkeys to feed you!" suggested one of the sentries. His companions chuckled, but did not let down their guard.

"Maybe you have something you can trade." Not wishing to appear entirely unreasonable, the officer eyed the pack on the traveler's back. Even unprepossessing southerners, it was said, sometimes carried interesting goods and artifacts with them.

"I am traveling light as it is. I need everything I have," the herdsman protested softly.

"That spear, for instance." The officer gestured at the slender weapon in question. "Barbaric design and decoration, pretty useless in a fight, but perhaps worth something in the marketplace as a curio."

"As I said, I need everything I have."

"Oh, surely not everything." The officer winked at his men a second time, then took a step forward. His mouth twisted. "That point, for instance. What kind of stone is that?"

"It is not a stone." Lowering the spear, Ehomba indicated the dark brown, serrated seven-inch-long spearpoint. "It is a tooth that has been turned to stone. It comes from a creature that no longer walks the Earth. The wise people of my tribe believe that the spirit of its owner still inhabits the stone."

"Ah, good! A fine story to go with the weapon. Together they ought to be worth almost a gold piece." Extending a hand, he held tight to the haft of his sword with the other. "Give it to me." Immediately, his men spread out to prevent the reluctant traveler from fleeing.

Ehomba studied the circle of armed men. "Very well," he replied at last. "Here." Lowering the spear, he gave it a short thrust in the officer's direction.

Instantly, swords were drawn and the guard stepped back. What happened next was a matter of some debate among those farmers and traders who were lined up waiting to enter the inner city. Most saw nothing, whereas those in front insisted that, for the briefest of instants, something monstrous had appeared before the town gate. Something like a dragon, only much bigger, with a head the size of a bullock cart, eyes like Death itself, and enormous teeth curved like scimitars. It had startlingly tiny arms, a long, stiff tail, and, unlike any common dragon, it walked on two feet like a man.

It bent low over the aghast guards and growled, the sound coming from deep in its belly. At this the men flung their weapons aside and fled, all save one, who fainted on the spot. Eyeing the prone individual, the beast bent low and nudged it with gaping jaws. But before it could snap the man up and devour him in a single bite, Ehomba drew back his spear. There was a rushing noise, as of air escaping into a vacuum, and the monster seemed (so insisted a dealer in herbs near the front of the line who claimed to have witnessed the whole business) to vanish, sucked back into the point of a spear wielded by a tall southerner standing beneath the gate.

Back in the line, rearing horses and panicked pigs fully occupied the attention of their owners, so that not all eyes were fixed on the drama by the entrance to the city. Without saying a word, the traveler entered, striding purposefully off in the direction of the bazaar. In the sudden absence of guards there was a rush to follow, as people and goods scrambled to take advantage of the opportunity to avoid the irritating inspection that usually befell all those attempting to enter from outside. As for the story, it swiftly lost currency as a topic of conversation as people immersed themselves in the necessary business of the day.

Ehomba located a plain but clean inn whose owner, in light of the fact that business had been slow lately, reluctantly agreed to accept some of the colorful Naumkib trade beads the tall stranger carried with him in lieu of coin. Settling himself on a real bed for the first time since he had left home, Ehomba unpacked and spread his belongings out on the floor to air. The fist-sized cotton bag of glassy gravel from the beach north of the village he placed beneath the pillow, both to remind him of home and because the pillow was too smooth and soft to sleep on. Rolling over, he could smell the sea stench that still adhered to the sack of pebbles.

In this manner he fell into a soundless sleep, awakening with the sunrise as was his habit. After washing up and repacking his gear, he retired to the dining room. It provided breakfast in the form of sausages, toasted breads enhanced by an interesting variety of seeds and chopped nuts, butter, jams, eggs of varying size and color, and meats both cooked and cold. It was an impressive and necessary repast, and when the herdsman departed it was with the satisfaction of having received fair value for goods given.

Already the bazaar was teeming with traders and farmers and craftsfolk hawking their produce. Colorful canopies of woven fabric shaded the stalls and benches while signs in several scripts beckoned buyers from above dark doorways. Wealthier shopkeepers sold everything from rugs to rambutan, silver to snake oil, fish to fine filigree work. Pancake makers hovered over hissing grills, competing in batter and patter. A heavyset woman clad in a silken blouse and denim trousers tried to sell him long pants to replace his woolen kilt, while from a narrow doorway a scrawny young mongoose of a youth attempted to inveigle the tall herdsman into purchasing (or at least renting) one of several lithesome young ladies packed into the shadows behind him.

All around Ehomba there was sound and discussion, with only a minimal amount of fury. Another time, he would have lingered in fascination. But he was in a hurry, to fulfill his obligation and to return home. Having eaten, he was able to ignore the frenetic blandishments of the food vendors. What he did need was information on boats or, failing that, on the best route north.

Several queries led him to a multistory mud-brick building, where a dark dwarf at the entrance directed him up a tiled stairway to the third floor. Reaching the top, he turned down an open hallway. One side was exposed to the city and to the light, in contrast to the dark stairwell he had ascended.

At the end of the porch-hallway he found a portal barred only by a curtain of dangling beads. In response to his query, a voice from within bade him enter.

He found himself in a spacious room filled with shelves

and dominated by a tinkling fountain of black and gray stone set near a far window. The stone was full of ancient animals that had been petrified, not unlike the tip of his spear. Moving close, he found he could sense their spirits, though they were not nearly as strong as the one that inhabited his weapon. Mostly they were of modest creatures that crawled and fluttered along the ocean floor.

The shelves and bookcases were filled to overflowing with specimens taken from the natural world, and with well-rubbed ancient books and scrolls. The room was very much the habitat of a scholar, well read and with extensive knowledge of the world beyond the town. He felt he had come to the right place.

"Be with you in a moment!" The voice came from a door set in the far wall. Finding an empty seat, Ehomba settled himself into it as best he could, taking care that the two swords slung against his back did not bump up against the embossed leather of the expensive chair.

A figure emerged from the unseen room beyond the doorway. It was not at all what Ehomba had expected. Extending a hand and favoring him with a cheerful smile, the young woman made motions for him to retain his seat.

"Good morning! I am Rael, of the school of Cephim. How may I help you?"

"I—please excuse my poor country manners. I was expecting . . ."

"Someone older?" Her eyes twinkled. "A superannuated, parchment-skinned man with a long white beard, perhaps? Or a lumbering fat woman with a crystal ball?" She laughed, and her laughter was the sound of summer waves lapping at a white sand beach. "I get that all the time. I'm sorry to disappoint you."

He tried not to stare. "I did not say that I was disappointed."

"Gentlemanly put. You are . . . ?"

"Etjole Ehomba. A herdsman from the south."

"Yes, I can tell that by your style of dress and your, um, bouquet." She settled herself behind a desk that was piled high with open books and specimens of insects, plants, stuffed birds, stones polished and rough, and colored glass bottles containing unknown liquids. "What do you need from me, Ehomba? Have some of your cattle gone missing?"

"No." She was teasing him now, he felt, and he determined to convey the gravity of his purpose to her in no uncertain terms. "It concerns an obligation put upon me by one who lay dying."

"Ah." Her mien grew serious and for the first time he saw, behind the unavoidable physical beauty and agile wit, a much deeper persona. "Tell me about it."

As he spoke, the air in the room seemed to chill slightly and the light pouring through the windows to darken. When he had finished, she sat in silence, eyes closed, contemplating all that she had just heard. When at last she opened them and focused on her visitor again, he noticed that they had changed color, shifting noticeably from blue to black.

"This is a serious business you speak of, Etjole Ehomba."

"Very much so, Rael."

"As to your question, there are boats that call regularly at Kora Keri. They ply the trade routes along the Kohoboth, traveling west with the current and returning eastward with the wind. But none that I know of would think of daring the wild currents of the Semordria. There are delta-based merchants who do leave the safe confines of the river. You might travel to its mouth in hopes of meeting one of them, but even they trade only along the coast. The idea of actually crossing the ocean would horrify them. They are interested in making money, not in noble exploration."

"I see," he replied resignedly. "Then I will have to continue northward until I find a captain and crew whom the notion of undertaking such a journey does not fill with terror."

She wagged a warning finger at him. "There is trouble in the north."

"So I have been told." Idly, he wondered if the gate guards had stopped running. At his feet, his spear stirred slightly, as if it were part of a cavernous mouth that was flexing in its sleep. "I do not fear trouble."

She eyed him intently, and he wondered at her purpose. With an effort, he forced himself to think of his wife. "What *do* you fear, Etjole Ehomba?"

He formulated a reply. "Ignorance. Prejudice. Eromakadi."

Her perfect eyebrows rose slightly. "So you are more than a mere herdsman."

"No. Nothing more." He waited silently.

After a moment, she grunted softly. "You are a tracker of certain things, I am a reader of certain things. I will give you instructions that will let you find the best route north, if you are determined to continue on. But first, for my interest, and because I like you, I will attempt to see what the future holds for you." Her expression conveyed a professionalism that worked hard to conceal a seething, underlying sensuality.

From a cabinet behind the desk she withdrew a crystal. Not round, as was the norm, but perfectly square. It was filled with embedded bits of other minerals. Rutilated quartz, he decided, or something even more exotic. Without waiting to be asked, he drew his chair close.

Setting the crystalline cube down on the desk between them, she began to make passes over its surface with her hands, caressing the transparent material with the tips of her fingers. Unwillingly, he found himself envying the stone. Within, the embedded shards of darker material twitched, shuddered, and began to move, realigning themselves according to cryptic patterns that meant nothing to him, but whose very activity he found fascinating. As near as he could tell, the stone cube was solid. Yet the deeply rooted inner crystals were clearly shifting their position within the rock.

The quartz cube grew cloudy as it embarked on a sequence of color changes. One moment it was morion, the next citrine, then amethyst, a squared succession of gemstone properties. Through it all Rael sat almost motionless, wholly intent on her task. Ehomba could only look on, equally entranced by the doer and the doing.

At last she looked up, closed her eyes, sighed deeply, and seemed to slump in on herself. The cube became colorless again save for the rutile and other inclusions. Opening her eyes, she blinked at him. Expecting a smile, he was disappointed.

"Go home, Etjole Ehomba."

He blinked. "What?"

"Go home." She laid one fine hand atop the cube. "It is all here. I saw it. Disaster, complete and entire. You are doomed to unremitting misery, your quest to failure, the rest of your life to cold emptiness. Unless you end this now. Go home, back to your village and to your family. Before it is too late. Before you die."

VI

STUNNED, HE SAT BACK IN HIS CHAIR. OUTSIDE, THE CACOPHony of the bazaar continued to rage raucously, the piquant odors of frying food still drifted up to the upper floors of surrounding buildings. But within the room something was different. Something had changed.

Despite her fervor, she was as beautiful as ever. Briefly, he wondered how that intensity of intellect might translate into physical passion. The moment passed, as circumstances compelled him to concentrate on other matters.

"I do not understand." He indicated the crystal cube. "What did you see in that thing to render so dire a warning?"

As she spoke, her eyes changed from black to green. "A woman of great—no, of supernal, beauty."

He pursed his lips. "That is not a sighting I would call a prelude to disaster."

"Then you know little of the real world, traveler."

His head dipped in barely perceptible acquiescence. "I cannot argue that. I am but a poor herdsman."

She eyed him shrewdly. "Are you, Etjole Ehomba? Looking at you, sitting here across from me, far from your animals and your village, I find myself wondering. A herdsman to be sure, and poor in the false coin of commerce perhaps, but there are other kinds of wealth, other means for measuring riches and the true worth of an individual. So, I wonder."

As always, he was uncomfortable when the subject was him. He gestured anew at the cube. "If your intent is to turn me from my chosen path, you will have to come up with a threat greater than the sight of a beautiful woman."

"My 'intent' is to do no such thing. I desire only to try and see what the future holds for you. The path you choose is your own, and only you can decide whether or not to walk it. Life is a noun, Etjole, and living it no more or less than a matter of adding adjectives." Her petite, fine-skinned hand brushed over the top of the cube. "I am here only to show you what adjectives may be added."

"The woman you saw is the Visioness Themaryl," he told her.

Her eyes widened. "So you have seen a little of the future yourself."

"Nothing of the sort." He crossed his arms casually over his chest and leaned back in the chair, rocking it gently. "It is the name of the woman abducted against her will, and was confided to me by the dying soldier Tarin Beckwith. It comes from my past, not my future."

"Well, it lies here in your future as well." The sensuous seer bent forward over the cube. "She is being held captive by a small man who commands great evil."

"Hymneth the Possessed."

"Yes." Rael frowned as she studied the rutilated innards of the crystal. "There swirls about him an air of great confusion. I cannot tell if he possesses this evil or is possessed by it."

"I would think the two would go together," Ehomba commented.

"As often they do, but the confusion and uncertainty here

are profound beyond anything I have ever encountered before." She glanced up from the cube, and her eyes were a pale yellow, like those of a cat. "I am a strong woman, Etjole. Confident in my abilities, secure in my knowledge. But I would never, never consider challenging a power like this that I see here. Because its body is hidden from me and impenetrable to my arts, I can discern only its effects. There are many methodologies of evil, and this one exceeds my comprehension. It frightens me even to apperceive it. I don't think I want to look into it any deeper. I might come to understand how it works.

"If you continue onward and manage to confront this Hymneth person-creature, you will be utterly destroyed. Try as I might, I can foresee no other outcome." She sat back from the cube and closed her eyes. With her sigh, the air in the room seemed to surge around him and then relax, like a wave rushing onshore only to lose all its substance and energy to the thirsty sand.

"I would have hoped," he told her in a small masterpiece of understatement, "for more encouraging words."

Her eyes opened. They were blue again. "I like you, Etjole Ehomba. Simple or not, smelly or not, it would trouble me to see you come to harm. But I can't stop you, nor would I if I could. Each of us chooses our own adjectives, our own modifiers. I choose to sit here, in this comfortable, sunny place, and parcel out my learning to those who will listen and pay. It's a good life." For the second time he saw the twinkle in her eyes. "I don't suppose I could convince you to stay with me a while. Given enough time, I might be able to talk you into saving your life."

Her body manifested itself in quiet ways that could not be ignored, not even when she was revealing matters of great import. He had been aware of it ever since she had entered the room. Now her gaze metamorphosed from penetrating to inviting, and the way she shifted in her chair produced sounds he could only hear with organs other than his ears. They were loud, and forceful, and they threatened to drown out his own inner voice.

"I can think of nothing that would please me more," he told her frankly, "if only I was not committed to fulfilling this obligation, and if I did not have a woman waiting for me in my house."

"Your house is a long way from Kora Keri, Etjole. Who is to say what your woman does to keep boredom from her door when you are not there?"

"I cannot worry about that." He rose. "I prefer not to create pain without foundation."

Smiling insidiously, she fondled the crystal cube. The inclusions within seemed to torque slightly in her direction. "I could look and try to learn the answer to that question for you."

He turned away from her. "I would rather not know."

The seer Rael sniffed, unable to mask her derision completely. "So you choose blissful ignorance. It strikes me a poor way to go into battle."

"Who said anything about bliss? And is this a battle I am fighting here? If so, whom am I battling? There is no one present except you and I, and I do not want to think that I am fighting with you."

Her lips, which in another time and place he would gladly have stilled with his own, tightened. "What a maddening man you are, Etjole Ehomba! You must pardon my forwardness. In my profession I am not used to dealing with men or women of principle. So I am having difficulty deciding what you are, and how to deal with you."

"I told you," he explained patiently, "I am—"

"A simple herdsman; yes, yes!" Rising abruptly from her chair, she turned away from him and stalked toward the rear portal. "A simple herdsman with an answer for everything. Worse, you are right." Whirling around, violet eyes blazing, she wagged a warning finger at him. "If you insist on pursuing the course you have chosen and succeed in following it to its end, you are going to die, Etjole Ehomba! Do you hear what I am saying; do you understand my words? You are going to die! What, finally, do you have to say to that?"

His voice was as calm and controlled as ever. "You have a very pretty finger."

Dropping her arm, she inhaled sharply. "I think you're right, and that I was wrong to ever think otherwise. You *are* a simple herdsman, uncomplicated and disingenuous. You're too naïve to be frightened. That—or you are the most subtle of sorcerers I have ever met." Her tone thawed. "Many are the men who have pursued me for months, years even, without success, but you have ensorcelled me in a matter of moments, and with me doing most of the talking at that." She shook her head slowly as she regarded him, a baffled look on her face.

"Who are you, Etjole Ehomba? What are you?"

Before he could reply yet again that he was but a simple herdsman from the south, she had spun on the heel of her slipper and vanished through the rear-facing beaded portal. The meeting was over. For an instant, he considered following her, to try to explain further, to do his best to assuage her upset and unease. But it might very well be dark in whatever back room she had vanished into, and the walls would certainly be closer to one another, his options for flight narrower. Nor was he entirely sure he would fight very hard to escape. Best not to place himself in a position where he might be forced to find out.

The entrance beckoned behind him. Leaving himself no more time to think, which might prove unsettling, or to feel, which could prove worse, he turned and departed.

It was only later, when he was safely back among the boisterous, jostling crowd in the bazaar, that he was struck by the realization that she had not charged him for his visit. Dipping one hand into a pocket of his kilt, he absently fingered the little sack of gravel from the beach near the village. The simplistic, repetitive activity always helped to remind him of the village and to strengthen his memories of home. The more he thought of the dazzling seer Rael, the more he needed that reinforcement. And if her words were to be believed, he had exerted as profoundly unsettling an effect on her as she had on him. Their lovemaking would have been volcanic.

But it was not to be. He pushed on through the crowd. There were preparations to be made. If, as she had told him, he would find no boat master in this country willing to attempt an ocean crossing, then he would have to seek farther north. That meant restocking the few basic supplies he could carry on his back. Salt, sugar, a few carefully chosen spices, some basic medicinal powders, and whatever else he could afford that might prove useful over the duration of an extended overland trek. If he was fortunate, he might learn of a caravan of some sort traveling north and join them for guidance and mutual protection. But since he could not count on doing so, he had to be prepared to press on alone.

Of the lands to the north of the Kohoboth he knew little, only what village oldsters like Fhastal and Meruba mumbled around communal campfires. Half and more of that might be as much sheer invention as literal truth. Fhastal in particular could be exceptionally imaginative when it came to telling tales of distant lands and strange peoples. He had never paid more than cursory attention to such ramblings because they had never functioned as anything other than stories, related for the entertainment of adults and children alike.

Now he struggled to remember what he could of those babblings, hoping to winnow a few kernels of fact from the dross of speculation. The region north of the Kohoboth was called the Unstable Lands. He did not know why. Was it because knowledge of it was so limited, or were there reasons more sinister? He would know soon enough, he realized. In the absence of access to an oceangoing ship, that was where he had to go next.

But first, restocking. And something else. He turned, heading back toward the inn that had provided him with such good food and sleep. Not because he was hungry, or even because he was ready to choose a place to spend the night, but because of something the beauteous Rael had told him. A small matter he intended to take care of even though she would not experience the resolution of it.

He did not think that he smelled, but he was willing to take her word for it. After all, she was a seer, and her word was to be believed, and until he left Kora Keri behind he would be forced to suffer the company of others whom he might not want to think the less of him. So he would sacrifice, and have a shower.

VII

It was raining when he left town early the following morning, a drab drizzle the color of liquid charcoal that dampened his spirits if not his determination. An image appeared unbidden in his mind: of Rael, lying naked beneath silken sheets in a warm room, with the cool, clean rain-swept air pouring in through an open window, chilling the interior just enough to make the sheets a welcome accompaniment, bending them snugly across the bed, letting them outline the curves of her sleeping form with gossamer gentleness, almost as soft as . . .

He wiped water from his mouth and eyes and pulled the hood sewn to the back of his collar lower on his forehead. Using his spear as a walking stick, he exited the old part of the city via the northern gate. It was considerably smaller than the one that ingressed from the west, there being far less traffic to and from the northern reaches of the city than from east or west or from the south, where the town faced the river. The two miserable guards stationed outside ignored him. They were huddled together against the rain and wholly occupied

with those travelers desiring entry. A glance showed that neither of them had been among the quintet that had, to their
detriment, harassed him on his arrival days earlier.

Despite the drizzle, men and women were out working
their fields, broad-brimmed hats and capes providing some
protection from the weather. Kora Keri was a modest town,
surviving both on trade and on the production of all manner
of growing things. Though the soil was barely adequate, the
river supplied a constant, reliable source of water. It was very
different from home, where potable water was as precious as
gold and the herds had to be moved periodically from water
hole to water hole, pasture to meager pasture.

Watching the farmers at work in their fields as he strode
past, he decided that he was glad he had not grown up in such
a well-watered land. Too much ease made a man soft, and
lazy. He was neither, nor were any of his friends back in the
village. If necessary, they could survive in the harshest desert
imaginable armed with only a digging stick and clad only in
a loincloth. He allowed himself a slight smile, wondering if
Rael had factored that knowledge into her predictions. The
Naumkib had survived many disasters. Surely he could survive one.

Who knew? Perhaps this Hymneth the Possessed would
prove amenable to reason, or even better, would have lost interest in his abducted lady by the time Ehomba reached the
land where he held sway. Even beautiful women were known
to bore powerful men eventually, and vice versa. The real trial
Ehomba faced might consist solely of reaching the sorcerer's
country—if indeed he was a sorcerer. For all her skill, Rael
had seemed uncertain as to his true vocation, if not his nature.

Well, Ehomba would find out. He hoped he would not have
to fight the fellow. Fighting was a waste of time when a man
could be looking after his herds and raising his family. Perhaps this Hymneth was not possessed by evil, but only by un-
happiness, or a choleric disposition. Ehomba was good at

making friends. Most people liked him instinctively. With
luck, so would this Hymneth the Possessed.

Water, mud, and saturated vegetable matter sloshed
through his toes. Boots would have kept his feet dry, but he
could not imagine wearing footgear that completely enclosed
his feet. A man's soles had to breathe. Besides, the air was
warm, and whatever liquid ran into the front of his sandals
quickly ran out the back.

Gradually he left the cultivated fields and struggling orchards behind. The modest road he had been following shrank
to a rutted track, then to a trail, until it finally disappeared in
undisturbed grass that rose to his knees. Startled by his approach, birds and small flying reptiles exploded from cover to
flee, squawking or hissing, in many directions. When he was
hungry enough, he killed something to eat.

Several days out from Kora Keri, he reached a broad but very
shallow river whose name he did not know. Wide sandbars
protruded from water that ran clear over gravelly shallows.
Unlike his crossing of the Aurisbub, here he confronted a wa-
tercourse that he would not have to swim.

Making sure his pack was secure, he hefted it a little higher
on his back and was preparing to make his way down the gently curving bank when a voice hissed, softly but distinctly,
"Man, I am going to kill you."

At first he could not find the source of the declaration. Only
when he lowered his gaze markedly did he see the snake lying
coiled in the grass where it gave way to the mud of the bank.
It was ten or eleven feet long and a light lavender color, its
scales shining brightly in the sun. No spots or stripes decorated its body, which helped to explain why he had not seen
it. It was within easy striking distance of the place where he
had put his foot. He knew that a poisonous snake that large
would carry a lot of venom, and even though he did not recognize the type, he doubted its words no less than its intent.

Pushing his lips close together, he responded in the language of the legless. The snake's head drew back at his reply. Plainly it was not used to being addressed by a human in its own tongue.

"You sspeak the wordss that sslither. What kind of human are you that you do sso?"

"Just a herdssman, long brother." To show that he meant no harm, and that he was not afraid, Ehomba sat down on the side of the bank, letting his feet dangle over the edge. "There are ssome herdssmen who believe that a ssnake sshould be killed on ssight, to protect their animalss. Mysself, I do not believe in killing anything unless it iss for a much more sspecific reasson."

The snake's head lowered and it eyed the seated man with great curiosity. In his seated, relaxed position, Ehomba was quite helpless before the serpent, and the snake knew it. Realizing that it could kill the biped anytime it wished, the inquisitive reptile slithered closer.

"Enlightened, as well as articulate. What if I were to kill one of your animalss? How then would you ssee me?"

Ehomba shrugged, gazing out across the river as if he had not a care in the world, including the impressively venomous reptile that had approached to within an arm's length of his exposed leg.

"All creaturess have to eat. Mysself, I am very fond of meat. So I undersstand."

"Is that sso? I have heard that ssome humanss conssume only fruitss and vegetabless."

The herdsman smiled down at the serpent. "Long brother, we each of uss eatss what ssuits our belliess. As for mysself, I cannot imagine ssurviving on a diet of nutss and grass."

The snake hissed appreciatively. "I, too, long for ssomething warm and bloody to sslide down my throat. It iss the most deliciouss feeling. But you are human: You burn your food before you eat it."

"Not alwayss. It sso happenss that I mysself also enjoy the occassional tasste of raw flessh."

Uninvited, the snake slid the upper portion of its body onto Ehomba's lap. It was heavy, and like the rest of its kind, as solid as a flexible steel cable. He could not escape now if he wanted to—but he did not want to. He was enjoying the conversation. Not all snakes were so voluble.

"What a remarkable human you are. I think maybe I will not kill you."

"I appreciate that. It would sspoil what hass otherwisse been a good day." Reaching down with one hand, he allowed the snake to slither onto it. Lifting it up, he found himself eye-to-eye with the business end of cold, smooth flesh. Personified by penetrating, slitted, unblinking oculi, Death loomed only inches away. For its part, Death regarded him cordially.

"Bessides," he added, "I am too large for you to sswallow anyway."

The serpent's tongue flicked out, delicately exploring Ehomba's lips. "You tasste good. Warm and wet. But you are right."

Gently, mischievously, the herdsman moved his hand from side to side, carrying the snake's head with it. The reptile did not object to the play. "Then why did you want to kill me?"

"You sstartled me. I don't like to be sstartled, esspecially when I am hunting. Alsso, I have not killed anything in many dayss."

"As far as that goess, long brother, I am hungry too." Lowering his hand, he let the snake's head slip back into his lap. "Would you sshare a meal with me? I will find ssomething of the right ssize to ssuit both our gulletss."

Raising its upper body three feet off the ground, the disbelieving reptile contemplated its unexpected new friend. "You would do thiss for me? After I promissed your death?"

Rising, the herdsman brushed dirt and mud from the seat of his kilt. "Why not? When I meet ssomeone else on the road I am alwayss willing to sshare a meal with them. That iss the right way of traveling."

"If thiss iss a trick, my brotherss will find you." The snake weaved back and forth as it spoke.

Ehomba smiled. "No matter. Your ssmall brotherss the wormss will have me one day regardless. Now come with me, and let uss ssee what we can find to kill. I am a good tracker."

"You have the advantage of height," the snake declared, "while I musst rely on ssmell, and on heat."

After several hours of searching, Ehomba found the spoor of a capybara and tracked it to an inlet of the river where a small herd of the giant rodents lazed in the warm shallows. Two juveniles provided more than enough food for both hunters. In deference to the sensibilities of his companion, the herdsman ate his rodent raw. The serpent was appreciative.

"The ssmell of cooked meat makess me nauseouss." Though coiled tightly next to the herdsman's campfire, the snake could not hide the bulge that now dominated its middle. Swallowing the young capy had been a slow process, and Ehomba had stood guard until the serpent had finished. "I thank you for your courtessy."

"You're welcome." Ehomba chewed slowly on a strip of haunch. It was greasy, as was all rodent meat, but not unflavorful.

"I want to give you ssomething, human. As thankss for your help in hunting, and as a reminder of our friendsship. Ssomething very sspecial. I ssee that you carry water with you."

The herdsman rested a hand on the leather water bag that was fastened to his pack. "I need it more than your kind."

"Bring it closse to me. I would go to it, but I am full."

Obediently, Ehomba removed the sloshing sack and placed it close to the snake.

"Open it." Puzzled, the herdsman complied.

Moving forward, the serpent promptly bit down on the

metal rim of the bag. Ehomba could just make out the twin
rivulets of poison that ran down the grooved fangs to filter
into the leather. When it had finished, the snake drew back.

"I have meassured the dose carefully, man. Drink it ss-
lowly, a little at a time. By the time you have finisshed the last
drop, you will be immune. Not only to my poison, but to
many other kindss." The scaly head bowed, pointing ground-
ward. "It iss my gift to you."

Gingerly, Ehomba used a patch from the repair kit that he
carried to reseal the two tiny punctures. Though dubious of
the snake's claim, he was willing to give it a try. He was not
worried about swallowing the diluted toxin. If the snake
wanted to kill him, it could do so easily, at any moment.

"Thank you for your gift, long brother." Leaning back on
the pillow of his pack, he let his gaze drift upward, toward the
stars. "And now I think we should ssleep."

"Yess." The serpent placed its head on its coils and closed
its eyes. "Try not to wake me in the morning, man. I will
ssleep for sseveral dayss."

"I will be quiet as a mousse," Ehomba assured it.

The sibilant hiss was already diffuse as the snake drifted off
into sleep. "I am quite, quite full. Sso pleasse: Do not sspeak
to me of food."

VIII

TRUE TO HIS WORD, EHOMBA MADE NO NOISE AT ALL WHEN HE awoke the following day. Ephemeral as a baby's breath on a cold morning, mist was rising from the shallow surface of the river. In the green-heavy trees on the opposite bank, a querulous parakeel screeched in solitary joy at having been granted another day of existence.

Gathering his gear about him, Ehomba parted from the serpent, reaching out to give it one final, friendly caress. Its skin was cool and dry to the touch. He had always marveled at town women who recoiled in horror from any snake, no matter how small or harmless, but who would without a qualm gladly dress themselves in snakeskin sandals or belt. The self-contradictions of his fellow man never failed to bemuse him. As for the serpent, it did not even stir, embalmed as it was in the arduous slumber of slow digestion.

Wading the gurgling, slowly running river, which at its deepest never climbed over his knees, Ehomba splashed as little as possible so as not to wake the snake—or any dozy, lurking river denizens. Slivers of silver shot past him as small schools of fingerlings twinkled like elongated stars around and past his legs. Their biology was not uppermost in his mind as he studied them thoughtfully. Unlike the great reptile he had left drowsing on the bank behind, Ehomba could still think about food.

He took an experimental sip from the water bag. The taste was slightly bitter, but not intolerable. At once, his heart began to race and a dull pounding thumped at the front of his forehead. But both faded quickly, leaving him much relieved. The snake had been true to its word.

He reached the far bank without incident. Soon the character of the landscape began to change radically. Instead of desert, or flat fertile plains, or river bottom, unchecked vegetation overwhelmed the land. He had entered true jungle, a riot of crackling greenery and noisy creatures. Such places had been only a rumor to him, as they were to anyone who had been raised in the dry, barren country to the south.

As he strode along beneath the towering boles he marveled at the variety and shapes of the growths that closed in around him. Who would have thought that the world contained so many different kinds of trees, so many varieties of vine, so many strangely shaped leaves? The plethora of insects that flew, crawled, and hopped within the forest was equally astonishing.

He had no trouble walking. The tallest trees spread their uppermost branches wide, blocking much of the sky and keeping the light from reaching the ground. There, the competition for life-giving sunlight was intense among seedlings and saplings. Gomo and his troop would love the place, he mused.

There was no trail. No traders came this way, no farmers tilled fields this far north of Kora Keri. He had to make his own way. That was a prospect that did not trouble him. It was something he had been doing all his life.

Brilliantly tinted birds whistled and sang in the branches,

dragoneels cawed, and small, uncivilized primates rustled the treetops. While watching them, he kept a sharp eye out for snakes and insects on the forest floor, where downed logs and accumulating litter made it hard to see the actual ground. Stepping over a rotting log, he was careful to avoid the bristly fungi that had sprouted along its degenerating length. Some mushrooms and toadstools were toxic to the touch, he knew, while others provided shade to tiny intelligences whose whimsical approach to existence he did not want to have to deal with right now.

A second, larger log lay ahead and he had prepared to clamber over it as well—when he saw that it was not a log. Slowing his approach, he reached out to touch the mysterious barrier. To his left it extended as far into the forest as he could see, while in the other direction it eventually made a sweeping curve northward. A splotchy grayish white, it was gouged and battered along much of its inexplicable length.

At first he thought it was made of some kind of stone, but up close he could not find a place where individual sections had been mortared, cemented, or otherwise fitted together. The surface was rough but not pebbly. About five feet high and flat on top, it was slightly wider at the base, giving it a triangular shape.

Who had built such a redoubtable structure in the middle of the jungle, and why? Looking around, he saw no evidence of other construction; no crumbling temples, no imploded homes, no collapsed warehouses. The ground offered up soil, leaves, fungi, insects, dung, and other organic material, but except for the wall, there was not a hint of artificiality. Not a shard of rock, shattered lumber, or disintegrating brick. There was only the winding, smooth-sided, unaccountable barrier.

Despite the damage that had been done to it, it was largely intact, giving evidence of considerable engineering skill on the part of its makers. Turning to his right, he followed its length until he came to a place where a foot-high section had been gouged from the top. The exposed interior revealed fine gravel in addition to the compositing material itself.

The break offered a slightly easier place to cross. Looking down the length of the wall, he considered following the rightward curve until it no longer blocked his way north. Or, he thought, he could cross the wall here and save a little time. Placing a hand on either side of the break, he boosted himself up, put his feet down in the modest gap, and stepped through.

The air changed. The forest, abruptly, was gone. And the shrieking organisms that ignored him even as they surrounded him were like nothing he had ever seen before.

A lesser man would have panicked, would perhaps have gone running out into the howling herds to be instantly trampled to death. More poised than most of his kind, Ehomba froze while he tried to take stock of his surroundings. Facing the utterly unexpected, he knew, was not unlike confronting a rampaging mammoth. Best to stand motionless, appraise the situation from every possible angle, and hope the wind was against you.

Given the chaos into which he had stepped, it was not an easy course to follow.

The very air itself stank of unnameable poisons. Reflecting its composition, it was as brown as the backside of a brick kiln. Barely visible through the haze, buildings taller than Ehomba had ever seen or heard tell of towered into a blistering sky through which the feeble disk of the sun struggled to shine. Then he saw that the raging herds of wailing creatures that surrounded him on all sides were not animals, but vehicles.

Whatever pulled them was invisible to him. Their roaring was continuous and unrestrained. That, at least, was not surprising. Crowded together as tightly as any herd of wildebeest or brontotheres, their need to communicate with one another was obvious. Each held, locked away from the outside world, anywhere from one to a dozen people. Perhaps because they whipped past him at incredible speed, he was unable to tell if they were utilizing these remarkable means of transportation of their own free will, or if such a method had been forced upon them. Studying their faces as best he could, he strongly suspected the latter. Certainly few of them looked happy. Most wore masks of pure misery.

Many of their expressions turned to startled surprise as they shot past him. A few even turned to look back, which, at the velocity they were traveling, struck him as tweaking Death far too boldly. Several managed to yell something at him in passing, but he did not understand their words.

Though he was sure the people were traveling within vehicles, like wagons or oxcarts, they conformed to a pattern that more closely resembled organized animal migration. Half raced helter-skelter westward, while the other half sped past in the opposite direction. As for himself, he pressed hard against the wall that divided these two flows of people and vehicles lest he be run down. None swerved in his direction, the area immediately next to the wall apparently being inviolate or protected by some magic spell. Though it was not always so, he reminded himself, remembering the damage he had observed along its length. Not to mention the break through which he had vaulted.

A vehicle different from the others was coming toward him, from the west. As it approached it slowed and drifted over until it was operating in the otherwise unused region proximate to the wall. The top of the vehicle boasted bright flashing lights that reminded the herdsman of the aurora that could occasionally be seen on long winter nights, or the colors that experienced conjurors could bring forth out of seeming nothingness.

It stopped some forty feet away from him and two people emerged from within. They wore strange, flat clothing that except for the absence of scales was not so very unlike the skin of his friend the serpent. Finding the similarity unnerving, he began to back away from them. They responded with shouts and gestures that left him feeling even more uncomfortable.

When they broke into a run toward him, he had only a split second to decide which way to go. Realizing that to charge out into the ceaseless migration of vehicles was to invite a quick death, he turned the other way and in a single bound, cleared the wall back the way he had come. If nothing else, it would separate him from the onrushing snake men. Behind him, he heard them yell.

He landed solidly on cushioning soil, decaying leaves, and other forest detritus. Almost as startled as he had been the first time, he whirled to look behind him. All that could be seen was dark green rain forest, stretching endlessly in all directions until it closed off every horizon. All that remained of his unsettling experience was the wall, which continued as before to run in a white line to the west and northeast. That, and his memory of the experience.

A hand reached out and grabbed him firmly by the shoulder, strong fingers digging deep into his flesh. Jerking around sharply, he saw that one of the men who had been running toward him and shouting was leaning through the break in the wall. His face was red with anger and excitement, and the peculiar headgear he wore lay slightly askew on his skull. Glaring furiously at Ehomba, he mouthed incomprehensible words as he started to pull on the herdsman's arm. Ehomba started to reach back over his shoulder for one of his swords.

Then the man glimpsed the forest behind his quarry, saw the soaring trees, the arcing vines, the struggling rain-forest plants and saplings. Heard the musical chorusing of the canopy creatures, smelled the pungent odors of decaying vegetation, inhaled the oxygen-rich air, and fainted.

Ehomba was never sure whether the man slid back over the wall or was pulled back, perhaps by his companion. Regardless, he did not reappear. Letting loose the haft of his tooth-lined sword, the herdsman turned away and resumed his hike along the wall. A couple of times he looked back uneasily, but there was no sign of his former pursuers.

No wonder he was traveling in what were known as the Unstable Lands, he reflected. Crossing the wall had seen him, for a few brief, unpleasant moments, stranded in another country. No, he corrected himself. In another world. One that, while superficially fascinating, he had no desire ever to revisit.

He eyed the wall, a constant companion on his left. If he jumped it again would he once more find himself in that same choking, clangorous place? It was a conundrum he had no desire to resolve. As for the hapless inhabitants of that world, none of them sprang forth to confront him again. Perhaps the wall, or the section of it that was easily crossed, was more readily accessed from Ehomba's side.

When the wall finally disappeared, leaving him free to turn in any direction, it did not sink into the soil or rise magically into the sky. It simply stopped. Frowning at the abruptness of it, he cautiously examined the terminus. Long, ribbed bars of metal as thick around as his thumb protruded from the end, giving it an unfinished look. Perhaps that was its status in that other world—incomplete. Mischievously, he plucked a large toadstool from the fallen log on which it was growing nearby and placed the beige-hued fungal disk carefully between two of the metal bars. That should give the inhabitants of that other world something to think about, he resolved with a grin.

Leaving the jagged terminus of the wall behind, he continued on his way. From now on, until he left the Unstable Lands, he would be careful what artifacts he handled, what doors he entered, and what walls he leaped.

The rain forest grew denser, packing in tight around him, the trees pressing together, impenetrable undergrowth more prevalent. Clouds gathered, turning the visible sky the color of wet soot. Without the setting sun to guide him, it became more difficult to maintain his bearings.

Unsheathing the sky-metal sword, he hacked a large arrow into the bark of a nearby tree. With its thin, greenish outer covering thus distinctively incised, the much paler inner wood was revealed. Yellowish white, it would be visible from a distance. Letting the blade hang at his side, he strode on.

He was preparing to blaze another tree when a glimpse of pale not far in front of him made him hesitate. Hurrying forward, he found himself staring at the same arrow mark he had incised only moments ago. The edges of the cut were still fresh. Turning a slow circle, he studied the intense verdure that engulfed him on all sides. It was impossible to tell one growth from another. Angles blended together, and one bush looked much the same as its neighbor. Amidst all the greenery, only the blaze mark on the tree stood out distinctively.

He would have bet a whole steer that he had hewed to a straight line through the forest, but the marked tree gave lie to that claim. There was no questioning it: Somehow, he had become turned around and walked in a circle. He was back where he had been not long before.

Even though he had seen no one for days, he took the precaution of adding a straight line beneath the arrow. Sheathing the blade, he walked forward. Every few seconds he paused to look back, until the blazed tree was no longer in sight. Satisfied, he continued onward, marking his progress carefully. If not in a perfectly straight line, he was certainly walking north.

A flash of diminishing light illuminated a trunk and his eyes widened. He did not panic. That was a concept known to Etjole Ehomba only through example. It was not an emotion he had ever experienced personally. If ever he was going to, though, now was probably an appropriate time.

There was the tree again, the hewn arrow shape stark on its side, the secondary straight cut gleaming prominently beneath it.

Consider every possibility, he told himself slowly. Ask the necessary questions, beginning first with the most obvious. That was what he had been taught to do as a youngster, whenever a cow or sheep went missing. The chances that the animal had been carried off by a giant bird of prey or an invisible spirit were invariably less likely than the probability that it had wandered off and become stuck in a ravine somewhere, or was lying ill from eating madroot.

Ehomba was not tormented by invisibilities of enigmatic purpose, nor had he eaten anything whose hallucinogenic potentialities he was not reasonably sure of. Therefore, this was the same tree he had already encountered twice this evening. Therefore, despite his certitude, he was still walking in circles.

No, he corrected himself. It was the same tree, definitely. He had been walking in circles, *possibly*. Approaching the greenish-barked bole, he prepared to make another mark on its side.

Overhead, branches rustled. "Don't you think that's about enough? Or does mutilating me give you some sort of twisted pleasure?"

As one might expect, Ehomba stepped back quickly. His eyes roved the trunk, but he could espy neither eyes nor mouth, nor any other recognizable organ. There were only branches, and leaves, and the voice in his head. The tree looked like nothing but what it was. Am I really hearing this? he thought uncertainly.

"Of course you're hearing it. Did you 'really' cut me?"

"I am very sorry." The herdsman spread his arms wide and bowed his head. "I did not mean to cause pain. It has been my experience that most trees are not so sensitive as you."

"Oh really? And how many trees have you asked, before you sliced into them?"

"Truth to tell, tall forest dweller, not a one. But in the land I come from, trees are rarely cut. There are very few of them,

and so they are treasured for their shade and companionship."
He gestured at the surrounding forest. "I can see more of your
kind from where I stand right now than grow within many
leagues of my home."

"A poor land that must be, to be so treeless." The growth
sounded slightly mollified. "Most of your people are far less
sensitive, though admittedly few of them pass this way. Most
that do never leave the Unstable Lands. They become lost—
or worse."

"That is why I made the marks." The herdsman hastened to
defend, or at least to explain, his actions. "So I would not pass
the same place twice. But it seems that I have been walking
in circles, because this is the third time I have come back to
you."

"Nonsense," the tree replied. "You have been following an
almost perfectly straight route north, and as a consequence I
have had some difficulty catching up with and passing you."

So it was the same tree, Ehomba reflected, but it had not
stayed in the same place. "Trees cannot move."

"For a man who confesses to coming from a land where
few trees live, you presume to know a great deal about them."
There followed a great rustling and shaking of branches and
vines, whereupon the tree promptly rose a foot or so off the
ground and skittered forward several feet. Plopping itself
back down, it reestablished its root system and regarded the
man.

"I withdraw my statement," Ehomba commented promptly.

Branches bent toward him. "Because of your lack of
knowledge of and experience with trees, I forgive you your
actions. But a warning: No more casual incising to mark your
way. In the lands ahead live plants less benign or forgiving
than myself."

"I appreciate the warning." Ehomba glanced at the cuts he
had made. Sap was already beginning to ooze over the

wounds as a first step in healing the marks. "Again, I am sorry."

"Good. Remember how much you value the trees in your own country, and accord my brethren here the same respect. In return, they will keep you cooled, and sometimes fed."

Ehomba nodded, turned, and nearly fell as he stumbled to avoid stepping on a tiny shoot that was poking its minuscule green head out of the damp rain-forest soil. After all, it was something's offspring, and if the example of the tree was to be believed, the vegetation hereabouts was exceedingly sensitive. What with watching for dangerous animals, he had enough to do without riling the forest itself.

In the depths of the jungle there was no wind, but his unfamiliarity with the high humidity was largely canceled out by his natural affinity for hot climes, so that he sweated continually but not excessively. Anyone from a more temperate climate would surely have collapsed from the combination of heat and humidity. Ehomba drank from his water bag and kept walking. With each swallow his body shuddered a little less.

As evening drew into night, he encountered a surprise: a stone. The flat slab of grayish granite protruded like a crude spear point from the moist earth. When journeying through a realm of dirt and decomposing organic matter, it was always unusual to find exposed rock. The smooth, immutable surface reminded him of home, where there was no shortage of rocks but a considerable paucity of thick soil.

Slipping free of his backpack, he laid it carefully down on the dry stone, laying his spear alongside. For the first time in days he allowed himself to do nothing: not to worry about what lay ahead, or about how he was going to find his way out of the jungle, or what he might encounter when he did. He did not concern himself with Tarin Beckwith's dying request, or how he was going to supplement his limited food supplies, or what dangers the Unstable Lands might still hold. He relaxed in the company of the rock that needed only direct heating to make it feel exactly like the rocks he had left back home.

Astonishing, he mused, the simple things that one misses. We take our environment, our surroundings, for granted, until we are forced to survive in completely different circumstances. He would never have thought he could miss something as straightforward and commonplace as rocks.

If the sky were green, though, he knew that he would miss the blue. If sugar turned bitter, he would miss the sweet. And if he someday turned old and mean, he would miss himself.

Finishing a simple meal, he stretched out on the broad palm of granite and lay back, wishing he could see the stars. But until he emerged from the great rain forest of the Unstable Lands he would have to be content with a roof of green, and with the soaking precipitation that arrived every morning in advance of the sun, like a trumpeter announcing the approach of a king.

IX

The Lord of the Ants

THIS IS A STORY THAT IS TOLD TO EVERY MEMBER OF THE colony on the day when they slough off the last vestiges of pupahood and graduate to the status of worker, attendant, or soldier. It concerns a most momentous event in the history of the colony, one that occurred not so very long ago, which affected the future of everyone from the Queen herself on down to the lowliest worker toiling in the refuse beds.

No one could remember when the war with the Reds had begun. They had come raiding from beyond the big log to the east and had surprised the outpost guards. But providentially, a small column of workers returning with food had espied them sneaking forward through the forest litter and had raced homeward to spread the alarm. All save one pair were run down and dismembered, but those two who made it back alerted the rest of the colony, their agitated pheromones preceding them.

That warning, fleeting as it was, gave the colony time to mobilize. Quickly, soldiers were dispatched to the main entrance while the largest workers took up positions in front of the secondary portals. When it came, the attack was relentless. Holding sturdy defensive positions, however, allowed the members of the colony to keep most of the invaders from penetrating to the nursery. While some pupae and eggs were lost, it was nothing compared to the devastation that might have occurred had the survivors of the foraging party not been able to sound the alert.

That was the beginning of the war. Establishing themselves in a hollow at the base of a great tree on the other side of the fallen log, the Reds continued to make periodic depredations on the colony. In turn, the All-blacks not only defended themselves vigorously but launched zealous reprisals against the Red colony. Pupae and eggs from both brooderies were regularly carried off, to be raised as slaves of the kidnapping colony with no loyalty to or regard for their place of birth. This was in the natural way of things.

Then occurred the remarkable event that is the subject of this recounting.

It was not long after a typically ferocious morning's battle that the visitation was first remarked upon. Ordinarily, such intrusions from the outside world are ignored. Ants pay no attention to them, and they pay no attention to us, and the world continues as before. But this time, something was different.

Instead of passing through with great speed and indifference, like a passing cloud, the visitant paused. Not only paused but stopped, stretching all of its great length on the nearby rock upon which, unlike all the surrounding earth, nothing grows or can be grown. It stopped, and consumed food common to its kind, and lay there at rest.

Scouts duly communicated this information to the Queen and her personal attendants and advisers. It was a matter of some interest, but hardly a profound imposition on the daily routine of the colony, until Imit took an interest. I have mentioned Imit the Unique before. A most unusual ant, he had an exceptionally large head, bigger even than a soldier's but without the soldier's great scything jaws. Most remarkable of all, he was a drone who did not die subsequent to the annual mating flight.

Yes, I know that sounds impossible, but it is the truth. Anyone in the colony can attest to it. He did not succeed in mating with the chosen Queen, he shed his wings as was normal, but he did not wither and expire. Instead, he was made a special adviser to the Queen, as befitted his truly singular status within the colony. When I was but newly emerged, I myself waited on him in the royal chamber.

It transpired that Imit had a plan, which he proceeded to communicate to the Queen and to her other advisers. As to its efficacy, the most enthusiastic were dubious at best, while those who were skeptical bordered on the contemptuous. But seeing little risk to any but a few expendable workers and Imit himself, the Queen bade him to proceed, in the hopes that where incredulity prevailed, a benevolent destiny might intervene.

So it was that Imit requisitioned a column of workers who loaded themselves down with supplies from the colony's storage chambers and proceeded southward toward the reclining visitant. It was there that the drone proceeded to embark upon an enterprise so bold, so daring, so un-myrmecological, that those who attended him could scarce believe it. That it was accomplished through the inculcation of the black arts no one could doubt, for it was whispered often and openly that Imit had the command of forces and resources denied even to long-lived Queens.

Without knowing how it was done, all present were able to swear that the thing happened. Somehow, despite the impossible disparity in sizes, Imit succeeded in attracting the attention of the visitant. And not only did he attract it, but a rudimentary form of communication, or at least of mutual understanding, was established. It is, and was, beyond the comprehension of common workers like me and thee, but although I was not present for the momentous happenstance, I was able to talk later with those who were, and they assured me that there was no mistaking what had occurred.

After establishing contact, Imit made obeisance to the visitant, subsequent to which the gifts of sugar carried by the column were presented as offerings. No one was more surprised than the workers who had done the carrying when the visitant responded. Not only responded, but consumed the gifts with apparent enjoyment. When the last of the presents had been handed over, Imit boldly approached the visitant itself, thus demonstrating either remarkable courage or blind stupidity. To this day, not one of those who was present for the encounter is prepared to say which description would be appropriate. Myself, I tend to think a little of both.

Those proximate were able to understand nothing of the exchange that took place, but when it had concluded, Imit related to them all that had transpired, thus explaining both his purpose and his intent. He aimed to enlist the visitant as an ally in the war against the Reds, utilizing not only its immense physicality, so far beyond that of even thousands of ants as not to be believed, but the shock value of its mere presence, to deal our enemies such a blow as they would never recover from. It was a notion as radical as it was daring, beyond the conceiving of anyone but an ant as peculiar as Imit.

Returning to the colony, the details of this incredible encounter were related to the Queen. Though wary and incredulous, she and her advisers were unable to dismiss the reports of both Imit and the workers who had witnessed the historic encounter. Furthermore, the temptation was too great, the opportunity too exceptional to be dismissed out of hand. It was resolved to proceed, but with as much caution as possible.

Imit was authorized to return to the visitant with a much larger gift of sugar, with the promise of at least half the colony's stores if it would consent to the alliance. Much pleased with himself, Imit set off at the head of a multiple column of workers, carrying the finest, most completely refined sugar the colony could produce. They were escorted on both sides by grim soldiers prepared to give their lives to fend off any attack. The presence of so much sugar was, after all, a temptation not only to enemy ants but to a great many of the forest's inhabitants.

They reached the rock without incident, the visitant seated thereon becoming visible long before the rock itself. Imit stated later that it appeared bemused, though how he could interpret such an entirely alien expression was and is the subject of much derision. Regardless, the column approached, intending to deliver its presents with as much fanfare and ceremony as Imit could muster. It was only when they began to mount the rock that they found themselves shocked into immobility.

Arrayed on the far side of the outcropping were several brigades of Reds, drawn up in neat columns opposite the visitant's enormous foot. When Imit and his troop arrived, these representatives of our sworn enemy were in the process of divesting themselves of a great load of processed sugar, which they placed in an ever-growing pile at the foot of the visitant. Directing them in this farcical protocol was a Red ant with a strangely swollen head and oddly deformed antennae.

It seems that the Reds, too, had among them a male anomaly who had mastered the arcane, and who had independently and coincidentally hit upon the same notion of making an ally of the visitant as had Imit.

As for the visitant itself, it clearly made no distinction between Red ant or All-black, and was content and no doubt even delighted to receive free sugar from both of them. Certainly it consumed the sweets offered up to it by the Reds with as much gusto and enthusiasm as it had those presented by us. No doubt the same thoughts were occurring to Imit's crimson equivalent, for it is reported that he looked every bit as startled as Imit by the unexpected confrontation.

One thing that all who survived can agree upon without dissention is that which happened next. Espying the obtruding Reds, Imit immediately gave the order to attack. Internal commands among the Reds followed at approximately the same time, with the result that the lower portion of the rock was soon engulfed in hostilities. Sugar was forgotten, as was their purpose in going to that place, as old enmities rose to the fore.

The trouble was, that in their haste to attack and dismember their enemies, everyone forgot that the visitant was not merely an available agent of change, but one with a purpose and mind of its own. As All-black and Red alike swarmed over its feet and possessions, the visitant reacted with the energy and fury that each side had hoped to procure for their own. Only instead of displaying an affinity for the members of either colony, the visitant proceeded to look solely and actively after its own intrinsic interests.

Rising not to the height of a tree but exhibiting considerably more mobility, the visitant proceeded to hop about, flailing away with its gigantic upper legs at any ant unlucky enough to come within reach. When it landed, its weight shook the earth and dozens of Reds and All-blacks died beneath its immense feet. It continued to dance about in this manner, indifferent now to the precious, scattered stocks of sugar, intent only on ridding its own colossal form and the rock on which it had been sitting of all intruders regardless of color or allegiance.

Many hundreds died that morning, smashed by huge hands or stomped to death beneath feet each of which weighed more than most of the colony. Only a few on either side survived the carnage and returned to their respective colony to relate what had happened. Imit was among them. You all know what happened to him.

After offering explanations as best he could, and apologizing for stepping beyond the bounds of what an ant ought to do when confronting the rest of the world, he was ordered ritually dismembered by the Queen and her advisers, a task that watching soldiers attended to with considerable enthusiasm. One might suppose that the same fate befell his Red counterpart, assuming that he survived.

As for the visitant, it was observed not long thereafter gathering up its exotic belongings and departing to the north. There followed the Second Battle of the Rock, but this time the objectives were clear to all who participated. Perhaps out of indifference, perhaps as a gesture of contempt, the visitant had left behind the sugar that both sides had offered up as bribe and tribute. No one could say, no one knew, because the only one among the All-blacks who might have been able to find out had been slain by order of the Queen.

Safe to say that while many more died, we recovered at least half the sugar and perhaps a little more, so on balance the day might be accounted a victory for the colony. Discounting the hundreds who perished in both battles, of course. Regarding the visitant, it has not been seen since. Nor do the Queen's advisers think it ever will be again.

Myself, I sometimes regret not being privy to the clumsy conversation that took place between the visitant and the remarkable if imprudent drone Imit. To actually communicate with so alien a creature, one so inconceivably much larger than ourselves, must be a wondrous and terrifying thing. Who can imagine what its perspective might be, how different from ours its view of the world? I think I would have the courage to try it, if I but possessed the ability. I think I would, but cannot really say. For who can envision standing before a titan and engaging it in small talk?

Now then, what lessons are there to be learned from this story? You, in the back, with the one antenna shorter than the other. No, it does not speak to us of the folly of trying to engage allies who are different from ourselves. I venture to say any outside help against the Reds would be gratefully accepted, even after Imit's luckless encounter with the visitant.

No, what there is to be learned is this: First, do not expect reciprocity from the giving of gifts; second, remember always that just because your prayers are answered it does not mean that your enemy does not have a similar pipeline to heaven; and third, request of the gods all that you will, but never forget that the gods themselves may have an agenda all their own—one that does not include insignificant creatures such as yourself.

That is enough for one day. There is the work to be done: foraging to help with, eggs to be brooded, pupae to be rotated and attended to, and perhaps a raid on the Reds to be planned. There is no room in the colony for those who do not perform their assigned tasks. Here, the lazy are dismembered and consumed. The gods are out there, yes, and when carrying a leaf larger than yourself or moving rocks from the entrance you may call upon them for assistance all you wish, but never think for an instant that they have the slightest interest in helping poor little you, or any of our kind.

X

IF HE WAS HOPING FOR THE JUNGLE TO THIN OUT OR THE TER-
rain to become easier, Ehomba was sorely disappointed. Not
only did the density of the enveloping vegetation increase, but
the relatively flat countryside gave way to ripples and then
folds in the Earth. Soon he was not only walking but climbing and descending, pushing himself up one growth-infested
ridge only to face the prospect of slipping and sliding down
the far side to confront the equally difficult base of another.

Muttering under his breath as he advanced, he looked longingly and more than once at the rivers that sluiced through the
narrow gorges between the ridges. But it was useless to consider utilizing them as a way out of the difficult country in
which he now found himself. The streams were too shallow,
rock-riven, and narrow to be navigable, even if he was willing to take the time to build a raft. Besides, they all ran from
east to west, racing toward the distant sea, while his obligation pushed him ever northward.

At first he thought it was simply more of the mist that
trailed from the tops of the green-swathed ridges, but on

closer inspection he saw that it was thicker than the rising forest-steam and that it behaved differently as it rose, crawling upward through the saturated air with a purpose foreign to mere fog. He knew it could not be smoke from a fire: Nothing left out in this sodden clime would burn. Whatever fuel was combusting on the side of the ridge he was climbing had to have been gathered and dried specially and specifically for the purpose.

He considered whether to ignore it and continue upward on his chosen course. What kind of hermit would elect to live in so isolated and difficult a terrain he could not imagine, but such individuals were inherently antisocial at best. But he was curious—curiosity being his defining characteristic, insofar as he could be said to have one—and so after a moment's hesitation he turned to his left and began making his way through the trees toward the narrow column of smoke. He approached cautiously. If from a distance the instigator of the fire looked unfriendly, Ehomba would simply avoid initiating contact and continue on his way.

The unprepossessing hut was perched on a bump on the ridge, commanding a fine view of the enclosing jungle in three directions. Fashioned of rough wooden slats, bamboo, and thatch, it was encircled by an almost elegant and inviting porch, a fine place on which to sit and watch the sunset—mist and fog permitting, of course. There were a couple of bent-wood rocking chairs and a small table, and well-tended flowers bubbled from wooden planters set on the decking and atop the railing. Hermit or not, the hut's owner was horticulturally endowed. A pair of small, iridescent purple songbirds flared their tiny arias from the confines of a handmade wooden cage. Far from being hostile or antagonistic, the isolated abode appeared calculated to draw a traveler in, as if frequent guests were expected.

Approaching along a narrow animal trail, Ehomba kept a tight grip on his spear. By asking many questions of his elders when he was a child he had discovered early on that in the desert, appearances were often deceiving. Many dangerous plants and animals were masters of camouflage. The brightly colored flower concealed toxic thorns, the garish pond frog poison glands within its skin, the slight bump in the sand a deadly snake. He had learned to warn himself within his mind: What looks like one thing can often be another.

So it was with the hut. Eager as he was for some company and converse after many days alone, he was not about to go barging in on anyone who willingly chose to live in such surroundings, cheery flowerpots, rhapsodic songbirds, and shady confines notwithstanding.

When he drew near he slowed and stepped off the trail and into the surrounding brush. Advancing stealthily, he approached the hut not via the steps that led onto the porch but from behind. If his choice came to be remarked upon he would be happy to explain the reasoning behind it. Living in isolation, the owner should understand.

Voices. There were two: one strong and persistent, the other querulous and a bit shaky. Occasionally the latter would strengthen for a sentence or so, only to weaken with the next phrase. From his position outside it was hard for Ehomba to tell if they were arguing or having a normal discussion. Both voices sounded human, at least. In the Unstable Lands he supposed that one could never be sure. On the other hand, being human was no guarantee of anything. Had he not recently dealt with a snake more honorable than many of his own kind?

Advancing silently through the forest, he crept to the rear of the hut. There were several windows there, which surprised him. He would have thought that anyone building in such a place would want to keep the less appealing denizens of the jungle at bay by restricting their access to the interior insofar as was possible. But all the windows were open to the forest. Raising his head slowly until his eyes were over the sill, he peered inward. He was looking at a large, comfortable room with access to the porch visible on the far side. Seated on mats on the floor were two figures: a man about his own age and another with his back to the window. As he stared, the man facing him caught him looking in and shot him a glance, though whether of helplessness, surprise, or warning Ehomba could not say.

Somehow the other figure simultaneously became aware of his presence. Perhaps it noticed the direction of the other man's gaze. Without turning, it announced in a tenor voice smooth as the syrup the women of the village made from distilled honey, "Come in, traveler. You are welcome here."

Ehomba hesitated. The other man was still staring at him. An urge to turn, and to run, welled up sharply within the herdsman. But that inviting voice was compelling and besides, as always, he was curious.

Walking around the hut from back to front, he mounted the porch steps and entered. Like the windows, nothing barred the doorway. It was a portal without a barrier. Like the rest of the hut, it was enticing.

"Come in, come in!" The larger figure seated in the rear of the main room beckoned encouragingly. As he entered, Ehomba noticed that the man already present continued to stare at him. "Take a seat."

Ehomba remained standing. "I do not want to interrupt a private conversation."

"Not at all, not at all." The figure in back smiled, though it was a doleful sort of smile, the herdsman thought. It was a ghost of an expression from which all honest sentiment had fled; a shell, a shadow, from which all real contentment had been wrung like washwater from a rag. Nevertheless, he took a seat, crossing his legs beneath him and setting his spear to one side.

As soon as he did so, the other man present let out a groan.

"Well, that's beggared it! We're both done for now." He dropped his head.

"Done for?" What odd manner of speech was this? Ehomba wondered. Up close, he considered the other occupants of the room more closely.

The man seated on the mat next to him was of average height, with heavily knotted legs and a stocky, muscular upper body. His black hair was long and tied up in a tail in back while his facial features were like none the herdsman had ever seen before, with narrow eyes and small nose set above a wide mouth. The face was inordinately round in contrast to the athletic build and the forehead high and intelligent.

He wore light leather armor that must have been a burden in the jungle heat. Beneath it could be seen a white shirt of some silken material. Below the waist the man was clad in very little: a loincloth that was bound up between his buttocks over which protective leather straps hung no farther than midthigh. This unusual raiment was matched by its owner's disposition, which was dyspeptic at best.

"Why couldn't you have just run?" he was muttering. "Didn't you see me trying to warn you off when you were peeping in the window?"

"I was not peeping," Ehomba explained decorously with a glance in the direction of the master of the house. "I was reconnoitering."

"Well, it sure as Gibra didn't do you any good. You're in here now, and he's got you, too." The speaker nodded in the direction of the third occupant of the room.

Unperturbed, Ehomba turned toward their nominal host. "Is what he says true?" he asked quietly. "Do you have us?"

"Oh, most certainly," the other replied in his lugubrious voice. "Once caught, none can escape me."

"That is strange. I do not feel caught."

"Don't worry about it. You are."

The speaker was not entirely human, Ehomba saw. Or perhaps he was merely representative of a type of humanity the herdsman had not previously encountered. One thing Ehomba was ever conscious of was his unabiding ignorance. That was why he asked so many questions. The habit had frequently driven his elders to distraction.

The squat shape confronting him was massive and blocky, rather like a squeezed-down, compact version of a true giant. It had a lantern jaw and dark, deep-set eyes. Perhaps its most notable feature was its great mane of red and gold hair, which swept back from not only the forehead but the cheeks to flow in a single continuous hirsute waterfall over its shoulders and back until it touched the floor. The nose was crooked and the upper body much too big for the lower, as if it had been grafted onto hips and legs from another person entirely. Ehomba would have called the face apelike had such an appellation not been denigrating to the monkey. It was ugly—there was no getting around it—but not grotesque. There was even a bizarre, alien warmth to it.

It did not warm the man seated next to him, however. "Don't feel caught, eh? Try getting up."

Ehomba attempted to comply, only to find that he could not rise from the mat. Looking down, he saw that the tiny fibers upon which he was seated were anything but inanimate. They were twitching and rustling in spasmodic silence. A fair number already gripped his lower legs and sandaled feet, but not by wrapping around them and holding them down.

They were boring into them, skin and sandals both.

Looking to his left, he saw that his neighbor was suffering from the same affliction. He was as tightly fastened to the mat as if he had been rooted there. Which was, in fact, precisely what was happening to him.

After waiting a moment for realization to strike the newcomer, the stocky figure extended a hand. "Too bad for you, but I can't deny that it's nice to have some company." He nodded curtly in the direction of their host. "I was fed up with being able to talk only to him."

"Tut," murmured their hairy host, "surely my conversation is not so intolerable."

"Of course it is, but I suppose you can't help it." Despite circumstances that were obviously less than conducive to casual joviality, he grinned as he looked back at Ehomba. "I'm Simna ibn Sind. I come from a country that's far to the northeast of here. And I sure wish I was there now."

"Why aren't you?" the herdsman asked him.

Simna looked away, still grinning. "Dispute seems to dog me the way a sweat bee pesters a runner. I find that I have to keep moving in search of outer as well as inner peace."

"Have you ever found it?"

The fine-featured face looked around sharply. Then the smile widened. "Not yet, but I understand that it's a condition devoutly to be desired. I'd hoped someday to be able to appreciate more than just the theory."

"I am sure that you will."

"Don't you get it, uh . . . ?"

"Ehomba. Etjole Ehomba. I am a herdsman from the south."

"Yeah, well, it's time to stop deluding yourself, friend. You're stuck here just like I am, and neither of us is going anywhere. We're going to sit here until we rot."

"Of course you are." Their host was most agreeable. "That is what people do in my company. That is what everything does in my company." He sighed resignedly. "I do so wish others wouldn't take such a negative view of what is after all a most vital and necessary process." The great-maned head shook slowly. "So few stop to consider what kind of place the world would be without me."

"And what is that?" Ehomba inquired with interest. "What are you? Who are you?"

"I thought you might have guessed by now, traveler."

Again the intimation of an imitation of a smile. "I am Corruption."

"I see. By whom were you bribed?"

"No, no; you don't get it, do you?" A man of short sentences and peppery disposition, Simna looked disgusted. "He's not corrupted. He *is* Corruption. Take another look around you. Take a good look."

Ehomba did so, and found that by squeezing his eyes tight together, certain aspects of his surroundings that had heretofore escaped his notice suddenly stood out in stark contrast to what he had initially believed he was seeing.

All those colorful flowers growing in planters and pots on the porch, for example. Gazing at them afresh, he saw now that they were wilted and dying; the petals wrinkled as the faces of old, old men, the stems shivered with disease. The stench of decay permeated the hut. Instead of a woven mat, he was sitting on a heap of moldering dung from which emerged the tendrils of corrupted fungi that were ever so slowly drilling into his feet and lower legs.

As if his eyes had suddenly refocused, he saw the hut in a new light, a dark and decomposing one. The walls were not made of wood, but of some crumbling earthen material resembling peat. Instead of thatch, the roof was composed of the yellowed bones of long-dead animals—and other things. And their host . . .

Pustules and boils covered the heretofore smooth skin while the great mane of hair was in reality a compact herd of composting worms that writhed and twisted slowly around and through the stolid skull. A palpable fetidness that oozed from every pore made the herdsman glad he had not eaten since morning, and then very little. Yet for all the quiet horror of his revealed self, Corruption exhibited no excitement at his new guest's realization, belched no bellow of putrefying triumph. He remained quiet and courteous. Ehomba found this only natural, patience being an important component of the nature of corruption.

"What do you want from us?" he inquired of their host.

Eyes that seethed like the sewage system of a great city turned to him, and maggots spilled from cracked lips. "What your friend said: for you to rot. Don't feel singled out or put upon. It is what I want everything to do." Around him, the hut moaned as the molecules of which it was made slowly collapsed.

"I am afraid I do not have time for it," Ehomba responded. "I have an obligation to fulfill and responsibilities to others."

Cackling laughter bubbled up from noisome depths and the rankness of the room pressed close around him. On his left, Simna turned his head away from their host and gagged. He did not throw up only because he had done so earlier. Repeatedly.

"You have no choice in the matter." Corruption was insistent. "You are rotten. All men are rotten. So is the rest of the world. It is true that I am spread thin, so it is a particular pleasure when I can give personal attention to individuals. I must say that I admire your calm. You will make a fine and entertaining guest until your tongue rots in your mouth and your lungs begin to putrefy."

"I think not."

Reaching back over his shoulder, Ehomba unsheathed the sky-metal blade and drew it across the tendrils that were growing into his sandals, feet, and legs. Normal steel they would have resisted, but against an edge drawn from the absolute purity of space they had no resistance. Corruption's dull eyes were incapable of registering surprise, but they focused more intently on the tall man who now straightened atop the pile of dung.

"Hey bruther, don't forget me!" Simna ibn Sind struggled against his own fungal bonds. Bending over, Ehomba rapidly and efficiently cut him loose. The garrulous traveler rose gratefully and removed one of a pair of swords from a single scabbard slung across his back. Corruption looked on, unperturbed.

"Right now, that's for you, you pile of shit!" As an opprobrium to Corruption, it was not very effective, but the apoplectic Simna was too excited and angry to hazard a more effective imprecation. Bringing his sword around and down in a swift arc, he swung at their host's head.

The blade struck the neck and stuck there. Teeth clenched, Simna tried to pull it free, to no avail. As the two men looked on, rust bled from Corruption's neck, crawling up the flat of the fine blade like water through a straw, turning the gleaming steel a dull red-brown right up to the bone haft. Bone and metal disintegrated simultaneously.

Taken aback but still full of fight, the emancipated traveler drew his second weapon and crouched warily. "Clever it is then, but I warn you: I'm not going to rot quietly."

"Everything rots quietly." Corruption placed the tips of moldering, sausagelike fingers together. "Whatever you do will only put off the inevitable."

"That is true," observed Ehomba.

Simna turned on him quickly, eyes a little wider, stance more tense than a moment before. "Hoy, what's that? You agree with this perversion? Whose side are you on, anyway?"

"The side of life," Ehomba assured him, "but that does not mean I cannot see things as others see them." He met the putrid gaze of their host without flinching. "Even Corruption."

"You are a man of the Earth." The thickset figure was bloating before their eyes, swelling with gas and putrescence, threatening to explode all over them. "I will miss your company."

"And I will not miss yours." Reaching into a pocket of his kilt, Ehomba felt of the beach pebbles there. They were not all he had brought along to remind him of home. What he wanted, he remembered, was in his other pocket.

He came out with a handful of . . . dirt. Simna stared at it in disbelief. "What are you gonna do with that? Offer to plant some mushrooms? This is a helluva time to be thinking about gardening!" He clutched the handle of his blade tightly in both hands, knuckles whitening.

Eyes that had become pools of scummed-over sewer seepage focused on the handful. "Even small contributions to the state of decomposition are always welcome. But it will not buy you your freedom."

"The Naumkib do not pay bribes." So saying, Ehomba threw the dirt at their implacably malodorous host.

It struck where the ballooning chest had been—with no apparent effect. The crouching, poised Simna was openly contemptuous. "Well now, that was useful! What was that you were trying to do, force him to take a bath? It's done nothing at all."

The herdsman did not comment, just stood and watched as Corruption continued to swell. And swell, and swell, until he filled half the hut. Now it was Simna's eyes that widened.

"I think—I think maybe we ought to get out of here and reflect on the situation from a distance, bruther." He turned to run. Though curious, Ehomba recognized the sense of the other man's aside and turned to join him. Within the room, the stench of rotten eggs had become overpowering.

They reached the door just as Corruption exploded, spewing every imaginable kind and variety of filth and muck in all directions. This mephitic fusillade struck them from behind as they threw themselves out the door and onto the porch. The discharge would have swallowed them up had not the wood of the porch been rotted through. It collapsed beneath their weight and they tumbled onto the heavily vegetated slope below. Decaying bushes broke under their fall, cushioning their descent. Healthy growths would have cut and torn at them. Corruption, Ehomba mused as he rolled to a halt, really did have its uses.

Simna was up and on his feet, sword in hand, with commendable speed. He stared up at the hut through the gap their bodies had made in the rotted porch. Very little was left of the building, most of the walls and all of the roof having been blown away by the explosion. What was left was encased in a coating of solid—well, corruption. Above them, nothing moved.

Breathing hard, Simna turned to look at his taller companion. Ehomba had picked himself up and was wiping distastefully at the mire with which he was covered. When he saw Simna staring at him, panting slowly and evenly, he smiled.

Simna grimaced huffily. "What in Gorath are you squinting at, traveler?"

"You are a mess." Ehomba's smile widened.

The other man looked down at his coat of exceptional filth. When his gaze rose again, he too was grinning. "S'truth, I am, aren't I? And you—if you sought refuge in a pig sty, the hogs would throw you out and hold their noses while doing it!" He started to chuckle.

"I have no doubt," Ehomba admitted.

The swordsman nodded upward. "That wasn't dirt you threw at our late unlamented host, was it?" Eager curiosity burned in his expression. "It was some kind of magic grit, or powdered thrall. Are you a sorcerer?"

Ehomba shook his head dolefully. "I am only a herdsman, from the south."

"Yeah, yeah, so you said. But what was that stuff?"

"Just as I explained: dirt." Ehomba eyed the obliterated hut speculatively. "But it was clean dirt, free of corruption, from my home village. In a desert country, soil that is good enough to grow food in is revered. It is a precious thing, and looked after with care. For what is more magical than the ability to bring forth food from the bare earth?" He nodded up the slope. "I kept it with me as a remembrance of my home. It came from a small plot that my wife tended that had been many times blessed by Oura, the mother of Asab, our chief. She is a wise woman, and skilled in the ways of the earth. I did not think its purity would suit Corruption."

"Suit him? By Girun, it gave him a damned bellyache, it did!" Simna started upward, fighting the slippery slope with renewed energy. "Now let's get after it."

"Get after it?" The herdsman frowned. "Get after what?"

"Why, his treasure, of course." Simna eyed him as if he had suddenly gone daft. "Everyone knows that wherever Corruption lingers for very long there is treasure. There are all kinds of corruption, you know. Somewhere up there should be a hoard of riches amassed from the morally corrupt, from crooked magistrates and bent politicians and backdoor guards."

Ehomba wanted nothing to do with any treasure that had been gathered by Corruption. But as always, his curiosity tugged at him more powerfully than common sense. "I thought you were traveling in search of inner peace?"

Using broken stems and branches to pull himself up the steep slope, Simna ibn Sind smirked back at him. "Gold pieces first, my friend. Inner peace later."

"I do not agree with your priorities," Ehomba grumbled as he followed behind.

The shorter man leaped slightly to grab a thick root protruding from the hillside. With the agility of a gibbon, he pulled himself up and continued ascending. "You saved my life, Etjole. So I'm not going to argue with you. But I give you fair warning right now: Whatever happens, don't ever try to get between me and treasure."

"I have no interest in treasure," the herdsman replied softly.

"Hoy, right, that's what they all say."

But as he continued to climb, the compact swordsman was

less sure of himself, just as he was less than certain of his quiet-voiced companion. An odd duck for sure, he thought. The concern did not linger. There was treasure to be unearthed and he was going to find it—even if it meant digging through untold layers of exploded, accumulated foulness.

XI

THEY FOUND NOTHING IN THE HUT, BUT THERE WAS A SLANTING cave behind it that was high enough for a man to enter, if he bent slightly. Remarking that corruption burned well, Simna fashioned torches for them both and started in. Ehomba was content to follow. If anything, the stench in the enclosed tunnel was even worse than that without, but nothing could compare with the odor that had momentarily filled the air during the detonation of Corruption himself.

"Who told you there would be treasure here?" Ehomba kept his attention on the well-slimed floor instead of his eager companion.

"You hear things." Simna kept flashing his torch from side to side to ensure nothing was overlooked. "Besides, doesn't money always follow corruption?"

"I would not know," the herdsman replied frankly. "There is none of it in my village, nor among my tribe."

"'Tribe,'" Simna muttered. "Hoy, that figures. You're not exactly a sophisticate from the big city, are you, bruther?"

"Kora Keri is the biggest town I have ever seen, and that only recently."

"Well, lemme tell you, Etjole—I can call you by your friendly name, can't I?"

"You just did," Ehomba pointed out pragmatically.

"Etjole, if there's one thing I know, it's corruption." If it occurred to Simna that admitting to this body of knowledge might reflect less than favorably upon him personally he gave no sign that he realized it. "And believe me, money follows it the way a honey badger tracks bees." His torch swept back and forth, the swinging flame leaving behind a wake of flickering light. "It's got to be here somewhere. It's got to!"

"Perhaps that is what you are looking for up ahead."

"What?" Simna had been gazing back at his companion. Now his attention shifted forward. Raising his torch as high as the tunnel would allow, he saw what he had hoped to find glittering back at him.

The gold was piled higher than a man, higher even than one as tall as the rangy herdsman. Coins, bracelets, rings, chokers, tiaras, bullion, slabbed bars, goblets, plates, and all manner of other devices lay in a single imposing heap, as if casually discarded during a trash pickup. Peering from the small mountain of gold like iridescent insects were jeweled earrings and buttons, rings and wristlets, and all manner of elaborately carved lapidary decorations.

Eyes wild as a mad kudu, Simna ibn Sind had prepared to take a flying leap onto the golden hillside when he felt a hand restraining him. Attempting to shake it off, he was startled by the strength of the grip. Tough and well built himself, he quickly became frustrated at his inability to loosen that unyielding grasp.

Cobalt blue eyes flashed at Ehomba. "What's the idea, bruther? Let me go! Or are you going to stand there like a disapproving priest and tell me you have no love for gold yourself?"

"Actually, I do not," Ehomba told him, quite honestly. "It is you I am concerned for."

Licking his lips in anticipation, Simna's gaze darted between his eccentric friend and the kingdom's ransom that dominated the chamber. "Don't worry about me. This will fix anything that's wrong with me."

"When I was young," the herdsman went on, still keeping a firm grip on the other man, "I learned that many delicious-looking fruits are safe from grazing animals despite their enticing appearance because they contain one form or another of deadly poison." He nodded at the hoard. "Here is the treasure of Corruption. Think a moment, my friend, on what we have just seen. Corruption corrupts everything it comes in contact with. The instant our eyes and minds cleared we saw that his house was corrupted, the furniture within was corrupted, everything that grew inside and nearby was corrupted. What makes you think this is any different? The fact that it is shiny?"

"C'mon, Etjole! This is gold, and jewels! Not plants or wood."

"It is the provenance of Corruption."

"Let go of me." The swordsman struggled furiously in the other man's grasp. Eventually, one flailing hand encountered the knife sheathed at his waist. "Let me go or by Gwetour . . . !"

Ehomba released him. Simna staggered a moment before regaining his balance. "Take it if you will, then," the herdsman said, "but do me one favor first. Pick only one piece, one coin, and examine it closely before you hurl yourself upon the rest."

Simna squinted at the tall southerner. "That'll shut you up?"

Ehomba nodded, just once. "That will shut me up."

"More than worth it, then." Pivoting, the slim swordsman bent and chose a coin from the bottom edge of the pile. It was a fine coin, lustrous as the day it was minted, with the silhouette of some obscure emperor stamped on one side and an obelisk surrounded by cryptic symbols on the other. Simna turned it over and over between his fingers, flipped it into the air, and caught it with the insouciance of an experienced juggler.

"There! Satisfied?"

"Let me see." Ehomba leaned forward and the other man held the golden disk out for him to inspect. "Yes, it is a large coin, and based on what little I know about such things, real gold."

"Of course it is!" Simna did nothing to try to hide his contempt and impatience. "What else did you expect?"

"I was not sure. Something like what is happening to your hand, I think."

"Something . . . ?" The swordsman blinked and looked down at the coin in his palm. "What are you babbling about?"

"Beneath the coin. See?"

Simna squinted, and then his eyes widened. With a yelp as if he had been stung by a hornet, he flung the coin away from him with a spasmodic twitch of his arm. Holding his wrist, he gaped open-mouthed at his hand.

A neat hole the exact diameter of the coin had appeared in the flesh. The edges of the quarter-inch-deep wound were black and festering. White pus oozed from the center and a mephitic miasma arose from the rotting meat. It was a stink with which both men were by now all too familiar.

"Ghontoh!" Simna exclaimed. Still tightly clutching his wrist, he started to tremble as he looked back over his shoulder at the gleaming, beckoning golden hillock. "If I'd gone and jumped onto that, buried myself in it like I wanted to . . ." He left the rest of the thought unvoiced even as he tried to expel the synchronal vision from his mind.

Ehomba had slid his pack off his back and was rummaging

through it. When he rose from the inspection, he had a small piece of sealed bamboo in one hand.

"Here," he said gently, "let me see it."

Shakily, the swordsman held out his ulcerated palm. The herdsman examined it thoughtfully for a moment, then unsealed the bamboo. Pushing a finger inside, he smeared it thoroughly with the milky sap the container held and proceeded to rub this across the injured man's open palm. After repeating the treatment several times until the wound was thoroughly invested with the sap, he resealed the bamboo vial and replaced it in his pack.

"Give me your other arm," he directed Simna. The swordsman obeyed without question. Ehomba promptly tore a long, winding strip from the sleeve of the other man's shirt.

"Hoy, that's Bakhari silk! Do you know what that costs in a Thalussian marketplace?"

Ehomba eyed him darkly. "Which is more important to you, Simna—your shirt, or your hand?" Wordlessly, he began to bandage the circular lesion with the silken strip. The swordsman did not comment further.

Satisfied, Ehomba stepped back and examined his handiwork. "The dressing should be changed every three days. If you keep the wound clean, it should be healed in a week or two."

"A hole like that? Are you crazy? Even if that goo you smeared on it is worth anything, it'll take at least a month for the flesh to replace itself."

"Oura is mistress of many unguents and salves. I have seen her reduced sap from the leaves of the kokerboom tree save a child from a mamba bite." He offered the other man a thin smile. "Of course, if you think you can do better, you are welcome to do so. Perhaps immersing it in gold bullion would be more to your liking."

"I never met a herdsman with a sense of humor," Simna

grumbled. His tone changed quickly. "That's the second time you've saved my life. How am I ever supposed to repay you?"

With a shrug, Ehomba turned. He was more than ready to leave the tunnel. He had been ready to leave before he had entered it. "I know that had our situations been reversed, you would have done as much for me."

"Oh, sure, hoy, absolutely." The swordsman nodded too vigorously. "I would've done so without a thought, bruther!" Holding his torch in his good hand, he followed Ehomba as they started out of the stench-filled cavity. "I guess you're not as green as you look. For a start, I expect you know more about certain kinds of corruption than me. Organic corruption, anyway. Meself, I'm more conversant with the societal variety. I just didn't think there'd be that much difference between the two. Urban corruption wouldn't have rotted a hole in my hand."

Ehomba glanced back at him, only half his face visible in the enveloping darkness. "Perhaps not, but presented with such a circumstance I would have a worry for my soul."

Simna trailed behind in silence for a while before venturing to inquire uncertainly, "Are you sure you're just a herdsman?"

"Cattle and sheep, with the occasional moa," Ehomba assured him. "I miss them even as we speak."

"Hoy, well, better you than me, bruther. Meself, I prefer the companions of my days and nights slimmer, smoother, and better smelling. Watch your step," he added solicitously. "Remember that big rock that sticks out of the floor near the entrance."

They emerged into sunlight that, mist-shrouded and dimmed as it was, seemed brighter than any either man had ever encountered before. Without a word, Ehomba turned to his right and began to make his way along the flank of the mountain, keeping to the open spaces in the rain forest while heading north.

"Hoy, wait a minute!" Surprised by the abruptness of the other man's departure, Simna ibn Sind hurried to catch up to him. "Where are you going?"

Without slowing or looking back at the swordsman, who continued to pace him, Ehomba replied succinctly, "North."

"North?" Simna echoed. "That's it? Just 'north'? North to where? North for what?" Somewhere nearby a flock of very large and throaty birds trilled in chorus like a carillon of silver bells.

"Just north." The herdsman stepped over a root that hugged the ground like a petrified snake. "You would not believe my purpose if I told it to you."

Licking his lips, Simna pressed close on the other man's heels. "Okay, okay, look—I'll tell you what I was really doing here, and then you tell me, okay? We'll each tell the other the truth." He eyed the tall herdsman eagerly. When no response was forthcoming to his offer, he added enthusiastically, "I'll go first.

"You say that you're going north? Well, I was heading south. Way south. Further south than a sensible man might be expected to want to go." He took a deep breath, framing his imminent revelation. "I'm looking for Damura-sese."

Surrounded by steep jungle, Ehomba halted and peered over at the swordsman. "That is too bad. I happen to be from the south, and as a southerner I can tell you that there is no such place as Damura-sese. All that exists of it is the name. I have heard about it all my life, and I can tell you with complete confidence that no such place exists on the face of this Earth."

Simna's expression turned sly. "Ah, but that's what they all say. I figure it's because anyone who knows anything about the place wants to keep it a secret until they can mount an expedition to find it for themselves." He slammed his closed fist against his chest. "Well, I'm an expedition! I'm going to find it, and all the riches the old legends say it holds, and buy myself a khanate or a kingdom. And then when the norics who've been hounding my heart come looking for me, I'll send a battalion of my household cavalry to harry them into the nearest river."

Ehomba listened to all this in silence. "Better to secure yourself an honest and stable position with some noble courtier, or learn a distinguished trade. You might even consider farming." His eyes seemed to change focus, to see far off into the mist-murky distance. "There is much to be said for working in close contact with the earth."

"You keep close to it." Simna tersely jerked a thumb back the way they had come. "Didn't you get close enough to the earth back there?"

"That was not the earth, but its dross." Again he looked over at his companion. "I tell you there is no Damura-sese, Simna ibn Sind. There are only stories that mothers use to amuse their children and see them off to sleep. That too is a sort of magic, but not the kind you seek. If you think you will make your fortune by finding it, you might as well try to market your dreams."

"Don't try to talk me out of it, because you can't." The swordsman pushed through a line of leafy branches, keeping a careful eye out for stinging insects as he bashed his way through. "Okay, now I've done my part and told you of my intentions. Now it's your turn. And since I've been pretty forthcoming, I think you owe me more in the way of detail than 'I'm going north.' "

Ehomba sighed heavily. Good-natured though he might be, the swordsman was tenacious as a leech. Clearly he was not going to let the matter rest until he heard something that would satisfy him. So the herdsman explained his purpose, and his intentions, in making his way northward, eventually to take ship to the unknown west.

Simna listened to it all in silence, occasionally nodding sagely as Ehomba made his points. When the herdsman finished, the swordsman grinned crookedly up at him and commented, "That's some story." He sidled closer and lowered his voice, as if there were someone besides bugs and birds present to overhear. "Now really—what are you up to? You're after treasure too, aren't you? Everyone's looking for treasure. Or you've been given some secret assignment by a high wizard, or better yet, by a banker. There's a lot of gold at stake here. I can tell. There has to be, or you wouldn't have come this far and gone through everything that you have already." He gave the taller man a comradely nudge in the ribs. "Come on, Etjole. You can tell old Simna. What are you after, really?"

Ehomba did not look over or break stride. Another steep-sided ridge loomed ahead, clad in its familiar coat of rain-forest green. "What I told you was the truth. The whole truth. There is nothing else."

The swordsman chortled aloud. "You're good, I'll give you that. One of the better liars I've encountered in my time. But not the best, not by a long shot. See, I've been around, Etjole. I can tell when a man's having me on and when he's telling the truth just by studying the way his cheeks twitch and his lips quiver. I look them right in the eye and I can tell. You're good, but you can't fool me."

Stolid and determined, Ehomba strode on. "You are right," he replied imperturbably. "I cannot fool you. You are too perceptive for me."

Simna beamed, well pleased with himself. "See? I knew better! Now then, what is it that you're on to? A sunken merchant vessel laden with scarce trade goods? A spice merchant's caravan on its way from far Narinchu? A pirate's abandoned lair, or jewels guarded by the spirit-wraith of a dead queen?"

"Something like that," Ehomba replied noncommittally. The ridge ahead looked less imposing than the last several he had crossed. Perhaps the mountains were beginning to subside. It would be good to travel on level ground once again. He was tired of climbing.

Simna pouted. "Fine then! Be that way. Keep the truth to yourself. I'm sure you'll tell me when the time comes."

Frowning, Ehomba looked over at him. "Tell you? Do you think you are coming with me? I thought you were bent on finding Damura-sese?"

"One expedition at a time," the swordsman replied. "Truth be told, bruther, when speaking of directions, 'south' is pretty generalized and offers little in the way of direction. You, on the other hand, seem to have a definite destination in mind."

"Not as definite as you seem to believe." Ehomba kicked aside a fallen branch that was decorated with spotted blue liverworts.

"More definite than mine, anyway. Wherever it is, Damura-sese isn't going anywhere. So I had this notion that I might tag along with you for a while." He indicated the knife at his belt and the remaining longsword slung against his back. "I can hold my own against any half dozen men in a fight, keep a dragon at bay, satisfy three women at once, outdrink the biggest primate in a tavern, and ride all day and all night while asleep in the saddle. I'm a boon companion with more stories to tell than any two professional guides, better songs than a tintinnabulation of troubadours, and I won't run out on a man in a tight spot. You'll do well to keep me in your company."

Ehomba could not repress a slight smile. "If you can handle that sword as well as you do your tongue, truly you would be a good man to have at one's back in a fight. But I do not need, or want, any company."

"Oh." Simna was momentarily crestfallen. But his irrepressible good spirits rapidly returned. "Want to keep all the treasure to yourself, eh?"

The herdsman's gaze rolled heavenward. "Yes, that is it. I want to keep all the treasure to myself."

"Well, don't worry. I'll only expect for what I'll earn. So you won't mind if I keep company with you for a little while?"

"It may be more than a little while," a somber Ehomba informed him. "As to you 'tagging along,' much as I might wish to do so, I cannot very well prevent it. I think you are like malaria: It can be made to go away for a while, but it always comes back to make a man sick and uneasy."

Simna lengthened his own jaunty stride. "Flattery'll get you nowhere, cattle-man. So this fortune you're on the trail of, how big is it? Are we after gold, or works of art, or what?"

By evening Ehomba was almost ready to use the spear on his tirelessly garrulous new companion, but he was too weary. Simna ibn Sind prattled more than a convocation of women gathered for the village's annual coming-of-puberty ceremony. The herdsman finally compared it to a forlorn steer bulling in the fields. Eventually and with an effort of will he was able to largely tune out the drone of the peripatetic swordsman's voice.

Briefly, he considered abandoning the man while he slept. Attractive as he found the imagery, however, he could not quite bring himself to do it. Since he could not courteously lose the fellow, he decided that he would have to find some way to tolerate him. The prospect did not concern him overmuch.

Once they had trudged another couple of hundred leagues or so north without encountering any sign of treasure, he decided, Simna ibn Sind would undoubtedly dissolve their little company of his own accord.

XII

His supposition was correct. Not about Simna ibn Sind, but about the lay of the land ahead of them. There were more jungle-clad ridges, but they continued to grow smaller and less difficult to surmount, the rain forest that flourished on their flanks thinning out even as the knife-edged ridge tops became more manageable.

Then, without warning, there were no more tree-crowned summits to ascend.

They found themselves standing on the last ridge top looking out upon a sea of grass that stretched, utterly unbroken, to the northern horizon. No rocky knoll poked its stone-crowned head above that perfectly flat green-brown plain. Not a single tree thrust its trunk or lofted its branches over the endless emerald sward. Unobstructed sunlight did not glint off isolated lakes or ponds, or flash from the mirrored surface of some lazily meandering stream. There was nothing, nothing but the grass.

"The country ahead looks like it's going to be easy to cross but difficult to hunt in." Simna held his chin in his hand as he studied the terrain spread out before them.

"It may not be so easy to cross, either," Ehomba commented. His eyes glistened. "What wonderful country!"

His companion gaped at him. "Wonderful?" He stretched out an arm to encompass the endless overgrown meadow. "You call that wonderful? There's nothing there but Gopuy-bedamned grass!"

Ehomba looked sideways at Simna. "I am a herdsman from a dry country, my friend. To one responsible for the well-being of cattle and sheep, forced to move them from place to place just to keep them from starving, this would be an earthly kind of paradise. Not all people see riches only in gold."

The swordsman eyed the tall southerner tolerantly. "You really *are* a simple guy with simple needs, aren't you?" Ehomba nodded, and the other man responded with a sly, knowing smile. "I've got to hand it to you, Etjole. I've crossed paths with some shrewd, closed-mouthed types in my time, but you're right up there with the best of them! How long do you think you can fool me with this 'simple herds-man' routine? Grass my ass! We both know what you're after, and you're not going to get rid of me that easily! It'll take more than cheap, obviously phony claims of ignorance to fool Simna ibn Sind!" He edged nearer.

"Come on, Etjole—you can tell me now. What is it you're after, really? A lost city like Damura-sese, only even richer? A bandit's abandoned cache? Clandestine merchant gold?"

Ehomba sighed tolerantly. "It is a shame, Simna. Having so narrow a vision, you must miss much of what goes on in the world. You are like a horse with blinders."

Annoyed, the swordsman stepped back. "Okay, okay. So don't tell me. I know you must have your reasons, and that you'll make everything clear when the time comes."

"Yes," Ehomba assured him candidly, "everything will become clear when the time comes." He started down the slope.

The last slope, for which he was grateful. Clambering over the jungle-wrapped ridges had been as tiring as it was dangerous. Seeking to change the subject, he said, "I would think you would know this country. Did you not come from here?"

Simna shook his head. Extraordinarily agile, he had an easy time picking his way down through the last trees. Where Ehomba had to step carefully, the stocky swordsman would simply hop or leap to the next clearing.

As they descended, the grass grew nearer—and taller. And thicker, and taller, until it became clear to both men that the country ahead was no ordinary veldt, and the grass they were approaching almighty unlike its humbler cousins elsewhere. They were unable to appreciate its true dimensions, in fact, until they were standing at the very bottom of the ridge.

"Nine feet high." A contrite Simna stood before the wall of solid green. "Maybe ten. How in Gerooja are we going to get through *that*?"

Stolid as ever, Ehomba regarded the seemingly impenetrable barrier. "We have blades. We will cut our way through. Make a path." He nodded skyward. "I can navigate by the stars. A lone herdsman out in the pasturelands learns early how to do so."

"That's all well and good, it is," Simna snorted, "but do you recall the panorama from the top of the ridge?" He nodded back at the slope they had just descended. "This extends farther than a man can see." Taking a couple of steps forward, he felt of the nearest blade of grass. Soft and fibrous, it was as thick and wide as his hand. "You know how long it will take us to cut a league or so deep into this? If the plain reaches beyond the horizon, it could take us months just to cut a path halfway through. And what are we going to eat while we're doing it? I'm no grazer."

"There must be game," Ehomba commented. "Surely so much rich forage does not go unutilized."

A skeptical Simna waved at the wall. "Hunt—in this? How

can you hunt something that might be standing right behind you without being visible? And anything that does live in there is bound to travel through it faster than a man."

"What would you have us do?" With his spear, Ehomba gestured toward the top of the ridge. Back the way they had come. "Retrace our steps? Over every ridge and canyon? Or go back the way you came, toward the east?"

"I didn't say that." A frustrated Simna slumped down on a moss-covered rock and cupped his head in his hands. "Of course not. An ibn Sind never retreats. But I don't like our prospects for advancing, either."

"We could camp here until inspiration strikes."

The swordsman managed a weak grin. "You mean like a rock to the head? If I thought it would do any good, I'd take the blow myself." He eyed the unbroken, ten-foot-tall rampart of green. "I can resign myself to the necessary cutting. It's the problem of finding food that worries me."

"We will manage." Reaching back over his shoulder, Ehomba unsheathed the sky-metal sword, the exposed blade gleaming grayly in the muted sunlight and glinting off the strange, sharp, parallel lines etched into the metal. Bringing back his arm, he prepared to begin the arduous task of cutting a lane through the overgrown veldt.

"Just a moment there, if you please."

Pausing with the blade held over his head, the herdsman turned toward the sound of the voice. So did Simna, who had been steeling himself to join in the path-cutting effort.

Emerging from the towering greensward just to their right was a man—or a close relation. Stepping out from between two ten-foot-high blades, he turned to confront them, sharp-eyed and unafraid despite his small stature. He was maybe three feet tall, slim to the point of emaciation, with high pointed ears, eyes that were small round circles of intensity, a bare snub of a nose, and a cone-shaped head that more than anything else resembled small blades of grass slicked up in the manner of some dandified courtier and glued together to form a perfect point. He wore nothing but a green loincloth that had been braided from strips of grass, and went barefoot. Fastened to his loincloth by a single loop was a comparably sized scythe of sharpened bone.

Like his loincloth and his surroundings, he was bright green, from pointy head to tiny-toed foot. No wonder they hadn't seen him until he had elected to emerge from hiding. Looking upon him, Ehomba decided their visitor might be a hundred years old, or two, but certainly no less than fifty. Of course, he was using the only referents he knew, which were human. The small green manikin was surely something else.

This their unexpected visitor proceeded to confirm, in prompt response to Simna's diplomatic inquiry of "What the hell are *you*?"

The figure drew himself up to his full, if unprepossessing, height. "I am Boruba-Ban-Beylok, sangoma of the Tlach Folk, the People of the Grass." He glared at Ehomba. "The grass gives life, the grass gives protection, the grass is the carpet on which the world treads. We do not take indifferently to its wanton cutting."

Hand on sword hilt, an uneasy Simna studied the impenetrable wall of high green and wondered if the blade might have found itself cutting down something more mobile and less indifferent than grass. There could be a hundred tiny green warriors hiding in there, a thousand, and he would not have known it. His senses were acute, but he saw and heard nothing. As near as he could tell, the only intruder that was rustling the grass was the wind. But he was on full alert now, trusting in his unassuming companion to defuse the situation. Simna was smart enough to know when to keep his mouth shut, aware that his chronic intemperance was more likely to exacerbate than ease the confrontation.

Ehomba lowered his blade but did not put it up. Instead, he let it hang loose from his right hand. "I was not being wanton." With his other hand he gestured at the green escarpment. "We are traveling to the north. The grass is in the way. If we could fly, we would choose that method of travel. But we are only human, so we must walk. To walk, we must make a path."

Boruba-Ban-Beylok shook his head disapprovingly. "Human you are, to think always of going through things. Never around."

"Very well." Ehomba was perfectly agreeable. "We will not cut the grass." Simna stared at his friend, but continued to keep his opinions and suggestions to himself.

Approaching the greensward, the herdsman pushed one blade of grass aside. Another was immediately behind it. "Show us how."

"You mock me," the little green sangoma snarled. Or at least tried to snarl. Like the rest of him, his voice was not very deep.

"Not at all," Ehomba replied. "I do not know how to go around the grass. If that is what you wish us to do, show us how. We will be glad to comply." He swung his blade in a short arc. "Cutting grass of any height is hard work. I would be delighted to be able to avoid it."

"And so you shall," the sangoma informed him, "if you can answer for me three riddles."

With a heavy sigh, Simna resumed his seat on the rock. "I knew there was a catch in this somewhere. When you're dealing with sangomas and shamans and witch doctors and spirit women, there's *always* a catch." Resignation underlay his words. "Sometimes it's deeds that have to be performed, or a magic crystal that needs recovering, or a sacred icon that has to be returned to its altar. Or bridges to be crossed, wells to be plumbed, cliffs to be scaled—but it's always something."

"What happens if we cannot answer your riddles?" Ehomba asked quietly.

The sangoma took a short hop forward. He was smiling

now. "Then you'll have to go back the way you came, you will. Have to go back, or a fate worse than any you can imagine will spring out at you from between the very blades of grass you seek to pass and rend you to fragments small enough for the beetles to feast upon, rend you with fang and claw and poison stinger."

Alarmed by this augury, Simna rose and retreated until he could stand with his back against a solid rock that protruded vertically from the base of the ridge. He held his sword at the ready and redoubled his continuous scrutiny of the green barrier.

If Ehomba was at all taken aback by the naked threat, he did not show it. "Ask your three riddles, then, Tlach-man."

Clearly enjoying himself and his role as ambassador of confrontation, Boruba-Ban-Beylok rubbed tiny green hands together as he primed himself. As they made contact with each other, the sliding palms generated a sound like bark being sanded. The sky did not darken and thunder did not roll—the Tlach sangoma was not a very big sangoma, after all—but the crests of the nearest grass blades tilted forward as if eavesdropping on the proceedings, and the rustling within momentarily grew louder than the slight breeze alone could have inspired.

"Listen close, listen careful, human." Trenchant green eyes stared deeply into Ehomba's. "First riddle: In the morning comes the sun, in the night comes the moon. But what comes at midday and is midwife to both? Riddle second: A fish is to a frog as a heron is to a crow. What is a Tlach to? Third riddle and last: The name of a man is how a man is known to others, but by what other means may he introduce himself?" With a confident smirk, the sangoma rested his hands on skinny green-skinned hips and waited for the tall trespasser to respond.

Observing scene and byplay, Simna had already resigned himself to finding a way back through the mountains. Sick as he was of climbing and descending, of fording rock-filled jungle streams and fighting off bugs and thorns, he struggled to accommodate them in his mind. Because it was clear that his simple, kindly friend, while a boon companion and pleasant fellow, was no towering intellect. In contrast, Simna was highly conversant with puzzles and conundrums of many kinds and origins. Quick-witted as he was, though, the solution to the three riddles of the Tlach was beyond him.

He eyed the impossibly lofty wall of grass apprehensively. If as seemed certain Ehomba failed to answer the riddles and they attempted to press on through the high veldt, Boruba-Ban-Beylok had all but promised them encounters with apparitions unpleasant. He studied the green escarpment intently, searching for signs of the brooding monstrosities the sangoma had assured them were lurking within, waiting for the right moment to spring upon unfortunate travelers. Just because he could not see anything did not mean there was nothing there. If it was green, like the sangoma, it could be standing right in front of them while remaining virtually invisible.

Ehomba stood quietly as he pondered the Tlach's questions. Then he slowly raised the sky-metal blade he was holding and silently aimed the point at the sangoma's chest. Simna tensed, while Boruba-Ban-Beylok eyed the much bigger man warily but did not turn and run.

"You cannot imagine what fate will befall you if you harm me," he growled darkly.

"I do not intend to harm you, but to answer your riddles." The herdsman advanced the tip of the sword ever so slightly nearer the sangoma's throat. "This blade is forged from metal that fell from the sky. See how strangely the sunlight shines on it? That makes it midwife to both the sun and the moon. As to your second riddle, a Tlach is close to Death, if he should come too close to such a blade. And it answers your last query as well, for with this sword I provide another way of introducing myself than by using my name." With surgical precision, he touched the sharp point of the weapon to the sangoma's neck, dimpling the green flesh just above the bulging Adam's apple.

"Boruba-Ban-Beylok, sangoma to the Tlach, meet the metal that comes from the stars."

The sangoma swallowed—not too hard, lest he awkwardly impact the location of the blade. Behind them both, Simna put a hand on the hilt of his own weapon as he tried to divide his attention between the two figures and the still quiescent wall of grass. At any moment he expected something huge and horrific to spring forth from between the stems. But the greensward remained still.

"Am I supposed to offer a greeting in return?" Eyes narrowing, the sangoma fixed the contentious interloper with a threatening stare. "I warned you. Now you must accept the consequences."

"I am prepared to do that," Ehomba assured him. "That is why I am still standing here holding this weapon at your throat instead of running away. I have never run from a confrontation in my life, and I do not intend to start now." He nodded at the grassy escarpment. "I have vowed to travel north until I can find a ship to take me westward across the Semordria, and north I will go in spite of spew, spirits, or spiteful sangomas."

Simna stretched as he tried to see over the tops of the grass. "Etjole, something's coming! I can hear it." He inhaled sharply. "And smell it."

"What is it, Simna?" The herdsman's blade did not waver. Boruba-Ban-Beylok was starting to smile.

"Can't tell. Animal of some kind. No—animals. More than one, less than a dozen. Big." He drew his sword. "If we're going to make a stand, we'd do better to find a cave to fight from, or at least higher ground."

"No." Ehomba kept his attention on the small green man

standing before him. "I stay here. Climb to safety if you want."

Simna stood with his back against the protruding rock, torn among common sense, personal desires, and admiration for the stupidly brave herdsman. The internal conflict found him in an agony of indecision.

"You know I can't do that! You saved me from Corruption, not once but twice. I can't run out on you!"

Ehomba nodded agreeably. "Good for me. Then stand, and be ready." He met the sangoma's stare with an unwavering gaze of his own. Startled by its unexpected depth and intensity, the Tlach stumbled slightly before recovering his balance.

"A herdsman, you say you are? Are you sure?"

Ehomba's tone was rock steady. "In the pastures a man must learn to stare down predators that threaten his herds and flocks. When one is used to doing that, locking eyes with another man-thing is never very intimidating."

Something large and heavy was smashing its way through the grass toward them. In spite of himself, Ehomba turned to look in its direction. Boruba-Ban-Beylok sniffed expectantly.

"Now you will learn the folly of challenging a sangoma of the Tlach! Your death approaches. Prepare yourself, herdsman! And don't say that I didn't warn you."

"They're coming!" Leaping from his rock, an agitated but determined Simna took up a defensive position alongside the herdsman's back, facing the green wall with his sword held firmly in both hands. "Whatever it is, is coming!"

The grass parted and a glowering brown face glared down at the three bipeds. A second facade, splotched with white, emerged nearby. Two flat-surfaced, sharp incisors protruded downward from the upper jaw, each longer than Simna ibn Sind's body. Black convex eyes stared down at them while the upthrust ears were each as big as a good-sized steer. The fur that covered each animal was thick and silky, and the round, compact bodies traveled on gigantic, immensely powerful feet.

Ehomba stared back while a gargling sound emerged from the throat of the startled Simna. They were hares, the herdsman saw immediately.

Hares as big as elephants.

XIII

Neither man laughed. Expecting something toothier, they nonetheless did not lower their guard for a moment. A small hare could bite off a man's finger, while a larger one like those that inhabited the Naumkib country could knock the wind out of a person with a single kick, or do real damage if such a blow struck a vulnerable area. Hares the impossible size of those they now confronted should be capable of biting a horse in half or kicking down a castle wall. Though not what was expected, they were no less potentially lethal.

Ehomba wondered at his own surprise. In a country of tree-high grass, what could be more natural than to encounter grass-eaters of equivalent size?

He was watching the triumphant sangoma carefully. He had not seen the little green man trace any arcane symbols in the air, nor had he been heard to enunciate any mysterious phrases. His voice had not been raised in alarm, nor had he uncorked a gourd or bottle of concentrated musk. Therefore the appearance of the titanic hares was most likely a conse-quence of their mere presence in the area, and a natural cu-

riosity about the source of human conversation. The boastful
sangoma might know their ways, but he had done nothing
thus far to indicate that he commanded them.

Which did not make their present situation any less potentially perilous. With an admirable effort of will, Simna held
his ground when his natural instinct was to run for cover
among the rocks behind them. That, Ehomba suspected, was
what Boruba-Ban-Beylok had intended to do the instant the
hares made their initial appearance. With his small size and
knowing the ways of the new arrivals as intimately as he
surely did, he was doubtless counting on finding a place of
safety long before the travelers did, leaving it to the hares to
finish off the unbelievers.

Ehomba put up his sword. Using his spear as a walking
stick, he marched straight toward the nearest of the immense
leporids. Still holding his own weapon out in front of him,
Simna made a grab for his tall friend—and missed. He did not
follow.

"Etjole, are you crazy? They'll bite off your arms—or your
head! They'll stomp you into the earth! *Etjole*!"

Ignoring the well-meaning swordsman's warnings,
Ehomba approached until he was within paw-length of the
nearest hare. Glowering, it leaned toward him, both front
paws extended. It could easily pin him to the ground, or pick
him up and, with a single snap, bite off his face.

Now, it is said that there is no talk among hares, and that
they reserve all such ability for their death throes, for as
everyone knows, the scream of a dying hare is as piercing and
soul-shattering a sound as exists in nature. But most men
know nothing of the lives of such creatures, for they are familiar with them only as garden pests, or a possible dinner.
Not so with Etjole Ehomba, and not by accident or chance.

The great ears inclined forward to listen to the softly speaking herdsman. With a single short hop that caused it to emerge
entirely from the grass, its white-faced companion moved in

imately close. Both enormous leporids remained quite still as
Ehomba whispered to them. Only their whiskers and over-
ized nostrils moved, quivering without pause.

Boruba-Ban-Beylok was positively beside his diminutive
green self. "What are you waiting for? Kill them! Kill them
both! They are intruders, interlopers, blasphemers! Tear them
o pieces, crush their bodies beneath your great feet! Take
hem up and hurl them—"

He broke off as the point of Simna ibn Sind's sword replaced that of Etjole Ehomba at the front of the sangoma's
green-skinned throat. The stocky swordsman was grinning
hastily. "Here now, bruther, that's about enough noise-making
out of you, don't you think?" He glanced significantly in the
direction of the soft-voiced conversation that was now taking
place between prodigious hares and easygoing herdsman.
"We wouldn't want to interrupt a friendly chat between man
and beast, now, would we?"

Ignoring the presence of the sword as much as it was possible to do so, a goggle-eyed Boruba-Ban-Beylok gawked at
he unreasonable trio, the two huge hare heads bent close to
he tall intruder so as not to miss a single word of his gentle
discourse.

"No—it's impossible! No man may talk with the great
grass-eaters! Such a thing cannot be!"

As time continued to pass without the immense herbivores
attacking, Simna grew increasingly at ease. "You have eyes,
don't you, wise man? Tiny, beady, nasty eyes, but eyes
nonetheless. Believe it: It is happening." He nodded in the direction of the most unlikely conversation. "My country friend
here may sometimes smell of cattle piss and sheep droppings,
but he is just full of surprises."

"This can't be happening." Moaning, the distraught sangoma dropped to his knees.

Moments later Ehomba broke off the talk and rejoined the
other two. Behind him the great hares waited, following his

progress with their bottomless eyes, noses twitching
whiskers as long as a man's leg quivering. The white-face
one turned away and began to gnaw at the nearest grass stalk
The green span disappeared into the oversized, mechanicall
grinding mouth as neatly as a log into the maw of a sawmill

Fully aware that his life was on the line, Boruba-Ban-Beylo
gazed up at the solemn-faced herdsman. "Don't kill me, war
lock of an unknown land! Please don't! My people need me
They rely on my knowledge and skills to help them survive i
the grass. Without me they will panic and perish."

"I doubt that," Ehomba replied. "I have no doubt that yo
are a person of importance among your tribe, and master o
some small competencies. But I think they would manage t
find another to take your place."

"Too right, bruther." Nodding agreement and smilin
wickedly, Simna shoved the point of his sword more firml
against the green man's neck.

"However," Ehomba went on even as he rested his fre
hand on the swordsman's arm, "I will kill another only to de
fend myself, and that is no longer necessary."

"Awww." Openly disappointed, Simna reluctantly drev
back his blade. The air went out of Boruba-Ban-Beylok. The
he rose and gestured in the direction of the hares, who wer
both now munching contentedly on the towering grass, indif
ferent to the small drama being played out in their vicinity.

"How?" he asked simply. "I have never seen or heard o
such a thing, magician."

"As soon as I saw what kind of creatures were threatenin
us, I was no longer worried. And stop calling me that." A
touch of irritation crept into the southerner's voice. "I am
herdsman; nothing more, nothing less."

"As you say, mag—herdsman. You were not worried? Yo
are the first interloper I have ever encountered who was no
terrified by the very sight of the giant browsers."

"That is because I know them," Ehomba explained. "O

ather, I know their kind. You see, I come from a dry country, and in dry country there is always constant competition for pasturage. Left to themselves, cattle will compete with sheep. There are also the wild animals: the antelope and the rhinoceros, the mice and the meerkats, the bushbuck and the brontotherium, the gerbil and the gormouth."

Simna's brows drew together. "What's a gormouth?"

"Tell you later." To the sangoma he added, "In the face of such endless competition for forage a herdsman can do one of two things: poison and kill those that compete with his herds for food, or try to work out some kind of mutually acceptable arrangement that satisfies all."

"And you," the sangoma asserted, "you are a compromiser."

Ehomba nodded. "The Naumkib are not a violent tribe. Our herds and flocks share with the oryx and the deer. They understand this, and so do the animals we claim for our own. To maintain this peaceful arrangement it is sometimes necessary for the parties involved to ratify and adjust, to discuss and debate. The talking of it is delegated to those of us who possess some small skill in conversation."

"And you," Simna declared bluntly, "you talk to hares."

"Yes." The herdsman nodded once. "I talk to hares." He glanced back over his shoulder at the quietly browsing brown behemoths behind them. "Among the Naumkib there is a saying for each species, for each of the grazing kind we have learned to deal with. For the hare it is 'Speak softly and carry a big carrot.' Unfortunately, I have no carrots to offer these, but I think it would not matter. To impress these would take a carrot the size of a sago palm.

"But they recognize a conciliatory spirit, and being of a nonviolent nature themselves, were quick to respond to my overtures." He looked down at the green hominid, who, while still wary, had managed to cease trembling. "I do not know if it is natural to your tribe, Boruba-Ban-Beylok, but you, at least, should learn some hospitality."

Immediately, the sangoma dropped to his knees and placed his forehead and palms upon the ground. "Command me! Tell me what it is you need of me."

"Well now, that's more like it, bruther." Strutting back and forth while picking at his teeth with the point of his sword, Simna considered the offer. "For a start we—"

"We need nothing from him," Ehomba declared, interrupting. "I take nothing from someone who is offering under duress."

"Duress? What duress?" Simna demanded to know. "I've drawn back my sword, haven't I? Besides, what's wrong with taking from someone who's under duress? D'you think he'd not do so if given the chance?"

"I do not know," the herdsman replied softly. "I know only that I am not him."

"Well, I ain't him neither," Simna protested, "but I do know that finding a way through this bulwark of bastard grass is going to be Gimil-bedamned difficult, and that he probably could show us the way!"

Eagerness shining from his face, the sangoma rose quickly to his feet. "Yes! I can have several of our youth guide you! Otherwise you will quickly become hopelessly lost and wander about until you perish." He waved an arm at the green barrier. "In the grass there are no landmarks, no way to determine direction. Even at night, the tops of the blades will shut you in and keep you from seeing the stars. Nor can you climb to find your position. The upper edges of the blades are too sharp, and can cut a person to shreds." He tapped his chest.

"Only the Tlach know the way, and are small enough to slip easily between the blades."

"We appreciate your insights," Ehomba informed him, "but we must move quickly. Therefore your offer is declined."

Sword hanging at his side, Simna gaped at his friend. "Declined? You think we're going to be able to travel faster through that mess without a guide?"

"Yes." Turning, Ehomba smiled reassuringly at his bemused companion as he started back toward the browsing hares. "And we are not going through the grass—we are going over it."

"Over—oh no, not me! Not me, Etjole!" Simna started backing away, toward the familiar, comforting, unmoving rocks. "If you're thinking what I think you're thinking . . ."

Reaching the haunch of the nearest hare, Ehomba turned to look back at him. "Come, Simna ibn Sind. I have a long ways yet to travel and therefore no time to waste. Is it so very different from mounting a horse?"

"I don't know." Uncertain, unsure, but unwilling to be left behind, Simna reluctantly took a step forward. "I've always had a decent relationship with horses. My own relationship with hares has been solely at the dining table."

"I would not mention such things around them." Placing his left foot on the brown hare's right, Ehomba stepped up. Using the long fur as a convenient hand-hold, he pulled and kicked his way upward until he was sitting on the broad chestnut shoulders just behind the great head. The enormous, towering ears blocked much of the view forward, but there was nothing to see anyway except the endless, monotonous field of grass.

"Why not?" Making an easier if more hesitant job of it than the herdsman, the always-agile Simna boosted himself into an identical riding position on the neck of the second elephantine hare. "You're not going to tell me they can understand us?"

"Not our words, no," Ehomba informed him, "but they are good at sensing things. Feelings, emotions, which way a predator is likely to jump. Helpless as the majority of them are, they have to be." Leaning forward, he spoke into the nearest ear. He did not have to whisper. With auditory apparatus the size of trees, the hare could have heard him clearly from the top of the final jungle-draped ridge.

With a turn and a leap, they were off, Ehomba holding tightly to the thick neck fur and maintaining his usual contemplative silence, Simna howling and protesting at every bound. With each mighty hop they cleared tracts of grass that would have taken men afoot many difficult, sweaty minutes to traverse, and with each jolting landing Simna ibn Sind seemed to find a new imprecation with which to curse the extraordinary method of travel.

They were not alone on the veldt, nor were the Goliath hares the only oversized creatures to be seen. The wind-whipped, emerald green food source was host to an abundance of equally remarkable creatures. At the apex of every gargantuan leap they could see down and across the soaring grassland. Tree-sized blades twitched where hippo-sized mice gnawed at fallen seeds. Caterpillars as long as dugout canoes felled stems like nightmare loggers at work in an unripened forest. Earthen ramparts that would have made any siege engineer proud were the work not of attacking or defending armies, but of bull-like moles and gophers that burrowed prodigiously beneath the rich soil.

Once they were attacked by crows the size of condors. Unceasing in their search for an easy meal, the black-feathered robbers struck boldly from all sides—not at the hares, which were far too big to serve as prey for them, but at the far smaller riders clinging to their backs. Simna had his sword out as soon as he saw the first bird approach, but he never had the opportunity to use it.

Sharp, barking caws and *cut-cut*s sounded on his right. Using his legs to maintain his seat, Ehomba was sitting up straight, hands cupped around his mouth in a most unusual fashion, and shouting back at the marauding crows as good as they were giving. To hear those clipped, guttural caws coming from his mouth was an entertainment any prince would

have paid to witness. Simna got it for free. Given the serious-
ness of the circumstances, his commentary following the
crows' departure perhaps ought to have been less acerbic.

"Wait, don't tell me!" The swordsman made a great show
of analyzing in depth what had just transpired. "I know, I
know—you can talk to crows, too."

Untutored herdsman though he might be, when it came to
unfettered sarcasm Ehomba was not above responding in
kind. "You are very observant."

Holding tight to the neck fur of his hare, Simna reserved his
rejoinder for the moments when he and his mount were sailing freely through the air above the grass. "So you've convinced me. You're *not* a sorcerer. You're just the world's
greatest talker. What else can you talk to, Etjole? Turtles?
Nightingales? Dwarf voles?"

"In my country there are many crows," the herdsman responded without a hint of guile. "Living there is as hard for
them as for hares or cattle, men or lizards. It is . . ."

"A desert country, a dry country, difficult and bleak—I
know, I know." Simna returned his gaze to the unbroken
swath of green that still stretched out in every direction before
them. "Not that I'm complaining, mind. I've always been
adept at the languages of man, but never bothered to try learning those of the animals. Maybe it's because I didn't know
they had languages. Maybe it's because no one I ever met or
heard tell of knew that they had languages."

"It sounds to me," his companion called across to him,
"like you have spent most of your life around men who only
talked and did not listen."

"Hah! Sometimes, they don't even talk. They just swing
things, large and heavy or slender and sharp. I'll make you a
deal, bruther. You take care of talking to the dumb animals we
encounter, and I'll take care of talking to the men."

"Fair enough," Ehomba agreed, "but there is one thing
more you will have to help me with."

Simna glanced over at his friend. "What's that?"

"How does one tell which is which?"

Onward they raced through the high green veldt, their mounts seemingly tireless, covering great difficult distances with each bound. Until, at last, it seemed that they were tiring. They were not. It was the universal perspective that was being altered, not the enthusiasm of the hares.

The first indication that something had changed came from Simna's observation that they were covering shorter and shorter distances with each bound. This was immediately confirmed by Ehomba, who was the one to point out that the hares were jumping as frequently and as powerfully as ever. It was not that they were covering less and less distance with each leap, but that they were covering less proportionately. Because with each hop now, they were growing smaller and smaller.

The hares shrank to rhino size, then to that of a horse, then a calf, at which point they could no longer support their human riders. After a very bad moment during which he thought he was shrinking as well, Simna realized that he and his companion were not changing in size. It was only the world around them that was changing.

They followed the hares forward until both fleet-footed creatures were reduced to the size of those that Simna knew from his travels in his own homeland and other countries: small brown furry creatures that barely came up to the middle of a man's shin. Their noses still twitched, their whiskers continued to flutter, and in every other aspect they were unaltered, even to the white splotches on the face of his own former mount. But the journey had reduced them from giants to the reality of the world he had always known. The real world, he decided—though in the company of a singular individual like Etjole Ehomba, who was to say what was real and what imaginary?

Along with the hares, the grass too had been reduced in size until the tops of the highest blades rose no higher than his waist, with a few isolated, more productive patches reaching to his shoulders. The taller Ehomba could see easily over even these.

Bending, the herdsman made unintelligible sibilant sounds to the two hares, who listened attentively. Following a light pat on the head of each, they turned and scurried back into the grass from whence they had all come.

Simna watched them go. "What will happen now? As they travel south will they start to return to their former extravagant size?"

"I believe so." Ehomba was trying to follow the progress of their mounts, but his efforts were defeated by the dense growth that closed in behind them. When not in their exaggerated state, small hares needed to be ever vigilant. Once back in the veldt of the giants, he reflected, they would be safe once again. Tilting back his head slightly, he glanced at the sky. Unless, of course, there soared among the clouds in the region they had just fled hawks and eagles that reached proportionate size. Such a winged monster would put all the tales of rocs and fire-breathing dragons to shame. What a wonder it would be, though, to see such a creature! An eagle with the wingspan of a nobleman's house!

He was glad they had been spared that particular marvel, however, because it would have meant that the monster would surely also have seen them.

Walking north, it was not long before they came upon a kopje, a rocky outcropping rising from the surrounding veldt. At its base was a small pool, not so shallow as to be too hot, not so stagnant as to prove distasteful. By mutual agreement it was decided to make camp there for the night.

When Ehomba announced that he would build the fire, Simna waited and watched eagerly for the herdsman to generate sparks with the tips of his fingers, or blow flame from his nostrils, or conjure it out of the thin dry air with closed eyes and staccato chant. He was sorely disappointed. The fire was started with flint and dry grass and much careful blowing on the tiny wisp of smoke that resulted.

Perhaps the tall herdsman was nothing more than he claimed to be: a simple master of cattle and sheep with an unusually adept skill at multispecies linguistics. One who would maintain that assertion even under torture or threat of death. He would have to, Simna knew.

Otherwise others might find out about the treasure he was after.

Smiling to himself, knowing that he knew the truth no matter what the disarmingly personable southerner might claim, Simna prepared for the coming night. Let the "herdsman" think that his traveling companion believed his fictions. Simna knew better, and that was enough for now. When the time came, he would confront his laconic companion more forcefully.

As forcefully as was necessary to ensure that he got his full share of what they were after. Whatever that was.

XIV

WITH THE BLACKNESS THAT FOLLOWS THE DAY PULLED OVER them like a speckled silk veil, the two men crouched around the fire taking turns trying to identify the sounds of the night. Occasionally, they argued. More often, they agreed. Ehomba was impressed by his well-traveled companion's range of knowledge, while Simna appreciated the acuity of his tall friend's hearing.

Not that it was always necessary to strain to hear the murmurings of the night creatures. A well-spaced assortment of screeches, yowls, roars, bellows, hisses, and whistlings surrounded them. A few they were able to identify, while the perpetrators of the majority remained as unknown as if they had come down from the dark side of the moon.

Once, the clear, still air resounded to the sounds of horrific conflict between unseen combatants. The noise of battle died away without any concluding scream, suggesting that the fighters had resolved their nocturnal dispute in nonfatal fashion. Not long thereafter, a high-pitched, lilting song that tinkled like running water made melody drifted across the grass, beguiling all within range, man and beast alike. And as they were about to retire, a small blue serpent whose back sported a pattern of pink diamonds slithered silently through the lonely encampment, passing directly and disinterestedly beneath Ehomba's ankles before disappearing back into the grass.

Simna rose abruptly at the sight of it and started to reach for his sword. When he saw that his companion was not only not afraid of the scaly intruder but actually indifferent to it, he slowly resumed his cross-legged seat on the ground.

"Do you talk to snakes, too, bruther?"

"Occasionally." The herdsman sipped from a leather water bag. "They have much to say."

"Really? It's been my experience they just bite, kill you, and go on their way."

"They should be forgiven the random burst of temperament. How would you like to go through life without legs or arms? Considering how unfairly Fate has dealt with them, limb-wise, I have to say that I find them admirably restrained." Finishing his drink, he recorked the container and set it aside. "Under the circumstances, I think I would find myself wanting to bite everything in sight, too."

"You know what your talent is, Etjole? In case you didn't know, I've just decided for you." Simna was preparing to turn in. "You sympathize with everything. You know what your problem is?"

"No. You tell me, Simna ibn Sind. What is my problem?"

The itinerant swordsman pulled the thin blanket up over his legs and torso. Upon it, a grieving maid had embroidered her feelings for him in certain and graphic terms.

"You sympathize with everything." With that he rolled onto his back and opened his eyes to the dark heavens. Everyone knew that the grains of sandy material that filled one's eyes and induced sleep were actually made of star-stuff. While lying beneath an open sky, this material would gradually sift downward to fill the corners of a man's eyes and gift him with a sound and healthful night's rest. Knowing this, Simna had never been able to understand how people were able to sleep indoors. No wonder so many of them tossed and turned uneasily in their beds.

The fire was burning low. A single distant but penetrating roar of particular resonance briefly jarred him, but he was too contented to let anything disturb him for long. They had crossed the seemingly impossible high veldt without injury or difficulty, saving weeks of difficult walking through dangerous country. He was traveling in the company of a mysterious but pleasant and unthreatening foreigner who was going to lead him to a trove of untold riches. True, this individual possessed abilities he refused to acknowledge until the time came to make use of them, but Simna had seen fakirs and magicians at work before, and was not intimidated by their ruses. Not even by those of one who could talk to animals. He was certain he was ready for whatever surprise his traveling companion might choose to spring next.

No he wasn't.

It was the light that woke him. Stealing in under his eyelids, prying at them with insistent photons, raising both his lids and his attention. The explanation was simple and natural: The sky had become lit by a rising full moon. Smacking dry lips, he prepared to roll over, away from the light in the sky. As he did so, he opened one eye to check on the position of the night's light. At the same time it occurred to him that there had been only a sliver of moon the night before, and that it was usual for the moon to move with stately and regular procession through its phases and not to jump from one-eighth full to wholly rounded.

He was wrong. The light did not come from the moon. He sat up, the thin but warm blanket sliding down to his thighs, his eyes now fully open and alert.

The campfire had been reduced to a pile of coals from

which curls of smoke continued to rise, taking flight into the night and making good their escape from the company of man. Ehomba sat cross-legged on the other side, staring not at the sky nor at his companion but at the intense glimmering that was drifting, will-o'-the-wisp-like, in front of him. No random, irregularly shaped glob of luminance, the light had form and shape.

What a form, an enchanted Simna thought dreamily, and what a shape.

It hovered in the air before the herdsman, draped in tight folds of silk in many shades of blue flecked with silver stars and laced with pearls and aquamarines. Though long of sleeve and skirt, the binding of the royal raiment was such that he could see the curves that folded upon curves. It was at once entirely modest and unrelievedly arousing.

The young woman who was thus encased, like a spectacular butterfly about to be born from a glistening cocoon, had skin the color of love and smooth as fresh poured cream. Her eyes were bluer than the silks she wore, and they sparkled more brightly than any diamond sewn to her gown. In striking contrast to the color of her skin, her hair was impossibly black, wavy filaments of polished onyx that spilled down her back and around her shoulders, as if a portion of the night itself had attached itself to her being.

She was staring not at the unmoving, attentive Ehomba, but off into the distance. Her expression was resigned, determined, wistful. What she was looking at Simna could not imagine. He knew only that he would, without hesitation, have given his very life to be the subject of that stare.

Something made her frown, and as she did so the light in which she was enveloped curdled like souring milk. A second presence stepped into the ragged splotch of efflorescence. It was huge, monstrous, and overbearing.

You could not see the eyes, concealed as they were within the depths of the horned helmet. Spikes and scythes protruded from the rough-surfaced black metal. Below the helmet began the body of a wrestler and a giant, immensely powerful, the muscles themselves occasionally visible beneath flowing garments of purple, gold, and crimson. The cape that trailed behind the figure, which Simna estimated to be close to eight feet tall, was decorated with the most horrible visions of hell, of bodies being torn limb from limb by demons and devils, all of whom were performing their dreadful activities under the supervision and command of that same towering, helmeted figure.

As both men looked on, there in the night in the middle of the veldt, the giant put a massive, mailed hand on one flawless bare shoulder. Instantly the woman whirled, her far-off look abruptly replaced with one of utter loathing and revulsion. Her reaction did not seem to trouble the giant. Though she did her utmost to remove his clinging hand, at first shaking and then grabbing at it, she was unable to dislodge the mailed grip even when pressing both hands and all her weight upon it.

Until now Simna had sat motionless, enthralled by the vision and the distant drama of what he was seeing. But suddenly, the giant was looking past the woman held in his bruising, unyielding grasp. Looking beyond the room in which he and his prize stood, beyond even the building where his prisoner was bound in unwilling consort.

He was looking straight at Etjole Ehomba, a herdsman from the dry, desiccated lands to the south.

With a bellow of outrage that dwarfed anything that the veldt had produced, the figure brought its other hand forward. Something that was the consequence of an unholy union between fire and lightning sprang from the mailed palm, leaping toward the seated southerner. Ehomba ducked instinctively and the blast of luminescent diablerie passed over his left shoulder to strike the center of the dying campfire.

Those flames that remained within fled in terror of a

greater fire than they could know. As the air screamed, the very molecules of which it was composed were torn and rent. The image of giant and entrapped beauty collapsed in upon itself, twisting and crumpling like a sheet of paper in the trembling fingers of a scandalized warlord. And then it was gone: giant, empyreal prisoner, and the light that had framed them, leaving behind only the veldt and the scandalized night.

Not a sound emanated from the surrounding leagues of grass. It was as if the earth itself lay stunned by the apparition. Then, somewhere, a cricket resumed its violining. A frog croaked from within its prized puddle. Night birds and insects resumed their timeless chorus.

Aware that he had neglected to breathe for a while, Simna ibn Sind inhaled deeply. The perspiration in which he was drenched began to dry and cool on his body, causing him to shiver slightly. Shunting aside his blanket, he crawled over until he was beside his companion. It took a moment, because he had to avoid the foot-deep, smoking ditch of scorched earth that occupied the place where their campfire had been and that now drew a line in the soil between them. It stank of carbonized malignance and inhuman venality.

"Pray tell, bruther, what that was all about? And in the same breath, deny to me one more time that you are a sorcerer."

Ehomba looked over at him and smiled tiredly. "I have told you, friend Simna, that I am but a simple herdsman. Believe me, I would rather be lying with my wife than with you, listening to my children instead of the growls and complaints of strange animals, and in my own bed than here in this alien land. But through no wish or desire of my own, I have become involved in something bigger than myself." Turning away, he looked at the patch of sky where the phantasm had appeared and subsequently burned itself out.

"I did not conjure up what we just saw. I did not call out to it, or beckon it hither, or ask it to appear before me. I recited no litany, cast no spells, burnt no effigies. I was having trouble going to sleep and, having trouble, thought to sit a while and contemplate the majesty of the sky." He shrugged so lackadaisically that Simna almost believed him.

"So that just 'happened'?" The swordsman waved at the space in the sky where the figures had appeared. The air there still shimmered and smoldered like distant pavement on a scorching hot afternoon. "You did nothing to make it happen?"

"Nothing." With a heavy sigh Ehomba lay back down on the comforting earth. "I was sitting, and it appeared before me. The auguries of a dead man, Simna. The burden of Tarin Beckwith of Laconda, North." He nodded at the disturbed patch of atmosphere.

"I believe that the woman we saw was the Visioness Themaryl, and the frightful figure that appeared behind her must perforce be her abductor, Hymneth the Possessed. She fits the allusion of comeliness the dying Beckwith described to me, and he no less the likeness of concentrated animus. How or why they should appear to me now, here, in this isolated and unpretentious place, I cannot tell you."

Simna nodded and was silent for several moments. Then he commented, "You really don't know what you're getting into, do you?"

"I never worry about such things. We are all fallen leaves drifting on the river of life, and we go where the current takes us." The herdsman looked up at his friend. "Do you worry?"

The swordsman let his gaze rove out across the veldt. "I try to. I like to have some idea what I'm in for." Pulling his gaze away from the veldt and whatever was out there, he looked back over at the herdsman. "That must be some treasure he's guarding."

Frustrated, Ehomba rolled over onto his side. "If what you just saw and experienced is not enough to convince you that I

am not doing this for treasure, then it is certain nothing I can
say will convince you otherwise."

"Oh, don't get me wrong," Simna declared. "The woman is
certainly worth saving." He whistled softly. "There are all
kinds of treasure, even some that come wrapped in silk.
Speaking of which, did you happen to notice that—"

"You are an impossible person, Simna ibn Sind."

"I prefer incorrigible. All right, so my intentions are base.
But my objectives are noble. I'll help you rescue this Visioness Themaryl, if you're bound and determined to return
her to her family as you say you've sworn to do. But as my
reward, or payment, or whatever you wish to call it, I claim
for myself any gold or jewels we can plunder along the way."

In the darkness, Ehomba smiled in spite of himself. "You
would pit yourself against the figure we saw, against this
Hymneth the Possessed, for mere wealth?"

"Take it from me, Etjole—there's no such thing as 'mere
wealth.' So he's big and ugly and can throw sky fire from his
fingertips. So what? I'll bet he bleeds like any man."

"I would not count on that. But I admire your bravery."

"I've found that in the face of danger, greed is a wonderful
motivator, Etjole. I suppose you're fortunate that you're immune to it."

"I did not say that I was immune. It is just that we covet different things, you and I."

"Fortunate for me, then." Rising, the swordsman returned
to his resting place and once again drew the embroidered
blanket up around his body.

His companion was not quite ready for sleep. "Simna, have
you ever contemplated a blade of grass?"

Already drifting off, the exhausted swordsman mumbled an
indifferent reply. "Look, I'd rather believe that I'm traveling
in the company of a sorcerer than a philosopher. You're not
going to philosophize at me now, are you? It's late, it's been
a tiring time, and we need to get an early start tomorrow

morning to cover as much ground as possible before the sun rises too high."

"You should look forward to walking when the sun is high. It keeps the snakes in their lairs. In the cool of morning and evening is when they like to come out."

"You're sure of that, are you?" Something brushed the swordsman's exposed left arm and he jumped slightly. But it was only, to his relief, a blade of grass being bent by the breeze.

"That is what they tell me."

"Hares I can accept, but snakes? Not even magicians can talk to snakes. Snakes have no brains."

He could almost see Ehomba scowling in the darkness. "I am sure there are many in this place, and I hope none of them overheard that."

"Hoy, right," Simna snorted softly.

"There is the universe we live in," the herdsman went on, as if the colloquial conviviality of serpents had never been a question under discussion, "and then there is a blade of grass." In the deepening shadows Simna saw his companion pluck a young green shoot from the ground and hold it above his reclining head, a tiny sliver of darker blackness against the star-filled sky.

"A wise man of our village, Maumuno Kaudom, once told me that there is a world whole and entire in everything we see, even in each blade of grass, and that if we could just make ourselves small enough we could walk around in it just as we walk around in this world."

Rolling his eyes, Simna turned over on his side so that his back was facing his suddenly talkative friend. "Just assuming for a minute that your wise man knew what he was talking about and that he wasn't speaking from the effects of too much homemade beer or garden-raised kif, and that you could 'walk around' inside the 'world' of a blade of grass, why would anyone want to? Everything there is to see in a grass blade can be seen now." Reaching out from beneath his blanket, he ripped a small handful of stems from the soil and flung them over his side in the direction of his prone companion.

"Catch, bruther! See—I fling a whole fistful of worlds at you!"

A couple of the uprooted blades came to rest on Ehomba's face. Idly, keeping his attention focused on the stem that he was holding, the herdsman flicked them aside. "One world at a time is enough to ponder, Simna."

The swordsman rolled back to his original position. He was weary, and had had about enough learned discourse for the evening. "Good! At last we're in agreement on something. Concentrate on this one, and forget about grass, except for the leagues of it we must march through tomorrow."

"But, think a moment, Simna."

The other man groaned. "Must I? It hurts my head."

The herdsman refused to be dissuaded. "If Maumuno Kaudom is right, then perhaps this world, the one we inhabit, is to some larger being nothing more than another blade of grass, one among millions and millions, that can be held up to contemplation—or flicked aside in a moment of boredom or indifference."

"They'd better not try it," the swordsman growled. "Nobody tosses Simna ibn Sind aside in a moment of anything!"

Gratifyingly, it was the last thing Ehomba had to say. The silence of the night stole in upon them, pressing close on the sputtering embers of the dying campfire until it, too, went silent. In the rising coolness of the hour the enormity of what Ehomba had been saying eased itself unbidden into Simna's thoughts.

What, just what, if the old village fakir his friend had been talking about was right? He wasn't, of course, but just—what if? It would mean that a man's efforts meant nothing, that all his exertions and enthusiasms were of such insignificance as to be less than noticeable to the rest of Creation.

Reaching down, he fingered another blade of grass that was struggling to emerge from the soil just beyond the edge of his blanket. Fingered it, but did not pull it. He could have done so easily, with the least amount of effort imaginable. Curl a finger around the insignificant stem and pull. That was all it would take, and the blade would die. What did that matter in the scheme of things? They were surrounded by uncountable billions of similar blades, many grown to maturity. And if this one was pulled, two more would spring up to claim its place in the sun.

But what if it contained a world, a world unto itself? Insignificant in the design of Creation, yes, meaningless in the context of the greater veldt, but perhaps not so meaningless to whatever unimaginable minuscule lives depended on it for their own continued existence and growth.

Absurd! he admonished himself. Preposterous and comical. His finger contracted around the blade even as his lips tightened slightly. It hung like that, the slightly sharp edge of the blade prominent against the inner skin of his forefinger.

Slowly, he withdrew his hand. The blade remained rooted in the earth. It was nothing more than that: a single finger-length strand of grass. No horse or hare would have been as forgiving, no hungry kudu or mouse would have hesitated before the small strip of nourishing greenery. But Simna ibn Sind did.

He was not sure why. He was only sure of one thing. The next time he and his impassive traveling companion were lying in some empty open place preparing for sleep, he was going to cram his bedsheet, or blanket, or if need be clods of earth, into his ears so as not to have to listen to what the herdsman had to say. It was an evil thing to play with a man's mind, even if, as it appeared, Ehomba had done so unintentionally.

Blades of grass as individual worlds! This world as nothing more! What lunacy, what folly! Fortunately he, Simna ibn

Sind, was immune to such rubbish. Slipping his forearms beneath his head to support it, he turned onto his belly and tried to get comfortable. As he did so, he found himself wondering how many blades of grass he was crushing beneath his chest. His closed eyes tightened as he vented a silent, mental scream.

Tomorrow he would do something to unsettle Ehomba twice as much as the herdsman had unsettled him. That promise gave him something else to think about, to focus on. With visions of cerebral revenge boiling in his thoughts, he finally managed to drift off into an uneasy, unsettled sleep.

When he woke the following morning his good humor had returned, so much so that all thoughts of retaliation had fled from his mind. Sitting up on his blanket, he stretched and let the rising sun warm his face. Ehomba was already up, standing on the other side of the campfire staring into the distance as he leaned leisurely against his long spear. Staring north, where they were headed.

A humble man, the condescending Simna mused. Some would say single-minded, but it was as easy to think of him as highly focused. As he prepared to rise from where he had been sleeping, the swordsman happened to notice the skin of his left forearm. As he did so, his eyes bugged slightly.

A neat line of red spots ran from wrist to elbow. Some were larger than others. All were grouped in twos. The pattern was plain to see. What sort of biting insect would make such marks? He rubbed his hand over the pale splotches that were already beginning to fade. They did not itch, nor had whatever had made them penetrated the skin.

The repeated double pattern reminded him of something, but for a long moment he could not remember what. Then it struck him: They were exactly the kinds of marks the fangs of a snake would make.

Hopping back onto his blanket (as if that would provide any refuge or protection!) he looked around wildly. When he bent low he found that he could make out marks in the grass and the dirt. Many marks, familiar patterns in the ground, as if he had been visited during the night by a host of serpents. A host who had left their signs upon him as a warning, and a commentary.

Straightening, he scrutinized the surrounding grass, but could see nothing moving. Only the tips of the blades disturbed by the occasional morning breeze, and the flitting of hesitant, busy insects.

"All right," he called out to the open veldt, "I apologize! Snakes *do* have brains! Now leave me be, will you?"

With that he turned to see Ehomba staring back at him.

"Well," he groused as he snatched up his blanket and shook it free of dirt, grass, litter, and assorted would-be biting fellow travelers no bigger than the motes of dust that swirled in the air, "what are *you* laughing at!"

"I was not laughing," Ehomba replied quietly.

"Ha!" Roughly, the swordsman began rolling his blanket into a tight bundle suitable for travel. "Not on the outside, no, but on the inside, I can hear you! You're not the only one who can hear things, you know."

"I was not laughing," Ehomba insisted in the same unchanging monotone. Turning, he gestured with his spear. "That way, I think. More inland than I would like to go, but I think there may be water that way. I see some high rocks."

Pausing in his packing, Simna squinted and strained. Despite the best efforts of his sharp eyes, the horizon remained as flat as the beer in the last tavern he had visited. But he was not in the mood to dispute his companion. It was too early, and besides, Ehomba had already proven himself more right than wrong about the most extraordinary things. When a man was right about visions of ultimate beauty and terror, much less about snakes, it made no sense to squabble with him over the possible presence of distant rocks.

Shouldering their kits, the two men struck off to the north, heading slightly to the east. As he walked, Simna found himself apologizing to the young shoots of grass on which he unavoidably stepped, and followed each apology with an unvoiced curse in his companion's direction. The red spots on his arm were nearly gone, but that did not keep him from carefully inspecting any open places in the grass ahead before he strode through them.

XV

"SCREAMING."

"What?" Simna had been watching a small flock of brilliantly colored parrots chattering and cackling in a nearby tree. The unprepossessing tree itself was as worthy of attention as its noisy, joyfully bickering occupants. In the open veldt, it was worth marking the location of anything above the height of a mature weed for use both as a landmark and a possible camping site.

"I hear screaming."

Maybe his eyesight was not as keen as that of the herdsman, but there was nothing wrong with Simna ibn Sind's hearing, which was sharp from untold nights of listening intently for the creak of doors or windows being stealthily opened, or for the ominous footsteps of approaching husbands. The instant that his tall companion had drawn the swordsman's attention away from the tree, he too heard the rising wail.

His brows drew together. "It's coming at us from the east, but I don't recognize it. If it's some kind of beast, it's a mighty great huge one to make itself heard at such a distance."

Ehomba nodded solemnly. "I have an idea of what it might be, but this country is strange and new to me, so we will wait and hope it draws near enough for us to make it out."

His friend spun 'round to face him. "Draws near! We don't want it to draw near, whatever it is. We want it to go away, far away, so that we don't hear it anymore, much less set eyes on it."

The herdsman glanced down at the other man. "Are you not curious to see what it is that makes such a consistent and ferocious noise?"

"No, I am not." Simna kicked at the grassy ground. "I am perfectly happy to avoid the company of anything that makes consistent and ferocious noises. If I passed the rest of my life without ever seeing anything that made consistent and ferocious noises, I would be well content."

"I am surprised at you, Simna." Once more Ehomba turned his attention eastward. "I am always questioning things, wanting to learn, needing to know. I am afraid it made me something of a pest to my mother and an enigma to my father. The other children would taunt me whenever I wanted to know the name of something, or the meaning, or what it was for. 'Curiosity killed the catechist,' they would tell me. Yet here I stand, alive and well—but still boundlessly ignorant, I fear."

"I wouldn't disagree with that," Simna muttered under his breath. The roar from the east was growing steadily louder. The problem now was not how to hear it, but how to avoid it. His gaze fell on the kopje. "Unless it's some harmless but large-throated creature coming toward us, we ought to be prepared to deal with it. For once we have the opportunity of some cover, however slight." He nodded in the direction of the prominent rock pile. "I suggest we avail ourselves of it."

"Yes." Ehomba smiled at him. "A question may be as easily answered from a position of safety as from one of exposure. You are full of good common sense, Simna."

"And you are full of something too, bruther Etjole." Putting a hand against the taller man's back, the swordsman gave him a firm shove in the direction of the granite outcropping. "But I am growing fond of you nevertheless. I suppose there is no accounting for one's taste."

"Even if I am not leading you to great treasure?" The herdsman grinned down at him as together they loped toward the looming rocks.

"Save your fibs for later, bruther." Despite his inability to match Ehomba's long stride, Simna easily kept pace with his companion.

Several small, yellow-furred rodents scurried for holes in the rocks as the men drew near. From the far side, a large bird rose skyward in a spectacular explosion of iridescent green and blue feathers, two of which trailed from its head and exceeded the rest of its body in length. Though it had the appearance of a songbird, its call was as rough and jagged as that of a magpie.

There were no caves in the rocks, but they found a place between two great sun-blasted whitish gray stones that was large enough to accommodate both of them side by side. While the depression did not conceal them completely, it afforded a good deal more protection than they would have had standing out on the open plain.

"See!" This time it was Simna who reacted first, rising from his crouch and pointing to the east. "It's coming. At least, something's coming." Shielding his eyes from the blazing sun, he squinted into the distance.

"It certainly is." Ehomba gripped his spear tightly. "And it is not an animal."

By this time the distant screaming had risen to a level where both men had to raise their voices slightly in order to make themselves understood to one another.

"What do you mean it's not an animal? What else could it be?"

"Wind," Ehomba explained simply.

Simna frowned, then listened closely, finally shaking his head. "That's no wind. I don't know what it is, but it's alive. You can hear the anger in it."

Crouching nearby, using the smooth rock for support, Ehomba leaned his spine against the unyielding stone. "What makes you think, my friend, that the wind is not alive, and that it cannot feel anger?" He gestured. "Not only does this wind sound angry, it *looks* angry."

The screaming grew still louder, rising with its increasing proximity. Then the source of the shrieking came into view, making no attempt to hide itself. It was like nothing Simna ibn Sind had ever seen, not in all his many travels. Frightful and formidable it was to look upon, a veritable frenzy of malice galloping across the veldt toward them. It displayed every iota of the anger the swordsman had heard in its voice, confirming all he had suspected. But to his wonder and chagrin, Ehomba's explanation proved equally correct.

The fiend that was racing toward them, howling fit to drown out a good-sized thunderstorm, was wind indeed, but it was unlike any wind Simna had ever seen.

That in itself was extraordinary, for the wind rarely manifested itself visually. Usually, it could be felt, or heard. But this wind could also be seen clearly, for it took upon itself a form that was as appalling as it was imposing. Rampaging across the veldt, it ground its way in their general direction even as it wound deliriously inward upon itself. Nor was it alone. Again Simna squinted eastward. No, there could be no mistake. Unlike the winds he knew, this one was advancing purposefully and in a decidedly unerratic manner.

It was chasing something.

"There's something running from it," Simna called out as

e put up his sword. Of what use was steel against an unchecked force of Nature?

"I see it," Ehomba avowed. "It looks like some kind of at."

"That's what I thought." His companion nodded agreement. "But it doesn't look like any kind of cat I've ever seen before."

"Nor I. It is all the wrong shape. But it is definitely running from the wind, and has not merely been caught out in front of it. See how it swerves to its right and the wind demon turns to follow it?" He turned away briefly as a rising gust sent particles of dust and fragments of dry grass smacking into his face.

"Not again!" Simna pointed over the rocks. "What kind of demonic hunt is this? Whoever heard of wind deliberately chasing a cat—or any other creature, for that matter?"

He expected the ceaselessly surprising herdsman to say, "I have seen . . ." or "In the south I once knew of . . ." but instead the tall spear carrier simply nodded. "Certainly not I, Simna."

"You mean you haven't experienced everything, and you don't know all there is to be known?" the swordsman responded sardonically.

Ehomba looked over at him, now having to shield his eyes from blowing debris. The wind was much closer, and therefore that much more intense. "I have tried to tell you on several occasions, Simna, that I am the most ignorant of men, and that everything I know could fit in the bottom third of a spider's thimble."

"I didn't know spiders used thimbles."

"Only certain ones." This was said without a hint of guile. "They have sharp-tipped feet, and it is the only way they can avoid pricking themselves when they are weaving their webs." Keeping low, he looked back out across the rocks.

"The cat is exhausted. You can see it in its face. If something is not done, the wind will catch it soon."

"Yeah, you can see how its stride is growing slo— What do you mean 'if something's not done'?" As warning sign flared in his brain, Simna eyed his friend with sudden wariness.

His worst fears were confirmed when the herdsman rose from his crouching position and moved to abandon the comparative safety of their rocky alcove. "Wait a minute bruther! What do you think you're doing?"

Standing atop the bare granite, Ehomba looked back at the other man, that by now familiar, maddening, doleful expression on his long face. "There is something strangely amiss here, my friend, that has led to a most unequal contest. I am by nature a peaceful fellow, but there are a few things that can rouse me to anger. One of these is an unequal fight." Lowering his spear, he stretched it out in the direction of the advancing wind and its failing prey. "Such as we see before us."

Simna rose, but made no move to follow the taller man. "What we see before us, bruther, is a contest of unnatural will and unreasoning Nature in which we are fortunate not to be a part. Leave circumstances alone and get back under cover. Or would you think to debate with a thunderstorm?"

"Only if it was a rational thunderstorm," the herdsman replied unsurprisingly.

"Well, this is no rational wind. I mean, just look at it! What are you going to do—threaten it with harsh language?"

"More than that, I hope." Gliding easy as a long, tall wraith across the rocks, Ehomba made his way down the slight slope of the kopje toward the onrushing disturbance. Behind him, Simna cupped his hands to his lips in order to make himself heard above the ever-rising howl.

"All right, then! If suicide is your craving, far be it from me to interfere!" As Ehomba bounded off the last rock and down into the grass, the swordsman's voice became a shout. "But before you die, at least tell me the location of the treasure!"

Perhaps the herdsman did not hear this last. Perhaps he did, and simply chose to ignore it. Looking back, he raised his spear briefly over his head in salute, then turned and jogged out into the grass, heading directly into the path of the onrushing cataclysm.

If the exhausted cat saw him, it gave no sign. Nor did it react by changing its course and heading in his direction. Why should it? What could one mere man do in the face of one of Nature's most frightening manifestations? Lengthening his stride, Ehomba hurried to intercept the storm's quarry.

Certainly it was the strangest and yet most magnificent cat the herdsman had ever seen. Jet black in color, with yellow eyes that burned like candles behind the old magnifying lenses of a battered tin lantern, it had the overall look and aspect of an enormous male lion, complete to inky black neck ruff. But the heavy, muscular body was too long and was carried on absurdly elongated legs that surely belonged to some other animal. An unnatural combination of speed and strength, its lineage was a mystery to the curious Ehomba. From having to guard his flocks against them, he knew the nature and countenance of many cats, but he had never seen the like of the great black feline form that came stumbling toward him now.

While its pedigree remained a mystery, there was no mistaking its intent. It was trying to reach the shelter of the kopje. Given the speed at which it was slowing, Ehomba saw that it was not going to make it.

Breaking into a sprint, he raced to insert himself between the faltering cat and the pursuing tempest. Once, he thought he heard Simna's anxious cry of warning rising above the growling wind, but he could not be sure of it. As he drew near, the great cat stumbled again and nearly fell. It was not quite ready to turn and meet its apocalyptic pursuer, but from studying its face and flanks Ehomba knew it had very little strength left in those extraordinarily long legs.

Spotting the approaching human through its exhaustion, the cat followed him with its eyes, eyes that were strangely piercing and analytical, as Ehomba slowed to a halt between it and the storm. Standing tall as he could, willing himself to plant his sandaled feet immovably in the solid earth, the herdsman confronted the storm and threw up both hands.

The storm did not stop—but it paused. Not intimidated, not daunted, but curious. Curious as to what a single diminutive human was doing placing itself directly in the storm's unstoppable path.

It towered above him, reaching into the clouds from where it drew its strength, a coiled mass of black air filled with flying grass, bits of trees that had been ripped from their roots, dead animals, soil, fish, and all manner of strange objects that were foreign to Ehomba's experience. It was wind transformed into a collector, running riot over the landscape gathering into itself whatever was unfortunate enough to cross its path. In shape it most nearly resembled far smaller windcousins of itself that the herdsman had seen dancing across the desert. But those were no more dangerous than a momentary sandstorm that nicked a man's skin and briefly rattled his posture. This was to one of those irritating dust-devils as an anaconda was to a worm.

Not surprisingly, its voice was all breathiness and barely checked thunder.

"What is this? Are you so anxious to end your life, man, that you presume to confront me? Before I suck you up and drink you like a twig, I would like to know why." It held its position, neither advancing nor retreating, swirling in place as it glared down at Ehomba from a height of hundreds of feet.

"I do not know what sort of deviate contest you are en-

gaged in with this poor animal." Ehomba gestured back at
the great cat, who had paused to try to gather its strength and
lick at a cut on its left flank. "But it is a patently unfair one,
for you have all the sky to draw upon for energy while it has
only legs and muscle."

A gust of wind blew in the herdsman's face: a tiny gust, a
mere puff of air, really—but it was enough to knock him
from his stance, and make him stumble.

"I was told of the creature's boasting," the tornado replied,
"that it claimed it could run faster than the wind. So it was he
who set the challenge, and not I."

Ehomba turned to eye the cat questioningly. Undaunted by
either the herdsman's stare or the column of frenzied air hovering behind him, it replied in a voice that was notably less
barbaric than those cat-tongues with which the southerner
was conversant. How and where it had learned to speak the
language of man was a matter for further discussion, under
less adverse climatic conditions.

"The wind demon speaks the truth. I did say that." Yellow
eyes rose past Ehomba to fixate on the column of air. "Because it's true. I am faster than the wind."

"There! You see!" Screaming, the storm corkscrewed violently against the Earth. "As weather goes, I am among the
least patient of its constituents. How could I let such an im-
pertinent claim go unchallenged—or unpunished?"

The calm before the storm, Ehomba queried the cat. "I
mean no offense, or disrespect, but you will pardon me for
saying that given the current state of affairs it does not appear
to me, anyway, that you are faster than the wind."

"I am!" Turning to face both the herdsman and the storm,
the cat was spent but unbowed. "But I am only flesh and
blood and cat-gut." It glared furiously at the towering,
watchful column. "I can and did outrun it, for a day and a
night. It tried, but could not catch me. But, unlike it, I need
to stop to feed, and to drink, while it can draw sustenance di-

rectly from the clouds themselves. Its food follows it, while mine wanders, and does its best to avoid me."

"Sensible food," Ehomba murmured knowingly.

The cat took a faltering but proud step in his direction. "This twisting thing refuses to accept the result of that day. Now it pursues me with murder in mind."

"Nature does not like to be embarrassed," Ehomba explained quietly. He turned back to confront the waiting storm. "Is what the cat says true?"

"A day, two days, a month—what does it matter? Nothing can outrun the wind!"

"Not even for a day and a night?" The herdsman cocked his head to one side and eyed the writhing tornado.

"This is not a matter for discussion!" The wind that blasted from the swirling pillar of constipated atmosphere threatened to implode Ehomba's eardrums. "I am fastest, I am swiftest, I am eternally triumphant! And now you, man, will die too. Not because you anger me, not because you take the side of the blasphemer, but simply because you are here, and unlucky enough to be in my way. I will rip your limbs from your torso and scatter them within my body like the summer flowers that decorate the shores of distant rivers, and I will not feel it."

"You know," Ehomba replied as he reached back over his shoulder for a sword, "not only are you not the fastest, but you're not even the greatest of winds. Against the greater gales you are nothing but a wisp of air, a summer zephyr, less than a child's sneeze."

"You are brave," the storm told him, "or demented. Either way it makes no difference. The death of a madman is still a death. Upon the face of the Earth nothing can stand against me. I cut my own path through typhoons, and dominate storms strident with thunder or silent with snow. Tropical downpours part at my arrival, and williwaws steal in haste from my sight." It resumed its advance, tearing up the ground before it.

Unable to run anymore, its hind legs paralyzed by muscle cramps, the cat could only stand and watch as Ehomba held his ground, plunged his spear point down in the dirt, and with both hands held the dull gray sword out in front of him. *The storm is right*, fatigued feline thoughts ran. *The man is mad.*

The tornado could not laugh, and if it could, the difference between laughter and its habitual ground-shaking howl would not have been perceptible. But it did manage to convey something of amusement.

"What are you going to do, man? Cut me? Take a bite out of my air?"

"You are right, storm," the herdsman yelled back. "Nothing can stand against you—on the face of the Earth. But anyone who looks at the night sky knows that this is not the only Earth, that there are many others out there in the great spaces between points of light. Hundreds, perhaps. I have spent many nights looking up at them and thinking about what they might be like, and have talked often about it with the wise men and women of the Naumkib."

A glow was beginning to emerge from his sword, but it was unlike any glow the cat had ever seen. Neither yellow, nor white, nor red, it was a peculiar shade of gray, a cold metallic radiance that was traveling slowly from the tip of the weapon toward its haft. Silent now, the cat stood on tottering legs and stared, its pain and exhaustion completely forgotten. There was a wonder taking place before his eyes, and he wanted to miss none of it.

"The wise ones say that the Great Emptiness that spreads over our heads, even over yours, is not as empty as it appears at night. It is full of incomprehensible but miraculous things. Bits of forgotten worlds, the memories of long-lost peoples, energies greater than a veldt fire, beings vaster and more wise than a woman of a hundred years. All that, and more."

"I am not impressed or dissuaded by the ravings of madmen." The tornado inched closer, teasing the grass, toying with the lone human standing before it.

By now the gray glow had enveloped the entire sword, which was quivering like a live thing in the herdsman's powerful grasp. Ehomba held it high, presenting its flat side to the surging column of tormented air.

"Then be impressed by this. Storm, meet your relations, your distant cousins and brothers and sisters—the winds that blow between the stars!"

XVI

Had he been able to, a dumbstruck Simna would have shut his eyes against the blast that came out of the herdsman's sword. But he could not. The thread of intergalactic cyclone blew his eyelids up toward his forehead and kept them there. It caused the grass for leagues in every direction to bow down away from it, and knocked the muscular black cat right off its feet as easily as if it were a house kitten. Rooted as they were in the ground from which they sprang, the very rocks of the kopje trembled and threatened to blow free, and the sky was instantly cleared of birds and clouds for a hundred miles around.

Fortuitously trapped within the rock-walled alcove like a bee in its hive, Simna found himself pinned flat back against the rocks, his arms spread out to either side of him, and knew that he was experiencing only the feeblest of side effects from the wind his friend had called forth. Knew because the strength of that wind, its full force and energy, was directed straight out from the sword, directly at the inimical advancing storm.

It was an unnatural wind not only in its strength. It brought with it an intense biting cold that threatened to freeze his skin as solid as a shallow lake in the taiga, and an odor—an odor of alien distances that clotted in his nostrils and threatened to blunt his sense of smell permanently.

Crackling with energies exotic and inexplicable, the wind from between the stars struck the tornado foursquare in the center of its boiling column—and ripped it apart. Overwhelmed by forces beyond imagining, from beyond the Earth, brought forth through the medium of a sword forged from metal that itself had been subject to the whims of the intergalactic winds, the mere column of air could not stand.

With a last outraged howl it came asunder, fell to pieces, and collapsed in upon itself. The great pillar of conflicted energy blew apart, hurling its internal collection of dead fish and broken branches and river beach sand and the limbs of the unfortunate dead flying in all directions. As the radiance from the sword faded and the unearthly wind it had called up died with it, Simna was released from his imprisonment and allowed to slump to his knees. Something smacked against the stone where his head had been pinned only moments before, and he turned to see the upper half of a carp lying on the rocks where it had fallen.

The boiling clouds from which the tornado had derived its strength shattered silently, their constituent parts dissipating into the resultant blue sky. In a little while all was as calm and peaceful as it had been before the storm's arrival. Lizards emerged from their dens in the rocks, small dragons took wing and resumed their singing in concert with the birds, and vultures appeared as if from nowhere to feast on the widely strewn, discarded contents of the tornado's belly.

Taking a deep breath of uncommitted air, Ehomba slipped the sky-metal sword back into the scabbard lying flat against his back and turned to reflect on the cause of all the commotion. The huge black cat was sitting on its haunches in the grass, which was only now beginning to spring back to the vertical from the effects of the deviant wind. Licking its left paw with a tongue thicker than the herdsman's foot, it was grooming itself silently, working its way from nose back to mane.

It did not let Ehomba's approach interrupt its labors. "You saved me."

"You speak well in a tongue not widespread among your kind."

"Humans presume to know too much about cats." A paw that could easily have taken the herdsman's head off with one swift stroke daintily combed through the long black ruff that formed the fluffy mane. Claws like daggers isolated individual hairs.

"That is certainly true. I am Etjole Ehomba, of the Naumkib." When silence ensued, he added as he leaned on his spear, "What am I to call you?"

"Gone, as soon as I can get myself cleaned up." The stroking paw paused and piercing yellow eyes met the herdsman's. "I am a litah."

"A litah," Ehomba echoed. "A small name for so big a brute."

"It is not a name." The cat was mildly annoyed. "It is what I am. My father was a lion, my mother a cheetah."

"Ah. That would explain your lines, and your legs."

Brows drew together like black ropes thick as hawsers. "What's wrong with my legs?"

"Nothing, not a thing," Ehomba explained hastily. "It is just that it is unusual to see such a combination of speed and strength in one animal."

"A lot of good it did me." Grumbling and rumbling, the litah set to work chewing on his hindquarters.

"What did you expect?" Out of the corner of an eye, Ehomba saw Simna ibn Sind approaching, slowly and cautiously. "For the wind to play fair?"

The litah turned back to him, his tongue scouring around his snout. "Animals as well as humans always expect too much of Nature. I was truthful, but tactless. I admit I did not think the wind would take it so much to heart, if heart it can be said to have had." Bright eyes glanced heavenward, searching the sky behind Ehomba. "You are a sorcerer."

"See? See?" Coming up alongside the herdsman, Simna chimed in his agreement with the cat's assertion. "I'm not the only one."

Ehomba sighed tiredly. "I am not a sorcerer," he told the litah. "I am only a herdsman from the south, bound by an obligation set upon me by a dying stranger to travel to the north and then to the west in hopes of helping a woman I do not know."

The litah grunted. "Then you are right. You are no sorcerer. Any wizard, human or animal, would have better sense."

Simna drew himself up proudly next to his friend. "He won't admit to it, but he's really after treasure. A great treasure, buried somewhere in the lands across the western ocean." Beside him, Ehomba was shaking his head sadly.

"I have no use for treasure," the litah growled softly. "I need water, and sex, and a place to sleep. And meat." With this last, he eyed Simna thoughtfully.

"Now wait a minute, whatever your name is." Putting his hand on the hilt of his sword, Simna took a step backward. In addition to putting a little more distance between himself and the cat, this also had the effect of placing him slightly behind the herdsman. "My friend here just saved your life."

"Yes, curse it all." Idly, the cat inspected the claws of his right foot, holding them up to his face as he studied the spaces between for thorns or bits of stone. "Since humans cannot talk without having names to address, and since you already know me as a litah, I suppose you may as well call me Ahlitah as anything."

"Very well—Ahlitah." Ehomba eyed the great black feline

uncertainly. "But why 'curse it all'? Most creatures express gratitude and not irritation when someone saves their life."

The heavy paw descended and the brute rolled over onto his back, rubbing himself against the grass and the ground with his paws flopping loose in the air. A wary Simna was not yet reassured, and continued to keep his distance despite the kittenish display.

"I suppose it's not in my nature. Therefore I am not especially grateful. I am, however and unfortunately, indebted. This is a legacy that both my lines are heir to, and I am sadly no different." Concluding its scratching, the cat twisted with unnatural quickness back onto its feet and began to pad toward Ehomba. The swordsman held his ground, as did Simna—behind him.

"Easy now," the swordsman whispered. "This Ahlitah's idea of gratitude may be different from our own."

"I do not think so." The herdsman waited, hand on spear, its butt end still resting unthreateningly on the ground.

The great cat finally halted, its face less than inches away from Ehomba's own. Its jaws parted slightly, revealing major canines more than half a foot long. From between them emerged a giant pink tongue that proceeded to slather the herdsman's face in drool from chin to hairline. The tall southerner gritted his teeth and bore the infliction. The sensation was akin to having one's face rubbed hard in the sand.

Taking a step backward, Ahlitah dropped to one knee and bowed his massive, maned head. "For saving my life—even though I didn't ask you to interfere—I swear allegiance and fealty to you, Etjole Ehomba, until such time as you have successfully concluded your journey, or the one or the both of us die. This I vow on the lineage of my father and of my mother."

"Oh now, that's not necessary," the herdsman responded. From behind, Simna nudged him in the ribs.

"Are you crazy?" The swordsman had to stand on tiptoes to

place his lips close enough to whisper into his companion's ear. "He's offering his help, Etjole! Willingly! When looking for treasure, it's always best to have as many allies as possible."

"It is not willingly, Simna. He is doing so out of a sense of enforced obligation."

"That's right," concurred the cat, who easily overheard every whispered word.

Simna stepped back. "And what's so wrong about that? Seems to me I know someone else who's doing something against his will in order to carry out an unsought-after obligation."

Ehomba's brows rose slightly as he regarded his friend. "Contrary to what many people believe, too much common sense can be bad for a man."

"Hoy?" Simna grinned challengingly. "For me—or for you?"

The herdsman returned his attention to the watching four-legged blackness. "I do not like the idea of having in a moment of danger to rely on another who accompanies me unwillingly."

Yellow-bright eyes flared and enormous teeth made their second appearance in the form of an exquisitely volcanic snarl. "Do you doubt the steadfastness of my vow?"

"Oh no, no, we would never do that!" An anxious Simna forcefully jogged his friend's arm. "Would we, Etjole?"

"What? Oh, sorry—I was thinking. No, I suppose you should be taken at your word."

Teeth disappeared behind thick folds of lip. "How very magnanimous of you," was the acerbic response.

"But this is not necessary. I did not help you with the intention of indenturing you to me. Maybe it would be best if you simply returned to your home."

The litah began to pace back and forth, looking for all the

world like an ordinary agitated house cat made suddenly gigantic. "First you doubt my word, now you scorn my help."

Ehomba did his best to appear reassuring without sounding condescending. "I speak to you out of neither doubt nor scorn. I am simply saying that your assistance is not required."

"But it is, it is!" Throwing back his head, Ahlitah let out a long, mournful howl that was a mixture of melancholy and roar. It was at once impressive, terrifying, and piteous. When he had finished, like a tenor at the end of a particularly poignant aria, he fixed his gaze once more on the empathetic herdsman.

"Don't you see? Until I have repaid you in kind for what you did for me—without your being asked, I might add—I can't proceed with a normal life. I couldn't go on with that burden resting heavy on my heart and thick in my mind. However long it takes, whatever the difficulty involved, I have to discharge it before I can again be at rest."

"For Gudru's sake, Etjole," Simna whispered urgently, "don't argue with him. Accept the offer."

"Your annoying friend is right." Sitting back, Ahlitah scratched vigorously at his belly with a hind foot. "If you send me away, you not only shame me, you spray on my soul. You say to me that my offer of all I can give is worth nothing." Scratching ceased as the great cat resumed its pacing. "You reduce me to the level of a jackal, or worse, a hyena."

"Oh all right!" Fed up, Ehomba waved a diffident hand in the litah's direction and turned away. "You can come along."

The cat dipped its head, its long black mane falling forward like a courtier's cape. "I cower before your unfettered magnanimity, oh maestro of the condescending arts."

"If you want to do something for me," the herdsman responded, "you might lose some of that feline sarcasm."

"Sorry. It's in a cat's nature to be sarcastic."

"I know, but yours seems in proportion to your size. Over time, I see it growing tiresome."

Teeth flashed in a grinning display. "I will try to restrain my natural instincts. Given present company, that may prove difficult."

"Do your best," Ehomba instructed his new companion curtly. He looked back at the kopje. "It has been a wearying day."

Simna let out a muted guffaw. "That's me bruther—master of understatement."

"We might as well rest here until tomorrow."

"Agreed." The litah turned and began to walk away.

Simna called after him. "Hoy, where are you going? I thought you were with us?"

The cat looked back over its maned shoulder. "I am going to find something to eat, if that's all right with you. Maybe a human can live on anticipation and fine words, but I cannot."

"Don't get testy with me, kitty," Simna shot back. "I'm as hungry as you are."

"As am I," added Ehomba. "If you truly want to be of assistance, you could bring back enough for us all to eat. We will make a fire."

"I'll enjoy the warmth," Ahlitah growled back. "We cats quite like fire. We're just not adept at fabricating it." He sniffed derisively. "You, of course, will want to use it to burn perfectly good meat." Turning, he surveyed the veldt. "I will be late, but I will be back."

"Why so?" Simna's expression became a smirk. "Are you like the male lions that let the females do all the hunting?"

Sliding smoothly through the grass, the litah did not deign to look back. "Idiot. Male lions hunt often and perfectly well—at night. During the day our dark manes are highly visible through the yellowed or green grass and give our presence away. That is why the females run the day hunt. For the same reason, I am a better night hunter than any lion, and can bring down larger prey than any cheetah."

Ehomba moved to stand behind his friend. "Do not taunt

him. He is unhappy at having to accompany us. If a man has one bad moment and strikes out at you, your face may suffer a bruise." He nodded out into the veldt. "If *that* one has a bad moment, he is liable to take off your head."

"Aw, he's all right," Simna insisted. "He's obligated to you, and I'm your friend, so he won't let harm come to me."

"Probably not as long as I am alive, no. So it is in your best interest to see that I stay healthy."

"Hoy, that's always been in my interest." Simna grinned broadly as together they turned toward the kopje. "If anything were to happen to you, I'd never find the treasure. Not," he added in haste, "that I'd want anything to happen to you even if there was no treasure."

"There is no treasure," Ehomba replied forthrightly.

The swordsman clapped the tall herdsman roughly on the shoulder. "Yeah, right—what a kidder! I'll bet among your fellow villagers you're considered a real comedian."

"Actually, I believe they think I am rather dry and somber." He smiled hesitantly. "Of course, I do not think so, nor do my children or my wife." His expression twitched momentarily. "At least, I do not think she does."

XVII

T HERE WAS ENOUGH DRY WOOD TO MAKE A FIRE ON THE KOPJE, but not a large one. Raised above the surrounding grass on the rocks, the blaze would still be visible for quite a distance. Even so, Simna especially was beginning to doubt the truth of the litah's words as evening gave way to night and there was still no sign of their erstwhile ally.

"Maybe he decided he wasn't so indebted after all." Using a long stick, the swordsman stirred the vivacious embers that winked at the bottom of the fire. "Maybe he met an obliging pride, or a lone female in heat, and decided some things were more important than tagging along with us."

"I do not think he would leave like this. He was very adamant." But as the night wore on and the moon came to dominate the speckled bowl of the sky, Ehomba was less certain.

"He's a cat. A prodigiously talkative one, 'tis true, but a cat still. Cats set their own agendas, and big or small, those rarely include tending to the needs of humans."

"Listen." Ehomba froze suddenly, his face highlighted by the glow of the campfire.

Simna was immediately on guard. "What is it? Not more wind, I hope." Visions of angry wild relatives of the demolished tornado appearing in the middle of the night to wreak vengeance on those who had murdered their brother swept through his thoughts.

"No, not wind. Something moving through the grass."

Ahlitah was almost upon them before the flickering blaze cast enough light to reveal even the outline of his massive form. In his jaws he carried the limp, bent body of a wandala, a medium-sized antelope whose horns had spread wide and thinned out until they formed a great membranous sail attached to the skull. Using this the animal could tuck its short, fragile legs beneath it and in a good breeze literally fly across the tops of the veldt grass, flattening its body to assume a more aerodynamic shape.

The successful hunter unceremoniously dumped his offering onto the rocks alongside the fire. "Here is meat. You may have the flanks. I know humans are fickle about what portion of animal they eat."

"Hoy, not me." Drawing his knife, an eager Simna set to work on the carcass. "When I'm hungry I'll eat just about anything."

"Yes, I see that. But then, one would never mistake you for the fastidious type." Settling himself down on the other side of the body, Ahlitah began to eat, ripping dainty chunks out of the hindquarters of the dead wandala.

"You were late," Ehomba declared accusingly. "We had begun to wonder."

Blood stained Ahlitah's muzzle as he looked up from the other side of the cadaver. "I had to wait until it was dark enough for the night to hide me. When I stand or stalk, I am taller than any other cat. Better a certain kill that takes time than a quick one that fails." Lowering his head, he thrust his open jaws into the wandala's soft belly. The ragged percussion of bones breaking drifted out across the veldt.

"This situation makes for an interesting puzzle to contemplate," the litah announced later, when cat and men had finished eating. "Here we sit, as companions if not as friends. I kill for you. But if we were in your homeland to the south, I would be hunting your herds and flocks, and you would be trying to keep me from doing so. Trying to kill me, if it became necessary."

"That is true." Ehomba watched Simna slice steaks from the side of the dead antelope, the easier to pack them for carrying. "Oftentimes it is not personal preference that makes friends and enemies, but circumstance." This time it was he who mustered the feral gaze, peering deeply into the eyes of the litah. "It is a good thing I trust your word, for fear you might try to eat me in my sleep."

"And I yours," Ahlitah replied, "or I might worry about you acting like just another man, ready to leap to murder at the first opportunity and skin me for my valuable coat. How fortunate that we have such trust in one another."

"Yes. How fortunate."

Just because Ehomba could survive comfortably on little food did not mean that he was averse to a filling meal. Knowing that the meat would not keep for very long and that they had no time to spare to jerk it, they ate their fill of delicious wandala. Nothing was left to waste, not even the marrow of its bones, as Ahlitah possessed an appetite to match his size. When the unlikely trio finally drifted off to sleep, more than content, it was with an ease in mind and body none of them had known for days.

Except Simna. Troubling thoughts woke him several hours before dawn. Nearby, Ehomba lay on his side beneath his blanket, his back to the swordsman. On the other side of the vanquished campfire Ahlitah snored softly, his shadowed bulk like a storm cloud that had, silent and unnoticed, settled to earth for a moment's unnatural rest.

He had seen Ehomba utilize the power of the sword smelted from sky metal, but until the fight with the spinning storm cloud he had never imagined the extent of that power. What not could a man do who possessed such a weapon? The herdsman had declared that, just as its substance was not of this world, so it had powers that were not of this world. Certainly whoever wielded it could defeat more than clouds and Corruption.

Sitting up, he gazed out across the veldt. Distant moans and occasional sharp barks broke the stillness of the night, but nothing troubled them on their isolated stony outcropping. Ehomba had yet to vary from his path northward. He, Simna, had come from the east. What if he were to return that way? Would the herdsman try to come after him, or would he accept what had transpired, absorb his loss, and maintain his course? How valuable was the sword to him, how important to his journey? A wondrous weapon it was, true, but it was only a sword. Simna would not be leaving him weaponless. Ehomba would still have his spear, and his other sword, not to mention the protective, intimidating company of the litah.

Visions of conquest swam through the swordsman's tormented thoughts. He had never been what one would call a greedy man. Acquisitive, yes, but hardly rapacious. Overlordship of a small city would be sufficient to satisfy his desires. With the sky-metal sword in hand, what minor nobleman or princeling would dare stand before him? Again he gazed at his lanky companion's sleeping form. Ehomba was a generous soul. Surely he would not begrudge a good friend the loan of a wanted weapon.

By Giopra, that was it! Not a theft, but a loan, a borrowing! A temporary adoption of a singular arsenal, to be returned as soon as vital objectives had been achieved. As he slipped silently from beneath his blanket, he reflected on the

worthiness of rationalization. The herdsman would understand. Humble and unsophisticated he might be, but he was
compassionate as well. While he might not feel the need to
take control of a town or trade route himself, surely he could
empathize with the preoccupation of another to do so.

Advancing more quietly on hands and knees than a beetle
on its six legs, he made his way over to where his friend
slept. With his back to the humans, Ahlitah did not stir. The
sky-metal sword lay alongside its tooth-lined bone companion and the strangely tipped spear, all three within easy reach
of their owner in case of emergency.

Ever so gently, as though he were handling a king's new-
born infant and heir, Simna slipped his right hand beneath the
fur-covered, quaintly beaded scabbard. It was heavy, but not
unmanageably so. At any moment he expected the herdsman
to turn over, or rise up, and innocently ask what the swordsman was doing with his property. But Ehomba never stirred.
He was worn out, Simna knew. Exhausted from his battle
with the elements. Poor fellow, the best thing for him would
be to forget all this nonsense and return home to his family
and his cattle, his flocks and his friends. He might have the
fortitude for this kind of journeying, but he most surely did
not have the zeal.

If it induced him to turn back, Simna decided virtuously,
then by borrowing the sky sword he was actually doing his
friend a favor. Probably saving his life, yes. Certainly the
herdsman's family would thank him for it.

Returning to his blanket with the sword gripped firmly in
one hand, he prepared to gather up his kit. The moon would
guide him eastward, and by the time Ehomba woke, Simna
would be well out of sight and on his way. He could move
fast when the occasion demanded.

But before departing, best to make sure he could make use
of the weapon. Though Ehomba continued to insist he was no
magician, Simna would look the prize fool going into battle

someday with a sword he could not draw. If he could but remove it from its scabbard, that would be enough to reassure
him that its owner had cast no locking spell on it.

Gripping the handle, he gave an experimental tug. The
polished metal was slick against his palm, and the oddly
etched blade slid effortlessly upward. The smooth, gray edge
with its peculiar right-angle markings gleamed dully in the
moonlight. No problem there, he saw appreciatively.

One series of cross-hatched markings in particular caught
his eye. They looked a little deeper than the others, though by
no means deep enough to threaten the integrity of the blade.
They drew his attention to smaller markings still, and others
still smaller, until he felt that he was looking into the very el-
ementals of the metal itself.

Suddenly the parallel scourings flew apart. It was as if he
had been staring at a painting, a painting rendered entirely in
gray, only to be drawn in, sucked down, cast helplessly into
a gray metallic pit. Now the picture's frame was flying to
pieces all around him, and he found himself falling, kicking
and flailing helplessly at ashen emptiness adrift in a leaden
vacuum.

Fiery globes of incandescent energy rushed past him,
singeing his skin and clothing. Around these colossal spheres
of coruscating hellfire spun worlds whole and entire, swarming with life-forms more fantastic than the word spinnings of
any storyteller. Immense, billowing clouds of luminous
vapor filled the spaces between the fire globes and their attendant worlds, along with tailed demons and rocks that
seemed to have been launched from God's own slingshot.

And in the middle of it all was he, tumbling and kicking,
screaming at the top of his lungs even though there was no
one to hear him. Not that it mattered, because despite his
frantic efforts, no sound emerged from his throat. Perhaps
because there was no air in his lungs with which to make
sounds. As this new horror struck home he began to choke,

gasping for the air that was not there. His hands went to his throat, as if by squeezing they could somehow force nonexistent air into his straining, heaving chest.

Something pushed at him, rocking him even as he fell. Invisible hands—or claws, or tentacles—were wrenching at his body, threatening to divert him from his endless eternal fall to a place where unfathomable horrors could be wreaked on his impotent person. Screaming, crying, he kicked at the unseen presence and flailed at it with his hands. Though he could see nothing, his extremities made contact with something.

He was struck across the face, the blow stinging but not hard enough to draw blood. Dimly, distantly, he felt he heard a voice calling his name. Gojura, the Lord of Unknown Places, or some other deity? He was in no shape to meet his sister's daughter, much less a god or two. Not that he had any choice. Beyond caring, long past mere fear, he opened his eyes.

Ehomba was leaning over him, looking down into his friend's tormented face. The herdsman's expression was full of sympathy and concern, notwithstanding the fact that he held one hand upraised and poised to strike downward.

A gruff, inhumanly deep voice somewhere off to his left growled, "There—he's around. No need to hit him again. Unless you're simply in the mood." The speaker sounded sleepy, and bored.

Ehomba lowered his open palm and sat back. Feeling of his body to assure himself it was still intact, the swordsman sat up. Around him were darkness, night sounds, veldt smells, and wistful moonlight. The comforting solidity of the kopje's naked rock chilled his backside.

Relieved, the herdsman leaned away from his friend. "You were having a bad dream, Simna. Bad enough to wake us. You were kicking and screaming in your sleep as if something was after you. What was it?"

"I . . ." The swordsman put a hand to his perspiring fore-head. "I'm not sure I remember, exactly. I was falling. Not into something, but through it."

"That is interesting." Yawning, Ehomba slipped back beneath his own blanket. "What were you falling through? The sky, or maybe the sea?"

"No—not either of those." Suddenly Simna tilted back his head, craning his neck as he stared open-mouthed at the night sky. "I was falling through everything. I—saw everything. Well, maybe not everything, but an awful lot of it." He lowered his head. "As much of everything as I think I ever want to see."

Lying prone beneath his blanket and tucking it up around him, Ehomba nodded drowsily. "I can understand that. To see everything would be too much for any man. It is hard enough to look at and make sense simply of that which is around us. Myself, I am content simply to see something. I have no wish to see everything."

Simna nodded without replying as he slowly settled himself back beneath his own blanket. As he did so, his gaze inevitably returned to the dome of the night sky and the tiny points of light that twinkled in the darkness. He knew what they were now, and shuddered. Few men are capable of dealing with the world around them, he mused, so how could anyone be expected to handle the immensity of everything else? Certainly it was too much for him.

It had been a terrible dream, but an efficacious one. From now on he would leave strange weapons alone, no matter how much they might tempt him. Even if they belonged to someone who was simply a fortunate herdsman and not a sorcerer. He was lucky he had only dreamed about stealing—um, borrowing—the sky-metal sword. Had he tried to take possession of it, the harrowing visions he had experienced while sleeping might have become real.

Turning away from the no longer amicable sky, he lay on

his side gazing in Ehomba's direction. Tomorrow they would resume their northward trek. With luck they would come to a river that could carry them to the sea, where they would find a town at which seaworthy vessels called. They would book passage westward, to the fabled lands of Ehl-Larimar, where dwelled Hymneth the Possessed, and the treasure he knew in his soul must be at the heart of the poor herdsman's quest.

As he lay still, his head resting in the cup of his right hand, he saw that Ehomba's weapons were no longer neatly aligned on the smooth rock above his head, but had been put askew. Perhaps the herdsman had disturbed them in his haste to awaken and free his friend from the anguish of his nightmare.

Ignoring the feathered spear and the tooth-edged sword, he found his gaze drawn inexorably to the scabbarded blade of wondrous sky metal. It seemed to be partly drawn, just enough to expose an inch or so of the metal itself. The Widmanstätten lines etched into its side caught the moonlight and twisted it the way a child would knot a rope. A nimble pain shot through part of his forehead as he felt his left eye poked with too-sharp perception.

He rolled over quickly and closed his eyes tight, resolving to look upon nothing save the inside of his eyelids until dawn renewed both the day and his trust in the authenticity of existence. Some dreams drifted too close to reality, and some realities too close to dream. In the company of a perambulating curiosity like Etjole Ehomba, he decided, it was important for one to concentrate with unwavering determination on the path between the two, lest one's world suddenly slip out of focus.

Opening his eye just a crack, it was filled with a flash of light. For a dreadful moment he was afraid it was one of those hellish globes of fire he had seen floating in emptiness. Almost as quickly as he started to panic, he relaxed. It was only the glint of moonlight off a chip of quartz embedded in the rock close to his face.

He closed his eyes again, and this time did not open them until the sun began to sneak its first rays over the eastern horizon.

XVIII

MORNING ARRIVED NOT WITH THE EASE OF AWAKENING WITH which Ehomba was most comfortable, but with a thunderous declaration of life that had both him and Simna ibn Sind erupting from their place of sleeping. Initially panicked, the men relaxed when they saw it was only Ahlitah, greeting the arrival of the sun with an ardent bellowing that all but shook the rocks beneath them as his robust roars detonated against the vast expanse of the veldt.

"Must you play the lord of all roosters?" Exhaling sharply, Simna sat back down on the smooth, cool granite.

Standing with his forefeet on the highest point of the kopje, the litah turned his great black-maned head to glower down at him. "I am king of this land, and must so remind my subjects every morning."

"Well, we're not your subjects," Simna snapped, "and we'd appreciate it if while we're traveling in each other's company you maybe just waved to your subjects every once in a while."

"Yes." Ehomba was already packing to depart. "I am sure

the mere creatures who inhabit the veldt already recognize your suzerainty, and that it is not necessary for you to remind them of it quite so loudly every morning."

"Oh, I do beg your pardon. From now on I'll do it like this." Looking away and throwing back his head, the massive jaws parted and Ahlitah let loose as resounding a meow as Ehomba had ever heard.

"Much better," Simna commented tartly.

"I am so pleased that you approve." Tomorrow morning, the great cat vowed, it would roar again as loudly as ever—making it a point to place his lips directly opposite one of the stocky swordsman's ears as he did so.

But he would not argue the point now, when they were about to set off for a portion of the veldt that was new even to him. While he was embarrassed at having to keep company with humans, a part of him was anticipating the forthcoming opening up of new territory. He looked forward to meeting the inhabitants, and to eating some of them.

As they descended the kopje, which had proved to be an agreeable refuge in the midst of the all but featureless veldt, Ehomba found himself again questioning the suitability of his companions. Given alternatives, he would have chosen otherwise. One was inhuman, tremendously strong, but reluctant to the point of apathy. He wondered how he was going to be able to rely on someone to watch his back who would do so only out of a sense of enforced obligation.

His other associate was fearless, wily, experienced, and tough, but interested in only one thing: the domineering illusion of false wealth. Again, not the truest motivation for standing behind someone in need. Still, he supposed it was better to have them at his side than not, to have company and companionship in strange country than to be traveling alone. If nothing else, it gave potential enemies someone else to shoot at. For all his unrelenting babble about treasure, Simna ibn Sind would prove useful if he took but one arrow meant for Ehomba. And Ahlitah the same if he did nothing at all but stand still and frighten off a single stealthy assassin.

Yes, it was better to travel in the company of an entourage, however small and however uncommitted. They would be of no use against someone as overawing and powerful as this Hymneth individual, but if they could simply help him to achieve that final confrontation then all would be worthwhile. Until that ultimate moment he would suffer their company, dealing with Simna's endless harping about treasure and Ahlitah's incessant muttering.

Another day's walking brought them within sight of a line of trees. This was greatly to Simna's liking since, as he put it, he had seen enough grass and weeds to last a million cattle the rest of their lives, and him not able to eat a blade of it. Ahlitah was more circumspect.

"Trees make good places to hide behind."

"Maybe in the veldt, where trees are few and far between." Simna was leading the way. "In lands where they're the rule rather than the exception, they're no more dangerous than taller grass."

But the trees did hide something: a river; broad, murky, and of indeterminate depth. Ehomba resigned himself to another swim.

"Don't be in such a hurry." Simna was leaning over the bank. It was a short drop, less than a foot, to the water. There was no shoreline, no beach of sand or mud. Short, stubby grass grew right up to the water's edge. "It *looks* shallow."

"Fine," commented Ahlitah. "You try it first."

The swordsman nodded at the big cat. "Your legs are longer than mine, but if you're that afraid of water, then I'll break trail for you."

Making sure that his pack was secure against his back, Simna stepped off the bank. The water barely reached to the tops of his ankles. Turning, he spread his arms and smiled.

"See? No swimming, Etjole. The bottom has the feel of fine gravel. We can walk across." He kicked water in the direction of his friends, causing Ahlitah to blink and turn his head away momentarily.

Snarling softly, the great black shape hopped gingerly into the moderate current. Water ridged up slightly against his ankles before continuing to flow westward around them. A disappointed Ehomba followed. Had the river been deeper, he would have entertained notions of building a raft and following it west to the ocean. He missed the sea very much. Surely they were far enough north now to resume walking up the coast. But any raft made large and strong enough to carry them for any length of time risked running aground every few yards in such shallows. Northward they would have to continue to trek.

He fingered the sack of pebbles that rested heavily in the pocket of his kilt, remembering the beaches back home, the way the cold water foamed and danced whitely over sand and rock. As always, in helping to bringing back memories, the sheer tactility of the rough gravel in the little cotton bag helped to soothe his thoughts and ease his mind.

Once, something that was softer than stone but harder than water bumped into his right foot. Glancing down, he made out an indistinct, elongated shape hurriedly darting upriver away from him. A freshwater eel, perhaps, startled by the presence of something long, straight, and moving through the water that was not a drifting tree branch. Some eels could give a man quite a nip. Thereafter he paid more attention to the water swirling around his ankles.

Halfway across, the strangest thing began to happen. It could not be explained any more than it could be ignored. While the river itself grew no deeper, patches and pockets and globules of water began to come into sight above the actual surface. At first they were no bigger than a man's fist, but soon much larger blobs began to appear. The largest were the size of small ponds.

At their highest, these individual drifting sacs of liquid were as tall as the trees that were now visible on the opposite bank. Some had transparent undersides while others were dark with accumulated muck and soil. Water lilies, reeds, and small bushes grew from these individual pockets of aerial swamp. Some plants put down roots that traveled through the intervening air to suck nourishment from splotches of water floating in midair beneath them. Wind roiled their surfaces just as it did that of the shallow river beneath.

Sometimes two wandering patches of water would flow slowly into one another and merge to form a larger pond shape. Elsewhere, ample globules would slowly break apart to form two or more separate aqueous bodies. It was quite the most extraordinary landscape any of the companions had ever encountered.

Ducking beneath a floating raft of pond weed as big as a boat, Simna jabbed a finger upward and pulled it free. The bottom-side surface tension stuck to his finger for an unnaturally long moment, clinging to the skin more like clear glue than water. Then the contents of the floating pond began to drain out through the finger-sized gap, as if the swordsman had punched a hole in a transparent, thin-skinned balloon.

Fascinated, they watched as water grass, tadpoles, struggling fry, black-shelled snails, and other inhabitants of the airborne pond spilled out into the river below. After a minute or two of free flow, the hole was blocked and sealed by a clump of soil that formed the root-ball of a water hyacinth. Amazed and delighted by the aqueous phenomenon, they resumed their crossing.

The river never bulked up against a far bank so much as it spread out to form a vast, shallow lake whose extent they probably could not have determined even if the view northward had not been blocked by more and more of the free-floating aerial ponds and lakes. Not only were these becoming larger, but they were also growing considerably more numerous, as if drawing strength and sustenance from the boundless, shallow inland sea beneath.

Of more immediate concern, the travelers began to encounter places where the underlying river-lake itself deepened. It was difficult enough to keep moving forward while avoiding masses of drifting water that rose higher than a man's head. Doing so while stumbling into hidden cavities that brought the water up to one's neck was not only harder, but frightening. In such an environment it was technically impossible to keep one's head above water, because individual blobs of water were constantly drifting past at levels higher than one's hairline.

Within an hour they were having to duck beneath a small airborne lake that completely blocked their path in all directions. Hunched over, Ehomba was more wary of the great mass of water that hung just above his head than he was of the foot or so they were sloshing through.

"No experiments here," he warned Simna. "Do not stick your finger into the water hovering above us. If it were to break and all come down in a rush, we would surely drown."

"Don't worry." The swordsman was walking next to him, bent over and eyeing the underside of the great shimmering mass uneasily.

They passed out from beneath it without incident, but were then forced to advance single file down a narrow corridor between two twenty-foot-tall bodies of free-floating swamp. The dark green walls that hemmed them in on either side were in constant, if lugubrious, motion, bulging and rippling with a great volume of water constrained only by thin, transparent walls of unusual surface tension.

"Guela!" Simna, who had momentarily taken the lead, suddenly let out an exclamation of surprise and stopped short.

Behind him, Ahlitah let out a warning snarl. A concerned Ehomba stopped short of the cat's flicking tail.

"What is it, what's wrong?"

"Look to your left." The great cat was pressed up against the floating swamp-sac on their right, his eyes focused in the indicated direction.

The crocodile that swam slowly past at eye level with the travelers was at least twenty feet long and weighed close to two tons. Its huge armored tail swayed slowly from side to side, propelling it languidly through the murky water. As it swam past, one eye swiveled to meet Ehomba's. The slitted yellow orb tracked the man standing next to the side of the aerial pond for a long moment. And then the hulking reptile was gone, turning back into the distant depths of the floating lake it called home.

"I don't understand." Simna's tone betrayed his lingering tension. "Why didn't it have a go at us? It could have broken out easily."

Ehomba considered. "We are making our way through air, not water. Perhaps it did not see us as part of its environment. Who can imagine how the creatures that have learned to live in such a remarkable place have developed? Possibly they consider each individual bubble of water, whether as big as a lake or small enough to fit in a bucket, an isolated world whose boundaries are not to be tampered with." Looking away from the dark green water that hemmed them in on either side, he tilted back his head to regard the narrow band of blue sky that still held sway directly overhead.

"Even our world could be like that. Stick a finger up high enough, hard enough, and you might puncture the lining of the sky and let all the air escape out into nothingness."

"That's ridiculous!" With a snort of derision, Simna turned away and resumed walking. But for a while thereafter, every so often he would sneak a glance at the clouds and resolve to suppress any impulse to make sudden, sharp gestures upward.

They emerged safely from between the two large bodies of oating water only to find themselves surrounded by a dense opulation of smaller but still sizable globules. While some of ese were clear and contained nothing larger than small ci- lids and kindred swimmers, others were opaque with flour- hing plant life, crustaceans, shellfish, and aquatic reptiles. hough still able to advance, their progress was slowed by aving to walk around or duck under the proliferating float- g bubbles.

Once they had to wade right through a drifting airborne ond too wide to walk around. As they did so, they experi- ced the most peculiar sensation of being soaked from sole ankle, then dry up to their waists, and then wet again up to eir necks. By lowering their packs so that they temporarily de not on their shoulders but on their hips, Ehomba and imna were able to keep their gear dry despite the double im- ersion.

All day they trekked through the unprecedented landscape, ucking beneath, walking around, or hopping over individual tervening patches of water, until the sun, a welcome harbin- er of the normal world, began to set. Certainly it was a most rious place to make a camp.

Simply choosing a suitable site presented unique problems f its own. Standing in six inches of water with not a sug- estion of dry land visible in any direction, the prospect of a re was out of the question, much less any thoughts of lying wn and keeping dry. Big as he was, Ahlitah would have no ouble keeping his head above water during the night, but it as not inconceivable that Ehomba or Simna could roll over their sleep and drown. Furthermore, soaking themselves to e skin for an entire night was not the best way of ensuring ntinued good health.

"Gembota, but this is awkward." Muttering to himself, imna sloshed through the tepid shallows in search of some- ace to drop his pack, and found none. "What are we going to do until morning?" He eyed the great cat's broad back speculatively. Correctly interpreting the swordsman's appraising stare, Ahlitah lifted a massive paw and shook his head.

"Put it out of your mind, little man. No one sleeps on me. Up against me, perhaps, for mutual warmth, but only if I am in a sociable mood. But on my back, never. It would be demeaning."

"We have to do something." A peevish Simna kicked at the omnipresent water. "We can't lie down and safely go to sleep in this. Never mind that we'd wake up sodden through and at risk of catching a fever. Isn't that right, Etjole? Etjole?"

Ehomba's attention was concentrated elsewhere. Instead of looking at their feet for a campsite, he was looking up. Specifically, at a small irregularly shaped hovering pond, the center of which boasted a small sandy island from which grew a trio of juvenile casuarina pines.

"Up there?" Simna sloshed over to stand alongside his tall friend. "But the island is floating. Put the three of us on it and our weight will make it sink to the bottom of this watery mass."

"I do not think so." Ehomba continued to study the drifting aerial pond. "If weight was going to do that, I would think the heaviness of the soil itself would be enough to sink it. And there are the trees it supports—not giants, it is true, but no saplings, either. I think we should give it a try.

"Besides, what is the worst thing that could happen? The island will sink beneath us and we will fall into the pond."

"And drown," Simna added. "That's a little too much of a 'worst thing' for me."

"We would not drown," Ehomba assured him. "Even if we sank to the bottom, all you would have to do is rip a hole in the pond's underside and all the water would come spilling out, along with the fish, and frogs, and plants, and us."

Simna was still dubious. "It doesn't make any sense. If

an poke a hole in the wall of one of these deluded bodies of water, why don't fish and salamanders and snails and tree roots do it all the time?"

"An adaptation to where they are living, I imagine." The herdsman pursed his lips as he regarded his friend. "We hike through a land where the lakes and ponds and puddles all float about away up in the air, where you can walk around and beneath them, and you wonder about such matters?"

Though still reluctant, Simna was willing to be convinced. Besides, the only alternative promised a night of little sleep and unrelenting wet. He glanced over at the patient Ahlitah.

"How about it, bruther cat? What do you think?"

Their feline companion shrugged, his ebony mane twitching as he did so. "Why put it to me? I am only a nomadic quadrupedal carnivore of commingled ancestry. Aren't humans the ones who are supposed to have the big brains? That's what you're always saying, anyway. Or are you experiencing some second thoughts about your own cerebral propaganda?"

A bemused Simna turned back to Ehomba. "Ask a simple question, get a biting discourse. All right, I guess it can't hurt to try. One way or the other, it looks like we're gonna get soaked. The question is, for how long?" He glanced upward. "It's getting dark, and I don't fancy trying to find a better spot in the middle of the night. Not in this muck."

"That is good." Turning, the herdsman positioned himself next to the transparent wall of the hovering pond. "Because you get to go in first."

"Me? Why me?" Simna hedged.

Looking back over his shoulder, Ehomba eyed his stocky friend considerately. "If you want me to go, you get to boost me up."

"No." The reluctant swordsman scrutinized the watery wall. "I'll go."

Scrambling up Ehomba's legs and back as the herdsman

braced himself against the transparent wall of water, Simna was soon balancing on the herdsman's shoulders. Gripping the upper rim of the pond, he pushed down and up. The rubbery wall gave a little, sending small fish scurrying in the opposite direction and letting water spill through the depression created between Simna's downward pressing hands. Then the swordsman was up and over the rim, swimming for the central island while doing his best to keep his kit as dry as possible.

Together, man and litah watched as Simna hauled himself out on the island and stood up, shaking water from his limbs like a slow dog. Experimentally, he jumped up and down a couple of times.

"Well?" Ahlitah growled impatiently.

"The ground gives a little, like a wet mattress, but I don't think it's going to sink under us. Come on over." Turning, he carried his pack inland and set it down beneath one of the shady pine trees.

Ehomba turned to eye his remaining companion questioningly. Grumbling but complaisant, the cat advanced and placed itself next to the bottom of the watery mass.

"Tread easily, Etjole Ehomba. No man who was not a meal has ever done this before."

"I will step lightly," the herdsman assured him. So saying, he placed a foot on the litah's right thigh and stepped up onto his back. From there he was able to pull himself up and over the rim of the pond into the water.

It was a short, easy swim to the island, where Simna was trying to dry himself with some large leaves he had scavenged. Wading out of the water, Ehomba settled down nearby and began to fumble inside his own pack. A violent splash made him look up. Ahlitah had negotiated the intervening height in a single effortless leap and was paddling toward them, his magnificent head held as high above the water as he could manage.

"One thing's for sure." Removing his leather armor and under-shirt, Simna hung them over a casuarina branch to dry. "If we can get a fire started here, we can let it burn high all night without having to worry about it spreading. Hoy—have a care, there!"

He threw up his hands to shield himself and Ehomba turned away as Ahlitah shook vigorously, sending water flying from his fur. A marinated cat was a comical sight, Ehomba knew, even as he was careful to keep his expression perfectly neutral. He was not certain that Ahlitah's pithy sense of humor extended to amusement at his own loss of dignity.

As it turned out, they were able to start a fire, but only a small one. Still, the additional warmth was welcome more for its aid in drying out their clothes than for their bodies.

"Not that this is very useful." Simna was lightly toasting his underwear over the cheery blaze. Nearby, Ehomba was fil-eting the fish Ahlitah had scooped out of the pond with a cou-ple of leisurely swipes of his huge paws. "We're only going to have to drench ourselves again tomorrow when it's time to cave and move on."

"Perhaps not." Ehomba, as he so often did, was looking not at the swordsman but past him. And as he so often did, Simna followed the direction of the tall herdsman's gaze and saw nothing.

"Why? Why not?" His expression brightened. "I know! You're finally going to do some real magic and float us out of here! Or call up a boat—no, that wouldn't work in water as shallow as that which covers the real ground below."

"I have told you," an exasperated Ehomba replied, "I can-not do magic."

"Yeah, right, sure." The swordsman winked at Ahlitah who, head resting on crossed forefeet, did not respond. "Then if not by magic, how are you going to keep us from having to get good and wet again?" He gestured at their surroundings. "Going to drain the pond with us in the middle of it? I'm not

sure that'd be such a good idea. The wondrous envelope tha
holds this water aloft might collapse in upon us, wrapping u
up like a holiday present and suffocating us in the bargain."

"I am not sure exactly what I am going to do. I was think
ing of assaying some engaging conversation."

"Really?" The other man swept his right arm around in
broad arc to encompass every inch of their aqueous surround
ings. "With whom? Fish?"

"Something like that." Turning away, the herdsman re
sumed wringing water from his kilt.

Simna grunted and looked over at the sleepy Ahlitah. "He'
going to talk to fish. Me, I don't see the use of it."

"*Can* he talk to fish?" the cat asked curiously.

The swordsman stole a glance in his companion's direc
tion. "I dunno. He's a funny sort, is Etjole. After we firs
hooked up together he told me a story about him spendin
time with some monkeys. I thought it was just that: a story
But the better I get to know him, the more I'm not sure."

"So you think you know him?" The litah's massive jaw
gaped in an impressive yawn.

Simna shrugged confidently. "Sure I know him! He's a sor
cerer, see? Only he won't admit to it. Hunting after a great lo
treasure he is, and I aim to help him acquire it in return for
share. He'll probably cut you in on the haul, too."

"And what would I do with the bastard currency of huma
exchange? A warm place to sleep, plenty of game—prefer
ably old and slow or young and stupid—and a pride of will
ing females one of whom is always in heat, and I would hav
all I could ask for. I am immune from and indifferent to th
driving need that you humans suffer from to accumulat
things. Spending so much time in accumulating, you forget t
live." He yawned again. "Your friend, however, is a breed o
human I have not met before."

"By Gwantha, he's a new breed of human to me as well,
the swordsman confessed.

"Then who knows? Maybe he can talk to fish." A guttural cough emerged from the muscular throat as the big cat closed his eyes and rolled over onto his back, all four paws in the air. "Me, I would rather eat them than talk to them."

"Don't see what good it would do us anyway," Simna muttered uncertainly. "Even if he could arrange for us to ride, what fish would be big enough to carry you? And every time we reached the far side of one of these lunatic floating blobs of water we'd have to get off our fishy mounts, scramble over the side, climb up into another and find new fish in the new pond to carry us. Be quicker to walk—provided the water covering the real ground doesn't get any deeper." He concluded with a deep breath: "Well, best to leave it to Etjole. He's the brains here."

Eyes shut tight, the drowsing litah barely responded. "Among the humans, anyway."

XIX

"THEY HAVE BEEN WATCHING US FOR A LONG TIME. EVER SINCE we crossed the river, I think."

"What?" Suddenly alarmed, Simna left off repacking his kit and looked around wildly.

Ahlitah lifted his head, nose in the air, nostrils working. "I see nothing. But I do smell something—unusual."

Without moving from where he was standing, the now wary swordsman turned a slow circle. Beyond the island in the floating pond and outside its transparent boundaries, hundreds of additional bodies of water drifted independent of one another, some the size of small lakes, others mere globules no bigger than a child's ball. Some squeezed together until their mysterious transparent envelopes merged to form a larger aqueous mass while others wrenched apart until they separated into two or more distinct hovering bodies. He tried to let his gaze touch every one of them, but nowhere did he see anything out of the ordinary.

"There's nothing out there," he declared conclusively. "Nothing but fish and frogs, newts and waterbirds."

"No, you are wrong." One hand shielding his eyes from the mist-shrouded sun, Ehomba was standing at the water's edge staring off to the east. "There is something else. Something greater."

"They're coming closer." Head back, nose in the air, Ahlitah was inhaling a scent still too subtle for human nostrils to detect.

"Where, by Gheju! I don't see anything, and I don't smell anything! Except you two." Frustrated, Simna stomped up and down the tiny beach, sending tide-zone insects and crustaceans scrambling for cover from the footprints he left in the soft soil.

They came from beneath the rising sun, distant dots at first that soon matured into rising and falling arcs of glistening pink, as if the morning had decided to hesitate in its brightening and mark the pause with a series of rose-hued commas. With the precision of experienced acrobats they advanced by leaping lithely from one hovering body of water to the next, sometimes entering those nearest the ground, then ascending skyward from pond to pond as if climbing a watery ladder. This they did effortlessly, soaring from floating lakes to drifting ponds in spite of the fact that a single missed leap would in all probability result in the slow, unpleasant death of the jumper. Because while they could live out of water, they could not do so for very long.

"Dolphins!" Simna exclaimed. "Here?"

"Yes, here," Ehomba murmured. "They have sharp eyes, and even sharper hearing, and ways of seeing the world at distances greater than either eyes or ears can match."

"But dolphins are creatures of the sea," Simna protested as he watched the school continue its approach, leaping from one drifting body of water to the next.

"Not always," rumbled Ahlitah. "I have seen these very same, or their relations, playing in the rivers that crisscross the veldt."

"There are sea dolphins and freshwater dolphins," Ehomb
informed his friend.

"I guess there are," admitted Simna. "Strangely colored
they are and—" He broke off, frowning. "Wait a minute.
You've been telling me that you come from a desert country.
Now you're saying that you know all about the different kind
of dolphins, even those that live in fresh water. Deserts aren'
known for a surplus of deep rivers. How do you know so
much about this kind of water dweller?"

The herdsman smiled gently down at his friend. "The dol
phins of the sea know well their inland relatives. Where rive
meets ocean they often meet and talk, and sometimes ex
change matings. I know about the river dolphins because the
sea dolphins told me of them."

"Ah. So you don't talk to fish. You talk to dolphins."

"No. No man talks to dolphins. It is up to the dolphins to
talk to men."

"And they just happened to settle on you?" Simna eyed the
tall southerner slyly. "Why would that be, Etjole? Because
you are making all of this up to keep from confessing what
I've known all along? That you are a sorcerer?"

"Not at all, Simna. They talk to me because I like to take
long walks by myself along the beach, and the shores of my
country are desolate. The currents there are swift and cold
There are men who kill dolphins, for food and to keep them
from competing for the catch. I would never do such a thing
How can one eat another who is known to be kind as well a
intelligent?"

Behind them, Ahlitah licked a paw. "I've never had any
trouble with that."

"Well, I could never do such a thing. I believe that they can
sense a kind and kindred spirit. I have been talking to dol
phins since I was a child."

"So you called them to us?" Simna wondered uncertainly.

"Nothing of the kind." Raising his gaze once more

Ehomba monitored the school's advance. They were quite near now, slowing as they debated which floating globules to use to make their final approach. "I doubt they have seen many humans in this place before, or perhaps none at all before us. Naturally curious as they are, I believe they have simply grown too interested in our presence here to stay away any longer." He began walking backward. "You should step away from the water."

"Why?" Then Simna noted the enthusiastic splashes the oncoming dolphins were making and hastily gathered up his gear, moving it to higher ground among the trio of casuarinas.

The dolphins arrived singly and in pairs, leaping magnificently from a second pond into the one where the travelers had spent the night. There were a dozen of them, including a quartet of youngsters. They took up much of the available water, forcing the indigenous inhabitants up against the transparent skin of the hovering pond or close inshore as the invaders dashed in energetic circles around the island, squeaking and barking joyously. With their bright pink coloration they resembled strips of flame shooting through the water.

If it was a form of ceremonial greeting, it was a dizzying one, as Ehomba and his companions struggled to follow the streamlined racers' progress around and around the little island. Eventually the new arrivals tired of the game and settled down to hunting out the fish and other pond dwellers who were trying to hide in the crevices and roots of the island.

One of the dolphins did not. Instead, it swam slowly toward the three travelers with effortless strokes of its broad, flat tail. Its head was different from those of its seagoing relatives, being narrower and with a prominent forehead in back of the long beak. Turning slightly to her left, she raised her head out of the water and parted tooth-lined jaws.

"I am Merlescu, Queen of the High River School and of the

central district of the Water-That-Flies. Who are you?" Danc
ing eyes tracked their every movement.

Simna leaned close to whisper up at his tall friend. "N
wonder you can talk to them. They speak perfectly."

"Of course we speak perfectly!" declared the queen. "Wh
would you think otherwise, man?"

"Oh, I dunno. Maybe because I've never before heard you
people do anything but squeak like oversized finned mice."

It was hard to tell if Merlescu was smiling, because he
kind were always smiling. Inherited physiognomy made an
other expression impossible.

"It suits us to speak our own language around humans an
to keep them ignorant as to our true abilities. Except," sh
added as she turned to face Ehomba, "a very few. You, mar
have about you a kind and sympathetic aspect."

"Oh really?" Simna made a show of inspecting his com
panion's face. "He looks pretty ordinary to me."

"What are you doing in the land of the Water-That-Flies?"

"We are making our way north," Ehomba explained, "s
that we may eventually book passage on a boat going to th
dry territories that lie to the west."

"So very far!" Pivoting on her tail, she squealed at he
school, whose members replied with energetic squeaks an
chirps. Looking back at the travelers, she professed, "I hav
never met anyone who has crossed the ocean. Not even oth
ers of my kind—though there was one who insisted she ha
talked to one who had talked to one who had done it. Wha
drives you three to undertake so extensive and dangerous
journey?"

"An obligation," Ehomba told her.

"Treasure," added Simna.

"The tall idiot had to go and save my life," fumed Ahltah

Merlescu nodded, a gesture that dolphins often used amon;
themselves, particularly when there were no humans aroun
to witness it. "I see that your motivations are as diverse a

your appearance." Turning her body around, she gestured with a fin. "Many, many days of difficult travel stretch out ahead of you before you will come to the end of the Water-That-Flies. This is country best suited to those with fins, or with wings. Not to those with awkward, many-jointed legs. North of here the Water-That-Flies becomes denser still. You will find very few places where you can slip between."

"I wanted to ask you about that." Walking right up to the water's edge, Ehomba sat down and stretched out his legs. Merlescu swam close enough to rest the tip of her beak on one of his bare ankles. Behind them, Ahlitah found himself contemplating a large and easy meal until Simna jabbed him hard in the ribs. The great maned head whirled on the human, but the swordsman, more familiar now and therefore more comfortable with the great cat's moodiness, did not flinch.

"I see what you're thinking, kitty. Don't. Can't you see that Etjole's working his magic on our behalf?"

"What magic?" The litah growled softly. "They are only talking."

"Ah, but that's how our friend Etjole works his magic. With words. At least that's the only way I've been able to catch him working it so far."

"Of what possible use to us can talk with these water dwellers be?"

"I don't know," Simna readily admitted. "But this I do know: Etjole wouldn't be wasting his time doing so if he didn't think we would benefit in the end. So let's just sit on our natural instincts for a while and see what develops, shall we?" Experimentally, he prodded the litah's belly. "This morning you ate more fish than both of us put together. Surely you're not hungry again already?"

"Watch your hands, man. You presume a familiarity that has not been granted." Settling himself back down on all fours, Ahlitah concentrated intently on the verbal byplay taking place between human and dolphin. "I am not hungry. I jus felt like killing something."

"Well, my furry friend, hold that thought." Ignoring the big cat's warning, the swordsman leaned up against the muscular flank, using it for casual support. "I have a feeling that before this little excursion is done you will have more than one opportunity to indulge it."

Merlescu drew back slightly, sliding deeper into the water "That is a fine proposition for you, man, but what do we get out of it? You ask much in return for nothing."

"I would never propose anything so one-sided." The seated Ehomba was quick to reassure her. "Your rewards for helping us will be many. For one thing, you will be rid of us and any lingering worries our presence in your territory may cause you. More importantly, you will have that rare chance to work together in a manner I know your kind delights in but can only rarely experience. It will require great precision and timing on the part of you and all the members of your school." He looked away and shrugged indifferently.

"Of course, if you are not the kind of school that delights in this type of activity, we can always try to make contact with another. It may be that you and yours are not up to the challenge. If so, I will understand. After all, that which is elementary is for those whose focus is forever on taking it easy."

"What, what?" Backing off, the greatly distressed dolphin churned the water as she spun in a tight circle. After several moments of this she reapproached the shore and spat a mouthful of dirty pond water straight into Ehomba's face. Simna straightened and next to him he could feel Ahlitah's muscles tense, but the herdsman did not appear in the least perturbed.

Calmly, he wiped water and plant matter from his dripping face. "That is not an answer. Can you do it?"

"Can we? Can we?" She took up another mouthful of water and for a moment Simna thought she was going to drench his friend again—but she did not. Slowly, the water trickled from her jaws. "It is not a matter of can we, but will we."

"I refuse to concede the point without proof. Will you?" Ehomba leaned forward and squeaked something at her. "It will be great fun—if you can make it happen."

"It is not up to me. We of the water do not work things as humans do. Not even queens." Turning and squeaking, she swam out into the deeper water of the pond, calling the members of the school to her. While they convened in a mass of squeals and barks, Simna sidled over to his friend. Ahlitah pretended disinterest as long as he could, but soon he too was standing within leisurely hearing range of the tall herdsman.

"What did you ask of them?" The swordsman kept his eyes on the garrulous, squawling dolphins.

"To help us," Ehomba explained honestly.

"Help us!" Ahlitah grunted. "How can such as they help us? Without filling our bellies, I mean."

"Remember what I said previously about engaging conversation?" Ehomba nodded toward the dolphins. "I have just had some. Be patient until they are finished with their squabbling."

So Simna ibn Sind and Ahlitah squirmed silently and waited to see what their lanky friend was about, wondering how it might involve the three of them with a pack of obstreperous, noisy water dwellers who were not fish but not human, either.

After what seemed like hours of raucous argument the school broke up, its members resuming their former activities of hunting, playing, mating, and chasing one another around and around the single island. Merlescu swam slowly back to land. Leaning back so that she was floating upright in the water, she once again addressed herself to Ehomba. But her words and her gaze encompassed all three of them.

"We will need to find some vines." As she spoke a trio of adults leaped clear of the pond, across the intervening open space, and into another, larger drifting body of water beyond. "This may take a little time." With that she turned her head and slipped back beneath the surface.

"Vines?" Simna frowned at his friend. "What do we need with vines?"

"I am not even marginally vegetarian," Ahlitah added.

"Have you ever wondered what it would be like to swim to the bottom of a pond and be able to stare right through the bottom? It must puzzle the fish." Stripping off his kilt and shirt, Ehomba kicked off his sandals and dove, naked and none too gracefully, into the water. A pair of the younger dolphins promptly swam up to him and, chattering and squeaking, began a game of tag with him as the divider between.

"Will you have a look at that." Simna was grinning and shaking his head even as he began removing his own accoutrements. "I suppose any chance to get clean is a welcome one."

"Not at all." Lying down on his side, the litah promptly dropped his head onto the soft earth and closed his eyes. Simna eyed the big cat disapprovingly.

"Going to sleep again?"

One piercing yellow eye popped open to fix him in its glare. "When not hunting or screwing I usually spend eighty percent of my time sleeping. It's what we big cats do. And we do it well." The eye closed and Ahlitah rolled over so that his back was facing the human. "Go soak yourself, if you must. It's a human thing."

Simna started to turn away, then paused. An entirely impish smile spread across his face. Searching until he found what he needed, he walked to the water's edge, knelt, and then retraced his steps, tiptoeing up to the back of the cat.

The litah's roar as the swordsman dumped the contents of the hollow gourd onto the big cat's slumbering face shook the transparent epidermis of the pond and caused cones to fall from the shading casuarinas. With a whoop of delight, Simna had spun around and raced for the water. He had just enough of a lead to beat his pursuer to the pond.

His face twisted into a black rictus of pure ferocity, Ahlitah paced rapidly back and forth along the shore. "You've got to come out sometime, little man. When you do, I'll twist you up so tight you'll have to drink your own piss!"

"Just as I've always suspected." Treading water, Simna made faces at the outraged feline. "The bigger the cat, the smaller its sense of humor."

His eyes bugged and his expression was radically altered when, with a warning roar, the litah suddenly crouched and sprang directly toward him. Ducking, the swordsman kicked frantically for the bottom of the pond.

Massive paws dug at the water, but not for long. Soon Ahlitah was bucking and jerking as first one dolphin then another prodded him from below with their snouts, or blew bubbles beneath his belly. A smiling Ehomba joined in, and the big carnivore's initial outrage was soon forgotten as humans, dolphins, and cat churned the surface of the pond to joyful froth.

It was midafternoon before the absent trio of water dwellers returned from their scavenging. Held in their mouths and wrapped around their upper bodies were long lengths of strong vine, some green, the rest brown. Ragged ends showed where sharp teeth usually employed in the catching of fish had torn the tough lengths of plant matter free.

While Merlescu and Ehomba conversed softly, man face-to-face with dolphin in the water, Simna and Ahlitah hauled themselves out onto the edge of the island to dry their bodies in the sun.

"All right," Simna puffed, "you win."

"Win what?" Alongside him, the great cat was even more fatigued than his human companion.

Simna looked to his left, gazing across sand, gravel, and grass. "I retract my earlier allegation. You do have a sense of humor."

The litah was sitting up and cleaning itself with one paw, attempting to aid the sun in removing as much water as possible from its ebony coat. "Of course I do. But fair warning, man: Have a care when you trifle with a cat's dignity."

"Hoy, I allowed as how you might have a sense of humor. Nothing was said about dignity."

They verbally lunged and riposted in that vein until Ehomba rejoined them, pond water coursing in long rivulets down his lean, muscular form. "Our friends will make ready. I have to help them." Tilting back his head, he studied the sky. "We will have to spend another night here and leave in the morning." His gaze dropped to his companions. "They will help us."

"How?" Simna let out a querulous snort. "By tying vines around us and dragging us from one floating pond to another?"

"You will see." Turning, he loped back into the water.

Simna wanted to find out what the herdsman and the dolphins were up to, but he was too tired from all the water play. Maybe Ehomba's occupation was the key, he mused. Perhaps the vines were to be used as whips, to urge and guide the dolphins as the school towed the three travelers from lake to lake. With a mental shrug, he closed his eyes.

Despite his ever-present skepticism, he had come to have a certain confidence in Ehomba, even when he did not always have a clue as to the herdsman's intentions.

He was awakened by a delphinic din of ear-splitting proportions. It sounded as if every member of the school was squealing and squawking at the top of its capacious lungs. Rising from beneath his blanket, he saw that Ahlitah was standing at the water's edge watching as Ehomba and the dolphins organized themselves for departure.

Dressing quickly, he hurried to join them. It took only a moment to see what was intended and finally to ascertain the purpose of the scavenged vines.

Secured around each dolphin's head in a crude bit and bridle arrangement, each set of vines terminated in a pair of reins that ranged from four to six feet in length. Belting his skirt of leather armor, Simna moved to stand next to the watchful Ehomba.

"What are we supposed to do with those? Grab hold and hang on while they drag us from lake to lake? I didn't know their jaws were that strong. It's going to make for awkward traveling."

"Yes," agreed Ehomba readily, "but not in the sense that you think." He nodded at the nearest brace of eager dolphins. "The reins are not for hanging on to, but for balance."

"Balance?" Simna's brows drew together, as confused as the rest of him.

"Like this." Stepping out into shallow water, Ehomba proceeded to demonstrate.

Watching him balance himself with one foot on the back of each dolphin, using their dorsal fins to brace his feet while holding a rein in each hand, both swordsman and cat were astonished at the speed and grace the dolphins displayed as they raced around the circumference of the island and the confines of the pond with the human on their backs. After several such high-spirited circumnavigations, they sped into shore and deposited their passenger next to his friends. So skilled, so controlled, had been the dolphins' run that the herdsman was barely damp.

He handed the ends of the reins to the suspicious swordsman. "Here, Simna. You try it."

The shorter man held up both hands. "Oh no. Not me."

"Hmph!" Wearing his inherent haughtiness like a crown, Ahlitah promptly padded forward. Two more dolphins arrived and positioned themselves. Holding the reins firmly in his jaws, the big cat stepped forward and allowed the two dolphins to convey him effortlessly around the island, riding their backs as easily and magnificently as any carved figure-head ever rode the prow of a ship.

Simna eventually did as well. Despite his initial skepticism about the unique means of travel, he was too experienced a horseman to incur a spill from the striking double mount. Thus familiarized with the behavior of their slick-skinned chargers, the travelers gathered up their gear and took up their riding positions.

"Ready then?" Merlescu queried in her high-pitched yet el-egant voice. Satisfied by an expectant vocal melange of squeaks, snarls, and shouts, she threw herself forward into the water and kicked violently with her tail. "Then—let's go!"

There were none to witness the departure but fish and sala-manders, frogs and birds, but even they must have been im-pressed by the sight of an entire school of dolphins soaring as if a single entity from one floating pond to the next—espe-cially with two humans and one great black cat riding upon their arching backs. The splash as they all hit the surface of the next airborne body of water more or less simultaneously was impressive. Water would cascade over the sides of the transparent enclosure thus struck, spilling into smaller pondlets of water and the vast, shallow, freshwater sea that covered the actual ground below.

In this manner the travelers progressed, their fingers wrapped tightly around green reins, their feet planted firmly behind rubbery fins, their legs and joints braced for the relief of each takeoff and the shock of each watery landing. From pond to lake, lake to pond they advanced, never in a perfectly straight line, but always crisscrossing and hip-hopping and hopscotching more or less northward.

With the assistance of the acrobatic, leaping dolphins they covered miles instead of yards, resting and camping on those lakes and ponds that boasted dry land, helping their finned friends to round up and catch enough fish to satisfy all. The humans supplemented their diet with everything from berries to watercress, while Ahlitah proved he was not above eating even snails and crawfish—though filling his belly, they did not offer much of a challenge in the way of a hunt.

Once they encountered a place where no proximate body of water large enough to accommodate the dolphins and their passengers loomed near. Simna was convinced they would have to waste time backtracking and then searching to east or west, but at the last moment Ehomba did something with the reins of his mounts. It was very subtle, and the swordsman was not entirely convinced he had seen anything at all, but it left him with something to ponder while he fought to balance himself on the back of his own steeds as they soared over the liquidless gap. They did just make it to the next, seemingly too-distant hovering body of water, their tails slapping down on the rim of the thin, transparent wall, their squeals of triumph and delight echoing in his ears.

Ehomba had urged them forward with words, Simna decided. Words, or a suggestion, or orders to alter their angle of approach. Or—something more.

There had been no flash of lightning, no burst of alchemic effulgence. Just a barely perceptible flutter of long-fingered hands. The hands of a musician, Simna had mused on more than one occasion. Or hands that could cast spells.

Without preparation, or magic powder, or wand or crystal orb? All Ehomba had was a spear and two swords, and while they rode the backs of the dolphins, those devices rode high and secure against the southerner's back. Simna shook water from his eyes. Was his tall, soft-voiced friend sorcerer or no? More often than not, he found himself absolutely confused on the matter.

He could not spare the time to cogitate too deeply the conundrum that was Etjole Ehomba. At the moment he was too busy toiling to keep from falling off.

XX

M ANY DAYS PASSED BEFORE THE FLOATING, AIRBORNE PONDS
and lakes began to grow dangerously infrequent. The dolphins had to work harder to clear longer and longer gaps between the drifting bodies of water. After a while it became
impossible to maintain a reasonable northerly heading. Too
much energy was being expended on leaping from side to side
instead of forward, like a sailing ship forced to tack into a
steadily decreasing wind.

There finally came a day and an hour when Merlescu and
Ehomba agreed that the time had come to call a halt and make
an end to the joyous and fruitful relationship they had established. Neither wished to risk pressing on until one of the
hardworking dolphins fell short of its goal and had to be
raised bodily by the travelers back into the nearest, lowest
body of deep water. That Ahlitah by himself could accomplish
this no one doubted, but any dolphin missing a jump who fell
to the ground would not find its fall adequately cushioned by
the six inches of water there. Neither the travelers nor Merlescu desired to see that happen.

For their final farewells they chose a pond large enough to aspire to be a lake. Its rippling, curved underside hovered no more than a foot or so above the surface of the endless shallow swamp that covered the ground. The school clustered close along the water's edge, looking on and offering encouragement as the travelers clambered over the side and, one by one, dropped to the pale, tepid shallows below.

Terse but heartfelt good-byes given, the dolphins turned and, as one, began their return journey southward, heading for the heart of the land of suspended lakes. The travelers watched them go until the last pink, curving back had arched out of sight.

Simna gestured at the dripping length of thin, tough vine Ehomba had been utilizing as a rein for days. It was wrapped in coils around the southerner's shoulder. "What do you plan to do with that? Rope us a couple of frogs to ride the rest of the way?"

"No. But I have a feeling we may eventually have to use it to rope something." With that he started off, heading due north. Simna marveled at the herdsman's ability to tell direction from an empty sky the way a thief senses a heavy purse concealed within many folds of garment. He followed without question while Ahlitah splashed primly alongside, occupying himself with scanning the languid shallows for edible mollusks and crustaceans.

By the morning of the next day they had reached a place where the vast, shallow river bay that underlay the hovering ponds had been reduced to streaks of fading dampness in the sand. Behind them, glittering and glistening like pearls hung on invisible cords, the floating ponds and lakes stretched south to the main body of the river and the veldt beyond.

Ahead lay gravel plains dotted with low scrub and clusters of bizarrely shaped succulents. Half a day's march later found them confronting a desert. The first dunes lifted smooth-sided yellow-brown flanks toward the deep blue sky.

"More fine country!" Simna spat and watched as the dry grains rapidly soaked up his spit. "I long for the green fields and leafy forests of home." The disgruntled swordsman looked up at Ehomba. "At least you'll be comfortable."

"What, in this?" The herdsman indicated the desiccated terrain that lay before them.

"Hoy, haven't you told me that you come from a desert land?"

"No, I have not. Dry, yes. Desert—well, to some I suppose it is. But where I come from there are mountains crowned with trees, and valleys that fill with grass and clover and flowers, and springs that nourish small lakes and give rise to flowing streams." He nodded northward. "I see none of that here. Right now, the only thing about this place that reminds me of home is the temperature." He looked to his right.

"Are you suffering, my four-legged friend?"

"Not at all. Not yet, anyway." Ahlitah was panting, the splotched dark pink of the heavy, thick tongue shockingly bright against his black lips. "I know that when the sun is up I get hotter than my kin because of my color, but I have grown used to it."

"We're going to need plenty of water." Grim-faced, Simna surveyed the ground ahead. "No telling what we'll find out there."

"That is what I kept this for."

Turning, Ehomba retraced their steps until he halted before a very small pond. Floating a yard or so above the ground, it contained no central island, no visible soil of any kind. Reflecting its diminutive size, only minnows darted in its depths.

Unlimbering the coil of vine from his shoulder, he turned to his companions. "Come and help me secure this."

"Secure it?" Simna started toward the other man. "Secure it to what? And why? You're not thinking of somehow bringing it with us?"

"And why not?" Ehomba challenged him as he began to

measure out the length of vine around the circumference of the pond. "Can you think of a more reliable source of water, or a better container?"

"I know it's small compared to many we've seen." The swordsman bent to help with the vine. "But it's still a lot bulkier and heavier than a couple of gourds slung over the shoulder. What makes you think we can move it, anyway?"

"It will move," Ehomba assured him. "Now when I tell you, pick up that side of the vine and press it tight against the water wall."

It took work and a while—the vine kept slipping against the smooth exterior of the pond—but eventually they had it snugged tight. The green rope dug slightly into the sides of the drifting pond but did not break through. Strange to think of water having skin, Simna mused. With his knife they split the free end of the vine in half. He took one end and Ehomba the other, and together they put their weight into it and pulled.

The pond did not budge until Ahlitah, with a snort of disdain, grabbed the vine in his teeth and tugged. Once set in motion, the pond moved easily, traveling as if on an invisible greased pad. As soon as it had acquired some momentum, one man could drag it behind him. It glided through the air more freely than they had any right to expect.

"We will drink our fill until it is half empty," Ehomba declared, "and that will make it even easier to pull. Meanwhile we will be able to sip more lavishly than any desert would normally allow."

Putting out a hand, Simna pushed against the side of the pond. He was careful not to poke it with a finger. The cool, transparent epidermis dimpled at his touch before springing back to its original shape. It took several seconds to complete the process and return to normal, the marvelous container reacting not unlike an old man's skin.

"Drink our fill? By Ghothua, we can have a bath!"

Ehomba regarded him with distaste. "You would swim in your drinking water?"

The swordsman blinked ingenuously. "Sure, why not?"

"Why not indeed," added Ahlitah supportively. It was the first time he had agreed with Simna on anything.

Ehomba simply shook his head. "It is true what the migrating traders say. Civilization and civilized behavior are matters of perspective."

"Aw, our customs are just different, Etjole." Simna gave the herdsman an amiable slap on the back, marveling as always at the dryness of the southerner's attire. No matter the time of day or the temperature, he never seemed to sweat. "If it'll ease your mind, I promise not to swim in your drinking water."

"I would appreciate that." Like his companions, Ehomba was enjoying the easy walking. For the first time in many days, the ground underfoot crunched instead of sloshed.

They kept to the dry, dusty washes that ran like rocky rivulets between the dunes. Soon these were towering overhead, their sandy peaks rising to heights of a thousand feet and more. Yet between them, in shadowed and sheltered places, desert plants thrived on subsurface sources of moisture.

Besides the more familiar bushes and small trees with their desert-adapted miniaturized leaves and green bark, they encountered the most extraordinary miscellany of cacti and other dry-country plants. Some had spines that were curved like fishhooks, while others boasted spikes fine as hair, rustred in color and threatening. Towing their floating water supply behind them, the travelers were careful not to brush up against any of these. In Ehomba's experience, such plants not only stung, but many also carried poison in their quills. Overhead, small, fringed dragonets soared and circled like tatters of torn tent, their outstretched membranous wings keeping them effortlessly aloft as they watched the progress of the

rekkers below. Enamored of carrion, they would track iso-
ated wayfarers of any species for days, hopeful and expec-
ant.

Ehomba's companions trudged along, sometimes locked in
heir own private silence, sometimes chattering briskly either
o him or to one another. What an odd trio of travelers we
nake, he meditated on more than one occasion. None of us
eally wants to be here. I would rather be home with my wife
and children, Ahlitah would surely prefer the company of
other great cats, and Simna doubtless misses the fleshpots and
garish excitements of more populous surroundings.

Yet here we are: I because I made a promise to a man now
long dead, whom until he lay dying in my arms I did not even
know. Simna because he thinks I am a sorcerer on the trail of
reasure. And the litah because I had the audacity to save his
ife.

I should go home. Abandon this foolishness. Calving sea-
son is over and the cows and ewes have dropped their young,
but summer does not last forever. There is much to be done
before the cold winds come ashore.

Yet Mirhanja would not want for help, he knew. The
Naumkib looked after their own. And his friends and fellow
villagers understood the nature of his obligation. None of
them would complain at having to help the family of an absent husband. Not for the first time, he was glad he was
Naumkib. In other tribes, he knew, an extended absence such
as his would water the flowers of resentment.

How he missed the sea! Its heavy perfume, the rolling chorus of the waves fondling the shore, the uncompromising purity of its rejuvenating embrace. He even missed its taste,
blunt and salty and steadfast in its distillation of every part of
the world. Around him desiccation had reduced the good earth
to powder, useful for taking the hair off a hide preparatory to
tanning but little else. Unlatching the flap that covered the
right-hand pocket of his kilt, he kneaded the sackful of beach

pebbles between his fingers, listened to them grind against one another, hearing the sounds of the ocean at night resonate between his fingers.

Days that could have been hotter and gratefully were not were broken by chilly nights during which distant creatures howled and screamed at the moon. Twice it rained lightly, not only cooling the travelers but also partially replenishing their drifting bubble of water. All things considered, the journey through the dunes was proving difficult but not harsh. No one had succumbed to the heat, no one had been bitten or stung or acquired an armful of cactus stickers.

The days would have passed more rapidly, however, if they had had some idea how far they still had to go before emerging from such desolate country. Though not overtly hostile, the land through which they were traveling rapidly grew dull and uninteresting. Even the appearance of a spectacular new succulent no longer drew more than a casual comment or mumbled observation.

"I saw something."

Head down, tongue hanging out, Ahlitah growled testily. "None of us are blind. We all see many somethings. It is hardly reason for excitement."

"No." Simna had halted in the middle of the wadi and was shading his eyes as he peered ahead. "This was moving."

Ehomba was more charitable. Stopping alongside the swordsman, he leaned on his spear and tried to follow his friend's line of sight. "What did you see, Simna? A rabbit perhaps? Roast rabbit would be good."

"Rabbit or rat, I'd thank you for either." Drawing in its tongue, the litah licked dry lips. "I'm hungry."

"You are always hungry." Ehomba spoke without looking over at the great cat. He was striving to see whatever Simna had seen.

"As Gwyull is my witness," the swordsman insisted tersely, "it was no rabbit. No rat, either."

"Then what?" the herdsman prompted him.

Lowering his shading palm, Simna looked uncertain. "I on't know. It was there for an instant, and then it was gone."

"Like any story." With a snort, Ahlitah resumed padding rward, his big feet kicking up dust at every step.

Camp that night was uninviting, but in the absence of any nd of shelter it was the best they could do. Ruddy dunes owered all around them as they spread themselves out on the oor of the dry ravine. Ahlitah was less grumpy than usual, anks to the den of rodents he had sniffed out and promptly onsumed. For a veldt master used to bringing down and illing much larger prey, this hunting of rats and mice was deeaning, but an empty stomach in need of meat does not disiminate against the nature of whatever the throat elects to rovide.

As they unrolled their blankets on the hard, unforgiving round, they were more grateful than ever for the floating ond Ehomba had thought to bring along. Half empty now, it as easier to tow. Everyone drank from it, so everyone shared the pulling.

Overhead, a swelling moon promised good night walking hould they chose to exercise that option. It was something to onsider if the heat grew intolerable. Lying on his back, lisening to the cautious scurrying of nocturnal insects and those odents who had escaped Ahlitah's attentions, Ehomba put his ands behind his head and tried to envision what Mirhanja as doing at that same moment. Lying in their bed, most kely, in the posture she usually favored for sleeping: on her eft side, with her back toward him, her knees bent up toward er smooth belly, the knuckles of one hand resting just below er slightly parted mouth giving her an incongruously childke appearance.

Except there was nothing behind her in the bed now except ool night air. The body, the man, who should have been

there, was lying on the rocky floor of a dry ravine far to the
north, dreaming of her as he hoped she was dreaming of him.

Soon, he promised himself. We will reach a large town with
a harbor, and I will travel on a boat across the sea to deal with
this Hymneth person on behalf of the man who died in my
arms. And then I will come back to you, covered if not in
glory, which I do not seek, but in the satisfaction and the inner
contentment no crown or generalship can match. *Soon.*

Pursing his lips, he blew a silent kiss at the moon, turned
over, and went to sleep with an ease no king or soldier could
equal.

XXI

IT WAS COLD WHEN SIMNA IBN SIND AWOKE. BLINKING, HE yawned silently at the polished bowl of night that filled the sky between the dune crests. While it was beginning to set, the nearly full moon still threw enough light for a man to see clearly by, if not enough to enable him to read. Simna had never been much for reading and was glad he was traveling in the company of individuals of similar mind. Certainly Ahlitah, despite his exceptional if acerbic linguistic talents, was no peruser of books and scrolls. He was less certain about Ehomba, but the untutored, unsophisticated herdsman did not strike him as much of a scholar. A master of magics perhaps, but no great reader. Certainly in the time they had spent together thus far he had never expressed any great longing for the printed page.

He grinned at the thought of Etjole standing watch over his cattle and sheep, balancing himself with his spear as he alternated standing first on one leg and then on the other, with weighty tome in hand. The spear fit the image; the book did not. He comforted himself with that thought. Simna had little use for scholars. They tended to look down on an honest hardworking man, and whisper about him behind his back.

Something nudged his right thigh, and he froze. Probably some harmless creature of the dunes come exploring under cover of night. A large desert beetle, black and preoccupied, or one of Ahlitah's scurrying snacks unwittingly tempting fate. But the drylands of his native country were home to their share of less benign nocturnal creatures, and in terrain as harsh as this there were bound to be hunters of the dark that used poison and fang and sting.

So he moved only his neck and head as he rose slightly to see what was repeatedly thumping his thigh through the blanket. Even with the slight movement he expected whatever it was to react: either by turning and racing off or pausing in its activity or skittering away from the movement and retreating in the direction of his feet.

He did not expect it to look back at him.

The warrior's diminutive form was clad in rough brown fabric woven from sisal or some similar plant. From fringed pants that reached to just below the knobby knees, short legs protruded, terminating in disproportionately large, splayed feet that were bare of any covering. The correspondingly undersized arms were gnarled and muscled. In his right hand the tiny fighter held a slim spear or lance. Bits of carved bone gleamed whitely against cuirass and shirt, serving to decorate as well as armor the upper body.

The head was a slightly squashed oval instead of round. Commensurate with the rest of the squat body, it gave the warrior the appearance of one who had been stepped on and had his whole self compressed and flattened out. The mouth was inordinately wide, the lips thin to the point of nonexistence, the eyes deep-set and intelligent. An oversized cap of finely woven natural fiber flopped down over the forehead. As a wide-eyed, motionless Simna watched in fascination, the soldier pushed the thick front of the cap farther back on his head, revealing the first tight curls of red-gold hair beneath.

His ears were remarkable: oversized, protuberant organs that stuck out from underneath the cap and rose to points higher than the head. They were also immoderately hairy. Unlike the curls that emerged from beneath the rim of the heavy cap, these hairs were straight as needles. But they were equally red.

Softly snapping something in a tongue Simna had never heard before, the warrior gestured brusquely with the lance. Taken in concert, the meaning of his tone and movement were unmistakable. Slowly, Simna sat up and raised his hands. He was wary, but far from intimidated.

After all, the fearless fighter was only five inches tall.

As soon as Simna complied with the order, his captor advanced toward him on his mount. This was a running bird of a kind that was also new to the swordsman. A mottled, spotted brown with flecks of white, it had a very long, broad tail, a slim bill, a tall topknot, and a highly intelligent gaze. Whenever it moved forward, its head dipped, the long tail stretched out behind it, and the topknot flared upward like a weathervane taking the mood of the wind.

Seated on the bird's back, the diminutive soldier rode on a perfectly miniaturized saddle. From bridle to stirrup, every fragment of avian tack was downsized to the point of airiness. An intrigued Simna noted that the arrangement would preclude any possibility of flight. Apparently the warrior's mount was a bird that preferred running to flying.

"I give up." He raised his hands even higher. "You've got me."

"Soh," the wee fighter responded curtly, "you speak *that* language." His voice was not as high and thin as Simna would have expected. Raising his six-inch-long lance over his head, he stood up in the stirrups, turned in the saddle, and ululated loudly.

Ehomba awoke to find the camp invaded by forty or so of
the bantam night riders. The intruders darted back and forth in
the quick, short bursts of speed that characterized their
mounts' natural agility. They looked and acted quite confident—until Ahlitah yawned and stood up. Eyes drooping and
tired, the great cat frowned at the intrusion, sniffed once, and
opened oculi that were two yellow moons flanking the night.

"Ah, how considerate—a midnight snack."

"Back, get back!" The warrior who had awakened Simna
was screeching frantically at his comrades. Observing the retreat, the swordsman discreetly lowered his hands. There had
really been no reason to raise them in the first place, and besides, his shoulders were getting tired.

Swinging his legs out from beneath the blanket, Ehomba
sat up and contemplated their visitors. He addressed them
with the same respect he would have accorded a squadron of
full-sized men, even though the arrivals were neither full
sized nor men.

"I am Etjole Ehomba. These are my traveling companions,
the swordsman Simna ibn Sind and the litah Ahlitah." He
eyed the big cat disapprovingly. "Put your tongue back in
your mouth. Guests are not for eating."

"Hmph." Disappointed, the litah slumped back onto his
belly. "My late-night entertainments are more fun than
yours."

The diminutive callers gradually relaxed. Trotting forward
on his feathered mount, the one who had awakened Simna
confronted the herdsman. "I am Loswee, Son of the Patriarch
Roosagin, of the Swick—the People of the Sand." His gaze
narrowed and the hairy oversized ears inclined ever so
slightly forward. "You are not agents of the Dunawake?"

Herdsman and swordsman exchanged a glance while Ahlitah remained relaxed, unmoving, and uninterested. Long legs
crossed, Ehomba looked back down at their interrogator.

Loswee's mount was pecking curiously at the underside of the southerner's well-worn leather sandal.

"What is a Dunawake?"

"Not 'a' Dunawake," the miniature warrior corrected him. "*The* Dunawake." In the subdued silver shimmer of the moon, his shudder was clearly visible. "I don't even like to consider the possibility that there might be more than one." Wide eyes looked up at the infinitely larger visitor.

"The Dunawake is a Terrible. There are many Terribles in the world, but the Dunawake o'ertops them all. You can't fight it. All you can do is get out of its way. And you'd better get out of its way, or you'll be mushed. Obliterated, my friend, even such giants as yourselves, as deftly as I would pulp a sweet ant. So we move. It's aching and arduous work, but we have no choice. There are those who are not as skillful or agile as we, and these suffer the unmentionable fate that befalls all victims of the Dunawake." He sat a little straighter in his avian saddle. "So far we have succeeded in keeping ahead of it. We Swick are quick.

"We would fight it, if we had the weapons. But spears and arrows are less than raindrops to the Dunawake. We need something stronger."

Simna considered. "Bigger spears, bigger arrows?"

Loswee's gaze narrowed, tugged down by heavy brows, and Ehomba was quick to intercede. "You must excuse my friend. His muscles and his determination are both stronger than his imagination. What would you need to fight this Dunawake?"

"Magic," the Swick replied promptly. "Magic such as you possess."

Ehomba blinked. "We have no magic. I am a herder of cattle and sheep, my friends unpretentious wanderers. We are not magicians." He was aware that Simna was watching him as closely as was Loswee.

"If you are not magicians," the Swick countered, pointing with the tip of his spear, "then how do you explain that?"

He had singled out the half-full pond that hovered behind the travelers. A few minnows still swam in its reduced depths.

Ehomba smiled gently. "We did not conjure the floating water, nor can I explain it. We found it and many thousands like it in a land to the south of here, and brought it with us so that we would have enough to drink in this dry country. You could do the same."

"To the south, you say?" Loswee reflected. "This is as far south as the Swick have ever come. And we would not have done so had the Dunawake not forced the journeying upon us." He squinted at the pond, which was tied to a rock outcropping so that it would not drift away during the night. "I'm not sure I believe you. I think you have more magic than you're admitting to."

Ehomba shook his head. "I wish you were right and I untruthful. There have been times when I could have done with a little magic."

Turning in his saddle, Loswee barked something at his squadron of armed fighters, then turned back to Ehomba. "Perhaps after we have talked further, you will feel like being more forthcoming."

"We have no objection to talking," Ehomba assured him noncommittally.

"Good. I see that you are traveling light, so you must be ready for a real meal."

"Giquina knows that's true!" Simna agreed heartily.

Ehomba frowned at his friend. "Look at this country, and the size of these people. They cannot have much to eat, far less anything to spare for visitors of our size."

"On the contrary," Loswee proudly disagreed, "we have more than ample stocks. We don't lack for food, and we'll be pleased to share. If not magic, then maybe you can give us some advice. Having come from the south, you must at least be the bearers of new ideas." Extending his arm, he pointed with his spear. "It's not far, and I promise you will be warmer in the castle than out here in this ravine."

Ehomba beckoned to Simna, and the swordsman was at his side in an instant. The two men conferred briefly.

"What do you think?" the herdsman asked his friend.

Simna exhaled softly. "Any free food, however small the amount, is welcome. Especially if I don't have to carry it. If they mean treachery, then their brains are as small as their fingers. You or I could probably give their whole army a good fight, and Ahlitah would simply stomp them at his leisure. Since I don't see them being that stupid, I expect that their offer is genuine."

Ehomba nodded. "Those are my thoughts as well." He turned back to the bird rider and smiled. "We accept. Give us a moment to gather our things, and to untie our water, and we will come with you."

"Excellent!" While Loswee's mount could not rear back in the manner of a horse, it could mirror its rider's enthusiasm by hopping about jerkily. "Wherever else you go and whatever else happens to you, you will never forget Swick hospitality."

The riders waited patiently for the travelers to collect themselves. A number occupied themselves hunting along the base of the dunes for edible insects and plants. But they had little time for scavenging, because Ehomba and Simna were packed and ready to go within a very few minutes. Ahlitah, of course, was always ready.

The Swick troopers led the way down the gulch. Expecting to have to moderate their pace so as not to overstride their diminutive hosts, the travelers found themselves having to hurry to keep up, so swift were the Swick's feathered earthbound mounts. They hardly had time to take note of their surroundings as the line of mounted warriors turned down a much narrower wadi between massive slopes of sand, and then just as rapidly down another.

Panting, Simna looked uneasily back the way they had come. "All these dunes look alike. Many more of these twists and turns and we'll never be able to find our way back to the main canyon."

"What makes you think it was the main one?" Ehomba was striding along easily beneath his pack. "Another day or two's walk and it might have become as narrow and winding as this one." He spared a glance at the sky. "At least we are still moving in a more or less northerly direction."

"Hoy," the swordsman agreed with a nod. "Didn't they tell us that's where this Dunawake was coming from?" He surveyed the encircling dune walls uneasily.

"Relax, my friend. I do not think they would run us right at their nemesis without any warning. I think they are taking us to their community, as they promised."

The swordsman squinted ahead, past the double line of mounted Swick speeding along in front of them. "I'm looking for tents or huts, but I don't see anything yet."

He still saw nothing when the troop piped to a halt and Loswee trotted back to alert them. "We have arrived. Welcome to the castle."

Simna's eyes widened as he surveyed the moonswept sand. A few ragged bushes puffed branches into the night sky. It was almost morning and he was freshly tired. Too tired for jokes.

"Castle, is it, wee bruther? I see no castle. I see not even an outhouse."

"Come around this ridge of sand." Oblivious to the swordsman's sarcasm, Loswee beckoned for them to follow. To their left, the rest of the Swick troop lined up, wing to wing, forming a guard of honor. The travelers, after securing their floating water supply to a well-rooted nearby bush, marched on past, trailing Loswee.

The entrance was far larger than any of them had expected, a dark, gaping hole in the side of the dune. Why the shifting sand did not spill down to cover it they could not understand. Though it was difficult to tell anything for certain in the dim light, it was clear that something was holding the sand above securely in place and keeping it from tumbling down to block the opening. Provided that he advanced in a hunting crouch, it was even large enough to admit Ahlitah.

While the mere existence of the unnatural ingress was unexpected, it hardly harmonized with Loswee's description.

"I was wrong," Simna declared churlishly. "It *could* serve as an outhouse."

"Come inside." Unperturbed and at ease, Loswee led the way.

Equally as remarkable as the undisturbed, unblocked entrance was the depth to which it penetrated the dune. Bending double to keep from bumping his head against the ceiling of the tunnel, Ehomba and his companions were uncomfortably aware of the many tons of loose sand that loomed overhead. But though walled with the same grains that constituted the shifting slopes outside, the tunnel showed no signs of instability.

After a while, the soft babble of many voices became audible. Light appeared ahead. Loswee straightened in his saddle, a miniature portrait of satisfaction as he chirped to his soldiers.

"Heigh up back there! Ware your posture!" In a less martial tone he explained to his guests. "We are coming into Barrick, and the castle is waking up."

Simna grunted. "Good for it. Me, I'm going to sleep."

Close behind him, Ahlitah growled warningly. "This better be good. I didn't trot all this way for a breakfast of beans and berries. On the other paw," he added after a moment's consideration, "some of these Swick look quite nutritious."

"Ahlitah!" Looking back past his hunched-over shoulder,

Ehomba glared at the big cat. "We are guests here. Mind your manners."

"Hoy that, long bruther," Simna admonished him. "Etiquette's not my style, but even I know the idea's to dine with one's hosts—not on them."

"But I'm *hungry*." Irked by the early morning run, the hulking feline did not try to conceal his displeasure.

He forgot it, as they all did, when the tunnel made an abrupt turn to the left and they found themselves gazing at last upon the castle itself. Outside, it would have been a wonder. Here, in the deep heart of the dune, its existence was nothing short of miraculous.

Simna's anticipated tents and huts were nowhere to be seen. Instead, it was a true castle that rose before them, complete to external battlements and towers, minarets and multiple keeps. Off to the right were commodious stables where the prized running birds were quartered. In place of miniature wagons, cleverly made sand sleds were parked neatly side by side, and blacksmiths were arriving to begin the day's work with tiny bundles of wood and bands of black iron.

As they entered, advancing down a central avenue just wide enough to accommodate Ahlitah's bulk, awakening Swick appeared on the innumerable side streets to gawk at them. Smoke rose from dozens of cooking fires, trailing out tall, crooked chimneys as it curled toward the high dome of the great artificial cavern that had been hollowed out of the inside of the dune. Holes bored in the ceiling drew the smoke, allowing it to find a way out.

Pens held captive food animals: mice and rats, lizards and snakes. There were tanneries and slaughterhouses, farms exuberant with domesticated mushrooms and other edible fungi, kitchens and schools, workshops and apartments. Ehomba marveled, Simna was struck dumb, and even Ahlitah, though he gave little sign of it, was impressed. Expecting to find an unpretentious encampment, they found themselves instead in a veritable underground city. Prepared to deal with a few dozens of Swick, they instead were confronted by the People of the Sand in their teeming hundreds, perhaps thousands.

Looking past the main castle, Ehomba found that he could not see to the far end of the chamber, so extensive was the excavation. There were side galleries as well, similarly quarried from the dune, that were home to still more of the same. And everywhere rose miniaturized battlements and towers from which hung innumerable flags and decorations. Despite its reduced size, the citadel had been constructed on a grand scale, notwithstanding its implausible location or the diminutive size of its inhabitants.

He found himself smiling at no one in particular. In actuality, he was thinking of Daki and Nelecha. Because they would prize this place as no one else could.

Who else but children could truly appreciate the grandest of all sand castles?

XXII

THEY WONDERED WHAT HELD IT ALL TOGETHER, MUCH LESS kept the dune from collapsing in upon them, until they saw the first of many eternally busy construction crews. Secure in their saddles, Swick engineers directed dozens of domesticated slugs and snails as they worked at maintaining and adding to the buildings and walls.

Moving more swiftly than Ehomba had ever seen their kind travel, these humble creatures spread thick, viscid trails wherever they went. Other Swick riding large, sucker-toed geckoes followed behind, using long-handled brushes to spread and position the natural glue before it could harden. Looking up and to the side, he observed one crew working on the ceiling, the Swick hanging upside down in their saddles and harnesses.

Reaching over, Simna felt a nearby castle wall. Though nothing but fine yellow-red sand that glistened in the light of the many town lamps, it was firm and rigid to the touch.

Loswee was watching him. "Go ahead—try it."

Simna hesitated, then pushed hard with a finger, and then

with his entire hand. To his astonishment, the wall held firm against his giant's push.

"You could stand on it." Loswee's words were suffused with pride. "The Swick build thick."

They were coming to a central square. Beneath their feet, sand sifted by color and brilliance had been collected in minuscule molds. Framed and then glued in place, it gave the plaza the appearance of having been paved with multicolored stone. Tall buildings topped with cylindrical towers rose around them, some soaring to heights that would enable a Swick to look down even on Ehomba. Overhead, the dome peaked at twenty feet, allowing the visitors to stand freely.

Multiple street lamps formed a glowing necklace around the plaza, whose fringes were now filling with curious Swick anxious for a look at the giant guests. The mounted warriors of Barrick filed away through a gate off to the right, leaving only Loswee behind. Trotting up to Ehomba's feet, he tilted back his head and raised his spear in salute.

"I go to announce your presence to the Elected and to arrange for your proper reception. I will be back in a moment." With that he turned and sped off, his mount sprinting out of sight in seconds.

The travelers settled down to wait, Ahlitah pacing three tight circles before settling down against himself. Looking out at the inquisitive Swick staring back up at them from the edges of the plaza, the swordsman whispered to his phlegmatic companion, "Wonder what he meant by 'proper reception'?"

"I would imagine food, like he promised." Ehomba looked around sharply to face his friend. "I thought you did not believe that these people posed any threat to us."

"That was when we were outside, bruther." Simna studied their surroundings, which were much more spacious than the entrance tunnel but still confining. "In here, we're trapped. Any folk that can train snails to do masonry for them could have all sorts of surprising tricks up their smelly little sleeves."

Ehomba chuckled softly. "You are too suspicious, my friend."

"Hoy yes. I'm also still alive."

"And noisy." Behind them, the litah fully extended his remarkably long legs and stretched. "Why don't you shut up for a while?"

"Long bruther, why don't you—" Simna started to retort, but he was interrupted by the return of Loswee.

"That did not take very long," Ehomba ventured in greeting.

The Swick officer dismounted, leaving his bird tethered nearby. "Arrangements are being realized even as we speak. Prepare yourselves for a true Swick feast, my friends! The bites may be small, but you will find the quality and satisfaction unsurpassed."

Breakfast arrived on sand sleds pulled by teams of running birds yoked in pairs. And arrived, and kept on arriving. Where the Swick stored such copious quantities of food Ehomba did not know, but despite his unease he accepted Loswee's assurance that the banquet would in no way impoverish the community or impact adversely on its stores.

There was finely cooked and flavored meat, the origins of which Simna chose not to question. There were wild berries and nuts, desert melon, and a dozen different varieties of edible fungi, all basted and broasted and sauced to a turn. There were insects, cooked crisp in oil, and even cracker-sized loaves of bread made from wild grains. After days of living on jerked antelope and fish and what they could scavenge from their surroundings, the travelers soon put aside all pretense at politeness and gladly gave themselves over to Loswee's invitation to indulge.

When tankard-sized barrels of home-brewed beer appeared, Simna was all but ready to apply for transient citizenship.

"Not such a bad place, by Gyofah." Wearing a contented smile, he surveyed their splendid if shrunken surroundings. "A man could get used to it, if they put in a few windows."

"I believe the idea is to hide from danger," Ehomba commented dryly, "and not give it a way to look in." He considered the endless and apparently untiring line of heavily laden sleds that continued to funnel food and drink to him and his companions. "I am so full I can hardly keep my eyes open. I wonder if one of us should stand guard while the others sleep?"

Simna tossed back a cup-sized barrel of beer and blinked at him. "Now who's being suspicious? I thought you trusted these people."

"I trust everyone to a degree, but in a new country among unknown people it is better to trust no one completely. Not at first."

"So maybe you're smarter than your sheep after all." The swordsman grinned.

"Go ahead and rest." Both men turned to where Ahlitah lay on his side, having eaten his fill. The great cat's eyes were shut tight. "My kind sleeps long but lightly lest we miss the footsteps of passing prey. Trust me. If our hosts prove duplicitous, I will be up and on my feet in an instant."

"Remarkable," Simna murmured.

One yellow eye popped halfway open. "That I should rest so lightly?"

"No. That you'd use a word like 'duplicitous,'" the swordsman replied. "What's it mean, anyway?"

"One who articulates with the apposite orifice." The eye closed. "Shut up and go to sleep."

"Might as well." Stretching out prone on the paved plaza, Simna found himself regarding the domed sand ceiling.

"Can't tell whether it's day or night in here anyway. Can you, Etjole?"

But the herdsman, never one to waste the opportunity, was already locked fast in slumber.

In the morning they were taken to another part of the underground castle-city to see how the Swick were able to extend and expand their living space. The method was not at all what Ehomba had envisioned. There were plenty of shovels in evidence, and teams of birds hauling away sled-loads of excavated sand, and slug and snail supervisors shoring up the finished walls, but the initial removal was accomplished not by digging but by a small choir around which the rest of the engineering activity centered.

"I wondered how you had managed to burrow all this out." Ehomba gestured around him. "If I had tried to do so, fresh sand would simply spill into any hole I tried to dig."

"See," Loswee advised him. "They are working on extending that small service tunnel."

The choir faced a small hole in the wall. As the visitors looked on, the choir master raised his stubby arms and brought them down. Simple, single notes poured from several dozen petite Swick throats. High and sharply pitched, the consequent tone was astonishingly loud to have been produced by such downsized lungs.

As the travelers looked on in bemusement, the sand in the back of the hole began to disappear. No, Ehomba noted as he bent over for a closer look. Not disappear. It was retreating, compacting away from the singing as if propelled by an invisible shovel. As the tunnel deepened and widened, the slime spreaders moved in to cement and stabilize the new walls. Meanwhile, the choir continued to pour forth high, extended notes. Among the Naumkib Ehomba was reckoned a fine singer in his own right, but at his best he could not have matched the staying power of the weakest of the Swick singers. Not only natural talent but also much strenuous vocal training was being put to use.

"Where is the sand going?" he asked their host. Eyeing him, Simna shook his head sadly.

"Who cares? Do you always have to ask questions? Must you know everything? Do you have any idea how exasperating that is to those around you?"

"Yes, hopefully. I know but cannot help it," the herdsman replied.

"The sand is not going anywhere." Loswee ignored the byplay between his guests. "Look more closely. The same number of grains are present. It is the air between them that is being disappeared. Have you ever slid down a dune and listened to it roar?" Ehomba nodded while Simna shook his head energetically. Ahlitah ignored them, bored with the entire matter and wishing they were back outside.

"That roaring," Loswee went on, "is caused by the movement of air trapped between the particles of sand. Our singing disturbs the air and pushes it out from between the grains. The sand that remains behind becomes consolidated. This not only opens up living space but helps to stabilize the sand. Our masons complete the task of stabilization before air can seep back between the grains and expand the pile or wall once again."

"Sounds like magic to me," Simna avowed.

"Not at all," Loswee countered. "It is simply sound engineering, in every sense of the term."

"It is a wonderful thing." Ehomba was openly admiring. "Of what other marvels are the Swick masters?"

"Come and I'll show you." Loswee led them back toward the plaza.

They were shown the vast underground storehouses and fungi farms, the workshops where Swick craftsfolk turned out superb works in leather and in fabric woven from desert fibers, the narrow-bore but deep wells that brought cool water up from unsuspected pools deep beneath the dune, and the extensive stables for the care and breeding of running birds and other small domesticated creatures. A dark seep at the end of a tunnel so long and low they could not enter produced an endless supply of fine black oil that kept the lamps of the community burning around the clock.

"This country is full of such seeps," Loswee told them. "I think there must be enough of the black liquid here to fill all the lamps of the world."

Ehomba's nose wrinkled at the thought. "It smells badly, though, and it stains clothes, and animals could become trapped in it. Give me a clean wood fire any day."

"Same here," agreed Simna readily. "The stuff's not good for anything else anyway. I say take what you need for your lamps and leave the rest of it in the ground."

"That is what we do." Loswee turned back toward the main square. "You have seen much in a short time. I am hungry again myself."

Simna rubbed his hands together. "I wouldn't have thought a man could get fat on such small portions, but your cooks are as adept as your singers."

It was as they were finishing the midday meal that Loswee reappeared to confront them in the company of half a dozen senior Swick. These Elders had long, curly white whiskers emerging from their chins, like gypsum helectites protruding from a cave wall, but not one could boast of sufficient chin hair to be labeled the father of a real beard. The two females among them had manes of scraggly white hair corkscrewing down their backs. Instead of the familiar Swick attire of shorts and upper garment, these respected seniors wore voluminous cloaks whose hems scraped the ground.

Despite their impressive appearance, both individually and as a group, it was still Loswee who did the talking. Ehomba found himself wondering if the Swick warrior had volunteered for the position of go-between or if he had been delegated to the task. Whatever the truth of the matter, he did not act like someone laboring under a compulsion.

"These are members of the Council of Elders," he explained. The half dozen senior Swick promptly kowtowed spryly. "As the first among Swick to encounter you, I have been asked by them to beg your help."

Leaning to his right, Simna whispered to his companion, "Hoy—here it comes. I knew all this food and friendship had to come with a price."

"Hush," Ehomba admonished him softly. "Let us see what they have to say." Louder he responded, "What kind of help?"

For such a small warrior, Loswee could muster an impressively steely gaze. "We want you to fight the Dunawake."

"I knew it," muttered Simna sourly as he put down his latest barrel of beer.

As always, Ehomba's tone remained unchanged. "You said that magic was necessary to battle this creature. We told you before you brought us to your castle-town that we had no magic. Nothing has changed since we first talked."

Loswee's demeanor began to show some cracks. "When I said that we wanted to beg your help I was being truthful. The Dunawake is very close and comes nearer every day. You have seen how much work has gone into the building of our home here. Can you imagine the effort involved for people our size?"

Ehomba nodded slowly. "I think I can."

"I told you outside that we cannot fight the Dunawake, that we can only try to keep ahead of it." He gestured expansively, taking in the central square, the surrounding towers and buildings and shops. "How many times do you think we have had to move? How many times do you think we have had to rebuild our homes starting outside the face of a virgin dune?" When none of the visitors responded, Loswee quietly informed them, "This castle in whose center you sit, this thriving community wherein we dwell, is our forty-fifth.

Forty-five times we have raised a castle-town like this, and forty-four times we have had to abandon it and move on, to keep clear of the Dunawake."

Ehomba did his best to imagine the effort of which Loswee was speaking, the heartbreak of picking up and moving everything, down to the last miniature shovel and hearth. Of hurrying off through the desert between inhospitable dunes that were hills to him and his friends but gigantic sand mountains to people the size of the Swick. Of starting again from scratch, with the first choir singing out the first hole in the base of a fresh, untouched dune.

Of doing it forty-five times and now having to face the unholy prospect of doing it for a forty-sixth.

He took in the wondrous construction surrounding them, all of it fashioned from nothing more than laboriously worked sand. Contemplated the humming, thriving community, alive with craftwork and farming and art. Considered, and tried to envision abandoning it all to inevitable ruination and starting over again from nothing.

His gaze returned at last to the waiting Loswee. "I am sorry, but we cannot help you."

Simna looked momentarily startled, then relieved. Clearly, he had been expecting a different sort of response from his friend. Behind them, Ahlitah rolled over and snored.

Loswee accepted the response gravely. "Outside, you agreed that if not help, you might be able to give us some advice."

Ehomba shrugged diffidently. "I said 'might.' Loswee, I do not know what to say. You told us that magic was needed to fight this Dunawake, and I replied that we had no magic. I am sorry to say that we have no advice, either. We do not even know what a Dunawake is. Believe me, I feel terrible about this. Men I know how to fight, and animals, and even certain circumstances of nature, but not a Dunawake. I have never heard of one, seen one, or had it described to me."

"Perhaps if you saw it you would know how to respond." Backed by his silently watching Elders, Loswee was unwilling to drop the matter.

"I do not see why. And if it is as dangerous as you say, and we confronted it without knowing how to respond or react, I imagine we would probably die. I do not want to die. I have an obligation of my own to fulfill that does not, regrettably, include the Swick, and also a family that I am missing more than I can say."

"Also friends," Simna added quickly.

"Yes, even that." Ehomba took a long, deep breath. "I am sorry, Loswee. For you and for your people. But it is not like you are unused to moving."

"It never gets easier," the Swick soldier told him. "But if there is nothing you can do, there is nothing you can do. These Elders and I will convey your response to the rest of the Council." Behind him, the senior Swick genuflected once again. They had spoken, and having had their say, now added not a word. "Finish your meal," Loswee advised as he turned away.

This the visitors proceeded to do: Ahlitah quietly, Simna without a thought, and Ehomba with perhaps one or two—but they were fleeting. He could not change the world, and in actual fact had no desire to try.

If their hosts in general or Loswee in particular held any resentment against the travelers for their refusal to help in the endless ongoing battle against their nemesis, they did not show it. The rest of the day was spent touring other parts of the remarkable underground complex and in learning more of Swick culture. It was ancient but not widely known, in large part because of the perpetrators' secretive style of living.

"There are other dunes in other desert parts of the world where our distant relations thrive," Loswee informed them, "and the human beings who live in close proximity to those dunes are completely unaware of our presence nearby. They see tracks in the sand, but the tracks are those of the birds and other animals we make use of."

"You are a very resourceful people," Ehomba admitted respectfully.

"Yes," declared Loswee with pride. "Our lands have always been safe from all trespass except that of the Dunawake, though I fear that someday this may change."

"Why's that?" inquired Simna, only half interested.

Loswee turned quite serious. "Humans have a great love for lamps, and our land floats on the liquid they use to fill them. I am afraid that one day they may come to take it, smashing down the dunes and trampling the plants in the ravines and wadis."

Ehomba looked up at the sand ceiling overhead. "Not these dunes," he commented reassuringly. "They are too big, and this land is too remote."

"I hope you are right, my friend." Loswee sighed, the diminutive exhalation comical in the enclosed space, like the wheezing of a mouse. "I am more sorry than I can say that you are not the magician we had hoped for."

"So am I." It cost Ehomba nothing to agree. Sympathy was cheap.

"I know that you must be on your way." The tiny fighter summoned up a smile. Given the width of his mouth, it nearly split his broad, flat face in half. "At least you have had the chance to experience Swick hospitality. That is a treat few human beings have enjoyed."

"We are grateful." As a courtesy, Ehomba dipped his head slightly. "We will take away good memories with us."

"And I, if not the Elders, will remember you fondly." It seemed impossible that Loswee's smile could grow any wider, but it did, defying the boundaries of his face. "Tomorrow morning I myself will conduct you back outside, and show you the easiest way to the north. Follow my directions, and you will not find yourselves pinched by the dunes and having to slog your way through sand. There is a particularly wide and flat gulch that runs all the way through this country. Keep your feet on it always and you will soon find yourselves once more in a land of green trees and running water."

"How far from there to the nearest river or seaport?" Ehomba asked him.

Loswee spread his small hands apologetically. "That I can't tell you. We Swick keep to the sand country, where we can live in peace and solitude among our dunes. Not all people are as understanding or kindly toward others as yourselves. Believe it or not, there are some who like to hurt anything and anyone who is smaller than themselves simply because they can."

"The world is full of bullies," Ehomba agreed. "I understand your desire to maintain your privacy. When people are squabbling over nothing, as often seems to be the case, I myself prefer the company of cattle."

"Tomorrow, then." Loswee backed away. "Sleep well, my friends, and dream of Swick choirs singing back the stars."

XXIII

THE TRAVELERS AWOKE REFRESHED AND RELAXED, READY TO resume their interrupted trek northward. After a final, sumptuous breakfast, Loswee himself escorted them away from the inner castle, through the rest of the town, and into the main tunnel that led to the world outside.

After the time they had spent underground, the unfiltered directness of the desert sun stung their eyes. They had to retreat back into the tunnel and reemerge gradually. It took almost half an hour before their eyes could once more handle the harsh clarity of the blue sky and the sun reflecting off the surrounding dune faces.

There was no shaking of hands as was the custom in Simna's homeland, nor clasping of forearms in the fashion of the Naumkib and related peoples, nor even licking of faces as was common among Ahlitah's feline tribe. Loswee simply raised a hand in farewell, then turned on his bird and rode back toward the tunnel that led to the wondrous subterranean world of the Swick.

But not before leading them around the base of the great

dune whose unsuspected secret was the flourishing inner community it concealed. There, radiating out from a small salt pan, three waterless meanderings wandered off in search of the far distant sea. Pointing to the one in the middle, Loswee informed them that if they followed it, not only would it broaden into a wide, easily hiked desert highway, but eventually it would lead them into greener and more populated country. From there they would doubtless have better luck finding the oceanic transportation they sought.

Towing their diminished but still significant water supply behind them, they thanked the diminutive Swick warrior before starting off in the indicated direction. True to his word, the narrow wadi soon expanded into a sun-blasted, relatively gravel-free promenade that promised easy access to wherever it led.

By late afternoon, enough clouds had gathered to provide some surcease from the intolerant sun. This was not enough to assuage the mood of the valiant swordsman, who without anything specific to complain about was feeling decidedly peckish.

"If we were back among the Swick it'd be lunchtime about now." Adjusting his pack so that it rode a little higher on his shoulders, he squinted at the cloud-masked sky.

From his position in the lead, Ehomba looked back at his companion. "Would you have ever left? I was afraid that we had overstayed our welcome as it was."

"Of course I would've left, bruther. The food was good, for sure, but the appearance of the local ladies was not only a tad gruesome for my taste, they were also most proportionately incommodious."

The herdsman was left shaking his head. "What a wastrel you are, Simna ibn Sind. You have built nothing with your life."

"As opposed to you, with your nagging cattle and daggy

sheep? If that's a legacy for a man to be proud of, I'll take cinnamon."

"Excess!" Ehomba actually raised his voice slightly. "Your
life is all about excess, Simna. Useless, wasting, scattergood
excess."

"And yours is about nothingness, Etjole. Empty, barren,
sterile nothingness!"

"Barren and sterile, is it? I have a most beautiful wife, and
two handsome, strong children to care for me in my old age."

Simna would no more back down from a verbal challenge
than from a physical one. "And when I claim my share of
treasure I'll buy a harem to care for me, and guards, and the
best physicians. That I'll enjoy while you toss and rot as old
women chant lamentations over your withered, dying body."

"You may be right about that," Ehomba conceded, "but
therein lies a difference between us."

"And what's that?" riposted the swordsman belligerently.

Ehomba held his head high. "Having already acquired my
treasure, I have neither the need nor the desire to claim another."

"What treasure?" Simna made a face. "Your 'beautiful
wife'? I've had, and will have, dozens, hundreds more of the
most beautiful. Gold, you know, herdsman, is the most potent
aphrodisiac of all."

"It will not bring you love," Ehomba shot back.

"Hoy! Love!" The swordsman laughed aloud. "Highly
overpriced as well as overrated. Keep your love, bruther, and
I'll have my harem."

"That is where you are wrong, Simna. If you are not careful, *it* will have *you*." Angry, he lengthened his stride, forcing
the stubbier swordsman to have to hurry to keep up with him.

"Is that so?" Simna really had no idea what his companion
meant by the comment but was unwilling to leave him the last
word. "I can tell you from experience that—"

"Scat on your experience! Be *quiet*!" Having viewed the

entire argument with jaundiced detachment, Ahlitah had lifted his great maned head high into the clear, overheated air and was listening intently. Ehomba and Simna immediately put their discussion on hold as they tried to detect whatever it was that had alarmed the big cat.

For alarmed he was, or at the very least, suddenly wary. It was manifest in his posture: every muscle tense, every sense alert. Both men looked around uneasily but could see nothing out of the ordinary. A lizard with unusually broad, flat feet scampered up the face of a dune to get away from them. White-breasted dragonebs circled on silent wings high overhead, hoping and waiting for one or more of the party to drop. Isolated insects buzzed about the fragmentary plants that clung to the dry ravine or fought the fringes of encroaching dunes. There was no noise, not a sound, as if the very constituents of the air itself had stopped moving. The stillness was as profound as stone.

Then a slight breeze picked up, ruffling the paralysis. The world, after momentarily holding its breath, seemed set in motion again. For an instant, Simna would not have been surprised to see one of the violent corkscrew storms they had battled on the veldt emerge from hiding behind one of the towering dunes. But all that showed itself was a pair of iridescent blue butterflies with white wing spots, flitting and fluttering about a common axis of anticipated procreation. That, and the slightly darker-hued sand that was blowing around the far corner of the dune on their left.

Except—far more sand was sifting from west to east than the barely perceptible breeze should have been capable of moving.

It was the color of powdered rust, stained with a hint of decay. Yellow blotches appeared here and there as the sand drift continued to increase. Now a small ridge a foot or two high where it was emerging from behind the motionless bulk of the other dune, it continued to pile up across the wadi. The first scouting grains had already crossed completely to the other side, leaving behind a rising, widening seam of dark reddish sand.

Ahlitah continued to sample the air, but it was Ehomba who called a halt. "That is odd."

A frustrated Simna was searching their immediate surroundings for a nonexistent danger. "What is?"

"That rising ridge of sand." The herdsman pointed.

Simna glanced distractedly at the unthreatening maroon granules that were drifting across their path. "I see a line of blowing sand. Nothing odd about that."

"Not in and of itself, no." The herdsman gripped his spear a little tighter. "But by its actions it heralds an approaching darkness. Not an eromakadi, an eater of light that can only be slain by an eromakasi, but some kind of more physical, less subtle relation."

"Hoy, what are you jabbering about, long bruther?" What he could not see made Simna more nervous than any visible opponent, no matter how menacing.

Adding to the swordsman's discomfort, Ehomba took a step backward, acting for all the world as if he were actually retreating from something. "The reddish sand advances—but the sand in front of it and across from it does not move." He glanced meaningfully at his friend. "Since when does the air select its wind-borne freight with such care?"

Simna's expression contorted as he mulled over his companion's words—and suddenly he saw the blowing, drifting red sand in a new light. It was true, only the sand the color of rust rushed and rambled across the width of the wadi. Before it and behind it, not a grain was stirring. That was peculiar, all right.

It was also more than a little frightening.

"Maybe we'd better go back." He had already started backing up. "Loswee's directions aside, there must be another way north. One that doesn't involve confronting animate sands."

Retreating, he bumped into the litah's behind. But the great at did not growl at him. He was holding his ground, facing ack the way they had come.

"I'm afraid it's too late for that, man." A rising breezed irred his jet black mane.

A second stream of reddish sand was whisking across the avine behind them, cutting off their only retreat. Simna aped at the steady flow and the rising dike it was creating.

"For Grentoria's sake, it's only sand! A man could still lear it in a single bound!"

"Maybe," Ehomba conceded, "if all it did was continue to low from west to east." Turning, he gestured sharply with e toothed tip of his spear. "That way, quickly! Up the side f the dune!" Obeying his own words, he started up the slick, ifficult slope. Glancing methodically from left to right, Ahli- h followed, his broad footpads having an easier time with e difficult terrain than the sandaled human.

Simna trailed behind, cursing with every step the sand that lid away beneath his feet and made upward progress a stren- ous ordeal. Seeing that the mysterious wall of red sand was ow ten feet high at either end of the gulch and still rising elped to spur him on.

They were halfway up the side of the accommodating dune hen the sky began to darken and a voice boomed behind em. It was the lament of something that was less than a east and more than a natural phenomenon, the unnaturally rawn-out moan of a fiend most monstrous and uncommon. Vith their feet planted ankle deep in the sand the fleeing trav- lers turned, and saw at last what had so subtly tried to am- ush them by trapping them within the ravine.

It looked for all the world (or any other) like just another une.

Except it was taller, and darker. Angry-red darker. And it dvanced not in the manner of a living creature, but in the ashion of dunes, by shifting that which composed its near

side forward, so that it in turn pulled the center. The cente
drew the rear portion forward, rolling on over the middle, an
so continuing the cycle. Back become middle become from
like a slow wheel spinning about a central axis; endless, eter
nal, indomitable.

It had no arms and then a hundred, no feet but one that wa
as wide as the base of the advancing dune itself, like the grea
lumbering foot of some muscular mollusk. Everywhere an
all of it was sand, dark red like all the rust that had ever af
flicted all the metals of the world rolled and bunched an
squeezed up together into a single swiftly shifting pyramid o
revenge. Loswee had spoken of roaring dunes, and indee
there were some such in Ehomba's own country. But neve
before had he heard of, or encountered, a dune that howle
and moaned and bellowed like some sky-scraping banshe
unwillingly fastened to the Earth.

And in the midst of all that displaced geologic fury, two
thirds of the way up the face of the oncoming mountain, wer
two eyes. An abyssal, lambent red, they pulsed like fires fron
deep within the sand, inclined forty-five degrees in opposit
directions, and focused fixedly on the three fleeing traveler
Why they, foreigners in a foreign land, should inspire suc
rage and determination on the part of the Dunawake, none o
the three could say. Perhaps the monster raved and raged fron
a deep-seated need to exterminate whatever life it encoun
tered within the dunes, no matter its origin.

Already, several small mammals and reptiles had bee
caught and smothered beneath the advancing skirt of sand, to
slow or too blinded by blowing particles to flee in time. Th
same fate now threatened those trying to scramble clear of it
reach. Blasts of maroon sand stung their backs while granula
tendrils clawed at their legs. High on the face of an indiffer
ent, inanimate dune, they were temporarily safe as long a
they stayed above and ahead of the abomination's advance.

But the Dunawake was bigger than the dune they wer

limbing. If it continued to flow forward it would eventually
engulf the sandy prominence, overwhelming both it and them.
Ehomba knew the far side would provide no refuge. Not when
their abrasive pursuer could send arms of sand racing around
the base of the dune whose summit they were about to reach.
They were trapped. They could only continue to climb until
they reached the top, there to wait until the steady advance of
the Dunawake overwhelmed them on their final perch.

Struggling upward as his sandaled feet sank inches deep
and more into the unstable slope, Simna drew his sword and
slashed repeatedly at the thin red tendrils that were clutching
at his legs. As he cut and hacked away, handfuls of sand went
flying in all directions. What held them together, what made
of tiny individual particles a coherent and persistent entity, he
could not imagine. Who would have thought that unadulterated rant would make so effective a glue?

For every clutching sandy offshoot he scattered, another
crept upward to take its place. Noting the dispersing effect of
his methodical, skillful sword strokes, he felt he could eventually cut the Dunawake down to size. Why, at the rate his
sword was strewing sand to left and right, the monster would
run out of granules with which to form grasping tendrils in
not less than a couple of million years! Unfortunately, his arm
was already growing tired.

Sorely vexed by the streamers of sand that flogged his
heels, Ahlitah whirled repeatedly to bite at the sinuous red tormentors, pulverizing them within his massive jaws. But biting
and spitting were ultimately no more effective than Simna's
sword-work. Furthermore, with each snap the great cat had to
spit out a mouthful of hot, red sand. He would have much preferred to battle an opponent with some taste.

"The sword!" Sweating profusely as he struggled up the
tenacious incline, Simna yelled at his tall companion. "Use
the sword of sky metal and blow this Dunawake to bits!"

Looking back down at his friend, Ehomba shouted above

the advancing shriek of animate sand treading corybantical
upon itself. "It will not work! I can fight wind with wind, b
rock and soil and sand are a weightier proposition."

"Try!" With an effort more of will than of muscle, th
swordsman used some of his rapidly failing strength to acce
erate upward, until he was standing alongside his frien
Wind squeezed forward by the advancing Dunawake tore
their garments and wilded their hair. "If you can't beat i
maybe enough wind in its face will discourage it."

They were nearly to the top. "Feeding the wind off a dur
face only encourages it. Its strength lies in its coherence. Yc
have seen how it may be cut and broken on the sword."

"Hoy!" Simna agreed as they reached the crest of the dur
together. Ahlitah turned and snarled, mane streaming bacl
ward in the hot, stifling wind, defying the elements both na
ural and unnatural. "And if Gupjolpa would give me te
thousand swordsmen we'd beat it back as surely as this hot a
scours my flesh. But there are only two, me and thee, and yo
won't fight."

"I did not say that." Having swung his backpack around
rest against his chest, the herdsman was busy within i
depths. "I suggested that it was futile to use the sword."

Simna looked back and down. Already the raw red sand o
the Dunawake was three-quarters of the way up the side o
their inadequate asylum and climbing fast. "Well you had be:
find something to use, by Gostoko, or in minutes we'll all th
three of us be good and buried, leaving nothing behind but ol
memories."

"Ah." Straightening, Ehomba withdrew something fro
the interior of the pack. Simna's hopefulness was replaced b
disbelieving eyes and lowered jaw. In his right hand his goo
friend, his resourceful friend, his knowledgeable friend
held—a rotund, stoppered clay flask smaller than his fist. .
single thin cord secured the rubber stopper to a ring carved i
the side of the bottle.

The swordsman struggled to remain calm. "Poison?" he inquired hopefully. "You're going to poison it?"

"Do not be an idiot." Closing up his pack to keep out the swirling sand, Ehomba turned to face the rising, oncoming bulk of the Dunawake. Absently he juggled the clay bottle up and down in his open palm. "You cannot poison sand. I told you, to affect it you must impact its integrity."

"With that?" Simna gestured at the bottle with his free hand. "Well then, by Gwipta, what's in the pharking phial if ot poison?"

Ehomba did not take his eyes off the oncoming Dunawake or the tide of red granules that would soon be lapping at their feet. Behind them, more rivers of red sand were creeping up he backside of the dune, further extirpating any lingering hope of flight.

"Whater," he replied simply.

Striving to retreat farther, Simna found himself slipping down the eastern, back face of their dune. "Water?" he mumbled, more like a drowning man than a moribund one.

"No." Ehomba gestured at the pond remnant Ahlitah had dragged up the dune face with them. "That's water. This is vhater."

Feeling more than a little taste of panic in his mouth, the baffled swordsman looked on as the herdsman carefully removed the stopper from the clay flask. The crest of the red dune was now very close to overtopping and swamping the dune on which the travelers stood. The glowing, fiery eyes had slipped up the face of the oncoming mountain so that they were now nearly level with Ehomba. Sliding farther down the backside of the crest, Simna bumped into the litah. The big cat snarled at him but held his ground, using his much greater weight and all four feet to keep them from tumbling down the steeper, unstable slope.

Above, they saw the herdsman lower the point of his spear and rap the bottle sharply against it once, twice. The clay

cracked but did not come apart. Then Ehomba drew back hi
right arm and threw the fractured container directly into th
face of the swollen, howling Dunawake. As he did so, th
shattered bottle came apart, its contents spilling onto the hiss
ing red sand. Simna strained to see, but it looked like the bo
tle contained nothing more than a swallow or two of water. C
whater, as his friend had insisted.

A mammoth curl of sand rose high, higher than the dun
peak, pausing before surging forward to crush the stoic herds
man and his companions beneath its hot, smothering weigh
And then a strange thing happened. Simna, for one, was no
surprised. He had already had occasion to observe that in mo
ments of difficulty, strange things had a tendency to transpir
in Etjole Ehomba's vicinity, and that at such times it was
good idea to be on the herdsman's beneficent side.

The unimaginable tons of sand that comprised the malevo
lent structure of the Dunawake began to shiver.

XXIV

It was a most peculiar sight, to see sand shiver. First the dune face and then the entire scarlet mass commenced to tremble, shaking and quaking and shuddering in place. Ahlitah's lower jaw fell, revealing huge canines in a gape of amazement instead of threat. Simna stared grimly, wondering how his tall friend had managed to freeze an entire dune with one tiny bottle of water. Only it was not water, he reminded himself. It was whater, whatever that might be.

But he was wrong. The Dunawake was not freezing, not turning from sand to ice or anything comparable. What it was doing was coming apart, shaking itself to pieces. How something that was already composed of billions of tiny grains could come to pieces was yet another wonder that the awestruck Simna had no time to ponder.

What was happening before their eyes was that the Dunawake was shivering itself into its individual components. A small dune of pure quartz began to rise alongside a sibling dune of feldspar. Next to them a glistening cone of mica rose from the desert floor, and beside it granulated black schist heaped up in dark profusion. There were other colors and cones, stacks and mounds, to which Simna could not put a name. Their identities did not matter to him. What was important was that none of them moved, and none glared up at him out of baleful, pulsing red eyes.

The once fearsome Dunawake continued to tremble and quiver until it had shaken itself apart. Where it had once loomed there now rose a dozen separate dunes far more modest in size, each composed of a single different, unadulterated mineral. The herdsman's companions climbed the short distance back up the east face of the dune from where they had sought refuge to rejoin their friend.

Thin as a stick stuck in a child's mud pile, tall and straight as a tree rooted in the depths of the earth, Ehomba was standing at the very apex of the yellow dune staring down at the disassociated remnants of the Dunawake. Wind whipped his shirt and the hem of his kilt. Had he suddenly raised his arms to the sky and drawn down lightning from nothingness Simna would not have been surprised. Nothing of the sort happened, of course. As the subject of the swordsman's stare would have been the first to remind him, he was nothing but a simple herdsman.

Coming up alongside him, Simna grabbed his friend's arm as together they gazed downward. "Tell me now you're no sorcerer, Etjole Ehomba. Tell me now to my face that you're not a man who can work magicks!"

"Sorry to disappoint you yet again, friend Simna, but I am not." Lips firm, jaw set, the laconic southerner looked down at his disbelieving companion.

"Oh, I see. And how, then, do you explain what you just did?" He nodded at the dozen or so new, unalloyed dunes that rose from the desert floor below where they stood.

"That was not me," the other man protested humbly. "It was the whater that did that."

"Perhaps we would understand better," Ahlitah put in from behind him, "if you told us what this 'whater' is? Or was."

Ehomba nodded agreeably. "Before I set out on this journey, the women of my village gave me several things to carry with me, to help me along the way. Old Fhastal, clever Likulu, bright-eyed Omura; even my own woman, Mirhanja, helped. It is a tradition among the Naumkib that when a warrior leaves for any length of time, the women get together to bundle useful items for him to take with him." His gaze angled downward once more, toward the remnants of the Dunawake. "Sadly, that was my only bottle of whater." He started down the dune, positioning his body sideways as he descended, the better to balance himself against the shifting sand.

Simna simply walked straight down, paralleling his friend and exhibiting the remarkable physical poise of which he was capable. The four-footed Ahlitah, of course, had no trouble at all with the steep slope. Not nearly as agile as his companions, Ehomba stumbled several times in the course of the descent.

"This whater," the cat asked, "what does it do?" The maned head nodded tersely in the direction of the neatly disassociated dunes. "What *did* it do?"

"It was for purifying water." Ehomba stepped over a rock that protruded from the lower dune face. "The women say that one drop of whater will make an entire basin of water fit for drinking. It purifies liquid by separating out all the dirt and scum and little bugs we cannot see from the water itself."

A much puzzled Simna wore a deep frown. " 'Little bugs we cannot see'?"

Herdsman and cat ignored him.

"So that's what you did to the Dunawake," Ahlitah mused aloud. "You 'purified' it."

"Into its individual parts." They were almost down, stepping back onto the hard, unyielding, blissfully motion-free bed of the ravine where the monstrous apparition had almost had them trapped. "In this instance, the sum of the parts is much less than the whole. A man would be no less," he added thoughtfully, "if he were similarly purified. Skeleton here, blood there, muscles in one pile, and organs in another."

Simna's mouth twisted. "Now there's a pretty picture. Remind me not to go sampling the contents of any other bottles you happen to be carrying."

"That was my only whater." Ehomba gestured at the half-full floating pond Ahlitah continued to tow. "We had better hope we always find good water from now on, because I have nothing left with which to launder the undrinkable."

"You did the right thing, Etjole. By Girimza, you did!" The swordsman clapped his friend reassuringly on the back. "Clean water's no good to a corpse."

"Hold up." Ahlitah lifted a paw and sniffed the air. "We are still not alone here."

Startled, Simna reached instinctively for his sword even though it had proven ineffectual against their last opponent. Then he relaxed. Relaxed, even though he was no less disconcerted.

Ehomba handled the unexpected confrontation with his usual sangfroid, smiling and nodding at the figure that now blocked their path.

"Hello, Loswee. I did not expect to see you again."

As the Swick's feathered mount advanced toward the travelers, a dozen other miniature mounted warriors trotted out from their place of concealment behind a pile of sand-swept rocks. Brightly tinted pennants flew from the tips of their lances, and they were clad in decorative ceremonial armor.

Leaning forward in his saddle, Loswee stared at the travelers for a long moment before sitting back and gesturing at something behind them. "For not-a-magician you seem to have not-dealt pretty well with the is-no-more Dunawake."

"It wasn't him," Simna interjected sarcastically. "It was just a bottle of whater that did that."

"Thum," murmured the Swick fighter. "It would be pointless for me to argue with you about your true natures. The People of the Sands do not care. What matters is that the Dunawake is done and the dreadful, persistent threat of it has been removed. For this deed you will live forever in the hearts of the Swick. One last time, I salute you."

He raised his lance as high as if he wished to pierce the sky itself. Behind him, his resplendent escort echoed the gesture. Five times they did this, each time giving forth a piercing ululation that seemed to rise up from the depths of the surrounding sand itself. Then they turned to go.

"Strange the ways of coincidence, is it not?" Ehomba watched the long tail feathers of the warriors' mounts bob up and down as they filed back behind the rocks from where they had emerged.

"What?" A bemused Simna turned to look up at his friend. "What coincidence?"

With a sigh, the herdsman started forward, formally resuming their trek northward and using his spear for support, like a tall walking stick. "The little people wanted us to fight the Dunawake for them. We refused, and so after wining and dining us they graciously bid us on our way. They even told us the easiest way to go to reach the lands to the north. Told us even though we did not ask directions from them. Soon after leaving, we run right into the Dunawake." Glancing over at the swordsman, he did something Simna had not seen him do very often. He laughed aloud: not only with his mouth, but with his eyes.

"Face it, my friend. We have been played the way a master musician plays his flute."

Simna's expression darkened. "Are you telling me, bruther . . . ?"

"That we have been the victims of a Swick trick." And the herdsman chortled afresh.

Realization landed on the swordsman like the news of an

unwanted pregnancy. "Why, those miserable little, lying-lipped, arse-mouthed, flat-faced fuggers!" Raising his voice, eyes wild, Simna drew his sword and rushed toward the pile of rocks where the diminutive warriors had disappeared. "I'll kill you all! I'll cut off your hairy ears and feed them to the scorpions!"

With an indifferent snuffle, Ahlitah changed direction until he was pacing the long-striding Ehomba. "He doesn't get it, does he?"

The herdsman shrugged diffidently. "Simna's a good man. He is just a little impulsive."

"A little too human, you mean." The big cat sniffed derisively. The penetrating yellow eyes of a great feline predator peered into Ehomba's face from only a foot away. Hunting, searching. "And you?"

The herdsman pursed his lips. "I do not follow you."

"What are you, Etjole Ehomba? Are you all human? Or is this a mask you choose to wear to fool the rest of us? I am thinking that the Swick are not the only ones who are good at tricks."

The rangy southerner smiled comfortingly as he poled the hard ground with the butt of his long spear the way a sailor would dig his paddle into water. "I am only a man, Ahlitah. I am only what you see here walking beside you."

"I will accept that—for now." With that, the litah moved away, the hovering pond bobbing along behind him as he put a little distance between them. Ehomba watched him with interest. For one who slept as long and often as the litah, very little escaped the big cat's notice.

Simna ranted and raged among the rocks for only a moment or two before resigning himself to the fact that his intended quarry had fled. More than fled, they had disappeared, utterly vanished from sight. Even the footprints of their mounts had evaporated like mist in the desert air. Muttering

o himself as he resheathed his sword, he rejoined his companions.

"The little buggers are fast, but I didn't think they were that
fast." He shook an angry fist at the dunes and wadi behind
them. "What I wouldn't give for one small gray neck under
my fingers!"

"Yes, they are fast." Ahlitah's black lower lip curled upward. "That'd make it a quick slick Swick trick, wouldn't it?"

"Oh, shut up, you imprecise venter of stinking bodily flu-
ids!"

Still grinning in its sly cat fashion, the litah did not respond.

"They did what they felt was necessary for their survival."
Ehomba tried to mollify his companion.

"Their survival?" The swordsman jabbed a thumb into his
chest. "They didn't give a sparrow's fart for *our* survival!"

"The grand welcome they gave us, mere passing strangers.
The escorts and the tours, the singing and the feasts, giving
freely, even extravagantly, of their food and drink. Did you
think that was all done out of impulsive friendship?"

Simna's anger dissipated as he considered the herdsman's
words. Eventually, he nodded agreement. "Yes, you're right,
Etjole. I, of all people, should have known better. I suppose it
was their size that fooled me. Who would have guessed that
their appetite for treachery was as great as their ability to
build structures out of sand?" With that admission the last of
his fury fled as effortlessly as it had originally consumed him,
and he was his old self again.

"Clever little dumplings, weren't they? I'll know better
next time. From now on I, Simna ibn Sind, won't accept hospitality from a mouse without first questioning its ulterior mo-
tives."

"I understand why they did what they did."

The swordsman glanced up at his friend. "You take their
side? 'What they did' nearly got us killed!"

"I know. But if it was my village at stake, my family, all my
friends, everyone I had ever known, I would also do whatever
was necessary to save it. At such times, under such circumstances, expediency always takes precedence over honor."

Simna drew himself up to his full height. "For a true hero
nothing takes place over honor!"

"Then you can be the hero, Simna. I want only to discharge
my obligation and return as quickly as possible to my family
and to my village. That is what is important to me. That is
what I have built my life around. Not abstract notions of what
may or may not be considered acceptable behavior among
those I do not care for and do not know." He nodded back the
way they had come, back toward the silent dunes and their
sand-locked, unseen mysteries. "That is how the Swick believe. I cannot condemn them for acting exactly as I would
have under similar circumstances."

The swordsman snorted. "Then you'll never be a hero,
Etjole. You'll never ride in triumph through the streets of a
great city, acknowledging the acclamation of the crowd and
the eyes of pretty women. You'll never be a noble in your own
land, much less a king lording it over others."

The lanky southerner was not in the least offended by his
companion's dismissive summation. "I have no desire to lord
it over even my children, friend Simna. As for drawing the
eyes of pretty women, I have never thought myself the type to
do so, and would not know how to react if I did. Besides, I already have the eyes of the one woman who means anything to
me. As for riding through the streets of a great city, I am content to walk, and am satisfied in place of cheers to receive the
occasional 'Good morning' and 'How are you?' These things
are enough for me."

"You have no ambition, bruther," the swordsman groused
at him.

"On the contrary, my friend, my aspirations are considerable. I desire greatly to live a long and healthy life in the com-

pany of my woman, to see my children raised up strong and of kindly mien, to have always, or at least most of the time, enough to eat, to continue to be able to watch over my animals, to enjoy the company of my friends and relations, and to walk once again along the edge of the sea, listening to its song and smelling of its perfume." His eyes glistened. "That, I think, should be enough for any man." Slipping his free hand into a pocket, he felt of the pebble-filled cloth bag there, wondering how much of the sea-smell still clung to the shiny rock fragments.

They walked in silence for some time before a wide grin came to dominate the swordsman's face, wiping out the indifference that had been extant there. "Hoy, now I see." He shook his head and guffawed delightedly. "Oh, you're good, good it is you are, Etjole Ehomba! You had me going for a while there. It's a clever, clever magician you are, but you can't fool me! Not Simna ibn Sind. I've been tested in the marketplaces of wily Harquarnastan, and gone toe-to-toe with the shrewd and shifty barkers of the Yirt-u-Yir plateau. But I'll grant you this: You're the subtlest and sneakiest of the lot!" He executed a joyful little pirouette, dancing out the delight of his personal revelation. Ahlitah looked on with distaste.

" 'Have enough to eat.' 'Walk along the edge of the sea.' Oh surely, sorcerer, surely! As a cover it's brilliant, as a mask unsurpassed. No one will think anything more of you, humble master of steer and sheep that you are. What a masquerade! Better than pretending to be a merchant, or storyteller, or unoffending pilgrim." While walking backward in the direction they were headed, he executed several mock bows, making a dance of it as he repeatedly raised and lowered his head and his outstretched arms.

"I concede to you the title Wizard of the Incognito, o masterful one! Herder of goats and sovereign of infants; that shall be your designation until the treasure is ours." Resuming his normal gait, he fell in step alongside his friend while Ahlitah padded along opposite. "You *almost* had me fooled, Etjole."

"Yes," the herdsman responded with a heartfelt sigh, "I can see that you are not a man to be easily deceived." He focused on a lizard that was scampering into a burrow off to their left. It was blue, with bright pink stripes and a yellow-spotted head.

"Just so long as you realize that," Simna replied importantly. "Hoy, but I'll be glad to get out of this desert!"

"The desert, the cleanness and the dunes, is all beautiful."

"Speak for yourself, devotee of dry nowheres."

"Yes."

Lifting his head, the litah let loose with a long, mournful *owrooooo*. It echoed back and forth among the dune slopes, escaping their sandy surroundings far faster than could they. When it was finished, the big cat eyed his human companions. "In this I side with the swordsman. I love tall grass and shady thickets, running water and lots of fat, slow animals."

"Then why are we lingering here?" A cheerful, composed Simna looked over at the great black feline. "So this long-faced drink of dark water can set the pace? If we let him determine it, we'll find ourselves dawdling in this accursed country until the end of time." With that he broke into a jog, stepping easily and effortlessly out in front of the others.

Despite the burden imposed by the hovering pond he was towing, Ahlitah stretched out his remarkable cheetah-like legs and matched the man's pace effortlessly. Ehomba watched them for a moment before extending his own stride. It would be useless to tell them that he had wanted to move faster all along, but had held himself back out of concern for their welfare. It was better this way, he knew. Healthier for Simna to have made the decision.

He did not smile at the way events had progressed. There was no particular gratification in knowing all along what was going to happen.

XXV

The Tale of the Lost Tree

THE TREE DID NOT REMEMBER MUCH OF WHAT HAD HAPPENED, or even when it had happened. It was all so very long ago. It had been nothing more than a sapling, a scrawny splinter of wood only a few feet high, with no girth to shield it from the elements, no thick layer of tough bark to protect it from marauding browsers.

Despite that, it had thrived. The soil in which it had taken root as a seed was deep and rich, the weathered kind, with ample rain and not too much snow. It had neither frozen in winter nor burned in summer. Though it lost leaves to hungry insects, this was a normal, natural part of maturing, and it compensated by putting out more leaves than any of the other saplings in its immediate vicinity. As a consequence of insect infestation, several of the others died before they could become more than mere shoots.

The tree did not. It survived, in company with several of its neighbors. In spite of the fact that they had all taken root at the same time, two of them were taller. Others were smaller.

Growth was a never-ending struggle as they all strove to

gain height and diameter. Though ever-present and neve
ceasing, competition from others of their kind was silent, a
was the nature of trees. In its fourth year one of its neighbor
fell prey to hungry deer during a particularly long and col
winter. They stripped the bark from the young growth, leav
ing it naked and unprotected, and when spring next cam
around it was easy prey for boring beetles. Another suc
cumbed to the benign but deadly attentions of a bear with a
itch. Scratching itself against the youthful bole, it snapped i
in half, leaving it broken and dying, its heartwood exposed t
the callous, indifferent elements.

But this tree was lucky. Large animals left it alone, insect
found others in the vicinity more to their liking, birds chose
not to strip its young twigs for nest-building material. Every
spring it budded fiercely, fighting to throw out new leaves an
to photosynthesize sugars before they could be consumed
Every winter it lay dormant and still, hoping the migratin
herds would leave it alone.

Then, just when survival and long life seemed assured, dis
aster struck.

It happened late in autumn and took the form not of any
thing with blood in its veins but of a vast and powerful storm
The terrifying weather swept up the coast of the land where
the tree grew, destroying everything in its path that was un
able to resist. Even some of the great old trees that formed the
bulk of the forest mass where the tree lived were not immune
Unprecedented winds roared down off the slopes of the west
ern mountains, descending like an invisible avalanche. As
they fell, the winds picked up speed and volume.

Trees that had stood for a thousand years were blown over
their roots left exposed and naked to the world. Others los
dozens or even hundreds of minor branches and many majo
ones. The forest floor was swept clean as leaves, logs, mush
rooms, insects and spiders, even small animals, were sucked
up and whirled away.

The sapling held fast as long as it could, but its shallow, young roots were no match for the unparalleled violence of the storm. It found itself ripped up into the sky, where it joined the company of thousands of tons of other debris. Since the storm had struck in autumn, the tree had already shut down in anticipation of the coming winter. Sap was concentrated in its heartwood, waiting for the warmth of spring to send it coursing freely once more throughout the length and breadth of the young growth.

Now it was at the mercy of the berserk elements, which tossed and flung it about as if it weighed even less than its slim self. How long it was carried thus, over water and field, mountain and plain, the sapling did not know. It might have been an instant or a month. A tree's sense of time is very different from that of most other living things.

Then it felt itself falling, tumbling crown over root, spiraling toward the ground. Nature is rife with examples of extraordinary accidents, and the fall of the tree was one of those exceptions. It landed not on its side as would have been expected, nor on its crest. It struck the ground with its slender trunk exactly perpendicular to the earth. Bare roots slammed into and partially penetrated the loose-packed surface, giving the tree immediate if uncertain support.

Expelled from the tail end of the swiftly moving storm, the tree shuddered in its farewell gusts but did not fall. The tempest continued on its way, wreaking devastation to the east and leaving the tree behind. It was surrounded by other debris that had been abandoned by the weather, but most of it was dead. That which was not soon died and began to decompose.

Only the tree survived. Along with wind, the storm had contained a great deal of water, which fell along its path as heavy rain. The soil in which the tree had providentially landed upright was now saturated, so much so that the sapling's roots were able to draw from this source for many months after its unwilling transplantation.

Against all odds, its roots took hold in the alien ground. Where winter had been approaching in the tree's homeland, it was summer where it had landed. Sap began to flow well in advance of the date determined by the tree's biological clock. This perturbation also it adapted to. Buds appeared on those branches that had survived the storm's wrath. Leaves sprouted and unfolded wide, drinking in the strong, unobstructed sunlight of their new home.

In this new land there were far fewer insects, and so the tree was able to grow even faster than was normal. Over the years its branches thickened and its trunk put on weight. It spread its arms wide to shade the ground on which it stood. This helped to preserve the rain that fell seasonally and rarely, much more so than in the land where the tree had first sprouted.

But beneath its roots lay a consistent, subterranean supply of water. This the tree tapped with roots that bored deep, assuring it of proper nourishment no matter how infrequent the annual rains. With no other growths in its immediate vicinity, it had no competition for nutrients. Only the sparseness of the land itself kept it from growing to even greater proportions.

Inherently unambitious, over the years and the decades and even the centuries, the sapling flourished and matured into a fine, tall specimen of its species, with numerous major branches and a trunk whose diameter far exceeded that of its parent. As the centuries unfolded, it observed the comings and goings of hundreds of creatures, from small beetles that tried and were unable to penetrate its dense, healthy layer of bark to migrating birds and other flying creatures that found grateful refuge in its branches. Occasionally, intelligent beings would pass by, and pause to enjoy the shade it gave freely, and marvel at its unexpected splendor.

Unexpected, because the tree was alone. Not only were there no other trees of its kind in the vicinity, there were none anywhere in sight. With none of the particular insects that were needed to pollinate its flowers, its seeds did not germinate, and so it was denied the company even of its own offspring. No lowly bushes crowded its base to make use of its protective shade, no flowers blossomed beneath its branches. There were not even weeds. There was only the tree, spectacular in its isolation, alone atop the small hillock on which it grew. An accident of nature had condemned it to eternal hermitage.

But a tree cannot die of loneliness. Every year it put out new leaves, and every year it hoped for the company of its own kind. But there were only visiting insects, and birds, and the occasional small animal, or travelers passing through.

Three such were approaching now, and an odd trio they were. Though it had no eyes, the tree perceived them. Through sensitive roots that grew just beneath the surface it sensed the vibration of their coming. It knew when they increased their pace, and felt when they slowed and stopped beneath it.

Two of the travelers immediately sat down at the base of its trunk, leaning their backs against its staunch solidity. The tree supported them effortlessly, grateful again for some company. Such visitations were rare and welcome. Lately, the tree had come to treasure them even more.

Because it was dying.

Not from senescence, though given its long lineage that would not have been unnatural, or even unexpected. Despite its great age it was still inherently healthy. But its roots had exhausted the soil in the immediate vicinity. Despite the extent and depth to which they probed, they could no longer find enough of the nutrients vital to the tree's continued health. The land in which the tree had taken root so long ago was simply not rich enough to support more than another decade or two of continued healthy life. And with no other vegetation nearby to supply new nutrients through the natural decomposition of leaves and branches and other organic matter, there was nothing to renew the supply the tree had mined when it had been planted atop the small rise by the ancient storm.

So it sat quietly dying and contemplating the world around it. There were no regrets. By rights it should never have reached maturity, much less lived a long and healthy life. Trees were not in the habit of regretting anyway.

It savored the presence of the travelers, silently delighting in the pleasure they took from the shade it provided against the hot sun, the support it gave to their tired, sweaty backs, and the use they made of the seeds that lay scattered all about. Most creatures found those seeds delicious, and these visitors were no exception, though there was one among them who refused absolutely to partake of the free feast. Apparently, despite the protein they contained, such vegetable matter was not to its liking.

No matter. Its companions gorged themselves. What they did not eat on the spot they gathered up and packed away for future consumption. All this activity the tree marked through its receptive roots, glad of active company on a scale it could easily sense. It had been a hale and robust life, but a lonely one.

Unlike many of the tree's visitors, these travelers were among those who employed a language. This was normal, since all motile visitors possessed a means for communicating among themselves. The insects used touch and smell, the birds song and wing, but spoken language was of the most interest to the tree. Sensed by its leaves, the vibrations words produced in the air were always novel and interesting. Though the tree could not understand a single one of them, that never stopped it from trying. It was a diversion, and any diversion in its lonely existence was most welcome.

Taking turns, all three of the travelers urinated near the base of the tree. This gift of water and nitrates was much appreciated, though the tree had no way of thanking the disseminators openly. It tried to provide a breeze where none existed, but succeeded only in motivating a few of its leaves. The travelers did not notice the movement. Even if they had, it's doubtful they would have remarked upon it.

They seemed content with the shade, however, and that pleased the tree. It was happy it could give back some of the pleasure the travelers were providing through their company. Had it a voice, it would have trilled with delight when they decided to spend the night beneath its spreading boughs. Curled up near the trunk, they relaxed around a small fire they built from fallen bits and pieces of the tree itself. The tree felt the heat of the flames but was not afraid. The travelers kept the fire small, and there was nothing around to make it spread.

In the middle of the night one of the visitors rose. Leaving its companions motionless and asleep, it walked a little ways out from their encampment until it stood beneath the very longest of the tree's branches. This pointed like a crooked arrow to the south, which direction the traveler stood facing for a long while. The moon was up, allowing him to view dimly but adequately his surroundings. But he looked only to the south, his stance barely shifting, his gaze never varying.

After what was for his kind a long while but which to the tree was hardly more than an instant, he turned slowly and walked back toward the encampment. But he did not lie back down on the ground. Instead, he walked slowly and contemplatively around the base of the tree, peering up into its numerous branches, studying its leaves. Several times he reached out to feel of the rippling rivulets that gave character to its cloak of heavy bark, caressing them as gently as he might have the wrinkles on an old woman's face.

Then he began to climb.

The tree could hardly contain its joy. The feel of the traveler's weight against its body, the sensation of fingers gripping branches for support, the heavy placement of foot against wood, was something it had never felt before. In all its long and insightful life, no other traveler had thought to ascend into its upper reaches. It relished every new contact, every fresh vibration and touch.

Eventually, the traveler could ascend no higher. Up in the last branches that would support his weight, he paused. Settling himself into a crook between two accommodating boughs, he leaned back, resting his upper back and neck and head against one unyielding surface. With his legs dangling and his hands folded over his belly, he lay motionless, contemplating the moonlit horizon. All his work and effort gained him a perch that allowed him to see only a little farther to the south, but to the traveler this seemed enough.

He spent the night thus, nestled in the upper branches of the hardwood, and it was difficult to say who luxuriated in it more: traveler or tree. When morning came his companions awoke and immediately rushed about in panic, wondering what could have happened to their friend. He let them agitate for a while before announcing himself. They reacted with a mixture of relief and anger, generating vibrations whose meaning was transparent even to the tree. It might have chuckled, had it possessed the means.

They gathered together beneath the heavy boughs to ingest nourishment. This was done in the manner of motile creatures, at incredible speed and with little regard for the pleasure of slow conversion. Careful consumers, they left behind very little in the way of organic scrap that might have nourished the tree. It did not mind. The company they had provided was worth far more to it than a few bits of decayable plant or animal matter.

When they had finished, they gathered up their belongings and struck off to the north. As with every visitor it had ever had, the tree was sorry to see them go. But there was nothing it could do about it. It could not cry out to them to stay just one more night, or wave branches at them in hopes of drawing them again to its base. It could only sit, and meditate, and pass the time, which is one of the things trees do best.

Before departing, each of the travelers had performed an individual farewell. A final gesture, if not of good-bye, then of acknowledgment of the comfort the tree had given them. The largest among them raised a hind leg and made water again, forcing it out at an angle that actually struck high up on the tree's trunk. As before, it was thankful for the small contribution, though it was not nearly enough to provide the quantity of vital nutrients it required for continued healthy life. The second traveler plucked a leaf from a low-hanging branch and placed it in his hair, over one ear, as a decoration.

The one who had spent the night high up in the tree's branches walked up to the base of the trunk and pressed his body against it. Spreading his arms as wide as possible, he squeezed tight against the bark, as if trying to press his much softer substance into the wood. Then he drew back, turned, and rejoined his companions. The tree felt the vibrations of their footsteps fade as they strode off to the north. It tuned itself to its most sensitive rootlets, drinking in the motion of their passage until the last faint trembling of animate weight against earth had gone.

Once more, it was alone.

However, it did not feel the same as before. When the one traveler had pressed himself tight against the trunk it was as if a part of himself had entered into the tree. Xylem and phloem quivered ever so slightly as a subtle transformation began to race through the tree's entire self.

It was as if the solid ground beneath its roots were giving way. Not for hundreds of years had the tree experienced the sensation of falling. But it was doing so now. Whether it was penetrating the ground or the ground was moving away beneath it the living wood had no way of telling. It sensed only that it was descending, not in the manner of a dying tree falling over, which was the only natural kind and style of falling it contained in its cells' memory, but straight down, without damage to branches or leaves.

It fell for what seemed like a very long time. Fell through the soil that had supported it, then through solid rock, and finally through rock that was so hot it was as liquid as water. The tree knew it should have been carbonized, burned to less than a cinder. Miraculously, it was not. It passed on through the region of molten rock as easily as, as a sapling, it had passed through wild, frivolous air.

Still sinking, it reached a region where everything was hot liquid, where the pressure of its surroundings should have crushed and shattered it. Nothing of the kind happened. Instead, it began to rotate, turning slowly, slowly, until it was facing in the exact opposite direction from the one in which it had spent its entire life. Meanwhile, motion never ceased entirely. It continued to sink. Or perhaps now it was rising. Or possibly it had always been rising, or sinking. The tree did not know. It was confused, and bemused, and although it had no means to show such emotion, the sensations were very real to the tree if not to the rest of the world.

Upward it went, or downward. It could not tell, could sense only the movement of motion. Through more of the molten rock, and then through solid stone, until it once again felt the cool, moist embrace of nourishing soil. But it was soil unlike that in which it had grown. Rich soil, thick and loamy, opulent with every kind and sort of nutrient. A veritable feast of a soil.

And then, air. Cool against its leaves, no longer hot and burning. Comforting and damp, encasing each leaf and branch in a diaphanous blanket of invisible humidity. Moving still, rising until the lowest branch was exposed, and lastly the base of the trunk.

Until finally, ascension ceased, leaving it free and exposed to entirely new surroundings. Around it the tree sensed other trees; dozens, hundreds. Smaller growths, and flowers, and grasses in their aggregate profusion. Birds different from those it had known quickly took perch in its outspread branches, and new kinds of animals began to inspect its base. It welcomed even the threatening explorations of active, dangerous insects. Anything that was new, and fresh. If a tree could have been overwhelmed by a surfeit of new sensations, it would have happened then and there.

Except the sensations were not new. Not the atmospheric conditions, not the birds, not the bugs. Certainly not the soil. Not new—simply very old, and all but forgotten. Not quite, though. Trees do not have memory. They *are* memory, in hard wood and soft presence. The tree was no different. It remembered.

This place, this grove: almost destroyed by a once-in-a-thousand-years storm. Renewed now, rejuvenated by time and nature's patience. The tree was back.

It had come home.

How and by what means it could not say, because it had nothing to say with. But it knew, as it knew the air, and the soil, and the vibrant mix of creatures that dwelled in the vicinity. Its wind-borne journey as a sapling had carried it over half the surface of the Earth. In the equally inexplicable course of its return, it had passed through the very center.

Long-starved roots sucked hungrily at the rich, fertile soil, commencing the slow process of replenishing the tree's nutrient-starved cells. In such bountiful surroundings the tree would have no trouble reinvigorating itself. It would not die but would continue to live, perhaps for another hundred years, possibly even longer. For this it did not know whom or what to thank. It knew only that it was going to survive.

Not only in the company of other trees, but trees of its own kind. All around it, hardwoods belonging to the same tribe thrust sturdy trunks skyward and threw out branches to all points of the compass. Birds nested in their boughs and small mammals and reptiles scampered among them. In this forest bees and wasps and bats and birds lived in plenty, more than enough to ensure thorough pollination of any plant that desired to reproduce. The tree would, after all, not die without having given a part of itself over to new life.

Renewed, the tree regretted only one thing, insofar as a tree could have regrets. Somehow, deep within its heartwood, within the solitary spirit that was itself, it knew that everything that had happened, the silent impossibility of it, was all tied in to the final, farewell hug that singular traveler had performed before he and his companions had taken their leave. How mere contact could have initiated the remarkable sequence of events that had led to the tree returning home the tree did not know, but it was the only explanation.

Or perhaps it was not. Refreshed and renewed, it had plenty of time to consider the conundrum, to stand and contemplate. It was the thing that trees did best, and this tree was no exception. If it came into an answer, that would be a good thing. If it did nothing more than continue to stand and grow and put forth leaves and seeds, that would be a good thing too.

It regretted only that it would never see that traveler again, and therefore could not give him a hug back.

XXVI

EHOMBA GLANCED OVER HIS SHOULDER, BUT THEY HAD BEEN walking for some time and there was nothing to see behind them that was not also in front of them. Sand and rock, rock and gravel.

"I still cannot get over that tree." The herdsman stepped over a small gully. "Standing out there all by itself, with nothing else growing around it, not even a blade of grass. And I have never seen that kind of tree before."

"I have." Simna kicked at a small red stone, sending it skipping across the hardpan floor of the wadi down which they were walking. "To the north of my homeland. There are lots of them there. They're nice trees, and as you found out, their nuts are delicious."

"They certainly are," the herdsman readily agreed.

Alongside him, still towing the remnants of their floating pond, Ahlitah snorted. "Omnivores! You'll eat anything."

"Not quite anything," Simna shot back. "I find cat, for example, stringy and tough."

"But why was it there?" Ehomba was reflecting aloud.

"Obviously so far from where its kind of tree normally grows, all alone on top of that small dune? It must have some important meaning."

"It means somebody else traveling through this Gholos-forgotten land dropped a seed or two, and unlikely as it may be, one took root on that knoll." The swordsman was not sympathetic to his tall companion's interest. "You ask too many questions, Etjole."

"That is because I like answers."

"Not every question has an answer, bruther." Simna avoided the disarticulated skeleton of a dead dragonaz. Fragments of wing membrane clung to the long finger bones like desiccated parchment.

Ehomba eyed him in surprise. "Of course they do. A question without an answer is not a question."

The swordsman opened his mouth, started to say something, then closed it, a puzzled look on his face as he continued to stride along. It was early, the sun was not yet at its highest, and the increasing heat disinclined him to pursue the matter further. Not wishing to clutter up the place with another of the herdsman's inexplicable commentaries, he put it clean out of his mind, a process that with much practice he had perfected some time ago.

Days passed without incident. Game began to reappear. Not in profusion, but sufficient to satisfy Ahlitah's appetite as well as that of his less voracious companions. Standing sentinel over abating desert, date, coconut, and ivory nut palms began to appear. Other, smaller flora found protection at the foot of these taller growths.

When the travelers began to encounter otherwise dry riverbeds that boasted small pools in their depths as well as more frequent traditional oases, Ahlitah kicked off the shackles he had been using to tow the remnants of the floating pond. It was nearly drained anyway, and he was tired of the constant drag on his shoulders. Despite the escalating ubiquity of freestanding water, the ever cautious Ehomba argued for keeping the pond with them as long as it contained moisture. For once, Simna was able to stand aside and let his companions argue.

Ahlitah eventually won out, not through force of logic but because he had simply had enough of the ever-present pond. Simna watched with interest to see if the herdsman would employ some striking, overpowering magic to force the big cat to comply, but in this he was disappointed. Ehomba simply shrugged and acceded to the cat's insistence. If he was capable of compelling the litah, he showed no sign of being willing to do so. Simna didn't know whether to be disappointed or not.

They continued on. Once, when water had been scarce for several days, Ehomba muttered something to the big cat about performing reckless acts in unknown countries. Ahlitah snarled a response and moved away. But this scolding ended the next morning when they found a new water hole. Fringed by bullrushes and small palms, it offered shade as well as water once they had shooed away the small diving birds and nutrias.

After that, Ehomba said nothing more about water and the need to conserve it. This left Simna sorely conflicted. If the herdsman really was an all-powerful wizard traveling incognito, why would he let himself lose an argument he clearly felt strongly about to a mere cat? And if he wasn't, how then to explain the sky-metal sword and the vial of miraculous whater? Was he really dependent for such expertise and achievements on the work of a village blacksmith and a coterie of chattering women? Where sorcery was concerned, was he after all no more than a vehicle and venue for the machinations of others?

Or was he simply so subtle not even someone as perceptive and experienced as Simna ibn Sind could see through the psychological veils and masks with which the tall southerner covered himself? Much troubled in mind, the swordsman trudged on, refusing to countenance the possibility that he might have, after all, allied himself to nothing more than a semiliterate cattle herder from the ignorant south.

Ehomba's reaction to the palace that materialized out of the east was anything but reassuring.

Simna saw it first. "It's a mirage. That's all." After a quick, casual glance, he returned his attention to the path they were following northward.

"But it is a striking one." Ehomba had halted and was leaning on his spear, staring at the fantastical phantasm that now glimmered on the eastern horizon. "We should go and have a look."

What manner of dry-country dweller was this, Simna wondered, who sought to visit something that was not there? "And just how would we go about doing that, bruther? I'm thinking maybe you've been too long on the road and too much in the sun."

Ehomba looked over at him and smiled innocently. "By walking up to it, of course. Come." Lifting his spear, he broke away at a right angle to their course.

"I was joking, by Geveran. Etjole!" Exasperated, and starting to worry if his tall friend really was suffering from the accumulated effects of too much sun, the swordsman turned to the third member of the party. "Cat, you can see what's happening. Why don't you go and pick him up by the scruff of his neck and haul him back like you would any wayward kitten?"

"Because his scruff is furless and I'd bite right through his scrawny neck, and also because I think I might like to have a look at that mirage myself." Whereupon Ahlitah turned right and trotted off in the wake of the departing herdsman.

Aghast, Simna called after them. "Have you both lost what little sense you possess?" He gestured emphatically northward. "Every day brings us nearer some kind of civilization.

ou can practically smell it! And you want to go chasing after irages? By Gwiquota, *are you two listening to me?*"

Sputtering inventive imprecations under his breath, the wordsman dropped his head and hurried to catch up to his ompanions. He calmed himself by determining that while it as a waste of time, the diversion wouldn't waste much of it.

But he was wrong.

"Interesting," Ehomba observed as they neared the object f their detour. "A real mirage. I have heard of them, but I ever thought to set eyes on one."

Simna had caught up to the others. "What do you mean, 'a eal mirage'? Is that as opposed to a fake mirage? Have you one completely balmy?"

"No, look closely, my friend." The herdsman raised his pear, which when walking he often held parallel to the round, and pointed with the tip. "An ordinary mirage would e fading away by now, or retreating from us. This one does ot wane, nor does it drift into the distance."

"That's crazy! Anyone knows that—" Simna broke off, his rows drawing together. "Offspring of Gupzu, you're right. ut how . . . ?"

"I told you." Ehomba continued to lead the way. "It is a eal mirage."

Right up to the palace gates they strode, tilting back their eads to gawk up at the diaphanous turrets and downy-walled owers. From their peaks flags of many lands and lineages treamed in slow motion, though not a whisper of a breeze tirred the sand and soil beneath their feet.

Stopping outside the great gates, which were fashioned of ale yellow and pink wood strapped with bands of pallid blue netal, they weighed how best to enter. Simna continued to efuse to acknowledge the evidence of his own eyes.

"It's impossible, bedamned impossible." Reaching out, he ried to grab one of the metal bands. His fingers encountered nly the slightest resistance before penetrating. It was like try-

ing to clutch a cloud. Drawing back his fingers, he stare
down at the handful of blue fog they had come away with.
lay in his palm like a puff of the finest dyed cotton. When h
turned his hand over, the vapor floated free, drifting lazil
down to the ground. There it lay, at rest and unmoving,
small fragment of mirage all by itself.

"Impressive walls," he found himself saying softly, "b
they wouldn't stand much of a siege."

"This is a special thing." The herdsman advanced and th
gate could not, did not, stop him. He walked right through
leaving behind an Ehomba-sized hole, like a cookie cutout c
himself. Instantly, the opening began to close up, the wall t
re-form behind him. Ahlitah followed, making an even large
breach through which Simna strolled in turn, a disbelievin
but triumphant invader.

They found themselves in a hallway whose magnificenc
would have shamed that of any king, khan, or potentate. Pi
lars of rose-hued cold fire supported a mezzanine that ap
peared to have been carved from solid ivory. Overhead, th
vaulted ceiling was ablaze with stained glass of every imag
inable pastel color. It was all vapor and fog, the most elegan
effluvium imaginable, but the effect was utterly stunning
Marveling at the delicate aesthetics of the ethereal architec
ture, they strode in silence down the vast hallway. Beneath th
pseudo–stained glass, the color of the light that bathed thei
progress was ever changing.

"So this is what the inside of a mirage looks like." Though
there was no compelling need for him to do so, Simna ha
lowered his voice to a whisper. "I never imagined."

"Of course you didn't." Ehomba strode easily alongside hi
friend. His sandaled feet made no sound as they sank slightly
into the floor that, instead of tile or marble, was paved with
mosaic ephemera. "No one could. The inside of a mirage i
not for human imagining, but for other things."

Simna's eyes widened as he espied movement ahead. "It's
ot? Then how do you explain that?"

At the end of the overpowering hallway was a throne, eight
eet high at the back and decorated with arabesques of rose-
ut gemstones. Pillows of lavender- and orange- and tanger-
ne-colored silk spilled from the empty dais to form a rolling
vave of comfort at its feet. Sprawled and splayed, reclining
nd rolling on this spasmodic bed of dazzling indulgence, was
clutch of sinuous sloe-eyed houris of more color and varia-
ion than the pillows they lolled upon. There was not a one
vho would not have been the pride of any sultan's harem or
nerchant's front office.

Giggling and tittering among themselves, they rose in all
heir diaphanous glory to beckon the visitors closer. Their
estures were sumptuous with promise, their eyes the lights of
he passion that dances like a flame at the tip of a scented can-
le: concentrated, burning, and intense. For the second time
ince he had begun his journey, Ehomba was tempted to for-
et his woman.

Simna suffered from no such restraints. Eyes alert, every
nuscle tense, a grin of lust on his face as pure as the gold he
oped to find, he started forward. One houri in particular
rew him, her expression simmering like cloves in hot tea.

Blackness blotted out the enticing, serpentine vision. The
lackness had four feet, unnaturally long legs, and muscles
igger around than the swordsman's torso. Simna started to
o around it, only to find himself stumbling backwards as a
nassive paw smacked him hard in the chest. More than his
ternum bruised, he glared furiously at the litah.

"Hoy, just because there's no cats here, don't go trying to
poil my fun!"

"There's no fun here, genital man." Ahlitah was staring, not
t him, but at the hazy, vaporous side corridors that flanked
he hallway. The ostensibly empty corridors. "Get out."

"What?" Two surprises in a row were almost more than

Simna could handle. Ehomba stood nearby, not commentin,
his gaze shifting repeatedly from the now frantic dem
mondaines to the litah.

"Get out. Get back, get away, retreat, run." As he delivere
these pithy admonitions, the great cat had turned to face th
vacant throne and was backing slowly up the hallway, h
massive head swinging slowly from side to side so as to mi
nothing.

Hesitant, but for the moment persuaded more by the cat
behavior than his words, Simna complied, keeping the litah
bulk between himself and—nothing. Or was that a flash,
flicker, a figment of movement there, off to his left? And a
other, possibly and perhaps, on the far side of the hallwa
dancing against the evanescent wall?

Ehomba had joined in the retreat. More importantly, h
held his spear tightly in both hands, extended in fighting po:
ture. Together and in tandem, the visitors backed steadil
away from the dais and its languorous promise of phantasm
carnal bliss.

"I still do not see anything," the herdsman murmure
tightly.

"Hoy, cat, what are we—"

Simna's query was interrupted as Ahlitah rose on his hin
legs and slashed out with his right paw. The blow would hav
taken off a man's head as easily as Simna could pull a cor
from a bottle. Four-inch-long claws tore through an unsee
but very real something, ripping it where it stood. The two hu
mans saw only reflections of the destruction, flashes of brigh
gold in the air in front of the cat. Something that was all long
icy fangs and shredded, glaring eyes howled outrage tha
echoed off the enclosing walls. Tiny individual droplets o
wet, red blood appeared from nowhere to fall as slow scarle
rain, crimson bubbles suspended like candy in the cloying at
mosphere of the hallway. The mist-shrouded floor sucke
them up greedily, hungrily. Thin, skeletal tendrils of the tene

rous surface under their feet began to curl and coil upward, clutching weakly at the travelers' ankles.

Whirling and roaring like the tornado he had once challenged to a race, Ahlitah snapped viselike jaws on something that had fastened itself to his back. An inhuman high-pitched scream split the sugar-sweet air, and fresh reflections emitted a second shower of rapidly evaporating blood. Simna had his sword out and was looking to cover the litah's rear, only there was nothing to cover against. Strain as he might, he could see nothing moving save his friends and the delicate feminine visions that seemed restricted to the vicinity of the magnificent, forsaken throne.

"Gronanka—show yourselves—whatever you are!" Close to him Ehomba was swinging the point of his spear from left to right and back again, sweeping it in a deadly arc over the floor as they continued their withdrawal. "Do you see anything, Etjole?"

"Not a thing, my friend!" Alongside them, two immense jaws came together with a thunderous clap, and a third something unseen died. Ahlitah's eyes were wide and wild as he dealt death to the invisible. And all the while the floor continued to scrabble and clutch at their feet with futile fingers of fog.

Two of the gesticulating, moaning houris left their pillows and came running toward them. Their arms were outstretched, their eyes pleading. They wailed and moaned in languages unknown to either man, but there was no mistaking the desperation in their gestures, the imploring in their eyes. They were beseeching the visitors to take them along, to remove them from the mirage in which they dwelled in unsolicited, unwanted, unloved luxury.

Something bellowed angrily and slapped at them, sending them flying backwards to land among the satiny fluff and froth-filled cushions that hugged the dais. Helplessly they lay

there, sobbing softly among their intimates, turning the
flawless faces away or dropping their heads into their hand

Meanwhile, the apprehensive, uneasy visitors continue
their steady retreat. Having picked up the pace a little, the tw
men strained every sense they possessed in search of a
sailants they could not see while Ahlitah continued to rag
and destroy corposants that could not be made visible but th
could bleed.

They backed right out of that grand and sumptuous hal
way, right through the walls of wisp that enclosed the deli
ium palace, until they were standing once more upon dry san
and rock. The splendid battlements and spires rose high abov
them, masking but not blotting out the sky.

"Now—run!" Ahlitah commanded.

Turning, they sprinted away from that place as fast as thei
inadequate human legs would carry them. Though he coul
have fled westward at ten times the speed, Ahlitah trailed be
hind, often looking back over his shoulder to make sure the
were not being pursued.

But a mirage cannot follow. Sooner than Ehomba woul
have expected, the litah slowed. "It's all right now. It's goin
away."

Out of breath, they turned and stared. In the distance th
fleecy, resplendent palace was fading from view, waning lik
a new moon obscured by clouds until, like a final shimmer o
heat pinched between earth and sky, it vanished from sight.

Simna sank to one knee, struggling to catch his breath
"What—what were we fighting in there? I never saw any
thing."

"Eupupa." Through his hands, Ehomba rested his weigh
on his spear. "I have heard of them, but never before encoun
tered any."

"How would you know if you had?" Taking an especiall
deep breath, the swordsman straightened and sheathed his
untested sword.

"I am told you can feel their presence around you. They live in the empty, dry places of the world. Only rarely do they come out of the mirages that are their homes. But on a long day, when the sun is high and hot, I am told you can feel them investigating your body, swimming around your cheeks and your chest, coming right up to you to peer deep into your eyes. Outside their mirages they have only the power to cloud one's thinking. Have you never wondered why so many people who are lost in the desert die only a day, or an hour, or sometimes less than that but a few feet from water, or help?" Looking away, he gazed back at the now ordinary, unmarred horizon.

"The Eupupa do that. They make you dizzy, and stare into the depths of your eyes until they have disoriented you, so that you stumble away from water instead of toward it, or walk in circles, or ignore the signs that would lead a dying man to salvation. And then they feed, beating even the vultures and the dragonets to the corpse, until they have sucked out its soul."

"Gwythyn's children," the swordsman muttered. "Too close, that was." He frowned. "But the ladies. Not Eupupa. Surely not Eupupa. If these are creatures that can't be seen, then the ladies couldn't have been these invisible ghoul-things." A part of him twitched at the burning memory of those naked, unconditional invitations. "Because I sure as Gelell's goblet could see *them,* bruther."

His mouth tightening, Ehomba dropped his gaze to the gratifyingly solid ground on which they now stood. "So could I, my friend. It was impossible not to see them. That was the Eupupa's intent, to use them to draw such as us into the deepest part of the mirage, where they could set upon us without having to wait for us to die. Where they could suck out our souls even while we still lived." He looked up.

"Those exquisite, sad houris. They were the souls of women who died in the desert. From thirst, from neglect, in childbirth, by falling over a cliff and striking their heads—from any and all means. They were the unlucky ones, whose souls were caught up and stolen by the Eupupa before they could escape spontaneously. Captured, and brought here to be kept in that mirage to serve them that we cannot see." He was gritting his teeth now.

"It is a most unnatural way to not-die, but there is nothing you or I or anyone else can do about it. No wonder they were so frantic for us to take them away. They are souls that want desperately to rest." He shut his eyes. "By what means those like the Eupupa can force a soul to do their bidding I do not know. I do not want to know." Opening his eyes, he turned away from the eastern horizon to look once more to the north.

"Let us leave this place, and try our best to think no more about what we have seen here."

"But wait!" Ehomba did not, and Simna had to hurry to catch up to the herdsman as he resumed walking. "They were all so ravishing, every one of them. No, they were more than ravishing. They were radiant. Surely not all the women who die in the desert are beautiful. Or do the Eupupa choose them that way so they'll make better bait for the unwary—like us?"

Striding along, tireless and exact as always, Ehomba did not answer immediately. When he did, it was with a feeling of disappointment. Not in their narrow escape, but in his companion who had asked the question.

"Simna ibn Sind, my friend. You who claim to know so much about women, and to have known so many of them in person. Did you not know that that is how every woman sees herself—inside?" Lengthening his stride, he pushed on ahead, forcing the pace as if he wanted to put not only their recent experience but also the memory of the experience out of his mind.

Simna considered his companion's words, frowned, shook his head, and caught up to the third member of the party. "Well, that's the first time I've had to try and fight something

I couldn't see. It was lucky for us you've seen these Eupupa before."

The litah spoke without turning his massive head. Both jaws, Simna noted for the first time, were stained dark beyond the black. Occasionally the thick tongue flicked out to lick at them.

"I never saw such before."

Simna blinked in surprise. "Then how did you know what to fight? How did you know they were even there?"

The wide, yellow eyes turned to meet the swordsman's. "Don't you ever see anything outside yourself, man? Haven't you ever watched a cat, any cat, suddenly tense and strike at what to you seems to be empty air? We see things, man." Killer eyes flashed. "There's a lot out there, everywhere, that men don't perceive. We do. Some of it is to be ignored, some of it is for play, and some of it"—he snarled under his breath—"some of it is to be killed." With that he lengthened his stride and jogged on ahead.

Left scratching at his chin, Simna watched the tufted, switching tail move out in front of him. "Well I'm glad *I'm* fugging visible, that's all I have to say!" With a shrug he moved to match the herdsman's elevated pace.

Once he thought he felt something brush his face. It was just the wind against his cheek, but he swatted hard at it nonetheless, and looked around, and saw nothing.

Nattering cat, he thought irritably. Filling a man's head with narsty scrawl. Ahead, he thought he could make out a line of trees, the first they had seen in many a night. With the sight of fresh foliage to boost his spirits, he held his head a little higher as he strode onward, and tried to forget all about the dismal events of the past hours.

"Cats and sorcerers," he muttered under his breath. A more morose and melancholy pair of traveling companions he would have had difficulty imagining.

XXVII

LACKING IN INNER SENSITIVITY HE MIGHT BE, BUT THERE WAS nothing wrong with the swordsman's superb vision. The line of trees he had espied from a significant distance was no mirage.

"At last," Ehomba murmured as they started down a final, gentle slope. Ahead lay a narrow but deep river lined on both sides with small farms and orchards. The leafy crowns Simna had spotted were fruit trees, pungent with blossoms, each verdant upheaval a small galaxy of exploding yellow and white flowers.

The swordsman eyed his friend. "What do you mean, 'at last'? Why should you be so elated by such a sight? I thought you were the dry-country type."

"It is true that I love the land where I live." Dirt slid away beneath the herdsman's sandals. "But that does not mean I cannot love this more. Any man can love a distant destination more than his homeland without forsaking the latter."

"Then why don't you move?" Simna asked him directly. "Why not bring your family, your whole village, up here, where there's plenty of water and good soil for raising crops?"

"Because obliging as this place may be, it is not our home." The southerner spoke as if that settled the matter. "Much as plentiful water and fertile land are to be desired, they do not make a home."

"Then what does?"

"Ancestors. Tradition. A warmth of place that cannot be transplanted like an onion. Certain smells, and sights. The air." He felt of the sack of beach pebbles in his kilt pocket. "The feel of especial places underfoot. The wildlife you live with." He glanced surreptitiously at Ahlitah, who was padding silently alongside. "The wildlife you fight with. In a new place all these things are different, alien, foreign. People are the easiest thing to pick up and move. The others—the others are much more difficult."

Simna shook his head sadly. "I feel sorry for you, bruther. My home is wherever I park my carcass. Preferably a place with good cooking, a soft bed, and a friendly lady. Or a soft lady and a friendly bed."

Ehomba squinted down at him. "Should I feel sorry for you—or should you feel sorry for me?"

"I feel sorry for all three of us." Ahlitah did not look up. "You two, for being clumsy, chattering, two-legged hairless apes, and me for having to put up with you." Turning away, he snorted wearily. "Next time save some other cat's life."

"I will try to remember," the herdsman replied.

They were following a marked path now. No more than a foot wide, it wound like a smashed snake through a leafy field of taro and yam. Yuca bushes shaded the more sun-sensitive young plants.

"Strange." Shading his eyes, Ehomba scanned the numerous fenced plots and the neatly pruned fruit trees they were approaching. "You would think someone would have emerged to challenge us by now. These fields are well tended.

Surely there are wild animals here that would feast on these healthy vegetables if the farmers did not keep them away. And the appearance of three strangers in a tillage ought to provoke some kind of reaction. We could be thieves come to steal their crops."

"Yes." With a mixture of curiosity and wariness, Simna studied the luxuriant acreage through which they were traipsing. "If this was my farm and orchard I'd have been out here with arrow notched and ready as soon as anyone showed themselves atop that last ridge we crossed."

"House," Ahlitah interjected curtly. Raising a paw, he pointed.

There were three of them, individual homes sharing a small thorn-bush stockade. The gate was open wide, presenting no obstacle to their entry.

"Hoy!" Simna shouted, putting his hands together around his mouth. "Commander of a legion of legumes, come and greet your guests!" There was no response. With a shrug, the swordsman started for the entrance.

The first house had windows, but the glass was of poor quality and did not allow them to see clearly what lay within. An uneasy Ehomba held back.

"I do not like intruding on another man's privacy."

"What makes you think there's anyone here? You can't violate privacy if there's no one present to claim it." Simna opened the door.

Ahlitah hung back with Ehomba, not out of any respect for the intangible called privacy, but because the interior of human habitations held no interest for him. On the single occasion when he had been obliged to enter one, he had found the interior malodorous and claustrophobic. The occupants, however, had proven a good deal tastier than their surroundings.

Looking more puzzled than ever, the swordsman emerged several moments later. "Empty. More than empty, deserted.

There's food in lockers in the pantry, and dishes and clean linen stored neatly in cabinets. Beds are made but haven't been slept in recently." He eyed the surrounding trees with fresh concern. "The people who lived here left not long ago but with no immediate intention of returning. It's my experience that folks don't do that without a compelling reason, and it's usually a disagreeable one."

"Let us try the other houses," Ehomba suggested.

This they did, only to find further evidence of well-planned departure.

"There must be a town somewhere nearby," the herdsman conjectured when they had concluded the brief search. "Perhaps everyone has gone there."

"Hoy, yes." Simna tried to view their eerily silent surroundings with some optimism. "Maybe there's a festival of some kind going on." His expression brightened. "I could do with a little old-fashioned country excitement."

"On the other side of the river, maybe." Ehomba gestured with the point of his spear. "There are more farms, more fruit trees, and beyond that I think I see some hills. If the town is fortified, it would naturally be sited in an area affording the most natural protection."

"Come on then." With a growl, Ahlitah started toward the river. "If we're going to have to swim, I'd just as soon get it over with while the sun's still high enough to dry my pelt."

But they did not have to swim. A perfectly adequate, well-maintained wooden bridge wide enough to accommodate an oxcart spanned the swift, high-banked waterway not far downstream. On the opposite side they encountered more of the tidily deserted habitations, some built of stone as well as wood that boasted several stories. Each showed similar signs of having been conscientiously abandoned by their inhabitants.

"Must be quite a festival." Simna was not yet willing to

concede that something untoward had happened to the occupants of the fastidiously tended farms and homesteads.

"I hope not." Padding silently alongside them, the big cat flowed like black oil over the packed earth. "I don't like a lot of noise—unless I'm the one making it."

"Maybe it's a carnival, or a jubilee." Simna put more than his usual strut into his walk as they approached the first of the foothills. "I could do with making a bit of noise myself."

As they entered the gentle, forested hills, the path they had been following widened into a narrow but serviceable road that showed evidence of having recently accommodated many wagon wheels and shoed feet. Before long they found themselves passing numerous transient camps filled with people of all ages and description. Men and women alike wore expressions that seldom varied between exhausted and sullen. Even the children were somber and reserved, watching the passing travelers from the haggard depths of eyes wide with silent hurt.

Old men sat motionless, resting stooped heads in wrinkled palms. Dogs chased wallabies around and beneath wagons and carts piled high with household goods, while cats posed imperiously atop piles of bound linens and towels. Cockatiels and gallahs, parrots and macaws squawked from within cages of wire and wicker, but even their normally boisterous cries seemed muted among their doleful surroundings.

Women cooked food over open fires built of wood taken from the surrounding forest. Ehomba saw no signs of starvation among the bands of wayfarers, or indeed any evidence of physical deprivation whatsoever. Except for their attitudes, all appeared to be in good health.

Some they passed even looked frustrated and angry enough to contemplate assaulting the travelers, but such attitudes underwent a rapid and radical change the instant the would-be aggressors caught sight of the brooding litah. For his part, the great cat ignored the increasingly dense clusters of humans, deigning to exchange glances only with the cats they kept as pets and companions. For their part, the house cats returned his gaze, affirming that each and every one of them knew their place in the hierarchy of felinity without a word, or a hiss, having to be spoken.

"What's going on here?" An increasingly perplexed Simna kept glancing from right to left as they trudged northward past larger and larger concentrations of dour, depressed people. "Where have all these folks come from?" He gestured back down the road they were walking. "Not from the farms along the river. Those houses still contained all their goods and furniture. These people look like they've brought everything they own with them." He scrutinized one face after another as they continued on, trying to divine from their disconsolate expressions what sort of calamity might have befallen them.

"Look at them—exhausted, dazed, like they have nowhere left to go and don't know how they're going to get there. I've seen people like this before. People at the end of their rope. Usually they've been driven from their homes by some natural disaster, or by some marauding hoard. But these—these folk still seem healthy and well fed. By Geesthema, it's not natural. Even the children look as if for the past weeks they've been spoon-fed nothing but hopelessness and despair."

Ehomba concurred. "And it still does not explain what happened to the farmers along the river who deserted their homes and fields." He lifted his gaze to the winding road that led onward into the hills ahead. "Something peculiar is going on here, Simna my friend, and I fear it has nothing to do with a fair or celebration."

"Hoy, bruther, one doesn't have to be a keen reader of men to see that. But what?"

"Perhaps the answer lies over the next hill. Or the last."

They marched on, the butt of Ehomba's spear striking the ground methodically with each of the herdsman's steps, marking their progress like the pendulum of a tall, thin clock. The range of hills was not high, but it was extensive. It took them almost a week to negotiate the entire length of the winding road.

The farther north they traveled, the more families and transients' encampments they encountered, until the hills resembled anthills swarming with displaced farmers and townsfolk. Every time they tried to approach someone to ask the meaning of the unaccountable diaspora, the intended recipient of their questions caught sight of Ahlitah and beat a hasty retreat. Not wishing to panic any of the already obviously frightened migrants and believing it unwise to leave the always hungry litah out of their sight, they continued on, confident that sooner or later they would encounter someone willing to stand and deliver themselves of an explanation.

One, of a sort, manifested itself when they reached the crest of the last hill. The panorama spread out before them was not what they had hoped to descry.

As far as the eye could see, a vast, fertile plan stretched all the way to the northern horizon. Isolated clouds of towering whiteness marched across the sky like floating fortresses, and numerous small rivers and streams filigreed the earth like silver wire. Neatly spaced pockets of construction marked the borders of field and forest, and several towns were visible in lesser or greater detail depending on their distance from the hill.

But no one was tilling the vast patchwork of fields, or working in the towns, or plying the rivers in boats equipped with nets and lines. No pickers worked the orchards, no farm animals roamed the scrupulously fenced pastures. Smoke there was, but it rose not from chimneys but from the burned-out husks of abandoned homes and mills, workshops and granaries. The destruction had been selective and by no means total, as if the devastation had been imposed in a precise and disciplined manner.

In the midst of the robust, healthy pastures and towns there stretched a wall. A hundred feet high, it looked to be made of some yellowish stone. Twenty feet in width, its top was smooth and wide enough to drive wagons along. Or chariots, Simna thought, or cavalry. Armored figures in their hundreds, in their thousands, could be seen running back and forth to position themselves along its length, a length that extended as far to the east and west as they could see.

Nor was the wall straight. Here it curved inward, rippling and twisting, to accommodate the path of a river flowing against its base, there it thrust out sharply to create an arrow-like salient. At quarter-mile intervals, battle towers rose another fifty or sixty feet higher than the rim of the wall itself.

Immediately behind it the travelers could see the brightly colored tents and flying pennons of an army on the march, though at this distance it was impossible to assign an identity to the marchers. The glint of sunlight on armor, however, was very much in evidence. Ahlitah could also make out, marshaled in temporary holding pens, much larger creatures clothed for war.

"Mastodons, I think." The big cat had to squint, as the distance involved was a challenge even to his exceptional vision. "And glyptodonts. Other elephants, and some balucherium as well."

Simna nodded. "Easy enough to see who they're fighting." He gestured toward the base of the hill.

Thousands of figures swarmed over the fields that had been tilled right to the base of the first incline, trampling the crops there, knocking down the neat wooden fences and hedgerows. There were people, of course. No doubt some of them called hastily forth from the first farms the travelers had encountered, called to arms to help defend their country against the invading host.

But there were also dwarves clad in traditional leather and coarse cotton, and arrets, the tall, thin, bark-brown forest people of the west. Among the crowd Ehomba thought he saw a giant or two, massive of brow and heavy of jaw. Unmistakable in their light armor were the chimps and apes, and the smaller monkeys were present in large numbers as well.

Evidently all had shared in the bounty of this land, and now all had gathered to defend it. But the field of battle made no sense, not even to a nonprofessional like the herdsman. On this side the many-varied citizens of the good and fertile country were drawn up in lines of defense, swarming back and forth as if hunting for a weak spot in the enemy-held wall, or for a purpose. But they were crowded in too tightly together, crammed between the wall and the hills.

"I know." Simna was scrutinizing the battlefield intently. "It doesn't look right, does it? Maybe the attackers just took the wall. Maybe it had been built by these people here to defend themselves against an assault from the south, and now they've been pushed back up and over their own defenses."

"I thought of that," the herdsman replied. "But if these people wanted to defend themselves from a southerly invasion, why would they exclude so much of their land? Why would they not build such a wall in the sand hills where we first saw the line of fruit trees, to protect that rich farmland and that country as well? Or at the very least, why not build the wall on this side of that river to the north in order to make use of it as a moat?"

"Don't add up, do it?" The swordsman waved an arm at the field of battle. "Yet here's this great huge long wall, stuck square in the middle of their fields and orchards. And in clear possession of the enemy. Or are these people we've been passing these past days the invaders, and the ones on the wall the defenders of their country?"

Ehomba shook his head. "I do not see it that way, Simna. Were they the defenders, it would not explain why certain farms and homes are burning on their side of the wall. The cultivated lands to the north are the ones that bear the hallmarks of having been invaded and despoiled, not those on this side of the barrier. And these people are the ones whose faces show the blank stare of the displaced."

"I agree. So what's going on here?"

Turning slowly to study the hills, Ehomba scanned the numerous encampments. Below, the assembled fighting forces of all the two-legged tribes in the vicinity were frantically trying to compose themselves for combat. Even from their location at the top of the hill, the travelers could see that chaos commanded more allegiance than order among the disorganized ranks below. Therefore they would have to seek explication elsewhere, among the unarmed and less intractable, whether the individual they settled on wished to prove tractable or not.

"We have to know what is going on," he murmured. "Ahlitah, go and bring back a suitable person."

Massive brows narrowed. "Why me?"

"Because I do not want to waste time arguing with several possibles, and I do not think they will argue with you."

The great cat snarled once before whirling and dashing off toward the nearest encampment. There followed several moments during which Ehomba and Simna occupied themselves trying to make sense of the incongruous situation below before Ahlitah returned with a middle-aged man in tow. Or rather, with the scruff of his well-made embroidered shirt held firmly in the big cat's jaws. The fellow was overweight but otherwise healthy, even prosperous in appearance. Perhaps he had bought himself out of the ongoing strife below.

As Ehomba had predicted, the man had chosen not to argue with the litah.

Disdainfully, the cat parted his jaws and let his prisoner drop. The man immediately prostrated himself before the two travelers. "Please, oh warriors of unknown provenance! I beg of you, spare an ignoble life!" Face pressed to the ground, arms extended before him, the poor man was shaking and trembling so violently Ehomba feared he would destabilize his brains. "I have a condition of the belly that prevents me from participating in the illustrious struggle. I swear by all the seed of my loins that this is so!" Raising his head hesitantly, he stole a glance first at Simna, then at Ehomba. Reaching into a vest pocket, he pulled out a rolled parchment and held it up, quivering, for the herdsman to see.

"Look! A draft of my physician's statement, attesting to my piteous circumstance. Would that it were otherwise, and that I could join our brave citizens and allies in desperate conflict!"

Simna snorted softly. "He's got a condition of the belly, all right. A condition of excess, I'd say."

"Stand up." Ehomba felt very uncomfortable. "Come on, man, get off your knees. Stand up and face us. We are not here to persecute you, and none of us cares in the least about your 'condition' or lack thereof. We need only to ask you some questions."

Uncertain, and unsteady, the man climbed warily to his feet. He glanced nervously at Ahlitah. When he saw that the great cat was eyeing his prominent paunch with more than casual interest, the chosen unfortunate hurriedly looked away.

"Questions? I am but a modest and unassuming merchant of dry goods, and know little beyond my business and my family, who, even as we speak, must be sorely lamenting my enforced absence."

"You can go back to them in a minute," Ehomba assured him impatiently. "The questions we want to ask are not difficult." Peering past the detainee, he pointed with his spear in the direction of the great wall and the roiling surge of opposing forces below.

"There is a war going on here. A big one. For days my friends and I have been passing through hills and little valleys filled with refugees. We have seen fine homes and farms abandoned, perhaps so their owners could join the fight while sending their families to a place of safety."

"There is no place of safety from the Chlengguu," the merchant moaned. Fresh curiosity somewhat muted his fear as he looked from Ehomba to the short swordsman standing at his side. The predatory gaze of the great and terrible litah he avoided altogether.

"Who are you people? Where are you from that you don't know about the war with the Chlengguu?"

Ehomba gestured casually with his spear. "We come from the far south, friend. So you fight the Chlengguu. Never heard of them. Is this a new war, or an old one?"

"The Chlengguu have ceaselessly harassed the people of the Queppa, but by banding together we have always been able to fight them off. For centuries they have been a nuisance, with their raiding and stealing. They would mount and attack, we would pursue and give them a good hiding, and then there would be relative peace for many years until they felt strong enough to attack again. They would try new strategies, new weapons, and each time the farmers and merchants and townspeople of the Queppa would counter these and drive them off." As his head dropped, so did his voice. "Until the Wall."

Ehomba turned to look down in the direction of the line of combat. "It is an impressive wall, but though I am no soldier, it seems to me to be in a strange location. We thought that perhaps it was your wall, and that your enemies had captured it from you."

"Our wall?" The merchant laughed bitterly. "Would that it were so! For if that were the case we would use it to push these murderous Chlengguu into the sea."

Ehomba started slightly. "The sea? We are near the ocean?" Strain as he might to see past the western horizon, he could detect no sign of the Semordria. He was surprised at how his heart ached at the mere mention of it. It had been far too long since he had set eyes on its dancing waves and green depths.

"You mean the Semordria?" the merchant asked. When Ehomba nodded with quiet eagerness the other man could only shake his head. "You really are far from your home, aren't you?" Raising one beringed hand, he pointed to the west. "The Semordria lies a great distance off toward the setting sun. I myself, though a man of modest means and varied interests, have never seen it." His arm swung northward.

"That way lies the Sea of Aboqua, a substantial body of water to be sure, but modest when compared to the unbounded Semordria. Upon its waters ships of many cities and states ply numerous trade routes. I am told that at several locations it enters into and merges with the Semordria, but I myself have never seen these places. I have only heard other merchants speak of them. And I have never heard of a trading vessel with captain and crew brave or foolhardy enough to venture out upon the measureless reaches of the Semordria itself."

Ehomba slumped slightly. "There is something I must do that requires me to cross the Semordria."

The merchant's heavy eyebrows rose. "Cross the Semordria? You are a brave man indeed."

"But if no ship will do that," Simna put in, "how are we supposed to make this crossing? I'm a good swimmer, but no fish."

"From the tales I have heard of the monsters and terrors that swarm in the depths of the Semordria, I believe it a journey even fish would be reluctant to take." The man rubbed his chin whiskers. "But it is rumored that in the rich lands on the far side of the Aboqua there are ports from whence sail ships grander than any that ply the smaller sea. Who knows? You might even find shipmaster and sailors stupid enough to attempt such a passage. Tell me, what do you hope to find on the other side of the Semordria, anyway?"

"Closure," Ehomba told him. "Now, about this Wall. It is a very impressive wall. Behind it I see fields and buildings, some of which have been burned. If it is not yours, then it must be a construction of these Chlengguu. But why build it here, and how did they manage to trap all of you on this side instead of the other, where your homes and villages lie?"

The merchant looked over his shoulder. "My poor family must be in an agony of apprehension at my absence."

Simna fingered the hilt of his sword. "Let 'em agonize a little while longer. Answer the question."

"You really don't know, do you?" The man heaved a deep sigh. "The Wall was not built here." Turning, he pointed to the northwest. "When it first appeared on the outskirts of Mectin Township, no one could believe that the Chlengguu had managed to raise so massive a structure in so short a time. Its true nature was not immediately apparent to the people of the Queppa. That we learned all too soon.

"There was nothing we could do. Our young men and women fought bravely, but the Wall is so high and strong it cannot be breached. The Chlengguu we fought to a standstill, but we could not stop the Wall."

Simna blinked at him, glanced sharply down at the line of battle then back at the merchant. "Are you telling us that these Chlengguu keep moving the Wall forward?" He stared at the unbroken barrier that stretched from far west to distant east. "The whole Wall? That's impossible!"

"Would that it were so, traveler," the other man agreed, "but the Chlengguu do not move the Wall. Each time it advances, it pins us tighter and tighter against the desert lands. That is why you passed so many people, so many refugees. We have nowhere else to go. We are squeezed between the Wall and the desert." He cast a sorrowful gaze downward. "These Relibaria Hills are our last refuge, our final hope. We pray that the Wall cannot surmount them. If it can—" He broke off, momentarily choked. "If it can, then we will be pushed out into the desert, where most of us will surely die, and the fertile lands of the Queppa will belong forever to the Chlengguu."

"I do not understand," Ehomba confessed. "If the Chlengguu do not move the Wall, then how . . . ?"

"See, see!" Gesturing with a trembling hand, the merchant was pointing downward. "Look upon the abomination, and understand!"

Below, activity had increased from the frantic to a frenzy. Scaling ladders were brought forth as the ragtag citizen soldiery of the united Queppa peoples mounted yet another assault on the Wall. Fusillades of arrows flew like hummingbirds but because of the Wall's height were hard-pressed to wreak much havoc among its well-protected defenders. Catapults and siege engines heaved rocks and bales of burning, oil-soaked straw at the crest of the tawny palisade. They were not entirely ineffective. Ehomba saw figures topple from the battlements, to fall spinning and tumbling into the melee of furious fighters below.

From the top of the escarpment the Chlengguu hurled spears and stones and arrows of their own at the attackers below. More ladders were brought up, and mobile siege towers as high as the Wall itself trundled forward. A few Queppa, battling madly, even succeeded in reaching the top of the Wall and pushing back some of its defenders. To Ehomba it looked as if, in one or two places along the line of battle, they might have a chance to overwhelm the Wall's defenders and push them back.

As he and his companions looked on, the Wall began to shiver slightly. At a distance it was difficult to tell if it was really happening. Ehomba rubbed at his eyes, Simna squinted doubtfully, and the singular activity even brought the largely indifferent Ahlitah out of his feline stupor.

There it was again.

"What was that?" Simna muttered uncertainly. "What just

happened there?" Reaching out, he grabbed the merchant firmly by the shoulder, sinking his fingers into the soft flesh hard enough to hurt. But the other man just ignored him, staring, his gaze vacant with lost hope.

"There!" Ehomba pointed. "Look there." Alongside him, Ahlitah was on his feet now, growling deep in his throat.

Below, the people of Queppa began to retreat, pulling back their siege engines and all their assembled forces. Atop the Wall, the hard-pressed Chlengguu quickly regained all they had lost. They lined the battlements, jumping up and down, their armor shimmering, yelling and screaming and taunting their fleeing, dispirited quarry. Those Queppa fighters who had taken parts of the Wall were surrounded and butchered, their bodies thrown like so much garbage over the parapets to land among their fleeing comrades.

Then the Wall stood up, all hundred feet and more high of it, all along its considerable impressive length, and took one giant step forward.

XXVIII

Simna TRIED TO BELIEVE WHAT HE WAS SEEING, SHAKING HIS head more than once as if that would make it go away. The hair on Ahlitah's back bristled and his lips curled in a snarl. Ehomba stood between them, holding firmly to his spear, staring at the inconceivable, improbable sight. Nearby, the distraught merchant wrung his hands and wept in silence.

Having advanced one step, the Wall hunkered down. Dust rose from its base as a long, drawn-out *Boooom* echoed across the hills. Atop the battlements, the victorious Chlengguu howled and pranced a while longer. Then, except for the few assigned to the watch, they drew away from the edge, filtering back down stairways on the other side of the barrier to the numerous tented camps that served to house their multitudes. Soon campfires could be seen smoking among the ranked canopies, inviting the advancing night. The abundant serpentine coils of smoke gave the land the aspect of a vast plantation for snakes.

In his mind Ehomba replayed the impossible spectacle he had just witnessed. All along its length the Wall had risen and sprouted hooves. Dark gray, bristle-haired, cloven hooves, with gigantic toes and glistening, untrimmed nails. Hooves whose ankles disappeared into the underside of the Wall. In unison, they had risen as much as they were able and stepped forward, in a one-step march of fleeting but irresistible duration. The merchant had been telling the truth. The Chlengguu had not moved the Wall. The Wall had moved itself.

The heavyset man was watching him. "You see what has befallen us. From the first appearance of the Wall we were doomed. The people of the Queppa have been dying a slow death. The Wall is relentless and invincible. We attack, and sometimes we force back the Chlengguu. But then the Wall moves, overwhelming our war engines, dumping and smashing our siege ladders, forcing us always back, back, until now we are trapped here between it and the desert." Helplessly, he spread his hands.

"What can we do? We cannot fight a Wall that moves. If our soldiers try to outflank it, it grows another length, another extension, until our people are stretched so thin they cannot be supplied. Then the Chlengguu pour down off their Wall and slaughter the flanking party. These hills are our last hope." Once more he peered downward. "The Wall can march. We pray it cannot climb."

Ehomba nodded, then smiled as gently as he could. "Go back to your family, friend. And thank you."

Much relieved, the merchant nodded and turned to go. Then he paused to glance back, frowning. "What will you do now?"

The herdsman had turned away from him and was staring at the terrain below. "To find passage across the Semordria I have to find a ship capable of crossing it. If all that you have said is true, to do that I must cross this Aboqua Sea and reach the lands to the north. So we will keep going north."

"But you can't!" Licking thick lips, the merchant found his attention torn between his nearby encampment and the eccentric travelers. "You'll never get over the Wall, or around it. Your situation is the same as ours, now. You can only go back." His jawline tightened. "At least your home is safely distant to the south, and you know how to survive in the desert. The people of the Queppa do not."

"Nevertheless, we will continue northward." Ehomba turned to regard him. "Go back to your family, friend, and do not worry about us. You do not have enough worry to spare for strangers."

"There is truth in that." The merchant hesitated briefly, then raised a hand in a gesture that was both salute and farewell. "Good fortune to you, seekers of a sudden end. I wish you luck in your foolishness." With that he turned and hurried off as fast as his thick, heavy legs would carry him.

Simna sidled close to his companion. "I've no more desire to turn and go back the way we came than anyone, but he has a point. How do we get over the Wall?" The swordsman nodded toward the imposing barrier. "I count a pair of guards for every thirty feet of parapet and fire baskets or lamps for light every forty. We'll have to try it at night anyway. We wouldn't have a chance in daylight." He nodded at the third member of the group.

"And what about our great black smelly eminence here? Cats can climb well, but a smooth-faced vertical wall is another matter. You and I can go up a scaling rope, if we can borrow or steal one from this disheartened mob of defenders, but what about him?"

The dark-maned head turned to face the swordsman. "I'll get up and over. One way or another, I will do it."

"You won't have to." Ehomba was not looking at either of them, but at the Wall.

Simna squinted at him. "Say what?" Then his expression brightened. "Hoy, right! You'll use your alchemical gifts. By Gyuwin, I'd forgotten about that."

"You cannot forget something that was not there to know,"

Ehomba corrected him. "As I have told you repeatedly, I have no alchemical gifts to use." Lowering his spear, he gestured with the point. "We will go down among the Queppa defenders and find a place to ourselves, one unsuited to fighting. The next time the Wall rises to advance, we will race beneath it to the other side. It needs longer than a moment to take its step— more than enough time for us to run underneath." Lifting his spear, he smiled confidently at Simna.

"It will be easy. The only care we must take is that no one trips and falls. There will not be enough time for the others to help him up."

"Underneath?" Gazing afresh down at the Wall, Simna swallowed, trying to envision hundreds of tons of yellow mass hovering just over his head. He marked his companion's words well. Anyone who tripped and went down during the crossing might not have enough time to rise and scramble to safety. The Wall would descend upon its hundreds of feet, crushing him, smashing him flat as a crêpe.

Ehomba put a hand on his shoulder, bringing him out of his sickly reverie. "Do not worry, my friend. There will be enough time. Remember—as we run to the north, the Wall will be moving one giant step to the south."

"Hoy, that's right." Simna found himself nodding in agreement. "Yes, we can do it."

"Easier than climbing," the litah pointed out, "and no guards to dispose of while making the passage."

"Okay, okay." Simna had grown almost cheerful. "A quick sprint, no fighting, and we're through. And these Chlengguu won't be looking for anyone to do something that daring." A sudden thought made him hesitate. "Hoy, if it's so easy and obvious, why haven't these Queppa folk tried it? Ghalastan knows they're desperate enough."

"Any group of soldiers large enough to make a difference in the fight would surely be spotted from the ramparts by the Chlengguu lookouts," Ehomba surmised. "Since they control the Wall, they could simply command it to cut short its advance and relax, thereby smashing any counterattacking force beneath its weight. It may be that the Queppa have already made the attempt and met such results."

"Yeah." Subject as he was to abrupt swings of mood, Simna was suddenly subdued. "Poor bastards. Having to fight every day and move their women and kids at the same time." His face was grim as he stared downward. "If that Wall can come up these hills then they haven't got a chance. And after seeing the size and number of those hooves, I don't see these gentle slopes being any problem for it."

Ehomba's eyes danced. "Why Simna ibn Sind—one would almost think you were ready to stand and fight on behalf of these people."

The swordsman laughed derisively. "There are certain diseases I fear, Etjole. Among them are the chills and fever the mosquito brings, the swelling of the limbs one gets from an infestation of certain worms, the closure of the bowels, the clap, the spotted death, leprosy, and altruism. I count the last among the most deadly." He glared over at his companion. "I don't see *you* volunteering to help these pitiful sods."

"We do not have the time." Looking away, the herdsman once more considered the Wall they were about to attempt. "I have family and friends of my own. One man cannot save the world, or even particularly significant portions of it."

"Hoy, it's thoughts like that that keep us together, bruther." The swordsman glanced at the third member of their party. "I don't suppose you have any thoughts on the matter?"

"*Snzzz* . . . what?" Ahlitah looked up, blinking. "I was cat-napping."

"I thought as much. Go back to your rest, maestro of the long tooth. You'll need your strength for running."

Once more the litah dropped his great head onto his forepaws. "I could make the dash ten times back and forth before you arrived on the other side. Look to your own legs, man, and don't worry about me." The yellow eyes closed.

"Get up," Ehomba chided him. "We need to make ready." Poling the ground with the butt of his spear, he started downward, trailed by Simna and a reluctant, yawning Ahlitah.

None of the dispirited Queppa who saw the unusual trio pass did more than glance in their direction. With so much of their land under siege by the Chlengguu, allies from many townships and counties had been thrown together. Men fought alongside apes they had never met before, and monkeys did battle in the shadow of lightly armored chimps. In such conditions, under such circumstances, the presence of one imposing, long-legged feline was not considered extraordinary.

The travelers descended until they were close enough to the base of the Wall to easily make out individual sentries patrolling the parapet. Turning eastward, they walked until they found themselves among an outcropping of jagged rocks. No Queppa soldiers were present. Such rugged, uneven terrain rendered siege engines and scaling ladders useless. Having the spot to themselves, they settled down to eat an evening meal from their limited stores.

Less than a hundred feet away, the base of the wall loomed. It had the appearance of limestone that had been washed or stuccoed with some thick yellow paste. To look at it one would never suspect it harbored within the underside of its substance hundreds of hooves the size of elephants.

Tearing off a mouthful of dried fish from the whitish lump he held in his fist, Simna chewed slowly and stared at the imposing barrier. "We'll have to be damn careful. These rocks will make for treacherous running."

"Only between here and the Wall." Ehomba sat nearby, arms resting on his angular knees, his mouth hardly moving as he masticated his supper. "Beneath it the rocks will have been crushed flat. With luck, it will be like running on a gravel road."

"With luck," a skeptical Simna murmured. "Well, once on the other side we should be fine. Might be an occasional Chlengguu pillaging party to avoid, but that shouldn't present much of a problem. We'll just give them plenty of room."

Nearby, Ahlitah sighed sleepily. "Should be lots of livestock running free. Easy kill, fresh meat." He growled softly in anticipation.

"Stay alert," the herdsman advised him. "We need to be ready to move at the first sign of activity from the Wall."

"Don't worry about me," the big cat assured him. "Just look after your own skinny, inadequate selves."

It was already dark when they heard, not saw, the first indications of movement: a deep-seated grinding and rumbling that emerged from the base of the Wall itself, spreading outward as a vibration in the rocks beneath them.

To all outward appearances sound asleep, Ahlitah was first on his feet, awake and alert, tail flicking back and forth in agitation as he glared at the Wall. Ehomba and Simna were not far behind in scrambling erect.

To left and right they heard the yells and screams of the Queppa defenders, and, behind them, up in the hills, the distraught cries of their families and other noncombatants. Once more, showers of arrows rose from the massed defenders while gobbets of blazing brush and oil were flung against the Wall. It was all to no avail, but Ehomba suspected the citizen soldiers felt they had to do something, to try. The flaming missiles did no more damage to the Wall than they would have to any stone monument, and up atop the quivering, trembling barrier the Chlengguu despoilers merely hunkered down out of reach and range.

"It's moving," Simna hissed as he stood watching. "Be ready!"

So near, the raising up of the Wall was infinitely more imressive than it had been from the top of the hill. Dirt and bits of weed and brush were carried upward by its bottom edge, a low vertical heaving of unimaginable mass. Living stone groaned as it ascended on many multiples of hooves to reveal gigantic nails and pads.

The travelers were racing forward well before the Wall had risen to its full stepping height, arrowing down a slight gap in the rocks. Ehomba sprang lithely from one slab of sharp basalt to another, while Simna bounced from stone to stone like a lump of rubber that had been formed into the shape of a man. As for the litah, it leaped nimbly from one outcropping to the next, clearing in an instant spans that mere humans had to traverse painstakingly on foot.

They sprinted beneath the overhanging awe of the Wall and were swallowed beneath its gargantuan mass. Ehomba could sense the volume above him, millions of tons of solid material balanced on pillarlike but still imperfect toes. Barely visible through shadow and darkness, a few lines of brightness ran through the underside of the barrier, though whether they were fractures in the rock or flowing veins he could not tell.

They raced past one of the immense hooves as it rose up and started forward, an action matched by every alternate hoof under the length of the Wall. When they descended in unison, so would the Wall itself, swallowing them up once again together with everything and anything too slow to get out of its way. But by the time those hundreds of cloven hooves had begun their downward step, Ehomba and his companions had already emerged on the far side of the barrier.

Pausing to catch their breath, they stood and watched as it completed its ponderous single-stride advance, descending quietly to ground with a single long, exhausted *Whoooom*. Dust rose again, scattered, and began to settle. It was done. They were through, across, under.

"Nothing to it," quipped Simna. He was, however, showing

more perspiration than the short sprint and tepid evenin[g]
ought to have generated.

"No room for mistakes there." Tilting back his head, th[e]
herdsman gazed up at the top of the Wall. No shapes or bod[-]
ies were to be seen. The Chlengguu were all on the far side[,]
watching for mischief among the Queppa. No need for ther[e]
to guard their impenetrable rear. "Let us go."

Turning, they headed north, traveling at an easy trot. N[o]
one came forth to question their presence or challenge the[ir]
progress.

They found an abandoned farm and, without any sense [of]
guilt, made themselves at home in the comfortable surround[-]
ings presently denied to the rightful owner. Discovering [a]
still-intact and unpillaged pen of domesticated razorback[s,]
Ahlitah quickly and effortlessly supplied a feast not only f[or]
himself but for his companions. With so many structures sti[ll]
smoldering throughout the length and breadth of the Quepp[a]
lands, Ehomba conceded a fire to Simna, who refused to e[at]
his pork uncooked.

There were fine, soft beds in the house, and linen. Whi[le]
the delighted swordsman guilelessly availed himself of th[e]
former, Ehomba discovered he could not go to sleep on any[-]
thing so yielding. He found peace by wrapping himself in [a]
blanket on the wooden floor and trying not to think of the fa[te]
of the thousands being squeezed between the Wall and th[e]
eternal sands of the south. Thousands for whom such plea[-]
sures as a simple good night's rest were denied.

XXIX

MORNING WAS FULL OF MIST, AS IF THE SUN HAD BEEN SUR-
rised in its bath and risen too quickly, spilling a blanket of
aturated sunlight upon the world.

It induced the travelers to linger longer in their appropri-
ted beds, a condition with which the always sleepy Ahlitah
vas wholly in accord. When Ehomba finally awoke and as-
ertained the true position of the fog-obscured daystar, he
ound himself unsettled in mind.

"What's wrong now, wizard of worries?" Sitting up in the
legant, carved bed, a well-rested Simna ibn Sind stretched
nd then scratched unashamedly at his groin. "We did our
unning, and all went well. Why don't you try relaxing for a
hange? Who knows? You might even find the sensation
greeable."

Quietly agitated, the herdsman was staring out a many-
aned window at the farm's mist-swathed environs. "I will
st when we are out of this ill-starred country and safe
board a ship bound for the far side of the Aboqua. Not be-

fore." He looked back. "Get up and cover your ass. We shoul
be away from here."

"All right, all right." Grumbling, the swordsman slid hi
legs out from beneath the heavy wefted bed sheets and bega
fumbling with his attire. "But not before breakfast. Wh
knows when we may again have a chance to eat like this? An
for free."

"Very well." Ehomba was reluctant, but understandin
"After breakfast."

While most of the dairy products that had not been loote
from the forsaken farm stank of spoilage, there remained
substantial quantity of dried and smoked meats. Another sec
tion of the walk-in larder was filled from floor to ceiling wit
jars of preserved fruits and vegetables. Rummaging throug
the stores, Simna found a couple of loaves of bread decorate
by only a few spots of opportunistic mold.

"We should fill our packs." He bit enthusiastically into
mouthful of meat and bread.

"This is not our food." Though uncomfortable at rifling a
other man's pantry, Ehomba consoled himself with the rea
ization that if they did not eat the bread and other perishable
they would go either to the Chlengguu or to waste.

"Hoy, that's right—leave it for the despoilers. Misplace
good intentions have been the death of many a man, bruthe
But not me!" Daring the herdsman to take exception, l
began stuffing strips of dried meat and small jars of olives ar
pickles into his pack. Ehomba simply turned away.

When at last all was in readiness they stepped out into th
fog. If anything, the herdsman thought, it had grown thick
since they had arisen. It would be difficult to tell north fro
any other direction. But he was not about to linger in th
homestead until the mist lifted. If they could see any p
trolling Chlengguu clearly, then the Chlengguu could se
them. Better to take their chances under cover of the lo
hanging vapors.

He was only a few yards from the house, turning in the di-
ction where he imagined north to lie, when a thunderous
ar shattered the tenuous silence. Whirling, he saw only the
st flash of motion as the heavy net landed atop Ahlitah. The
eat cat bellowed furiously, claws ripping at the material,
werful jaws snapping, but to no avail. Whoever had de-
gned the ambush had made their preparations well: The
esh was made of metal, woven into finger-thick cords like
pe. Ahlitah could dent but not tear it.

Chlengguu seemed to come from everywhere: back of the
rmhouse, behind bushes, over fence rails, everywhere but
raight up out of the ground. Dozens more dropped from the
of to clutch frantically at the fringes of the net, for while the
ah was unable to break it, his convulsions were sending pan-
ked Chlengguu flying in all directions. It took forty of them
ally to pin down the net and the outraged, wild-eyed feline
thin.

No nets came flying at Ehomba and Simna. Instead, they
und themselves overwhelmed by another half hundred of
e forceful Wall masters. The herdsman had hardly begun to
wer his spear and Simna to draw his sword when rough
nds fell upon them, wrenching their weapons out of their
nds and reach. Hobbles were brought forth, and their hands
ere bound behind their backs. Thoroughly trussed and teth-
ed, they were shoved rudely forward as their captors barked
comprehensible commands at them in the exotic Chlengguu
ngue.

"I hope you enjoyed your breakfast," Ehomba muttered as
ey were marched away from the farmhouse and into the fog.

"That I did, bruther." Exhibiting considerable aplomb in
e face of a less than sanguine situation, the swordsman stud-
d their captors. "They're not especially big, but the little
ggers are fast." He smiled amiably at the Chlengguu war-
or striding along next to him. "Ugly, too." Unable to under-

stand, the soldier marched along stiffly, looking neither to l
nor right and certainly not at the grimacing captive.

Behind the herdsman, dozens of warriors bore the fr
trated, spitting Ahlitah aloft. So tightly wrapped and rolled
the steel net was the litah that he was unable to shift his lim
Nor if they had any sense at all would his captors allow hi
the slightest range of movement. If so much as a single set
claws slipped free, Ehomba knew they would find their w
into one of their abductors' necks. Always cautious, t
Chlengguu were taking no chances with the biggest and m
powerful of their prisoners.

They were excessively thin, the herdsman saw. Slim enou
that he looked bulky beside them, and Simna positively squ
They had narrow, sharply slanted eyes that were set almo
vertically in their faces, long hooked noses, and small mout
The two canines protruded very slightly down over the low
lip. Their ears were thin and pointed as well, and the narr
skulls showed no hair beneath their tight-fitting, emboss
helmets. Many of these were decorated with long quills a
spines appropriated, no doubt involuntarily, from sundry u
known animals.

Coupled with the narrowness of their skulls and faces, t
slight natural downward curve of their jawlines gave them
permanently sour facial cast. In hue their skin shaded fr
dark beige to umber heavily tinged with yellow, as if they we
all suffering from jaundice. Fingernails were long, thin, a
painted silver. Their finely tooled leather jackets, leggings, a
boots were engraved with diverse scenes of mass unpleasa
ness. The great majority of these were also tinted silver, b
Ehomba saw gold, bronze, and bright red bobbing among t
argent sea as well.

Most carried two or three tempered lances no thicker th
his thumb. A finely honed sickle hung from each waist–
particularly nasty weapon in close-quarter combat. A few

the more discriminating soldiers favored slim-handled spike-studded maces over the more delicate lances.

"I wonder what they have in mind for us?"

"By Gnospeth's teeth, not wining and dining, I'll venture." Simna continued to make faces at his guards, who resolutely ignored him. "Though there's some dancing houris I wouldn't mind introducing them to. Where's the soul-sucking Eupupa when you need them?"

They were marched on in silence for more than an hour before the mist finally began to lift. Tents began to materialize around them. From time to time Chlengguu soldiers busy attending to their bivouac glanced up to examine the prisoners. Those that made the effort to do so generally ignored the two men in favor of the trussed and bound black litah.

Probably they think we are ordinary Queppa prisoners, Ehomba decided. Simna and I look not so very different from the poor people whose land they are stealing.

With sinking heart, he saw a familiar sight looming up in front of them. The Wall. They had lost all the distance they had gained during their flight of the night before.

They were paraded past several large and elaborately decorated tents until the officer in charge halted outside one that was a veritable villa of cloth and canvas. Multiple standards of red and gold flew from its poles. Ehomba was sickened to see the flayed skins of human bodies alternating with the silken pennants, the grisly trophies snapping noisomely in the wind.

The periphery of the ornate shelter was embellished with threads drawn from precious metals. Two unusually large Chlengguu flanked the twin support posts of an imposing rain flap. Silk drapery provided privacy to those within. Each pole, the herdsman noted expressionlessly, was grounded in the bleached skull of a great ape.

One of the few among their captors who was not clad in silver leather paused to speak to the guards. Conversation was brief, whereupon a bony hand jammed hard into Ehomba's back, sending him stumbling forward. He heard Simna curse behind him as his companion was subjected to similar indelicate treatment. As for Ahlitah, the cat had been quiet for some time. Biding it, the herdsman decided.

If the outside of the tent had been designed to impress, the interior was calculated to overwhelm. Peaks of fabric soared overhead. Sewn into the material, fine jewels simulated the constellations of the night sky. There was richly carved furniture whose lines reflected the slenderness of its owners: tables, chairs, lounges, comfortable but not luxurious. The tent was located in an arena of war. While impressive, its furnishings were anything but dysfunctional.

A quartet of aged Chlengguu seated at an oval table looked on with interest as the prisoners were marched inside. Customarily slight of build, these withered specimens looked positively skeletal. But their sharp, inquisitive eyes belied their physical appearance. They muttered and mumbled among themselves while making cryptic gestures in the direction of the prisoners.

Ahlitah's cortege did not depart until the big cat had been securely staked to the floor. Without even room in which to struggle, the muscular black specter lay still, with only the steady, infuriated heaving of his chest to show that he was alert and unharmed except in dignity.

Three Chlengguu rose from a table groaning under the weight of food, drink, maps, and assorted alien accouterments whose functions the provincial Ehomba did not recognize. One of them was female, though the extraordinary lankiness of the Chlengguu form made it difficult to sex them at first glance. Spidery fingers resting on all but nonexistent hips, the nearest of the trio cocked his head sideways to peer up into Ehomba's face. The sharply angled eyes were unsettling. The herdsman had encountered eyes vertical and eyes horizontal, eyes round and eyes oval, but never before had he gazed back into angular oculi that were anything like those of the Chlengguu.

"*Sirash coza mehroosh?*"

Ehomba kept his face blank. "I do not understand you."

The Chlengguu noble tested the same phrase on the silent Simna, who to his credit had sense enough to keep his extensive farrago of ready retorts locked away in a corner of his brain where they would, hopefully for the duration of the foreseeable future, not get him killed.

Retracing his steps to confront the much taller herdsman the noble asked, in the common voice of men, "Who are you and where do you come from?" His voice was as soft and prickly as hot grease. Gesturing at Simna, he added, "This one could be Queppa, but you—you are different. You have the look about you of someplace else."

"We are both from the south," Ehomba replied. "As is our pet." Behind him he thought he heard the litah stir, but he did not turn to look. From the noble's manner he surmised that turning away from him while he was engaged in his interrogation might be construed as an unforgivable insult. Judging from their extravagant surroundings and the carriage and posture of their interrogators, he and his companions would have to be careful not to give even the slightest offense.

"The south." Daintily, the noble tapped the tip of a painted fingernail against one excessively long canine. "Why should I believe you?"

"Why should we lie?" Ehomba imperceptibly shifted his weight from one foot to the other, an instinctive herdsman's adjustment. "The Queppa hate the south. Who of them would claim to come from where you are driving them?"

The corners of the nobleman's tiny mouth twitched slightly upwards. "If you are not Queppa, how do you know what they hate or where we are driving them?"

"They told us." Ehomba chanced a nod in the direction of

his homeland. "Coming up from the south, we had to pass through them to get here."

"You had to pass through more than the stupid Queppa to get here." The female fairly spat the accusation. "The only way from south to north is over the Wall. That is not possible."

"We did not go over the Wall," Ehomba corrected her. "We came under it."

This claim set the quartet of oldsters to arguing agitatedly over their table. It also prompted the third member of the interrogating trio to speak up. "No one is half-witted enough to try digging under the Wall."

"Who said anything about digging?" Simna was smirking now, virtually strutting in place. "We just waited for it to make ready to step, and when it rose up, we ran under."

The initial questioner dropped his finger from his lips. "Such a thing is possible, of course." He nodded once, curtly. "Very well. I, Setsealer Agrath, accept your explanation. You are courageous half-wits."

"This is not our fight," Ehomba told him somberly. "I personally have no quarrel with the Chlengguu and no affection for the Queppa. This lasting strife is your own. Let us go."

Turning slightly away, Agrath chose a long, thin knife, very much an oversized stiletto, from the assortment of cutlery lying on the table behind him. "Why should we?"

"I have business in the west."

"The west?" Agrath snickered slightly to his associates. "I thought you told us your destination lies to the north."

"I have to go north," Ehomba informed him, patient as he would have been with a child, "in order to find a ship willing to take me west."

"Across the Semordria?" The Chlengg did not laugh so much as hiss breathily. "Now you try my intelligence."

"It's true." Simna jerked his head sharply in his friend's direction. "He's deranged, he is."

"Yet you follow him?"

The swordsman dropped his gaze and his voice. "What can I say? I have perverse tastes. Who can explain it?"

"Who indeed? When we are finished here we will remand you to the custody of specialists whose work is famed even among the Chlengguu. Perhaps they will get the real explanation out of you."

"Hoy, now wait a minute, you—"

The mace that descended struck only a glancing blow to the back of the swordsman's skull or he surely would have died on the spot. As it was, he only crumpled to the carpeted floor, where he lay motionless and bleeding. Ehomba glanced wordlessly in the direction of his friend's unmoving body, then returned his attention to the three Chlengguu nobles. They were watching him expectantly.

"You are not angry at this treatment meted out to your friend?"

Ehomba's voice was entirely unchanged. "Of what use would it be? You want to test us. You might as well have struck me to provoke him. It makes no difference."

"None whatsoever," Agrath agreed, "except that you are standing and he is unconscious." The noble shrugged. "As you say, it could as easily have been done the other way. But I am more curious about you than him. Contrariety is a welcome diversion from the boredom of our inexorable advance."

"We were told it was not always so."

"No." The other male's voice darkened. "Before the Wall it was very different. Now"—he did not grin so much as sneer—"after the Wall, it will be more different still."

"I really don't care whether our specialists work on you or not." Agrath ran the edge of the stiletto along his elongated palm, drawing a thin line of his own blood. His expression never changed. "But I do so enjoy the occasional uncommon curiosity." Removing the blade from his skin, he flicked the point to indicate something behind Ehomba.

Moments later, two soldiers came forward. They were carrying the weapons confiscated from the travelers. These they placed on the already crowded table. After genuflecting twice to the nobles, they carefully backed away and rejoined their comrades.

While the skeletal oldsters continued to bicker and squabble in the background, the nobles proceeded to inspect the outwardly unimpressive weapons. The woman hefted Ehomba's spear, sniffed contemptuously, and dumped it back on the table. Agrath picked up the tooth-studded bone sword, having to use both hands to finesse the weight, and whipped it back and forth a few times. One swipe passed very close to the herdsman's face, but Ehomba did not flinch. If his captors were struck by his stoicism, none of them remarked upon it.

"Bone and teeth." Agrath was singularly unimpressed. "A suitable device for a primitive tribesman."

Sliding the pale white weapon back into its goatskin sheath, Agrath then drew the sky-metal blade from its protective covering. His angled eyes could not widen, but he nodded appreciatively. As he had with its weighty predecessor, he required the use of both strong but thin wrists to support the weapon parallel to the floor. Maintaining this grip, he swung it slowly back and forth. Diffuse sunlight filtering through the fine material of the tent glinted off the exotically forged iron.

"This is more like it." Bringing the flat side of the blade up to his face, he eyed the peculiar lines etched into the metal. "Whoever worked this design into the blade is a master armorer."

"The design was not worked," Ehomba told him. "The lines are inherent in the metal, but must be brought out by dipping the finished blade in acid."

The noble's face squinched up tight as a snake trying to slip into a too-small hole in pursuit of prey. "Nonsense. No such metal shows such lines naturally." Using both hands, he held the sword high, admiring the play of light on the internal crystalline structure. "Perhaps when we have conquered the south I will bring this marvelous armorer into my own service." Lowering the point abruptly, he swung it around until it was dimpling the reawakened Simna's chest. The swordsman tensed, but held his ground.

"Tell me, southerner. How sharp is the edge? How strong the alloy? What could one do with such a blade?"

Ehomba deliberately avoided his companion's face lest the look frozen there cause him to hurry his response. "It can cut through any bone, even that of an elephant or mastodon. The point will penetrate most armors, be they metal or fabric. Striking it with a flint will make a quick fire. And," he concluded, "if held high enough for long enough, I am told by the old women of the Naumkib that it will draw down the moon."

XXX

THE SOFTLY CONVULSED MODULATED EXHALATION THAT PASSED
for laughter among the Chlengguu filled the tent. "Does he
take us for idiots?" the other male declared sharply. "Or does
he think to play with our minds and thereby somehow deflect
his unavoidable fate?"

"If he says it's so, then you'd better watch out." Simna
struggled with his restraints. "He's a mighty sorcerer."

Plainly amused, Agrath turned back to the stolid herdsman.
"Well, southerner? Does your friend speak true? Are you a
'mighty sorcerer'?"

"Note his clothing," opined the female disdainfully. "He
doesn't even look like a mighty breeder of rabbits."

Keeping an eye on Ehomba, Agrath raised the sword high,
as high as he could manage, aiming the point at the ceiling.
Straining with the effort it required, he let go with one palm
and maintained the difficult pose, balancing the weapon in a
one-handed grip. A couple of the guards commented approvingly.

"There!" The wicked slash of a mouth parted to reveal

white teeth. "What now, southerner?" Still holding the blade aloft, he turned toward the command tent's entrance. "It is early enough and the sky clear enough that I can still see a bit of the moon. Though it is more difficult to tell during the day, it looks unchanged to me, and certainly unmoved. Behgron! Please be so good as to check on the position of the moon for me."

One of the officers among the company that had brought in the three prisoners executed a quick, sharp half bow, whirled, and darted outside. His voice came back to those inside clear and crisp.

"It looks the same to me, Your Overlordship. The same color, and it surely has not moved."

"There now." Still holding the weapon aloft, greatly pleased with himself, Agrath eyed his tallest prisoner coldly. "What have you say to that, 'sorcerer'?"

"*I* did not say that it would bring down the moon," Ehomba responded humbly. "I repeat only what the old women of the village have told me."

The Chlengguu noble gave a curt nod. "Well then, it would appear that we have proof that the old women of your village are a bunch of prating, ignorant whores." He waited for the herdsman to say something, but Ehomba kept silent.

"Your pardon, Overlordship." It was the voice of the officer who had gone to stand just outside the entrance to the tent.

"Yes, what is it?" Agrath snapped off the response impatiently. The officer was interrupting his fun.

"It is true that the moon is unchanged, noble Agrath—but there is something else."

"Something else?" The Chlengg's expression twisted uncertainly. "What 'something else'? Explain yourself, soldier."

"I can't, Overlordship. Perhaps you should come and see for yourself."

"We'll do that, and if there is no good reason for this interruption . . ." He left the promise of unpleasantness hanging in the air.

Accompanied by Ehomba and the groaning, recently awakened Simna, the three Chlengguu nobles strode to the entrance of the tent. The senior officer Behgron proceeded to indicate a point in the sky. An irritated Agrath followed the line formed by the slim arm.

"What ails you? I see nothing."

"There, Overlordship." The officer pointed again. "To the left and below the curve of the moon."

"I see a bright star." His anger was growing. "You called us out here for that? As the sun rises it will soon be gone."

"Watch the star, noble Agrath. It's not fading with the rising sun. It is getting bigger."

"Don't be a *noukin*! Stars do not—"

The female noble stepped forward, her head tilted back, her narrow, slanted gaze inclined upward. "Behgron is right. Look at it!"

Not only was the glowing spot in the sky growing steadily larger even as they stared in its direction, but a small streak of light had begun to appear in its wake, like the feathery tail of the splendid white macaw.

"The sword!" Taking a step away from Agrath, the other male pointed a shaky finger in the direction of the weapon. Natural physiological constraints aside, it was possible that his eyes did widen slightly. *"Look at the sword."*

An ethereal blue-black light now bathed the weapon, engulfing it in an unearthly halo. This put forth no heat. In fact, if anything, the startled Agrath found the sword suddenly ice cold to the touch. Dropping it as quickly as if he had found himself clutching a cobra, he retreated backwards, pressing up against a knot of nervous, wide-eyed guards.

As soon as the blade struck the ground it sprang upward. As everyone present watched in awe and amazement, it rose slowly until it was hovering at chest level above the ground.

Still interred in the stunning steely effulgence, it adjusted its position slightly until the sharp terminus was pointing directly at the dilating orb overhead.

By now that fierce ghostly globe had swollen to dominate the sky, having grown larger even than the sun. The tail that trailed behind it was a streak of stark incandescence against the cobalt blue of the heavens. Among the assembled Chlengguu, troops and nobles alike, the first traces of panic had begun to surface.

"What is this, southerner?" Droplets of brown sweat had begun to bead on the noble Agrath's forehead. "I can still see the rim of the moon, so that is not the moon. What is happening?"

Squinting at the sky, Ehomba contemplated the onrushing orb. "I do not know," he informed his interrogator candidly. "I am only a simple herdsman." Lowering his gaze deferentially, he turned back to gaze down at the now highly agitated Chlengg. "To know the answer you would have to ask the prating, ignorant whores of the Naumkib."

The atmosphere was infused with a dull thunder. Unlike ordinary thunder, it did not announce itself and then steal away into the clouds in a series of gradually diminishing echoes. Despite the efforts of their officers to maintain discipline, a number of the guards had broken ranks and were running wildly in several directions. A number of their superiors looked as if they wanted to follow them.

Overhead, the steady thunder had become a screaming, a piercing shrillness that sounded as if the sky itself was coming apart. Hovering in midair, the sky-metal blade continued to emit the same spectral shine, a deep blue light that was almost black. As he eyed it interestedly, Ehomba found himself wondering how something could glow black.

Alarm was now endemic among the Chlengguu. Not only were the guards panicking in the face of the collapsing firmament, so was the rest of the army. Kicked aside in the mad rush to escape, cook fires latched on to tents. Soon, flames from numerous blazes were licking at the sky as if eager to greet their falling sibling. Soldiers clutched and clawed at one another in mad panic, and their massed screaming nearly rose above that of the descending colossus.

Watching the flawlessly organized bivouac plunge into madness and chaos, Ehomba wondered what the reaction was among the Queppa. Powerless to stop what Agrath had set in motion, he could only hope the thousands of refugees were managing their hysteria better than their tormentors.

"Do something!" A trembling Agrath had finally sunk to the level of his terrorized troops. "Turn it from us, make it go away!"

"Free me," Ehomba ordered him.

"Yes, yes, immediately!" With his own gold damascened sickle the noble cut the herdsman's bonds. As he stepped back, his terrified, tapering face was drawn inexorably to the lunatic sky. "Now do something!"

"I will." As mounting hysteria raged around him, Ehomba calmly walked over, stretched out one hand, and reached through the dark aurora to take hold of the radiant sword. The haft was cold, colder than he had ever felt it, but it seemed to warm a little at his touch. Or it might just have been the air itself, which was growing very warm indeed as the onrushing monolith approached the Earth.

Gripping the sword tightly in his fist, he turned around to face the shaken, fearful Agrath. The noble's two companions had vanished back into the tent, as though the sheer magnificence of its decoration might somehow impress the fiery plunging immensity and save them from destruction. Putting his left hand below his right, the herdsman drew back the blade and brought it around in a single swift, sweeping arc.

The expression on Agrath's face did not change even as his head was neatly severed from his shoulders and sent flying toward the entrance to the tent. It bounced a couple of times before coming to rest in the dirt. To their credit, a couple of the guards overcame their panic long enough to draw their weapons and rush toward Ehomba. Pirouetting as nimbly as if he were the lead dancer in a traditional Naumkib ceremony, the herdsman showed them the sword. That was enough. The pair promptly joined their comrades in hysterical flight.

Simna was hopping backwards toward his friend. "Cut me loose, bruther! We've got to get out of here." Lowering the blade, Ehomba swiftly sliced through the swordsman's restraints. "By Golontai's gonads, that's icy!" He rubbed at his emancipated wrists. "How do you hold on to it?"

Ehomba was running back into the tent. "In the winter, the nights in my country can get very cold. A man still has to stand watch over his herd."

"Cold, is it? Hoy, but you've sure given these pinch-faced bastards a chill!" Grinning wolfishly, Simna followed him into the tent.

If not for the naked fear rampant on their faces, the demeanor of the two nobles huddled and trembling beneath one of the carved tables would have been comical. On the opposite side of the tent, the four elder Chlengguu sat with eyes closed, lips moving silently as they recited whatever personal mantras they felt would best prepare them for Death. Nearby, Ahlitah fought futilely against the steel net.

"Lie still!" Ehomba barked as he brought the sword down. Simna looked on respectfully as the blade sliced through segment after segment of the tough metal mesh.

Once his front paws were free, the great black predator was able to push hard enough to snap numerous links and lengths of chain and give the herdsman some help. With Ehomba working his way down to the cat's hind legs, Ahlitah was soon free. He stretched magnificently, fighting to loosen cramped muscles.

"No time for that!" Simna yelled as he recovered the rest of their weapons from the table. The Chlengguu cowering be-

neath made no move to stop him. "We've got to get awa
from here. The sky is falling!"

"What is the hairless ape prattling about?" Ahlitah fol
lowed the herdsman as they hurried out of the tent.

"You will see," Ehomba assured the litah. And as soon a
they were outside, he did.

The piece of sky was close enough now for the scramblin
travelers to see that only its nucleus was solid. The remainde
of the globe was composed of gases and vapors that were boil
ing off its surface and streaming back behind to form the now
immense but nebulous tail. Actually, the solid portion of the
sphere was not very large at all. They did not have time to as
certain exactly how big it might be because it was very nea
and coming toward them very fast.

It shrieked over their heads, passing just behind them, and
hit with a sound like a million banshees all sobbing at once.

"Get down!" Even as he was shouting the warning to his
friends, Ehomba was diving into a cramped irrigation ditch
Simna and even Ahlitah imitated his headlong leap without
question. He felt the overheated mass of the big cat slam up
against him.

Then the sky erupted. Howling winds tore at his body and
clothing but largely shrieked past overhead. Out of one eye he
could see tents and Chlengguu caught up by the detonation
being scattered like toys in every direction. Many of the invaders were screaming, though they could not be heard over
the force of the concussion.

As rapidly as it struck, the great wind passed. Rising tenta-
tively from their providential if muddy refuge, Ehomba
looked back the way they had come. All around them was
desolation. The Chlengguu bivouac, much of the assembled
army itself, its murderous equipment and lodgings, trees and
surrounding vegetation, had been blown away or in many in-
stances humbled beyond recognition.

Rising from the ditch, the travelers gathered themselves as

they gazed southward. An enormous hole had been blasted in the Wall where the falling piece of sky had struck. Thousands of moaning, whimpering Chlengguu soldiers still clung to the untouched portions of the Wall that stretched away unbroken to east and west. The barrier was quivering, trembling slightly from the force and extent of the great wound it had incurred.

Then, to the accompaniment of hundreds of hopeless screams from as many hoarse and hysterical throats, the mortally injured Wall toppled slowly forward and fell, perishing with a reverberant crash and ensuing upheaval of dust, dirt, and Death. Dozens upon dozens of gigantic, gleaming hooves protruded from its upturned underside, stationary and unmoving. Among the cloud of debris that was raised by its collapse was a cloud. Not a dark cloud, but a cloud of darkness. This quickly dissipated into the sky, the wind whisking it northward. A tight-lipped Ehomba followed it with his eyes until it was lost from view.

As the echo of the Wall's fall faded, a new sound could be heard: the cries of thousands of displaced Queppa as they gathered themselves to swarm down upon the dazed and demoralized Chlengguu who had survived. Battle quickly became butchery. Ehomba turned away, disinterested in the outcome. As he had tried to tell representatives of both sides, theirs was not his fight. But no one had listened to him.

Taking a deep breath, carefully stepping over a pair of Chlengguu corpses that had been twisted out of all recognition, he accepted his spear and bone sword from Simna and prepared to resume the trek northward.

The swordsman paced him effortlessly while Ahlitah hung back slightly, pausing repeatedly to groom his ruffled and mussed black fur.

"Please now, bruther," Simna queried respectfully, "tell me once more how much the sorcerer you are not."

The herdsman looked down at his more than slightly skeptical companion. "Nothing has changed, my friend. I am the same man, boasting the same lack of skills beyond a knowledge of cattle and sheep, desert and ocean." Reaching back over his shoulder, he touched the hilt of the sky-metal sword where it rested once more in its scabbard. "The blade did all this, not I. Another made the blade, and others presided over its final forging. If you must have an explanation, talk to Otjihanja the Smithy or the old women of the Naumkib. Not I."

"But you knew what it could do." Simna was nothing if not persistent. "You ran for cover as soon as you could."

Ehomba nodded. "I knew, because I was told by those who know. Not because I carry with me any great store of necromantic knowledge. We were lucky."

"Lucky." Searching his friend's face for hint of cool concealment or calculated mendacity, the swordsman found none. Could it be as the herdsman claimed?

"Well, whatever the explanation, we're alive, and that's what matters." He put a little spring into his step. "Time enough later for clarifications." Shading his eyes with one hand, he squinted at the rubble they were approaching. From a distance, it appeared to be the ruin of a substantial building, perhaps a modest Queppa fortress. Shreds of Chlengguu banners hung limp from its crushed battlements. Shielded by the outer walls, the inner keep appeared to be relatively intact. Nothing moved on the damaged parapet, on the wind-scoured ground outside, or within.

"Let's have a look," he urged his tall companion.

"Why?" Ehomba's gaze narrowed slightly. "We still must reach the Aboqua and find passage north."

Concentrating on the small fortress, Simna muttered distantly, "The Chlengguu had to have a headquarters safely distant from the field of battle. Even with the Wall to protect them, that would be just common military sense." He nodded at the ruins. "Given the number of banners hanging from its stones, this looks like it might have been it."

"So?" Ehomba commented disinterestedly.

Simna smiled up at him. "Please allow me a minute, my laconic master of new lambs. I just want to have a quick look around."

The herdsman sighed tolerantly. "Very well. Otherwise I will hear about it for days."

"Yes you will. Come on." Increasing his pace, he raced on ahead.

Ahlitah watched him break into a sprint. "What ails the ape?"

"I do not know." Ehomba lengthened his stride. It would not do to let Simna out of his sight. The overeager swordsman might stumble into a nest of surviving invaders ready and frustrated enough to take out their anger on the first non-Chlengg who came their way. "But I can guess."

XXXI

THE SWORDSMAN WAS NOT TO BE FOUND IN THE VACANT courtyard of the fortress. Nor was he in the deserted stables, or the unpretentious, high-ceilinged entry hall. Everywhere was evidence of hasty departure on the part of the Chlengguu who had been stationed in the sturdy stone structure. With every uncontested breeze, scattered scrolls and abandoned papers scooted across the floor like whispering, bleached vermin. Goblets and cups of indeterminate liquid posed forlornly on tables and in alcoves, waiting for drinkers who would never come. Erratic spills stained the floor. Gaps in the rafters showed where a few banners had been ripped from their braces and carried off by the fleeing soldiers.

They found Simna in a back room lying on a bed of gold. The room was small and showed signs of having been partially looted, but enough riches remained to satisfy even the most avaricious. There was some silver extant, and platinum presentation disks, and several chests of jeweled pins and medals. The swordsman lay on his back atop the pile, arms spread wide to encompass as much of the hoard as possible.

His eyes were closed and a look of bliss reposed on his face as snugly as a perfumed hot towel.

Ahlitah took one glance at the heaping knoll of inedible metal, sniffed, and padded off in search of something valuable. Ehomba stepped through the open doorway, noting as he did so the broken lock and seal, and knelt to examine a handful of the coins. They were six-sided and stamped with an assortment of profiles and adornments. All of the sharply minted faces were Chlengguu.

"What was that you've been trying to tell me about no treasure?" As he slid down the front of the flaxen gradient, gold bunched up beneath the swordsman's undergarments. He did not find the sensation unpleasant.

Straightening, Ehomba surveyed the accumulation. "All Chlengguu coin and manufacture. This room in this fortress must have been used as the army's treasury. The troops were paid directly from this stockpile."

"And now there is no army." Simna smiled beatifically. "So it's ours." Lifting a fistful of coins, he let the gold trickle out between his fingers and spill across his stomach.

"Yours." Turning away, the herdsman prepared to head off in search of the litah.

"Hoy, bruther! Wait a moment." As Simna sat up, gold tumbled from his arms and chest. Coins bounced musically off the hard floor or ran away and hid against the base of the thick stone walls. "What do you mean, it's mine? Share and share alike, by Gloriskan!"

Pausing, Ehomba looked back at his friend. "I do not want any of it, Simna. It is all yours. I have all I can do to carry wood and water and weapons and a few essentials. Even a little gold is heavy when one has a long ways to walk."

"Not to me it ain't." Hoisting a handful, the swordsman tossed it into the air for the sheer pleasure of watching it catch the light as it fell. "To me it weighs next to nothing. In fact, the more I have to carry, the lighter my step becomes."

"If it makes you happy, you should enjoy it." Ehomba smiled good-naturedly. "There is little enough happiness in the world. I am sure you will be able to find Queppa who will be delighted to help you take charge of your good fortune." He eyed the pile appraisingly. "I do not know a great deal about gold or money, but I think there is enough there to keep you in comfort for the rest of your life. Not enough to buy a kingdom, perhaps, but nearly anything else." He started through the door.

"Hoy, what's your hurry?"

The herdsman smiled back at him. "I am on a journey that leads to a destination, remember? I hope to reach the shores of the Aboqua in a few days. Be well, my good friend, and have a long and contented life." With that he strode out into the corridor and headed back in the direction of the main hall in search of the litah.

Simna ibn Sind sat contemplating more gold than he had ever believed could be found in one place. Lifting back the lid of one of the small metal-banded wooden chests that floated like carracks among the coins, he let his gaze linger on its contents: military decorations and awards wrought in the semibarbaric and florid style of the Chlengguu. There were formal lapel pins of fine filigreed gold inlaid with emeralds and sapphires, tsavorites and pearls; medals prominent with ivory and amber cameos of unknown nobles; satin ribbons from which hung intricate scenes etched into the faces of rare crystals by master engravers. Each worth a pocket fortune, and all his. The riches of a lifetime.

Rising abruptly, jaw set, he flung the chest aside, causing its contents to spill in an instant of sparkling evanescence across the pile's front slope. He found his companions at the entrance to the main hall, preparing to depart.

"Oh no you don't!" he shouted at Ehomba. Pausing in the act of adjusting the straps of his backpack, the herdsman looked back curiously.

The swordsman stomped up to the taller southerner and got right in his face. "Think you're all too clever, don't you?"

Expression innocent of guile, Ehomba regarded his friend. "Simna, I do not know what you mean."

"Like Grestel's choice you don't!" He gestured angrily back the way he had come. "Thinking you can buy me off with a pittance like that!"

"Pittance? My friend, from what little I know about gold, I would think what you have here enough for any man."

"Leave him to his counting." Ahlitah growled impatiently. "We should make some distance before nightfall."

Simna shot the big cat a look. "You keep out of this, masticator of minor mammals." Not even deigning to respond, the litah sighed and settled down on his belly to wait out the rest of the confrontation. When humans were arguing, it was all one could do. "That's what you want me to think, isn't it?" the swordsman told Ehomba accusingly. "That this is enough. First you tried to convince me you weren't after treasure, and now you're doing your best to use this trifle to bribe me to stay behind. Well, it's not going to work."

Ehomba smiled and shook his head slowly. "My friend, nothing of the sort ever—"

Simna would not let him finish. Instead, he raised a hand and waved it in the herdsman's face. "No, no—don't try to deny it!" A broad grin on his face, he began walking toward the exit. "You may as well forget the whole idea, Etjole. You're not rid of me that easily. I'm sticking to you like a father to his daughter in a naval port until we find the *real* treasure!" With that he marched imperiously through the portal, forcing himself not to look back in the direction of the storeroom and its glittering riches.

Lifting his mane, Ahlitah yawned conspicuously. "Can we go now?"

Shaking his head, the quietly exasperated herdsman followed in the swordsman's wake. "Sometimes, my feline friend, I think I understand sheep better than humans."

Unwinding itself from the floor, the great ebony cat padded along close beside him. "That's because sheep are more sensible than humans. Now, for real intelligence and common sense, you need to talk to a cat."

They emerged into the courtyard. No longer having to compete with a fiery, angry visitor from beyond, the sun shone placidly down on the ravaged expanse of the Queppa lands.

"So then tell me," the herdsman inquired as they began to catch up to the boldly striding Simna, "how does sleeping nineteen or twenty hours a day really affect the quality of your life?"

Predator's eyes swung around to meet his own. "You ask a lot of questions, Etjole Ehomba."

The herdsman smiled agreeably. "It is my nature."

It was farther to the Aboqua than Ehomba had hoped, but not as far as he feared. Keeping to a major north-south trade route that followed a convenient canyon through the range of coastal mountains, they soon found themselves sharing the way with a people who called themselves Maliin. They had fine homes and were not much for farming, tending to concentrate in numerous bustling towns and villages. Reports of the invasion of the Queppa had suffused their daily lives with apprehension and dread, so they were much relieved to hear that the cold, cruel Chlengguu had once again been defeated.

As the bearers of such good tidings, Ehomba and his friends were received with good cheer wherever they stopped. Eager for the latest news from the interior and relieved that it was, for the most part, all good, enthusiastic townsfolk took pleasure in tending to the needs of the quaint trio of pilgrims. Anointed a herald by the grateful populace, Ahlitah had to suffer the attentions of giggling, delighted children. They pulled his tail and buried themselves in his mane. Ehomba was gratified to see the great cat handle it with dignity and forbearance, even if he did spend many moments grinding his teeth in exasperation at the attention.

"I know you would rather eat them," he whispered to the litah during a private moment, "but a guest who devoured the offspring of his hosts would not continue to be regarded with favor. Restrain yourself a while longer, until we can find ourselves a ship."

The litah's tongue lolled as he stared unblinkingly at a pair of particularly plump six-year-olds. Saliva trickled from one corner of his open mouth. This did not unsettle their hosts, who thought the big cat was merely cooling himself.

"Find one fast, man, and tell our friends to keep the meat coming, or as surely as blood runs red I am liable to forget myself."

It was therefore for an assortment of reasons that Ehomba was relieved when, employing some of Simna's Chlengguu gold, they finally were able to book passage aboard a single-masted, square-rigged merchantman departing for the northern shores of the Aboqua. While more than a few members of the crew were leery about having so large and ferocious a feline running loose onboard, they took heart when his "keepers" demonstrated their control over it.

"Is this really necessary?" Reposing on the open deck with his forepaws crossed and jaws parted wide, a mildly annoyed Ahlitah held a pose while Ehomba placed his head deep into the cat's cavernous, gaping mouth. Behind him, sailors whistled and cheered their approval and admiration. The herdsman withdrew himself and the cat slowly shut his jaws.

"That should be enough to reassure them you are tame," Ehomba said under his breath.

The litah's eyes widened slightly. "Tame, am I? They'd better hope this vessel's supplies are adequate or they're liable to see how 'tame' I really am." Looking to his right, he inhaled deeply. "I've heard about the sea but never expected to see it.

It smells like certain shallow lakes in late summer. All brine and brittle."

"The voyage will not be long, as such journeys go, and I think you will enjoy it." Ehomba ruffled the big cat's mane. "The captain assures me there will be fresh fish for the duration of our crossing."

Half closing his eyes, the litah placed his head down on his crossed paws. "Then I'll be content. I quite like fish." Within moments, he was snoring softly.

"Make sail there!" the first mate was shouting from his post alongside the helmsman. "Let go your main braces! Pulleys and haul. Ware the jetty cleats!"

Simna joined the southerner forward, where the truncated bowsprit thrust boldly out over the water. All around them, men were busy preparing to depart the tidy, compact harbor, with its freshly swept streets and innumerable pots and boxes of flowers.

"Been some time since I've sailed across anything wider than a lake." He nodded northward. "Onward to treasure and glory, hoy?"

"To the fulfillment of my obligation," Ehomba countered evenly.

"Aye, right, whatever." Grinning expansively, the swordsman clapped his friend on his narrow back. For the first time in many weeks they were without the burden of packs and weapons, these having been placed in their private cabin belowdecks.

"It was good of the townspeople to recommend us to this ship's master for passage." The sea here was calmer, warmer, less fractious than the one that washed the beaches below his village, the herdsman reflected.

"Hoy, I never saw so many relieved faces as when we told them of the Chlengguu's overthrow. I think they were grateful enough to buy us a boat, had we but asked them for one."

"This is better." Crossing his arms, Ehomba bent forward to lean on the wooden railing. "I am no sailor."

"Naturally not." Edging close and lowering his voice to a whisper, Simna gave his rangy friend a conspiratorial nudge. "Of course, with your powers you could have commanded a ship to sail itself, right?"

Ehomba sighed wearily. "When will you get it through your head, Simna, that I am nothing more than a humble herder of chewers of cud?"

"Oh, I don't know." Turning away, the swordsman also directed his gaze to the open sea that lay before them. "Maybe when I'm in your company and Corruption doesn't falter, great winds don't perish at your hand, and your sword doesn't call down a shard of heaven to scatter and confuse our enemies."

"All that was accomplished through the knowledge and work of others. I was only a means of conveyance. We have been damned lucky."

"Right. And I am a monk, one much versed in disguise." He chuckled affably. "I'll give you one thing, though, Etjole Ehomba. You're one of the most skilled liars I've ever met. Not the best, by any means, but the most persistent."

"Oh, very well," the herdsman snapped, "believe what you will."

"That's the spirit!" Simna's face was full of admiration. "Stick to your story no matter what." He nodded forward. "It may help us on the other side."

"You have never been to these northern lands?"

"More questions." It was the swordsman's turn to shake his head tiredly. "No, not to these." He jerked a thumb back in the direction of the friendly seaport whose citizens had been so accommodating. "Among the Maliin, those who've made the crossing say that the northern lands are nothing like here, or where we've come from. They say that the level of civilization and enlightenment is such that they're embarrassed to visit there. It makes me wonder what these northern eminencies will think of us. I've been around, but you'll be out of your depth, and the cat will be little more than a novelty."

"I will manage." Ehomba wished he felt more confident. Villages and hamlets he was familiar and comfortable with, but a proper city was something entirely different. No matter. He had no choice. They had to go north to find a ship large and capable enough to cross the Semordria.

The Aboqua chose to be kind as they set out. There were waves, but they were curious rather than threatening. There was movement, but it was calming to the spirit instead of disturbing to the digestion. Flying fish exploded from the water in front of the ship's onrushing prow, shooting away like silver darts to port and starboard before splashing and sinking anew into the welcoming whitecaps. Gulls harassed the stern, taking their ease on the mainspar and railings as they nagged the cook for scraps.

As paid passengers, the travelers were mostly left to themselves, though when Ahlitah would come on deck to nap in the sun the more courageous among the crew would make a game of tiptoeing near for a better look. It was a matter of some merriment among the mariners to see who could creep the closest. There was betting, and a fair amount of money changed hands until Ahlitah, irked at having his naps continually interrupted by the seamen's chatter, finally favored one of the brave sailors with a nip on the leg. That put an end to the encroachment, though for the rest of the voyage the seaman involved wore the bite marks like a medal of honor.

They were several days out when the sky began to darken.

XXXII

INITIALLY, THE CAPTAIN FOUND NOTHING AMISS WITH THE SUD-
den change in the weather. Although the Aboqua was a com-
paratively benign body of water, it was no stranger to the
sudden storms that could affect any sizable sea.

The usual precautions were taken. The mainsail was reefed,
hatches were battened down, the pumps were made ready, and
all hands were sounded to stations. After being apprised of the
situation and the possible dangers, passengers were left to
their own devices. Ehomba and his companions could remain
belowdecks, relatively dry and warm, or they could wander
about above to experience the as yet undetermined vagaries of
the weather. All that was asked of them was that they stay out
of the way of working seamen.

The nearer the storm drew, the stranger became its aspect.
Neither lightning nor thunder announced its impending arrival. Even more astoundingly, there was no wind. Though
black as night, the approaching clouds did not writhe and
roil. They simply came closer and closer, blotting out first the

horizon and then the sky, like the unrolling of some vast cumbrous black blanket.

Every man stood ready at his station. They were an experienced crew that had run safely before many storms, some mere rain squalls, others of impressive dimensions. But not sailor aboard could recall ever encountering anything like this.

The dark clouds swept over the ship, enveloping it in heavy, damp gloom. And still there was no wind. It was as if the storm entire consisted only of the eye of a hurricane, the ferocity of the tempest having absented itself elsewhere.

Uneasy now, the heretofore self-assured and confident mariners nervously eyed the baneful murk that had engulfed them. Where was the driving rain, the strobing lightning, the crashing seas that were the harbingers of any honorable storm? The ship drifted forward on calm seas, her stays barely rattling, her helm responding to the lightest of touches.

First they noticed the smell: a faint, fetid stink that portended no good. It was not the distinctive odor of rotting fish or seaweed. One mate declared that it reminded him of the ancient sewers of the abandoned city of Vra-Thet, whose people had been dead for thousands of years but whose decrepit essence still lingered in its multifarious catacombed depths. Another contended that the stench must have been carried hence on the wind from some great far-off battle in which tens of thousands had perished.

Ahlitah, whose sense of smell was infinitely more sensitive than that of any man aboard, wrinkled his nose so tightly it threatened to curl up and hide beneath his upper lip.

"What is it, cat?" Simna warily eyed the darkness that had swallowed the ship.

"Don't know. Decay, putrefaction, rot. But of what I can't tell."

The swordsman turned to the tall southerner, who was star-

g out across the bow, one hand holding on to a trembling
ay fashioned of finely corded rope.

"How about it, Etjole? As a herder of cattle you should be
timately acquainted with stinks. Any ideas?" The other man
d not look back. "Etjole?" Taking a step forward, Simna
abbed his friend by the arm.

"What?" Blinking, Ehomba looked back at his compan-
ns. "I am sorry, Simna. Yes, I know what it is."

"Then tell us," Ahlitah prompted him. "I'm not familiar
ith the smells of the sea, but I know storms, and this reeks
ke no storm I have ever encountered."

The herdsman's mouth was set in a thin, tight line. "That is
ecause this is not a storm."

Cat and swordsman exchanged a glance. "It's clouds,
tjole," Simna avowed gently. "Racing black clouds usually
erald the coming of a storm."

"These are not clouds, either. They are the substance of
hat has engulfed this ship."

Simna ibn Sind did not like the sound of that. Especially
homba's use of the word "engulfed." "Then if not a storm,
hat?"

Tilting back his head slightly, the herdsman looked upward,
canning the sky from side to side like someone standing at
e bottom of a deep well searching for a ray of light. Having
verheard, several sailors had left their posts and were hover-
ng nearby, watching the rangy foreigner intently.

"It has been following me for a long time, gathering
trength. I first saw it when I helped the People of the Trees
efeat the slelves."

Simna's expression twisted in confusion. "The what?"

"It was before you and I met. You may have seen this also,
riend Simna, when we fought Corruption. It gyred through
he winds that helped to propel the Dunawake, and its essence
vas everywhere in the shattered lands of the Queppa. Espe-
ially in the Wall." He was silent for a moment as he consid-

ered the lowing sky. "Ever since the time when I was with t[
People of the Trees it has been tracking me, waiting for t]
right moment."

"The right moment?" Staring at the sky, Simna tried to pe[
through the raven clouds, to see something else where to th
naked eye there appeared to be only arching blackness. "T]
right moment for what?"

Ehomba was as somber and serious as the swordsman ha
ever seen him. "To swallow."

That conjured up an image even less palatable than the on
that had been induced by the herdsman's use of the word "e[
gulfed." "You mean this whatever-it-is is going to try and e[
us?"

"It already has." With unshakable calm, Ehomba studie
the ominous dark. "We are inside it now. But it has not begu
to swallow. It must be stopped before it can."

"Hoy, right, I am in agreement with you there, bruther[
Wide-eyed but undaunted, the swordsman beheld their su[
roundings anew. Had anything changed since the black clou[
had first enveloped them? Yes, everything had grown eve[
darker, black as the inside of a chunk of coal. And it wa
pressing tight upon them, congealing like oil, a cloyin[
oleaginous mass that was acquiring more weight and su[
stance than was natural for an honest cloud even as the[
spoke.

A sailor struck out at a limb of murk as it threatened [
crawl up his arm. At the blow the gloom broke apart, but th
pieces hung in the air, ebony wisps floating in a sable dusk[
ness. Around the ship, a deathless night was descending
threatening to overwhelm and suffocate everyone on boar[
Sailors brushed at themselves, and cursed in frustration, b[
their efforts were proving increasingly futile. It was like try
ing to fight a cloud, a shadow, and that shadow was growin
stronger by the minute. Stronger, and all-consuming.

Simna flailed at the deepening gloom as if assailed b[

ant, ephemeral black bugs. It was midmorning, but not a
splinter of sunshine penetrated the ambient obscurity that had
enveloped them. Ahlitah snapped at the lazily coiling lengths
of deeper blackness that curled around his muscular form like
indigo snakes. They broke apart, re-formed, and drew
strength and sustenance from the deepening shadow all
around them.

"What is it?" Like the rapidly panicking crew, Simna was
brushing and slapping furiously at the terrifying blackness.
"By Gidan's eyeteeth, what is it?"

"Eromakadi." Ignoring the suffocating blackness that
swirled around him and threatened to invade his ears, his
eyes, his mouth, Ehomba held tight to the rigging. "Eater of
light. It consumes the light around us as well as the light that
is life that emanates from us."

"From us?" Next to the swordsman, the litah was tiring as
he struggled to do battle against something without substance.
His jaws were still mighty, his teeth still sharp, but it is hard
to take much of a bite out of an evanescence.

"Our thoughts, our souls, the way we project our animate
being into the world. Life is light, Simna, and the eromakadi
cannot stand light. Sometimes they are weak and scattered,
sometimes potent and powerful. The eromakadi are why bad
things happen to good people. Their allies are pestilence and
war, bigotry and ignorance. A tiny eromakadi will flock to a
contemptuous sneer, a larger one to a gang beating, a great
and more powerful one still to a politician's lies. This one has
grown especially focused."

Much of what his friend declaimed made no sense to
Simna. It was babble and gibberish of the most impenetrable
philosophical kind. But whatever it was, the darkness closing
tight around them was real enough. He had never been afraid
before because his fears had always assumed physical shape
and form. Anything that would respond to a sword could be
dealt with. But this—it was like trying to fight air.

As he spun about and flailed madly against the insisten
encroaching gloom, he saw Ehomba climb up onto th
bowsprit and stand facing the silently boiling blacknes
alone. As the swordsman looked on, his lanky friend method
ically removed his clothing and let it fall to the deck behin
him. Naked, a lean and slender scarecrow of a man wh
looked even slimmer devoid of his simple raiment, the herds
man braced himself against a pair of stays and spread his arm
wide as if invoking the sky.

The frantic crew ignored him. Those among them who sa
what was happening thought he had gone mad, and not a fe
expected to join the tall passenger in madness at any momen
Because the final blackness was closing in tight around them
suffocating sight and sound and thought, if not yet heaving
straining lungs. Could a man be suffocated while still breath
ing?

Etjole Ehomba stood alone on the bowsprit, detached fror
the rest of humanity. Stood there by himself, and inhaled.

His chest expanded. Simna could hear it, even above th
cries and wails of the raving crew. The sound was that of a
ordinary man inhaling deeply, but what happened next wa
anything but ordinary.

Tiny wisps of blackness began to drift backward, and not c
their own volition. They vanished into Ehomba's wide-ope
mouth, sucked down, away, and out of sight. More volumi
nous coils of gloom followed, straining to sustain their posi
tion but unable to resist. They too disappeared into the innard
of the herdsman. And all the while Ehomba continued to in
hale, not pausing to breathe normally, his chest distended in ;
steady, unvarying inhalation.

For the first time since the ship had been overtaken by th
darkness, wind assailed its mast and spars and deck. Gusts ar
rived forcefully from over the bow, but also from abeam an
from athwart the stern. It howled down out of the sky, and u
from the supporting surrounding waters.

Ehomba never paused, never faltered. He inhaled, and inhaled, and in so doing sucked up that all-encompassing gloom
and shadow as if it were essence of cinnamon and myrrh,
drawing it all down into him, into somewhere within himself
that Simna could not begin to imagine. And still the herdsman
did not stop to breathe. Clinging exhaustedly to the rail for
support, Simna looked on and wondered at the southerner's
stamina. How long could he maintain the suction, keep up the
pace? Would what he inhaled fill him up until he exploded, or
was it after all nothing more than evil air, a malignant atmosphere that in actual gist amounted to no more than a desolate
burp?

Light appeared above the ship: healthful, heartening, natural sunshine. The crew saw it, felt it fall upon them, and set
up a ragged cheer. And still Ehomba continued his unnatural
insufflation, until the last of the blackness had vanished,
drawn deep down within himself. Only then did he close his
mouth, give a slight shiver, slump, and fall backwards, limp
as a child's cheap ragdoll, onto the hard deck.

Simna was at his side in an instant, and Ahlitah as well, the
big cat looming anxiously over the fallen herdsman. Solici-
tous members of the crew crowded close, wanting to help,
until an angry Simna ordered them to stand back and give the
fallen herdsman some air.

Putting a hand beneath his friend's head, Simna raised it
gently. "Come on, Etjole—breathe! Open your mouth and
breathe. Drink in the fresh air of the sea and clear your lungs
of that murderous blight." He jiggled the head slightly.
"Breathe, damn you!"

The herdsman's eyelids fluttered like small moths on a chill
morning. Then his head jerked upward as he coughed, not
once but several times. A tiny puff of black vapor squeezed
out from between his lips. No bigger than a cotton ball, it
drifted upward until it finally dissipated beneath the pellucid

blue of the cloud-flecked sky. Simna followed it with his eyes until he was sure it was gone.

Inhaling sharply, exhaling slowly and wearily, Ehomba opened his eyes. When they met Simna's, and Ahlitah's, he smiled. "My friends." Looking around, he frowned to himself. "Why am I lying here like this? Help me up."

A plethora of willing, eager hands made themselves available to exalt the herdsman. Standing by himself, he took stock of his surroundings, then walked forward to where he had dropped his clothes and began to dress himself. When that was done he crossed his arms and leaned forward against the railing, resuming the position he had favored before.

Vigorously discussing among themselves everything that had transpired, the crew returned to their duties. The captain had many questions, but courteously restrained his curiosity. No doubt the remarkable southerner needed some time to himself. Queries about what had happened, however burning, could wait until later.

Simna operated under no such restraints. He was at Ehomba's side as soon as the herdsman had finished dressing. "For the last time, my friend—tell me you are not a sorcerer."

The herdsman glanced sideways at him and smiled. "It will not be the last time, Simna, but I will say it again anyway. I am not."

"Fine. Good. I accept it." The swordsman let his arms dangle over the railing. Dolphins ran before the ship's prow, energized by its presence, glorying in the pressure wave it pushed before it. "All you have to do is explain to me what just happened. I remember you mentioning this thing, this eromakadi, once before. It was when we were about to confront the Dunawake." He struggled to remember. "You said then that nothing could slay it except an eromakasi."

Ehomba hardly heard him. He was thinking of the warm, dry, clean homeland that now lay far to the south. Of a small and unprepossessing but accommodating house, of the music of children's voices at play, and of the woman who was his wife. The remembrances warmed him from within, and made him feel better about continuing to live. Made him feel that he had greater reason, and sweeter purpose, for being.

"I told you the truth, my friend. The eromakadi are eaters of light. They cannot be killed—except by an eromakasi, an eater of darkness." Turning his head sideways, he peered direct and deep into the swordsman's eyes.

"I am a simple herder of cattle and sheep, Simna ibn Sind—and I am also eromakasi. A man can be both." He returned his unblinking gaze to the sea ahead, and to the shore that could not yet be seen but that he knew was there. "That does not make of me a necromancer."

By his side Simna was silent for some time, until the ship's bell rang three times to announce the serving of the midday meal. "Perhaps it does not, Etjole, but you can't deny that it makes you something more than an ordinary man."

Removing his arms from the rail, Ehomba straightened. "Not something more, friend Simna. Not something more."

"Well then, bruther—something other. No, don't try to explain it to me. Not now." The swordsman grinned broadly. "Some days you talk like the most ignorant backcountry bumpkin I ever met, and other times I can't make up or down of your manner of speaking, much less what you're actually saying. Are you genius or imbecile? Idiot simpleton or sorcerer supreme? For the life of me, I can't decide."

His tall friend smiled gently. "Perhaps I am a genius imbecile. Or idiot adept."

Simna ibn Sind shook his head slowly as he rested a comradely hand on his companion's shoulder, having to reach high to do so. "Time enough yet to descry the truth. Doesn't matter one way or the other so long as there's treasure in it. Now come, and let's have something to eat. I'll wager you could use a drink."

Pushing out his chin, Ehomba rubbed appraisingly at his neck. "To tell you the truth, my throat *is* a little sore."

So it was that Ehomba the Catechist and his ill-matched companions came safely to the great harbor city of Lybondai, which lies on the silver coast of the kingdom of Premmois, beneath the perpetually snow-capped Mountains of Nerimabmeleh. There they discovered that in so worldly and cosmopolitan a community not even an Ahlitah was cause for much comment, and their presence among thousands of other travelers from all over the known world went largely unremarked.

All this was consoling to Etjole Ehomba, who was very tired. But being interested in everything, and everything in which he presently found himself being subsumed in newness, he found that he was able to lift his spirits by the asking of questions, a habit too deeply ingrained in him and too much a part of him to break even in unfamiliar surroundings.

Exasperated by his companion's continual querying of every other individual they encountered, Simna finally blurted, "Etjole, must you know everything?"

"Yes," his friend responded without hesitation.

"Must there be an answer to everything?"

The herdsman looked at him as guilelessly and openly as it was possible for one person to look at another. "Of course there must be, Simna. To everything. Otherwise, why would I be here? Or you, or Ahlitah, or anyone else? Why would I be looking to find a Visioness Themaryl, or chancing the wrath of this Hymneth the Possessed? Why would—"

"I'm sorry I asked." Ignoring the bustle and noise of the tavern in which they were presently tarrying, the swordsman buried his face in the simple ceramic goblet before him. "Shut up and finish your drink." At their feet, curled up tight beneath the table, Ahlitah stretched, extended enormous curved claws, yawned, and slipped indifferently back to sleep.

The adventure continues . . . in
INTO THE THINKING KINGDOMS
Now available from Warner Aspect

The world is larger than Etjole Ehomba had
dreamed. No sooner does he cross one menacing desert, one range of mountains, than
another challenge rises in front of him. The
lands of Hymneth the Possessed still lie far,
far away, and the kidnapped Visioness
Themaryl remains in his hold. But Ehomba
has sworn to return her to her family, and as
a man of honor, he will keep that promise.

As Ehomba and his friends, the cynical
swordmaster Simna and the great feline
Ahlitah, traverse vast landscapes they must
face challenges of all kinds—yet none will
stop the simple herdsman in his quest
for justice.

Here is a short excerpt from
INTO THE THINKING KINGDOMS,
available April 1999 in Aspect hardcover.

I

The most powerful man in the world couldn't sleep.

At least, Hymneth the Possessed thought of himself as the most powerful man in the world, and since those few who might have contemplated disputing him were no longer alive, he felt comfortable with having abrogated the title to himself. And if not the most powerful man, then he was certainly the most powerful mage. Granted that there might be a handful of imprudent individuals foolhardy enough to stand before him as men and women, there were none who dared confront him in the realm of the arcane and necromantic. There <u>he</u> was the Masters of masters, and all who dabbled in the black arts must pay him homage, or suffer his whims at their peril.

Yet despite the knowing of this, and the sum of all his knowing, he could not sleep.

Rising from his bed, a graven cathedral to Morpheus that had taken the ten finest woodcarvers in the land six years to render from select pieces of cobal, redwood, cherry, walnut, and purpleheart, Hymneth walked slowly to the vaulted window that looked out upon his kingdom. The rich and populous reach of Ehl-Larimar stretched out before him, from the rolling green hills at the base of his mountaintop fortress retreat to the distant, sun-washed shores of the boundless ocean of Aurel. Every home and farm, every shop and industry within that field of view acknowledged him as supreme over all other earthly authorities. He tried to submerge his soul in the warmth and security of that understanding, to let it wash over and burnish him like a shower of liquid pleasure. But he could not.

He couldn't shake the accursed dream that had kept him awake.

Worse than the loss of sleep was his inability to recall the details. Nebulous, hazy images of other beings had tormented his rest. Awake, he found that he was unable to remember them with any degree of resolution. His inability to identify them meant it was impossible to deal with their condition or take steps to prevent their return. He was convinced that some of the likenesses had been human, others not. Why they should disturb him so he could not say. . . .